ITHAKA

Also by Adèle Geras:

OTHER ECHOES

HAPPY EVER AFTER

TROY

ITHAKA

Adèle Geras

David Fickling Books

OXFORD · NEW YORK

ITHAKA
A DAVID FICKLING BOOK 0 385 60391 6

Published in Great Britain by David Fickling Books,
a division of Random House Children's Books

This edition published 2005

1 3 5 7 9 10 8 6 4 2

Papers used by Random House Children's Books are natural, recyclable products made
from wood grown in sustainable forests. The manufacturing processes conform to
the environmental regulations of the country of origin.

Set in New Baskerville by
Palimpsest Book Production Limited, Polmont, Stirlingshire

DAVID FICKLING BOOKS
31 Beaumont Street, Oxford, OX1 2NP, UK
a division of RANDOM HOUSE CHILDREN'S BOOKS
61–63 Uxbridge Road, London W5 5SA
A division of The Random House Group Ltd

RANDOM HOUSE AUSTRALIA (PTY) LTD
20 Alfred Street, Milsons Point, Sydney,
New South Wales 2061, Australia

RANDOM HOUSE NEW ZEALAND LTD
18 Poland Road, Glenfield, Auckland 10, New Zealand

RANDOM HOUSE (PTY) LTD
Endulini, 5A Jubilee Road, Parktown 2193, South Africa

THE RANDOM HOUSE GROUP Limited Reg. No. 954009
www.**kids**at**random**house.co.uk

A CIP catalogue record for this book is available from the British Library.

Printed and bound in Great Britain by
Clays Ltd, Bungay, Suffolk

For David Fickling,
who has waited with a patience
worthy of Penelope

Acknowledgements

I'm very grateful to several people for their support during the writing of this novel. Laura Cecil, Sophie Jones, Jenny Geras and Linda Newbery were extremely helpful readers and Linda Sargent has followed the book's progress from beginning to end and helped it enormously. Anne Jackson provided classical backup and early enthusiasm and Moi Ravenscroft gave a fascinating insight into the ancient methods of weaving and knitting.

My editors, David Fickling in the UK and Karen Grove in the USA, have been terrific, and Norm Geras has, as always, been in my corner. My thanks go to all of them.

Author's Note

After the end of the Trojan War Odysseus set out for his home in Ithaka. His long journey was fraught with difficulties, and these adventures – with the Cyclops, with Circe, with the Sirens, Calypso, Nausicaa and others – are recounted by Homer in *The Odyssey*.

This book is not a version of Homer nor a retelling of *The Odyssey*, but a novel written under the influence of stories which I first read as a young child and which I've loved ever since.

I have chosen to spell Ithaka with a 'k' because that is the spelling adopted by C. F. Cavafy in his poem of the same name. This is also how the word appears in the edition of Homer I consulted before writing the novel: *The Odyssey of Homer*, translated by Richmond Lattimore (HarperPerennial, 1999).

. . . my husband's life
hung from a thread, coaxing through my fingers.

All is made by the design of my hand.
What I weave is where and how he travels.
He sails on glittering tides. I weave.

Penelope Shuttle

BEFORE THE WAR

Odysseus, his wife Penelope and their baby Telemachus are sitting on a woollen coverlet spread out in the shade of a pomegranate tree. It's early in the morning. The baby, recently fed, is drowsing on his back, his hands flung out above his head, his mouth a little open and his eyes half closed. Penelope is trying hard not to cry. She's blinking to stop the tears from falling. She's turned her head away from her husband.

'Listen to me, Penelope,' he says. 'Look at me. Don't turn away. I have to go. Anyone who calls himself a man has a duty to go.'

'It's not your war. It's not your fight. What's Agamemnon ever done for you? Stay here. Stay with me and Telemachus, I beg of you, Odysseus. Look at your son. How can you bear to leave him?'

Odysseus shakes his head. 'I tried. You saw me trying. I did my best not to go. Didn't I? Didn't I pretend I was mad so as not to have to go?'

'It didn't work, though, did it?'

1

'Did you want me to run my plough over the body of my son?' Odysseus shakes his head.

'Agamemnon's as cunning as you are. He knew you were only pretending to be crazy. The ruler of Ithaka ploughing his own fields and sowing them with salt!' Penelope's voice breaks as she speaks. 'I saw the look on his face as he picked our baby up and laid him down on the ground, right in the path of your plough. He knew you were putting on a show. Tricking him.'

Telemachus stirs, makes a moaning noise and wakes up. He starts to grizzle and his mother gathers him up into her arms, nuzzling her face into the soft folds of his neck. Odysseus looks at his wife and child and tears stand in his eyes.

'Listen to me, Penelope. I'll come back. I swear I will. On the life of my precious son and on the love that fills me when I look at you, I'm telling you that I'll return. Don't stop waiting for me, my darling. You have to believe me. Please, Penelope. Say you believe me.'

'How can you ask such things of me? And how can you swear to come back? It's war, Odysseus, and men die in wars. They're wounded. They're torn apart. They're buried far from home.'

Her tears are falling now and Telemachus touches the drops that flow from his mother's eyes with his small fingers, enchanted by this novelty.

'I will fight in Troy,' Odysseus whispers, 'and I will come back to you. I give you my word.'

He leans over and puts his right arm around his wife's shoulders and draws her to him. She turns her face up to his and he kisses her on the lips.

2

'You are my life,' he says. 'My life is nowhere else but here. On Ithaka. With you.'

The sun rises higher in the sky and the light filters through the leaves of the pomegranate tree, scattering gold in Penelope's hair as she clings, weeping, to her husband.

'I believe you,' she tells him. 'And I will wait for you.'

THIRTEEN YEARS LATER

Pallas Athene in her owl shape flies over the water. The sky above the horizon is streaked with gold and pink as the burning chariot of the sun, driven by her brother, Phoebus Apollo, and pulled by his fire-footed horses, plunges down into the dark waves. Below her lies an island washed around on every side by the wide blue ocean. This place is beloved of everyone who lives there. Beloved too of one who is sailing towards it, and who has been longing to return to his home for many years. The white bird hovers on a breath of wind and fixes her amber eyes on Ithaka.

Mountains rise from a coastline that curves into coves and bays and inlets where the sand is pale and silvery and where rocks fringe the shore and caves stand with their black mouths gaping wide. The lower slopes of the green-clad hills are terraced and planted with vines, and wherever the land lies flatter, farmers have cultivated groves of olives trees and almond trees, and orchards where figs and peaches and lemons grow.

The owl soars over the harbour: a natural curve in the

landscape, with small boats and fishing vessels tied up along the seafront. Down on the quays, even though the clamour of the port is hushed, fishermen are working on their boats in the dim light of lanterns. They will set out before dawn to cross the seas around the island, and fill their nets with silver fish. A town has taken root here, gathering together those who live from what they can take from the sea and trade with their neighbours. They sell their fish, and buy the produce of those from distant lands whose ships, laden with metal and cloth and spices, sail into Ithaka's waters. The market is quiet now, and the stalls lie covered up for the night, but light spills out of the doors of taverns, and in kitchens everywhere fires are dying down after the evening meal.

Away from the harbour and up and up to the great gates of Odysseus' palace, the bird follows the road that leads from the town. Many are sleeping, but here and there a light shows at a window: a mother tending a feverish child, perhaps, or someone who is finding it hard to escape into dreams. Silence lies over everything, but from time to time a groan or a sigh floats into the cool air.

The rulers of Ithaka live in a palace built around two courtyards, one leading from another, like squares joined together by covered passages. The white owl comes to rest on a fig tree that grows below Penelope's chamber. This is the only room in the palace where a light is still burning. This is where she is needed.

Penelope is wide awake. It happens to her often that she falls into a black sleep as soon as she lies down and then wakes a little while later, tormented by dreams. Then it is hard to *rest again. Tonight she finds herself gripped by a terror so strong that she has difficulty drawing breath. She goes to stand at the window, and leans out into the fresh night air, trying to calm herself by looking at the branches of the fig tree that grows against the wall and spreads itself almost into her chamber. How happy they were, she and Odysseus, when they used to sit under this tree and the rest of the palace seemed to fade away till there was nothing left but the two of them under a green canopy of leaves. She sighs. Those days seem very distant now.*

Behind her is the bed that her husband carved out of a single olive tree before they were married. She has slept there alone for so many years that she sometimes thinks of it as a kind of desert. The headboard, carved into intricate patterns of flowers and garlands, reaches up to the ceiling of the chamber. Every one of the pillows has a cover that she has made with her own hands. A chest, its lid inlaid with mother-of-pearl, stands in one corner. It holds all her clothes, and whenever she opens it, a fragrance of cedar wood fills the chamber.

She turns to look at the small loom that has been set up for her here, where she spends so much of her time. It is somewhat shorter than she is and narrower than the span of her arms: a wooden frame with threads stretched across it from top to bottom. Next to the loom lies a large basket woven from dried reeds, and this is where Penelope keeps her wools: skeins and balls in brown and green and purple and red and yellow; pale shades and dark ones in each colour; thick strands and fine ones that she can push between the threads already on the frame, backwards and forwards, again and again, until a small piece of fabric is finished: a wall hanging, or a decoration of some kind. The loom is placed to the right of the window to take advantage of the light. When she sits at her work, if she lifts her eyes, what Penelope sees is a white wall. All the beauty of the island is behind her as she weaves.

Suddenly she notices a movement near the sill. She leans out to see better, and catches sight of a white owl settled on a branch of the fig tree. She thinks: how beautiful and how peaceful this creature is! and feels joy flowing through her, filling her whole body. The bird is near enough to touch, but she doesn't dare to put out a hand because the whiteness of the feathers is so perfect that she is frightened of marring it in some way.

Be brave, *says the owl, or maybe Penelope hears the words in her head. It is looking at her out of its amber eyes.*

She says, 'Will my husband come back to me?'

The owl steps on to the sill. Penelope hears its answer as though the words are being spoken in her head: His life is in your hands, Penelope. It is bound up in the threads you have tied to your loom, and as long as you are here, unchanged and unchanging, he will come to no harm. Pallas Athene will guide him home.

Penelope closes her eyes, dizzy with a mixture of relief and anguish.

'I'll never stop weaving,' she says to the owl, 'but how cruel of Pallas Athene to lay the burden of Odysseus' life on me! What if I should fail? What then? Unchanged and unchanging. There's so much I can't control. So many ways in which I'm powerless.'

You must be strong. *The owl's words ring in her ears.* Nothing will be easy.

'I'll try. I'll try to be strong, but I'll need the Goddess's help. I'm afraid. So afraid.'

Penelope listens for some words of comfort, but the white owl is silent. It steps from the window and on to the branches of the fig tree, and then it spreads its wings and Penelope watches it flying away, pearly white as moonlight against the dark sky.

ON THE SHORE

'Stop it!' Ikarios blinked and shook his head. 'You're kicking sand in my eyes.'

'I didn't mean to,' said his twin sister Klymene. 'I'm bored, that's all.'

She took hold of her long brown hair, twisted it and fixed it on the top of her head with a thin little stick that happened to be lying beside her on the sand. It was very early in the morning, with the sun still low in the sky, but the day was already hot. She waited for every wave that raced towards her to swirl cooling foam around her feet. We're on the beach, she thought, and he's making something out of sand. He's been doing the same thing since we were small children. She knew what he was building because he kept pointing out features of the structure.

'It's not an ordinary hill,' he said, piling yet another handful of damp sand on to the lump that he'd already made. 'It's a citadel. The citadel of Troy. Later on, we can line up some stones or something to show where the Greek lines were, across the plain.'

'I don't care what it is,' said Klymene. 'It's boring.

The war in Troy ended long ago and still you and Telemachus keep playing Greeks and Trojans. I wish everyone would shut up about it.'

'Telemachus' father was the hero of the war,' Ikarios said, his voice full of awe. 'It was his idea to build a horse and fill it full of soldiers.'

'I hate that story. They set fire to everything and the whole city burned down. Imagine how horrible that must have been.'

'But we won!' Ikarios looked at his sister in amazement. 'That's what matters.'

'But it's not all that matters,' Klymene said. 'People getting killed and burned alive matters too.'

Ikarios sighed, and Klymene knew what he was thinking: girls are weak and stupid and don't understand about important men's things. Boys' things. She knew he didn't feel like arguing about it because he said: 'Anyway, Odysseus was the one. The one who helped us win. He's the cleverest of all the Greek kings.'

'I know,' said Klymene. 'And he's *our* king. Everyone says he's dead. They don't say so in front of Penelope because they're frightened of making her even sadder than she is now, but that's what they're saying. Odysseus is never coming back.'

'He is. He's not dead,' Ikarios said. 'That's kitchen gossip. Telemachus told me he knows his father's alive.'

'He doesn't know anything. He's showing off, that's all. And comforting himself, I expect, too.'

She kicked a little sand up with her foot, trying not to send it in her brother's direction. All the boys on Ithaka, their island, where Odysseus ruled before he went off to the war, did nothing but play at being heroes. Klymene thought that these games weren't proper games at all, but excuses for rolling around, wrestling and fighting, and she couldn't understand why the boys enjoyed them so much.

As though he had read her thoughts, Ikarios said, 'Playing heroes is not as boring as playing princesses.'

Klymene shrugged. She could sometimes read what was in her twin's mind, and he had the same gift. Nana, their grandmother, said it was because they'd shared the same womb before they were born. They had grown from one seed, like a plant with two flowers blossoming on a single stalk. It meant that they could understand one another, but it didn't prevent her from sometimes being irritated by her brother's quietness and slowness and she often wished that she'd been born the boy. If I had, I could have been a fisherman like our father and sailed away from the shore all over the ocean, and I wouldn't have to waste my time in the kitchen, staring into pots to make sure the soup doesn't burn.

Klymene was happy to leave the war games to her brother and Telemachus, but she liked going with them when they explored the rocks above the town, or picked pears and figs from trees that grew in the orchards.

'You have my permission,' Telemachus often said, laughing, pretending that he was the king while Odysseus, his father, was absent, and that all the fruit growing on Ithaka was his to pluck from the trees and share with his friends.

Ikarios' voice interrupted Klymene's thoughts. 'You're thinking about Telemachus again,' he said.

'We were talking about him, that's why. We often talk about him. He's our friend.'

Ikarios said nothing. Klymene pushed at him with her foot. 'Come on,' she said. 'Stop being so annoying, Ikarios. You want to say one thing and you're saying another. Something's troubling you.'

'Not troubling me. Not really.'

'But?'

'But nothing. It's just . . .'

'Oh, come on, Ikarios. Getting you to talk is like squeezing juice from a lemon.'

Ikarios took a deep breath. 'You think of Telemachus all the time,' he said.

'I don't,' Klymene answered and then: 'and even if I do, what's wrong with that?'

'You love him. That's what I think.'

'Don't be ridiculous. I don't. At least, I do, but we're too young, Ikarios. We're not supposed to think about . . . well, such things.'

'But you do. Admit it, Klymene. Sometimes you do think of him in that way. You know what I mean.'

'Rubbish. Telemachus is like another brother to me. And to you, Ikarios, don't forget. Perhaps you're jealous. Have you thought of that? Maybe you think he likes me better than he likes you.'

Because Ikarios didn't answer, Klymene knew that what she'd said was true. She'd only said it to move attention away from herself, but now she understood. Ikarios feels left out, she thought. She was searching in her mind for something to say that would change the subject, when her twin spoke.

'Maybe if we found a piece of wood the right size,' he said, 'we could make a wooden horse, just like the one Odysseus filled with soldiers. The one that the stupid Trojans took into their city.'

'I don't want to make a wooden horse,' said Klymene, trying not to sound too bored. She was grateful to her brother, whose thoughts often mirrored her own, for deciding to talk about something else. 'We've made hundreds of wooden horses and I'm sick of it.'

'You stay here, then, and I'll go alone. I won't be long. There's always wood along here somewhere.'

As Ikarios went off across the sand, Klymene looked at the ocean. The sun was a little higher now, and where its light fell on the water, the green and blue became sparkles of gold. She knew why she enjoyed playing princesses: it was because she felt as though she really *was* one. Odysseus' wife, Penelope, had treated her like a daughter ever since she'd been a baby, and she'd spent more of her time in the royal chambers than in her grandmother's apartment, which sometimes led to quarrels. Nana's my own mother's mother, Klymene told herself, so of course I love her, but she annoys me and irritates me sometimes, and I like being with Penelope and helping her much better than I like working in the kitchen with Nana.

Behind her, rocks and scrubby grass and olive trees with their trunks pushed close to the earth by the force of the winds grew along the path that she and Ikarios took when they came down to the shore. It led through the town and up a long sloping hill through clusters of small dwellings. At the top of the hill stood the palace. Its enormous wooden gates were always open, by order of Penelope, in case her husband should return unexpectedly.

Ikarios and I, Klymene thought, are like Telemachus' brother and sister. We've always done everything together. He was only one year old when we were born, and because our mother died before we were weaned we were all looked after together.

'How could the Gods take my daughter from me?' Nana still cried sometimes, covering her white hair with a black scarf so that you couldn't see her eyes. 'A fever burned her up and she is now in Hades with the Immortals and lost to us in this life.'

Not having a mother was sad, but she couldn't remember her properly. She dreamed sometimes of a tall, dark woman bending over her bed, and in the dream there was singing, but it faded away as soon as she woke up. She thought that her twin saw their mother in his sleep too, but he never spoke of it.

Ikarios mourned for their father, Halios, who had been one of the best fishermen on the island, bringing silver fish to the town and the palace in a boat that had black eyes painted on the prow. He had drowned in a terrible storm when his children were five years old. His body had never been found. Klymene missed him too, but not as much as her brother did. She'd never told anyone how frightened she had often been of the big, hairy man who used to toss her up in the air like a doll to show his love.

'Still mooning over Telemachus?' said Ikarios.

'Don't be so pathetic. I see you've found your wood.'

'Are you going to help me, then?'

'No, I feel like going to look in the cave.'

'Do you mean the cave of the Naiads?' said Ikarios. 'We're forbidden to go there. Nana'll shout at us.'

'I'm not going to tell her. Are you?'

'What if something bad happens?' Ikarios said.

'It won't. You always think things will happen. You just sit and wait for the Gods to throw something at you from Olympus.'

'Sssh!' said Ikarios. 'What if they hear you?'

'I'm not being disrespectful to *them*. It's you. You're silly. I'm going for a walk. I won't go to the cave, don't worry. I'll go in the opposite direction.'

She set off across the sand. In the distance there was a small outcrop of smooth rocks and beyond them, if you climbed over into the next bay, a place where the shells lay thick near the water line and you could gather spotted ones, and pearly ones, and sometimes huge, spiky ones that were pale pink in their deepest, most hidden parts. She thought about what Ikarios had said about the Gods and wondered, not for the first time, whether her twin had ever seen a God. I've never spoken to him about it, she thought, because I'm not sure it's true, but I've seen things. She shook her head. She would never tell anyone that she thought she'd sometimes seen the Gods themselves, in case the dwellers on Olympus punished her for her presumption. And what if those things she thought were manifestations of divinity were nothing but a kind of dream? She'd look a fool if she spoke of them.

Klymene's feet made wet prints in the damp sand, and she looked over her shoulder to see how the waves smoothed them away. The rocks were easy to clamber on to, but still, she was careful where she trod. Soon she could see the whole of the next bay.

Two women stood at the edge of the water. Klymene recognized one of them. It's Antikleia, she thought, and then: it can't be. Why would an old, old lady come down to the beach so early in the morning? And who is with her?

She hesitated, wondering what she ought to do. Would it be impertinent to go and speak to them? Something about the way they were standing, something about the silence everywhere and the stillness of the water stopped her. Every wave was taking much longer than it usually did to travel across the sand. Could that be?

Suddenly the air above Klymene's head darkened. She turned to look back at the distant figure of her brother, and where he was the sky was still blue and the sun shone on bright water. The figures of Antikleia and her friend hadn't moved, but the waves at their feet . . . Klymene shivered as she stared at them. Maybe it's an earthquake coming, she thought. Poseidon shaking the island, as he did sometimes when he was angered. Even though she wanted to run away, she couldn't take her eyes off what was happening to the sea. It had ebbed, as though gathering itself into a giant breaker, and then it had parted, divided, and now instead of a flat, shining surface, the water was heaped up into two towering masses higher than a house, walls of translucent blue and green in which fishes and seaweed were trapped like flies in amber. In between the two cliffs of solid ocean lay what looked like a wide, white path, a carpet of sand.

Klymene climbed down from the rocks and began to walk towards the women. I might be dreaming, she thought. I might wake up in my own bed and this, all of it, will vanish. She couldn't see the sun, and yet what surrounded her was not darkness but a light that shone strange and livid, as if the air had turned to metal.

The woman standing next to Antikleia turned and started to walk towards Klymene. Oh, Ikarios, help me, she thought. Come and find me. Who is she? What if she's angry with me for being here? Should I run away? I can't. I can't move. Maybe I should scream and then he'd come. Klymene blinked as the woman approached. She was tall and wore a gown of shimmering bronze. Her eyes were clear and grey and as she made her way along the beach, a white owl flew above her head, following where she led.

'There is nothing to fear, child,' said the woman, putting out a hand to touch Klymene on the shoulder. 'Antikleia is weary of her life. She is going down to the Kingdom of the Dead.'

'But she can't!' Klymene burst out. 'She's Odysseus' mother. How will she go to Hades when she isn't sick or mortally wounded? Who are you anyway? If you were a friend to Antikleia you'd help her. Let me go to her, I implore you. What'll Odysseus say if he comes back from the war to find his mother dead?'

'I am Odysseus' friend,' said the woman, and her voice was like a song in Klymene's ears. 'His most caring helper. It is Antikleia's fate, and you can do nothing to prevent it. Watch now, and remember.'

Klymene gazed at Antikleia. The old woman took her cloak from her shoulders and laid it on the sand as tidily as if she were preparing herself for sleep. Then she walked slowly, calmly along the white path, the way that led between the water-cliffs.

'I can't see her any longer,' Klymene cried. 'Where's she going?'

'She will be safe in the realm of Poseidon,' said the woman. 'The fishes will take her down and down, and she will know nothing of sorrow any longer. You must tell them, tell them at the palace, how gently she died. Tell her husband, Odysseus' father Laertes. He will mourn her and cry for her, but you must tell him.'

A sound filled Klymene's head like a thousand horses at once drumming their hooves on the earth. She put her hands up to cover her ears and saw the glassy walls of water shifting and moving and swelling and she held her breath as they crashed together and broke in a fountain of foam that seemed almost to touch the dark sky and hang in the air before it fell back to the shore again, and broke on the beach in a line of gigantic waves that roared up as far as the path to the city, and ebbed back and back and broke again, over and over, till Klymene was deafened with the noise of it and shivering with fear.

'The sea is calmer now,' said the woman. The owl had settled on her shoulder with its white wings folded. 'Antikleia is lost to this world. Go and tell them at the palace, child. Tell them Athene guided her.'

'Pallas Athene is a Goddess,' said Klymene and the woman smiled.

'Recognize her, then.'

Klymene sank to her knees. How could she not have seen? How did she not know at once? Of course – this tall lady with the owl on her shoulder. Of course it was.

'Lady,' she breathed, and bent down with her head on the sand, her mind racing, as she wondered what she would tell Ikarios. Would he believe her? Would anyone? When she raised her head, Pallas Athene had disappeared. Klymene looked all around, but the only sign that the Goddess had spoken to her was the sight of the white owl, disappearing towards the horizon. Klymene got to her feet and began to run to the rocks, back to Ikarios, shouting as she went.

'Ikarios! She's dead! Antikleia's gone. She drowned. Ikarios, come, we have to tell them at the palace. Pallas Athene says we have to tell them.'

He couldn't hear her, she knew. She was still too far away, but some sound must have reached him because he was looking at her. Should she have mentioned the Goddess? It was too late now. She half slid, half jumped down the rocks as quickly as she could, and then raced across the sand to where her brother was digging a trench around the sandy citadel of Troy he'd made.

'What're you on about? Pallas Athene! The sun's gone to your head.'

'She was there. On the beach with Antikleia.'

'What did she look like then? Tell me.'

'I can't remember exactly. There was an owl. A white owl. And I remember Antikleia walking between two walls of water down to the kingdom of Poseidon. Oh, come on, Ikarios, we must tell them. Come quickly.'

'I'm not going to tell anyone that a person's drowned till I've seen a body.'

Klymene stamped her foot. 'You're an idiot. I *told* you. She walked into the water. She's gone to Hades. There isn't going to be a body.'

'Well then, I want to see the place. Show me, go on. And then I'll come with you to the palace.'

Klymene turned and ran back to the rocks. 'Come on then, if you're going to be obstinate. It won't do any good. There won't be anything there.'

Ikarios went first and Klymene followed. At the top of the outcrop, he stopped and pointed.

'What's that, then?' he said. A black shape lay on the beach, half in, half out of the water, with small waves breaking over it.

'I don't know. A log. A fallen tree. Rubbish.'

'It isn't,' Ikarios said. He made his way down from the rocks and began to walk across the sand. Klymene followed him. She knew he was right. It was a body, and as they approached she recognized the black fabric

20

of the robes swirling around it. Poseidon had left the corpse here so that funeral rites could be performed.

'It's her,' she told her brother. 'It's Antikleia. Now do you believe me?'

'Yes,' said Ikarios. They were standing over the body now. 'Should we turn her over? I don't want to look at her, but surely we can't leave her lying with her face in the sand?'

'Turn her over, then, if you're so brave,' said Klymene. 'I think we should run. We have to tell them.'

'I daren't,' Ikarios whispered. 'The dead look at you without seeing you. I'm frightened, Klymene.'

Klymene sighed. She wanted nothing more than to be safe in the palace, cool in the shade, away from this beach and the blinding sun, which was burning the back of her neck now. But Ikarios was right. The old lady ought to be facing the sky. She bent down and held her breath.

'Help me, at least,' she said. 'She can't hurt us. Her spirit will be grateful for our kindness. Help me to turn her.'

Together, the twins turned the body over.

'Oh, it's horrible,' Ikarios said. 'Her skin is so white and slippery and her eyes are like stones. She's staring at us, Klymene. Look!'

'Come on,' Klymene whispered, covering the old woman's face with a corner of her own sodden garments, unable to gaze at her any longer. 'Run. Run faster than you've ever run before.'

Ikarios set off at once up the path to the palace,

with Klymene behind him. Even though no one in the town could hear them, she started to shout: 'Help! The old queen is drowned. Help us! A drowning on the beach. Help!'

ANTIKLEIA'S FUNERAL

Klymene's and Ikarios' grandmother, Eurykleia, was in charge of all arrangements for the funeral. Everyone, from King Laertes to the lowliest servant and her own grandchildren, called her Nana because that was Odysseus' childhood name for her. She had been nurse to him and later to his son, Telemachus, and she had been housekeeper in the palace for many years.

Now, she was preparing Antikleia's body. It seemed strange to Klymene that something that had already been so thoroughly cleansed by the sea needed to be washed all over again. Nana wept as she anointed the pale limbs with the finest oils and wrapped the embroidered shroud around them and covered Antikleia's face. Klymene could see from her place by the door that the dead woman had lost many of the wrinkles she had had in life. The skin, even though it was white and slightly swollen from being too long in the water, looked smooth and clear.

Nana had done her best to shield the twins from the sight of a body being prepared for burial. She had sent them out to the hillside behind the palace to gather wild herbs to strew over the shroud. Klymene knew what her grandmother would be doing while they were gone: closing the queen's eyes and placing coins on them to pay the ferryman for the journey across the river that divided this world from that of Hades, God of the Dead.

'My poor Antikleia!' Nana sighed, and wiped her red eyes when Klymene returned with the bunches of rosemary and wild thyme. 'I washed her clean after she gave birth to Odysseus. I remember it so well. I washed the baby too. What a happy day that was! You should have heard him crying, as if he was telling us: *I'm Odysseus. Look at me!* And now, here we are: Odysseus' mother dead, dead and her child dead too, more likely than not. Or if he's alive, then he's lost to us. Aie, this is a life of sorrow, Klymene. Poor woman!'

She bent to kiss the head under the shroud and Klymene shivered as a sudden chill touched her flesh.

The queen's body lay in a darkened room for two days. Nana had turned her attention to the funeral ceremony and was now in the kitchen, preparing the feast that was to follow it. Klymene was with her, waiting to see what needed to be done. She would rather have been almost anywhere else, but today wasn't the day to pick a fight with Nana. She said, 'Can't you rest a little? You haven't stopped working for three days. I can help you, if you like.'

'You're a good girl. But it'll soon be over. There's a lot of work goes into funeral feasts.'

Klymene poured herself a cup of cool goats' milk from the jug that stood on the wooden table. Nana went on, 'This death reminds me of other deaths. Your mother's death. How could the Gods take my own daughter from me?' Tears stood in her eyes.

'I can't really remember her,' Klymene said. 'When I'm sad about her, it's for you, and not for me.'

Nana began to baste the roasting meats with a mixture of olive oil and chopped rosemary. Klymene looked around the kitchen. The sun was a little higher now, and its light made squares of gold on the floor. She could see, in the passage just outside, some of Nana's flowerpots, each one brimming over with geraniums – scarlet and pink and white – surrounded by lush green leaves. Her grandmother loved these flowers and looked after them carefully, making sure they were well watered in the hot weather and cutting away the foliage when it grew dry and brown. Argos, Odysseus' ancient dog, was stretched out in the coolest part of the room, as far away from the fire as possible.

Nana smiled at her granddaughter. 'Penelope has been almost as good as a mother to you. She's fond of your brother, of course, but to you she speaks as freely as though you were of her blood. But enough. Enough of the past. All this was long ago, and now there's another funeral to see to. Hades, the God of Death, visits us often.'

Nana left the meat roasting on the spit and sat down at the kitchen table, saying: 'Now, let me see. What remains to be done? The wine, the scattering of fragrant herbs. And speaking of fragrance, I'd thank you if you took that smelly dog out of here and went to find Telemachus. He won't be ready for the burial and that'll be my fault.'

'Come on, Argos,' said Klymene. 'Nana is busy again. In spite of having servants to help her with the funeral arrangements, she has to do everything herself. She has to make sure things are done as she likes them.'

'If you do something yourself, it gets done properly. I've always said that. But you'll be helping me if you can find Telemachus.'

'What should I tell him – if I do find him?'

'To go and bathe before the funeral rites begin and to make sure that his hair isn't standing on end. He's too old to let me smooth it for him, but I used to do it for his father and I'm happy to do it for him, if he's willing.'

'He won't be. He thinks it's babyish to have a nurse.' Klymene put a hand on Argos' collar and the old dog stood up at once, eager to follow wherever she led.

'Good dog,' she said, and turned to her grandmother. 'He *is* a good dog. He always likes coming with me.'

Argos had been Odysseus' hunting dog. He spent most of his time lying on his side, panting in the heat of the day and occasionally giving a snuffly snore that shook his whole body. There was a time when he was the scourge of the palace cats. These had always been allowed to roam freely near the storeroom where the grain was kept to drive the rats away. Now the cats were sometimes to be found in the inner courtyard and near the kitchen door, and Argos hardly noticed their existence. He was nothing but a fur-covered skeleton of a hound, and so ancient that everyone agreed it was probably thanks to a God taking a fancy to him that he was still alive. Penelope thought he was waiting, just like her, for his master to come home, and she was superstitious about him.

'As long as Argos is alive, I can hope,' she often said. 'He'd know if Odysseus were dead.'

'You're the only person,' Nana said to Klymene, 'who loves him enough to get close to him. He's so old now. I'm surprised he hasn't dropped dead long ago.'

'Don't listen, Argos!' Klymene bent down and spoke into Argos' ear. 'Nana's being horrible. You're a good dog and a happy dog. Aren't you a happy dog?'

Argos wagged his tail feebly and Klymene said, 'There you are! He's happy.'

'Are you going? If not, I'll find someone else to look for Telemachus.'

'No, I'm going. Really.'

She left the room and Argos trotted after her, his claws making clicking sounds on the stones of the kitchen floor.

'Telemachus could be anywhere,' Klymene said. Everyone in the palace was quite used to her speaking to Argos as though he were human. She told him what was in her thoughts as they walked about the island; she wept into his fur whenever she was troubled; she whispered secrets to him that even her twin didn't know. This dog was her friend and she loved him. Was there something a little peculiar about holding long conversations with a creature who couldn't answer? Aloud she said, 'But you do answer, Argos, don't you? In your own way. A doggy way, but I can understand what you're saying. That's all that matters. Now, where d'you think Telemachus is?'

Argos sniffed the air and set off down a long covered passageway that ran along the side of the great hall of the palace. Klymene went after him, anxious suddenly at the thought of talking to her friend. Her heart was beating fast, and she felt her cheeks flaming. You never knew with Telemachus. Sometimes he was in a good mood; at other times a cloud of sullenness came over him and it was hard to get him to speak at all. She always looked forward to seeing him, though, and couldn't help feeling pleased that Nana had sent her to find him and not Ikarios.

Someone was walking along a little behind her and she turned to find out who it was. Then, scarcely able to believe what she was seeing, she stood motionless. A young woman dressed in shining white and carrying a quiver full of arrows tipped with silver stood close to her. Pale light came from her eyes; her hair was the colour of moonlit water and was bound up with silver threads. Argos, sensing something happening behind him, came back to sit at Klymene's feet.

'You are kind to the dog Argos,' said the young woman. 'I thank you for it.'

'I love him,' said Klymene. 'Are you . . . ?' She didn't dare to speak further, for fear this shining white vision would disappear.

'I am Artemis, Goddess of the Hunt and of the Moon. I care for this dog and for young women too. In his youth, Argos could sniff out prey on the other side of the island and follow it to the death.'

The Goddess began to travel along the passageway, skimming over the stone floor in her silver sandals. Argos trotted after her, and Klymene followed him.

'Wait, Argos, wait. I'm coming.'

Artemis had vanished. Klymene shivered. I'll say nothing, she thought. She felt suddenly happier, comforted. I won't tell anyone I've seen her.

'It'll be our secret, Argos, won't it? You won't tell and neither will I. And I know where you're going now. To the armoury because it's your favourite place.'

This was the room where all the weapons that belonged to Odysseus were kept. There was a pile of old skins in the corner where Argos liked to sleep in the afternoon, and Ikarios had put a bowl in the room. Klymene kept it filled with water. Now the dog was pushing the door open with his nose and Klymene followed him in.

'Clever Argos!' She stroked his ears. 'Here he is. You knew, didn't you?'

Telemachus was sitting on the floor with his knees drawn up to his chin and Odysseus' enormous bow on the floor beside him. In his hand was a small knife and he was stabbing repeatedly at a piece of wood he'd found on the floor. When he saw Klymene, he put the knife away in a leather purse that hung around his waist. He scowled at her as she stood in the doorway.

'Telemachus! What's the matter?' She sank down next to him and put an arm around his shoulders.

He shrugged it off. 'Nothing's the matter with me. Come here, Argos, good boy. Come and lie down next to me.'

Argos sank to the floor and put his legs in the air and Telemachus began to rub his stomach. Klymene would have felt jealous if Argos had behaved like this with anyone else, but she knew that the old dog thought he was a sort of bodyguard to Odysseus' son and that Telemachus for his part had loved him since they were all children together. She didn't mind if Argos rolled over for Telemachus.

'Are you sad?' she said. 'There's nothing wrong with that. It's the day of your grandmother's funeral. I'd be weeping if my grandmother was dead.'

'I was *not* weeping. It's womanish to cry and I don't. I never cry.'

'But you loved Antikleia and your sorrow honours her memory.'

'You don't know anything.' Telemachus rested his forehead on his knees.

He sounded sad and not angry as he spoke, so Klymene went on: 'Nana says she'll help you prepare for the rites. She's in the kitchen.' She tried to make him smile and added, 'She thinks she ought to smooth your hair.'

'As if I'd let her do that!' said Telemachus. 'What does she think I am? A toddler?' He looked as though he were on the edge of being normal again; of being less sad than he was before. He had picked up the end of the bow and now he was holding it up to show Klymene. 'If you really want to know, I'm not sad. Well, I am, of course, but that's not . . . I'm just . . . I don't know. Angry. Or something. I don't know what to call what I feel.'

He looked at her out of clear grey eyes fringed with long dark lashes and pushed a mass of dark brown hair away from his brow. Klymene felt a kind of weakening in her stomach, as though something were turning over inside her, and it was all she could do to stop herself from stroking Telemachus' bare shoulder, which was brown and smooth and very near her own. They'd grown up together. They'd played together every day since they were tiny babies. Telemachus was as close to her, almost, as her twin, and yet Ikarios was right. The feeling she had for him was not what she felt for her brother. When she and Telemachus were alone, if he chose to be with her instead of with Ikarios, or with the two of them, a kind of warmth filled her, as though a glowing fire had been lit in her heart. She'd begun to dream about Telemachus at night too. Ikarios almost never appeared in her dreams, and that, Klymene thought, meant that her love for Telemachus was different from what she felt for her brother. She said, 'Whatever you feel, I'll comfort you. You've always told me everything. You still can. Whatever it is.'

31

'I know,' Telemachus said. 'I shouldn't lie to you, Klymene. Haven't we always been friends? I *am* sad. I'll miss Antikleia. She told me the stories . . .'

'About Odysseus?'

Telemachus nodded. 'This was his bow. Look at it, Klymene. Will I ever grow strong enough to use something like this? There's not one chieftain in the islands who could do it. It's a bow for a hero. You know the song. We've been singing it all our lives, haven't we?'

He started to sing:

> *'Odysseus can bend the bow.*
> *No other mortal that we know,*
> *humble or highborn, swift or slow.*
> *Only our king can bend the bow.'*

He broke off abruptly and turned away from Klymene. 'Sometimes . . . there are days when I feel so furious with my father that I don't know what to do. I go and scream at the rocks or run and run till I can't move any more, because how could he do it? How could he leave me all alone and never come back? Where is he, Klymene? I want to see him. I want him to hold me in his arms and call me by my name. I've never said that to anyone before.'

Klymene put out a hand and laid it tentatively on Telemachus' arm. He didn't shrug it off so she kept it there as she spoke. She was almost whispering as she said, 'But Telemachus, what if he's dead? What then?'

'He's not. I know he's not. I feel it. I'm going to go and search for him. As soon as I'm old enough. I swear it, Klymene. I will.'

'He was in a war,' she said quietly. 'Many were killed at Troy. You've heard the tales.'

'There aren't any tales about him dying. And there would be, wouldn't there? Someone would've told us. He'd have died a hero's death and the singers would have sung songs about it. We'd have heard.'

'If he's alive,' Klymene said, 'he'll come home.'

Telemachus turned to face her and she saw that his eyes were brimming with tears again. 'What if he doesn't? What if he's found somewhere else to live? Someone else . . .'

'But your mother . . .'

'My grandfather told me' – Telemachus spoke so quietly that Klymene had to bend her head close to his to hear him – 'that men sometimes . . . if they're far away from their wives for a long time . . . well . . . they find other wives. Other women to live with. He says it happens quite often. And if they find wives . . .'

Telemachus fell silent and began to draw patterns in the dust of the floor with the toe of his sandal.

'What?' Klymene said. 'If they find wives . . . then what?'

'Those wives might have sons, mightn't they?'

'Yes,' said Klymene, understanding at once what he meant. 'They might have sons, but they wouldn't be you. Your father loves *you*, not the son of another man. You don't really think he'd forget about you?'

'I was very small,' Telemachus said. 'When he left

for Troy I was still a baby. Just crawling. He doesn't know me. He can't . . .'

He kicked at the floor. 'What am I going to do, Klymene? Everything's so sad. So awful.'

'You'll be brave,' said Klymene. 'Like your father's son.'

'Yes, I will,' Telemachus said. 'You're right. I'll come and find Nana with you. Help me lift this bow up on to its hook.'

Klymene struggled with her end of the bow, but at last they raised it up to its place on the wall. Telemachus left the armoury and Klymene went over to where Argos was fast asleep in his nest of skins.

'You stay here now,' she told the dog. 'It's too hot for you to go up to the cemetery for the rites. You sleep till I come and fetch you.'

Argos snuffled happily and opened one eye. He looked at Klymene and laid his head obediently down again.

The temple on Ithaka had been built in a clearing in the foothills behind the palace and beside it was the cemetery where the royal dead were buried. An avenue of cypress trees led up to it from the town. On the morning of Antikleia's funeral, the procession set out early from the great gates of the palace, before the sun had risen over the black mass of the mountain. First came the bier carried by four servants, bearing the shrouded body of the dead queen. Behind it King Laertes, his grey beard blowing in the breeze from the sea, walked with his head bowed. Tears, which he made no effort to wipe away, flowed down his cheeks. He was finely dressed in purple garments and he wore a mourning wreath of laurel leaves on his head like a crown. But even though his body was that of a ruler, his face was white and there were dark rings under his eyes. He looked like a confused old man: someone who didn't know exactly what was happening; someone who was bewildered by the events he was witnessing. Telemachus walked beside his grandfather, holding his arm to support him, and Klymene noticed that his hair had been tidied and flattened. He held his head high.

Penelope walked a little way behind them. Nana always said that as a young girl, Odysseus' wife had been lovely: graceful and slender, dark-eyed and with hair that gleamed like glossy chestnuts. Today she was as thin as a bone. Sleepless nights had left bruises under her eyes, fretting had made her cheeks pale, and her skin had become so thin that you could see the blue veins beneath. But even so, how beautiful Penelope was! Her gown was of white cloth, richly embroidered, and she had a scarf drawn over her head to cover her hair. Klymene thought, She looks like a queen: noble and silent and sad.

Everyone on the island had left their work and come out to line the way up to the cemetery. From where she was standing at the top of the path, near the burial place, Klymene could see them: old men, young men, women with their heads covered, children and babies, all gazing after the funeral procession and singing songs of mourning to mark the death of the queen. Fishermen had come up from the shore, their garments still wet from the sea. Farmers from the other side of the island had walked over the hills to watch the procession. The fruit had just been picked from the vines and from the trees in the orchards, and they were carrying baskets heavy with grapes and figs.

Klymene caught sight of Ikarios standing almost opposite her, on the other side of the path. Why hadn't he come to stand next to her? Now she would have no one to talk to while the offerings were made and the libations poured on the earth. All the palace servants had gathered to say farewell to their mistress. Nana was standing very close to Penelope, ready, Klymene knew, to help her if she fainted.

'A fine funeral,' said someone. 'This queen was loved by her people.'

Klymene turned to see who was speaking to her and saw a tall figure, cloaked in grey from head to foot. A man, she thought. No woman is so tall. This person wore the hood of his cloak pulled up over his head and it hid his face from view. She felt a chill coming from his body and she shivered and stepped away a little. She said: 'Yes, Antikleia was a good woman.'

'Good and bad, everyone comes to me in the end,' said the man. His voice was soft, and part of Klymene was surprised that she could hear it so well, considering the noise of weeping all around and the beating of the funeral drums.

She was about to ask his name, when he spoke.

'I am Hades, God of Death,' he murmured. 'This is my domain.'

Klymene took a step away from the God. Immediately she felt warmer. She looked away, towards the place where the bier had been placed on a raised platform and heaped with branches of olive and myrtle. When she turned back, there was no sign of him. She trembled and bent her head as Laertes stepped forward to make his funeral oration.

Laertes raised his hand and everyone in the crowd fell silent to hear his words. Before he began the king looked around, as though searching for someone, and from time to time he sniffed and wiped his eyes, which were red from weeping. Then he spoke and his voice shook: 'My beloved wife, Antikleia, will soon be laid in earth and we will beseech the Gods to be kind to her. The tears will dry on my cheeks, but in my thoughts they will flow for ever. I beg you, my people, to remember your queen. I gave the ruling of this island to my son when he married, for I would rather be a farmer than a king, but my wife was always the queen and now that she is dead that title passes to my dear daughter-in-law. I grieve for Antikleia. She could not bear to live without our son, Odysseus. She thought – I know this – that she might meet his shade in Hades, but . . . I hope. I still hope . . .'

Laertes' voice failed him and he stumbled. Telemachus went quickly to his grandfather's side and put an arm around him. Laertes nodded his thanks and wiped his eyes, and Telemachus led the old man to a stone bench and sat down next to him.

Penelope came forward and went to stand near the edge of the grave. Suddenly she fell to her knees on the ground and, covering her face with her hands, began to keen and cry and beat her fists on the earth. Nana rushed to her. Telemachus left Laertes' side to run and help his mother, and Klymene would have gone too, but her way was blocked by the crowds who had gathered around the grave.

'My husband . . . my Odysseus . . .' Klymene heard her words, even though they were muffled by the fabric of the scarf she was wearing. 'How will I live? Where are you, my love?' Penelope's sobs rose into the air.

'She's scared,' said a sour-looking woman, pushing Klymene aside in her eagerness to see more, hear better. 'Odysseus is probably dead too, and this funeral reminds her of it.'

'She thinks he's coming back,' another woman said. 'Or says she does. But of course you're right. Look at her now! You can't tell me anyone would weep like that over a mother-in-law.' They started to giggle under their breath and Klymene wanted to hit them, but she contented herself with an exasperated sigh and made sure to dig her elbows into one of the women's ribs as she pushed her way closer to the front of the crowd.

Penelope was helped to her feet. Telemachus whispered to her, and she stroked his face. Then she stood for a moment with her head bowed. When she looked up, her eyes were red and her lips trembled, but she seemed calm. She pulled her scarf over her head as she stepped forward to speak.

'My grief is great today. You have all seen me over-come by sorrow and I'm not ashamed of it. I'm not accustomed to speaking before so many people, but with my husband's mother gone from us, I want to say two things. The first is: I do not wish to be called Queen while my husband is not by my side, so I thank my dearest father-in-law and promise that I will do all he wishes me to do, but I would rather keep the name I have grown used to: Penelope. The second thing I have to say is this: Queen Antikleia found she could not live without her child, but I – I am quite sure that Odysseus is alive and will be restored to us when the Gods will it.'

Some people in the crowd began to murmur and Klymene could not tell whether this was because they agreed with what Penelope was saying or because, like those two stupid women, they thought she was deluding herself. The queen's voice was soft and trem-bled as she spoke. She went on: 'I don't know if the love of a wife for her husband can be compared with that of a mother for her child, but I live for the day when Odysseus comes home to Ithaka. He will return, I am sure of it, for he is under the protection of Pallas Athene and I will make offerings to her and pray that she may bring him back. I have spoken to King Laertes and we have agreed that each year a day at the end of the harvest will be set aside so that all may honour the Goddess and offer sacrifices for the safe return of my beloved Odysseus.'

Penelope stopped speaking, and Klymene noticed that she was holding the end of her scarf a little too tightly between her white fingers. She stepped back and bent her head, and then the crowd began to sing dirges: songs about Antikleia, and how loved she was, and how she had given birth to the great Odysseus, for which she would be remembered by both Gods and men. The music wailed and swooped and Telemachus, sitting next to his grandfather on the bench, was beginning to look bored. He was scuffing his feet on the ground, already eager to leave the cemetery, Klymene could tell. She knew how he felt because she too was longing to be out of the sun's heat and back in the cool of the great hall, helping to pour the wine at the funeral feast. There would be more singing in praise of the queen there, but it would be good to sit down and eat and drink. I wish it could be over, Klymene thought. Argos'll be wondering where I am. He'll have finished his water in this heat and his bowl is bound to need refilling.

'Where I am taking Antikleia, she will be out of the sun for ever,' a voice whispered almost in Klymene's ear. She turned at once and found herself face-to-face with Hades again. She tried to look into his eyes, but just as they had been earlier, they were hidden by the hood of the garment he was wearing. 'My kingdom is always cold.'

Klymene could see waves of heat shimmering over the earth, but she felt as though an icy mist were drifting around her. She blinked and when she opened her eyes, the God had moved. She saw him making his way through the mourners and going to stand next to Laertes. The old king was leaning over the grave, weeping and throwing clods of earth on to the shrouded body of his wife, and behind him the grey shape of the God loomed like a gigantic shadow.

WEAVING

Everything was much simpler when Telemachus and the twins were tiny, Penelope thought. In the days following Antikleia's funeral, that time came into her mind more and more often. Life then was like making a plain blanket from wool of a single colour. There was no need to consider patterns, changes, complications. She had passed from one task to another: feeding the infants, handing them to their nursemaids, playing with their pretty naked toes as they lay in the shade of the trees in the courtyard, singing songs to them while she rocked their cradles – songs that had no real words, only nonsense she'd spun from her love and her care. The fabric of life then was plain, and because children are all-absorbing, also tiring. There were many, many nights, Penelope remembered, when all she'd had energy for was to take her clothes off before falling into a deep and untroubled sleep until Telemachus woke her in the morning. Since he'd been weaned from her breast, he woke up earlier than anyone in the household and she, his mother, had charge of him till the servants came to attend to his morning meal.

'He's up before Phoebus Apollo,' Nana always said. 'That shows energy and a love of life.'

Penelope said nothing, in case a God overheard her complaining about her child and sent sickness and infirmity as a punishment, but secretly she wished that her son would sleep at least until everyone else was awake.

Later, when Nana's daughter died, her twins Klymene and Ikarios became like Penelope's own family, and there were times when her father-in-law smiled at her and said: 'You're more like a nursery servant than a queen, my dear. All your days are spent on the floor pushing toy horses along the tiles and making dolls for all the babies to play with. You'd be better off attending to the farms and lands your husband left you in charge of.'

Penelope never answered back. There was nothing to be gained from contradicting Odysseus' father, who hadn't changed an opinion of his since before the war against Troy, so she merely smiled and said: 'You are the person who knows best what's to be done on the farms and with the livestock. All the tenants are devoted to you.'

'Hmph,' Laertes would mutter, stroking his beard. He was so pleased to hear her flattering words that he quickly forgot he'd chided her at all and began to tell her of his plans for this or that piece of land; this or that crop.

It's easy to please him, Penelope reflected. Antikleia had been harder to deal with but then it's probably always so. A mother is jealous of her son's wife. I shall be jealous of whoever Telemachus brings into this house, because his love will no longer be directed only to me. Now that Antikleia is buried and at peace, she thought, now that the funeral is over, I can return to my loom.

She picked from the basket a thread of blue that was the exact shade of the ocean she could see in the distance, and sighed. How much more difficult it was to bring up a child when its father was absent! She spoke of Odysseus to his son every day, keeping the memory alive in him of a parent he'd barely known, never spoken to, and it was she who had made her own son obsessed with his heroic father's deeds. Telemachus was so determined to believe that Odysseus was alive and would come back to them that she never, ever let him know her secret fears. There were times when she knew so completely that her husband was dead that she could almost smell the blood as it flowed from his body and soaked into the sands of the Trojan plain.

They passed, these moments, but when they were upon her, there was nothing she could do to hide them but pretend sickness. She used to tell everyone – Nana, Telemachus, Laertes . . . everyone – that her head was breaking into pieces with the pain and then she would lie on the wide bed that her husband had fashioned with his own hands and weep and weep and offer up prayers to Athene, whom Odysseus worshipped, to take these terrible visions from her.

The bed itself had always been a great comfort to her. Everyone in the palace knew about it. It was famous in the whole of Ithaka and beyond and travelling minstrels sang songs about it. When she became betrothed to Odysseus, he had cut the topmost branches from the handsomest olive tree on the island, and from the piece of the trunk that remained in the earth he carved a headboard and polished the wood till it shone.

'We'll make our marriage couch here,' he told her. 'I'll build our chamber around it, and when I've done that, I'll make a whole palace for us to live in until we grow old together. We'll die in the same bed we sleep in all our lives.'

Penelope remembered those days. Odysseus told everyone he was making a home for her; for his beloved. Laertes had thought they could all go on living in the old rooms, which had served the family for genera-tions, but Odysseus told him that only a magnificent edifice was fit for his new bride. Penelope smiled as she recalled how bad-tempered Laertes and Antikleia became while the building was going on. Odysseus brought together the best carpenters and masons in the island, and even from other islands nearby, to lay foundations for the palace around the olive tree and the bed that was now part of it, like a living thing planted for ever in the earth. They'd laid floors and put up walls and raised the pillars of the courtyard to a noble height. Then they'd hammered the roof into position over all the rooms that spread out and out from around this very chamber. The palace Odysseus built as a home for his bride was the glory of Ithaka.

The bed stood in the very centre of the room, out

of reach of any comforting wall. I sleep alone here now, Penelope thought, and it's as lonely as lying in the middle of a field or a plain. Antikleia, when she was alive, was always trying to persuade Penelope to leave this chamber and move to another. 'Just until Odysseus comes home,' is what her mother-in-law said; but she had refused. Whenever the subject was broached, Penelope simply went to the window and stared at the horizon to calm herself, wondering whether a passing breeze might whisper to her; tell her where Odysseus was and why of all the Greeks who fought in the ten-year-long war at Troy, he had to be the one who hadn't returned to his island; to his wife and son. But the owl – the owl *had* visited her. Since she had seen Pallas Athene's bird, her faith was much stronger, and whenever any doubts crept into her mind, she tried to recall exactly how happy, how relieved she had felt on that night.

There was so much to see to. Sometimes Penelope felt as though she were holding the reins of a dozen horses, all pulling her in different directions. Laertes, she knew, couldn't say anything to her, but she could guess what he was thinking. He wishes it had been me, she told herself. He wishes that *I* had walked into the sea and not his wife. *I'm* the one who ought to have gone to Hades to look for Odysseus. She wondered whether it was true that she had failed in her duty.

But he's still alive, she thought. I know he is. I'll wait for him and be brave, just as I promised, but how my body hums with longing! Penelope shook her head and felt herself suddenly stretched as taut as the wool on the loom in front of her. The palace was very quiet. Everyone was sleeping. Sometimes she wished she could leave the room, and leave the wooden structure that held her as fast as any cage. I can't, she said to herself. I can't leave the loom because the picture is there and until it is done, I have to weave it. I have to find it. How impossible it would be to explain this to anyone: her hands needed to move.

She bent over the loom in front of her, and the bed behind her, with its carved headboard, rose up towards the ceiling like a wall of wood. Penelope stood and stared at the threads stretched tight on the frame, and after a time her eyes grew misty and she felt in her fingers what the colours should be; where the shuttle needed to go. She knew then how the work would be done. Her hands moved as though they did not belong to her and the threads began to weave more than pictures. They wove a story.

blue and green now
a land full of grass for pasture
caves high in the hills   the sky clear
something dark on the mountain
blue wool   thin spun green   one black thread the
*   ship*
weft warp   forth back   weft warp
back forth   warp weft   back forth
red red red   yellow for sun
forth warp   back weft

The Cyclops Polyphemus lies asleep.
A fire burns and burns in the black cave
and flickers gold and scarlet in the dark.
Odysseus has in his hands a branch
that glows white-hot from lying in the flames.
He plunges it into the giant's head.
The Cyclops screams and stumbles to his feet
and writhes and groans and vainly tries to pluck
from his huge, melting, suppurating eye
the fiery spear on which he is impaled.
Odysseus and his men wait for the dawn.

thin watery blue   egg white white
back forth   weft warp
blue green   more blue   one black thread the ship
back forth   weft warp
forth warp   back weft

Argos dreams

deer and rabbit and wild boar and more fresh bloody meat than I could eat once and now nothing but old smells and waiting and waiting and on the wind today the stink of ancient bones and roasted sheep meat and blood soaked into the earth and goat dung and black smoke from charred flesh and cold ashes

THE CAVE OF THE NAIADS

After the three days of mourning for Antikleia were over, Telemachus and Ikarios went down to the seashore to explore the cave of the Naiads. Ikarios still felt nervous about it, but what could he say when Telemachus was so determined? He didn't want to be called a coward. No sooner had they reached the mouth of the cave than Telemachus disappeared inside and called over his shoulder: 'Come on, Ikarios! What's the matter with you? I thought you were following me.'

His voice sounded strangely echoey. Ikarios hesitated at the entrance, not really wanting to go with his friend into the clammy darkness but knowing that if he didn't Telemachus would laugh at him and call him a coward. The sun was hot on the white sand. The sea lay like a cloth striped in blue and green from the shore to the horizon, and you could see the fishing boats in the distance. The fishermen will be singing, Ikarios thought. They'll be throwing the nets out over the water and dragging in the fish to squirm and leap over the deck. He became aware of someone sitting

50

on a rock and watching him. Ikarios squinted to see better, but this person was no one he recognized. An old man, with a long beard that seemed to glitter in the light as though fish scales had been caught up in it and not been washed away properly. A fisherman perhaps. His clothes seemed to hang from his thickset body like rags. He was getting down from the rock and walking towards Ikarios.

'Good morning, sir,' Ikarios called out politely, hoping the old man would walk straight past him and leave them alone. As he came closer, Ikarios had to hold his hands down by his sides or he'd have pinched his nostrils together to stop the odour of raw fish and salt and seaweed from burning the back of his throat. The smell that surrounded the old man was over-whelming.

'My shore,' the stranger said as he passed Ikarios. 'Remember that.'

'The shore belongs to no one,' said Ikarios. 'Or perhaps to the rulers of the island. To Odysseus and his family.'

'Nonsense. It's mine. No one crosses Poseidon, boy. Bear that in mind. See those rocks? I could toss them up like a baby's bricks and rearrange them with one breath. You've felt the land shake under your feet sometimes, have you not? That is my doing and I could do it again.'

Ikarios hesitated before he spoke. Was this man truly Poseidon or just a fisherman with madness in his eyes? Klymene had seen Pallas Athene not far from here, on the day they found Antikleia's body. That, anyway, was what she said. He was her twin, grown from the same seed, Nana always said – could it be that he too had seen gods in his life and not known it? He said, 'I think you've had too much wine, old man. Perhaps you ought to go and lie down.'

'Lie down?' The man's voice was like the rumble of thunder on a distant mountain. 'You don't believe me, do you? Foolish boy.' He turned towards the blue ocean. 'See that? Flat as a shield, is it not? Calm as a lullaby. Watch.'

He made a soft blowing sound with his lips, breathing out as you do to cool the broth on a plate, and the water began to withdraw. It was as though someone unseen was pulling a cloth away from a table, wrinkling it up and leaving the wood exposed.

Ikarios stood with his mouth open in amazement. Where were the waves? What had happened to the ocean? Now there was nothing but sand almost as far as the horizon . . . shining like polished bronze in the air that had suddenly become heavy, as though the light had thickened and become solid. He turned to the old man and said: 'Lord Poseidon, I'm sorry. I'm sorry I didn't know you. Please, bring the sea back . . . can you bring it back?'

Poseidon frowned. 'I can do anything I choose to do.' He lifted his arm, and Ikarios noticed that the skin was scaly and iridescent, like that of a fish. The God made a gesture with his fingers, and Ikarios heard something: a whisper of noise. As he watched, the ocean returned. A wall of water, curled up into one long wave as high as the tallest trees, skimmed over the sea bed towards the shore, and Ikarios had to cover his ears because the air was filled with sound like the drumming of a thousand hooves and the roaring of a thousand wild beasts. He wanted to shut his eyes but couldn't. The blue-green wall was nearly upon him now. He'd be drowned if he didn't move, but his legs had turned to stone. Telemachus. Telemachus in the cave. He'll die, Ikarios thought. The wave'll break and the cave'll fill up with water and he'll drown.

'Lord Poseidon!' he shouted. 'Stop the wave! I implore you! Telemachus will die. I'll die too, but he's the son of Odysseus. He'll be our king on Ithaka. He can't die! I beg you, Lord Poseidon!'

Ikarios sank to his knees and covered his head with his hands. Klymene. Nana. Telemachus. Hades. He waited, unable to think, hearing the beating of his own heart in his ears, louder than the water. It must be nearly here, he told himself. The wave'll break at any moment. Terror ran through his veins like ice, and he felt cold and as though every breath had been pushed out of his chest.

'Get up, lad,' said Poseidon, and Ikarios stumbled to his feet. The wave had frozen into an arch above his head, and what he could see was a translucent high ceiling of solid unmoving water.

'Lord Poseidon, I thank you.'

'So you should. Odysseus' son. I don't know why I should have such a care of him, considering his father's treatment of my child. I will never forgive Odysseus for that. There is much I won't forgive him for, but that is the worst. A father's vengeance is terrible . . . terrible.'

Ikarios saw him put out a hand and wipe something from his eye. Was the God weeping? Poseidon sighed deeply before he spoke again. 'Never mind,' he murmured. 'Not this time, eh? I've still got a trick or two. Not today. Today I'm grieving. I can wait.'

The wave withdrew from above their heads, and before Ikarios could find the words to thank the God again, it had shrunk back to become the sea Ikarios knew: lines of gentle wavelets trickling on to the shore and breaking in tiny frills of foam over the sand.

'You have not seen the last of me,' said the God, leaning in close, so close that his breath, stinking of old fish and dark waters, filled Ikarios' nostrils. 'I have a plan, you know. But I will say farewell until next time.' Poseidon walked briskly away. A sea breeze blew the stench of him towards Ikarios again, but he'd gone.

Ikarios peered into the cave mouth. The silence was unsettling. Telemachus wasn't usually so quiet.

'Come out, Telemachus. It's safe now. I've saved your life,' he shouted in a voice he hoped sounded cheerful and brave.

'What nonsense have you got into your head now?' Telemachus' voice sounded strange, booming from the cave. He emerged from the darkness, blinking a little.

'Poseidon. I've just seen him. He . . . he sent a wave that nearly flooded the shore and the cave and everything else but I . . . I told him you were in there and he made it all go away. He's gone now.'

'And you're moonstruck. Poseidon, right? You're making it up.'

'I'm not. I saved your life.' Ikarios could hear himself. He sounded aggrieved, like a sulky little girl. He added, 'I don't care if you don't believe me. I know what I saw. And you know we're not allowed in the cave of the Naiads either. If your grandfather finds out, he'll have you beaten. And shout at you. Let's go climbing. Really good rocks over there. Come on.'

'There's nothing to be frightened of. You don't believe that Naiad stuff, do you? They're no truer than the Poseidon story you just told me. It's women. They make up those stories to frighten us away, Ikarios. You spend too much time with your grandmother and your sister. You'll become like them: womanish.'

'No, I won't,' Ikarios said, though he feared that indeed that might happen to him. Telemachus had always been much more daring than he was. He'd been like that even when they were small children. He was always ready to climb the most difficult-looking tree, risking a fall without a second thought. I look ahead too much, Ikarios told himself. Telemachus doesn't care a fig about what could happen. He never thinks anything can possibly harm him. I wish Poseidon had waited till both of us were on the shore before he showed himself. He felt anger sweep through him. The one and only time that he'd had something astonishing happen to him; the one and only time he'd been brave and actually stopped Telemachus from dying, and he wasn't believed. He kicked out at a small shell lying on the sand and sent it flying.

'Stop looking so glum,' Telemachus said. 'Why d'you care whether I believe you or not?'

Because I want you to be grateful. Because I want you to think I'm as brave as you are. Because I want you to like me better than you like Klymene. Ikarios couldn't say the words because they would make him look weak and stupid. Better to keep silent.

Telemachus said, 'I'm going to explore in here, so if you don't want to sit on the sand all by yourself, you'd better come too.'

'I'm coming,' Ikarios said, and the two boys stepped into the darkness together.

'It's always cool in caves,' Telemachus said. 'Good to be out of the sun.'

'Cold, more like.' Ikarios didn't add that it was dark and that the rocks beneath their feet were becoming more and more slippery with each step they took.

'Shout something,' Telemachus said. 'There'll be an echo.'

Ikarios didn't want to shout. If there were any Naiads watching them from secret hiding places, shouting might disturb them, and if they were disturbed, who knew what they'd do? He didn't want to find out.

'You're scared, aren't you?' Telemachus laughed, and began to shout himself: 'Are you listening, Naiads? Spirits of this cave, I'm summoning you. Ikarios here is terrified, but I'm not! I'm the son of the hero

56

Odysseus and when I grow up I'm going to be a warrior, just like him. Speak to me!'

'Telemachus, don't! You can't call them like that . . .'

Telemachus laughed. 'Come on, then, let's go and climb your stupid rocks. It's no fun being here with you. You're making me nervous. Come on.'

He set off in the direction of the cave mouth again, and Ikarios was relieved. He'd heard something, or someone, breathing in the cave and his heart was hammering in his chest. He'd been on the point of mentioning it and now he wouldn't have to. When they were safely out in the sunshine again, the two boys went to sit on the sand near the water line. Little waves rushed up over their feet and into the hole that Telemachus was idly digging with one hand.

'Did you hear it?' Ikarios asked.

'What?'

'I don't know. I heard something breathing. I think.'

'I didn't.' Telemachus picked up two handfuls of wet sand and threw them at Ikarios.

'Stop it!'

'Try and make me . . .'

'Right,' said Ikarios and he launched himself at Telemachus, wrestling him backwards till he was lying on the ground. 'Now . . . you can't move, can you?'

'I can—'

'No you can't. I've got you pinned down. You couldn't get up. I'm bigger than you.'

'Fatter, you mean—'

'No, just bigger. Stronger.'

'But not braver. Or cleverer. Also, you never follow through with a threat. You lose all your advantage. I'm not like that, as you know. I've beaten you often enough. Come on, Ikarios, this is boring. Let's go and climb those rocks.'

'Say you heard it.'

'I didn't hear anything.'

'You're lying.'

'All right, I admit it. I'm lying. Let me up. Go on.'

Ikarios rolled over and allowed Telemachus to sit up again. 'You only said that because you wanted me to release you, didn't you?'

Telemachus was suddenly serious. 'No. I really did hear something. I thought . . . Well, I thought it was you at first, but then it seemed to be coming from the wrong place. An animal hiding in the cave, I expect.'

'Naiads,' said Ikarios. 'Everyone knows that's their cave.'

'You believe that? Honestly?'

Ikarios nodded. 'I'm not the only one, either. When your grandmother died . . . when we found her . . . that day, Klymene saw Pallas Athene. Don't tell her I told you.'

'She's a girl,' said Telemachus. 'They're always imagining things.'

'She wasn't imagining it. What are you saying, Telemachus? That you don't believe in the Gods?'

'Of course I believe in them. They have charge of everything. And I believe in Pallas Athene who's a friend to my father. I believe she protects him. But . . .'

58

'What? What were you going to say?'

'Sometimes I wonder, that's all. It's hard to keep on believing when nothing happens. When the seasons go by and he doesn't come home.'

'He will,' Ikarios said.

'You're just saying that. You don't want me to get in a mood.'

Telemachus was right. Ikarios knew it was wise to go along with his friend, who was capable of keeping up a gloomy silence for a very long time if he was in a bad temper. You could almost see a cloud of misery hanging around his shoulders when that happened. Klymene was good at lifting his spirits, but Ikarios had no idea how to go about cheering Telemachus and so he generally said nothing and just waited till his good temper came back all by itself. Also, what he'd just said was quite true. In his deepest soul, Ikarios didn't know whether Odysseus would return to Ithaka or not. Probably he was dead and had been in Hades for a very long time. Antikleia, his own mother, had thought that, so maybe it was true.

Argos waits

and the days are passing and the moons are turning and the waiting is long and the nights follow one after another and the sea moves around the land and the land sleeps and wakes and breathes

MELANTHO

Klymene was sitting under one of the peach trees in the orchard. Soon it would be time to go up to the cemetery and take part in the annual ceremony of prayers and offerings to Pallas Athene, beseeching her to send Odysseus back to his island. It had been held on the same day for the past two years – the anniversary of Antikleia's funeral – and everyone called it the Remembering.

'Talking to Argos as usual, I see.'

'Telemachus! You shouldn't sneak up like that. You gave me a fright.'

'Your grandmother sent me to fetch you. Are you ready?'

Klymene nodded. She pulled at Argos' collar and began to walk towards the palace with Telemachus beside her. He was already dressed for the ceremony and Klymene thought she'd never seen him looking so handsome. She blushed and wondered why it was that she found it harder to know how to *be* with Telemachus than she used to. He'd changed. His arms were not a boy's arms any longer. They looked stronger, harder: almost like the arms of a man. He wasn't tall, but his body was slim and strong and his hair hung down on to his shoulders in brown curls that should have made him look girlish but somehow did not. His eyes, which Penelope said were inherited from his father, were such a pale grey that they seemed luminous, and they were fringed with thick, dark lashes. Nana had often told Klymene how she used to kiss him when he was a baby and say, *These eyelashes are wasted on a boy. Quite wasted.*

Now, very soon, his beard would start to grow properly and he would have to scrape the hair away with a sharp blade. I used to wrestle in the sand with him, Klymene thought, and climb trees with him and Ikarios, but now I'm supposed to be a young woman, and Nana says it's unseemly to pick up my skirts and run races on the seashore.

She glanced at Telemachus as they walked and wished that he would say something. Ikarios had been right after all, and what she was feeling now for her childhood friend was like nothing she had known before. Was this love? Certainly she found that whenever Telemachus and she were alone, she became short of breath and quite often blushed when he spoke to her. Lately she'd begun to daydream about him, which meant that when they were together what she'd been imagining came between her and the real person she'd known all her life. Sometimes, as she lay in her bed at night, she would imagine Telemachus' arms around her. His mouth on hers . . . what would that feel like? Thinking about such things left her tossing and sighing and clutching her pillow to her breast as though it were flesh and blood.

'I'll take Argos to the armoury and then I'm ready. Can I come with you to the cemetery?'

Telemachus smiled and wrinkled his nose. It was what he always did when he knew that you wouldn't like what he was going to say. Klymene wondered what was coming.

'I have to walk with my grandfather and my mother. I'm sorry, Klymene. It's expected now. I'm supposed to act more like a prince these days. I'll see you later, though. And Ikarios. Tell him I'm sorry, won't you?'

Klymene nodded and Telemachus waved at her as he hurried to Laertes' chamber. She and Argos set off in the direction of the armoury. I should've expected it, she thought. Telemachus wouldn't have been allowed go on fooling around with us at the back of the crowd for ever. Penelope will need him to stand at her side more often, now that we're older. Klymene felt a sadness come over her. They still did so many things together, she and Ikarios and Telemachus, but how long would it be before it was decided that a servant's children were not suitable companions? There wasn't time to think about it now. She could hear the sound of drums and singing coming from the harbour. Everyone would be there already, down at the water's edge. For the last two years the Remembering had turned into a celebration. Everyone was in a happy mood because the fruit crop had been safely gathered in, and the wine was passed from hand to hand in leather bottles and the songs went on being sung till late at night.

'Gracious Goddess, send him homeward,
bring him safely back to shore.
Guard and keep our good Odysseus
safe and happy ever more.
We, his people, long to see him.
We have waited through the years.
Send his ship home, send it quickly.
Hear our song and dry our tears.'

The words rose from the throats of hundreds of people, all singing together, and Klymene knew that the tune would be winding its way through her head for a long time. No one knew who first sang it, but there it was, the summer after Antikleia's death, and by the next time the ceremony was celebrated everyone on Ithaka knew it by heart. Even Argos could probably bark the melody, Klymene thought, smiling to herself as she left the palace and walked down the path to the harbour. He hears it from me all the time.

She looked for Telemachus and there he was, looking a little uncomfortable standing with his mother and his grandfather on a specially built platform. Ikarios, who had lately become apprenticed to the palace carpenter, Ikmalios, had helped to put it up. Penelope was wearing a blue robe and her head was crowned with a garland of flowers. This gift had been brought to the palace yesterday by a group of young girls from the inland farms. Klymene was the one who'd had to find a basin for it and make sure that it kept fresh till this morning, and she felt proud to see how beautiful it looked.

Laertes stepped forwards to speak. 'My people, I am touched to see how many of you have come here to join me in remembering my dear wife, Antikleia, who died three summers ago, and my son, Odysseus, who is lost to us for now, but not, I pray, for ever. I have ordered new wine to be distributed to the taverns, and I beg you to pour a little of it on the earth as you drink, to please the Gods and show them that you remember them. May the fruit you have picked this year give you nourishment for many months. If the Gods are willing, we will meet here again next summer.'

Telemachus took this for a signal to leave the platform, and Klymene saw that he was making straight for her. Happiness filled her heart. He hasn't forgotten about me, she thought. He *does* want to be with me. There's no need to worry.

He said, 'Aren't you glad that was nice and short, Klymene? I am. My grandfather obviously also thinks it's too hot to stand around in the sun. Have you seen Ikarios?'

'He's with them, over there.' She pointed in the direction of a crowd of palace servants standing in the shadow of a tavern.

'Right. Only we arranged to go out in the boat. I'll go and remind him.'

He was gone before Klymene could say a word. She could feel her face turning scarlet. Why didn't he ask *me* to go with them? Why is it always Ikarios who gets to go everywhere with Telemachus? She turned and almost ran up the path to the palace. It's because I'm a girl, she thought. I was good enough to play with when we were little children, but now I'm different. I'm separate from the boys. They treat me as if I'm some other kind of creature now. I wish we didn't have to grow up. I wish we could have stayed children for ever.

When she reached the armoury, Argos struggled to his feet and came to greet her. Klymene sank to her knees and hugged him tightly around the neck.

'Oh Argos, you'd never do that, would you? Stop wanting to be with me? Of course not. You never change. I could be an old, old woman and you'd still love me, wouldn't you?'

The dog began to lick Klymene's face, and she allowed herself to cry. No one was going to see her. Telemachus preferred her brother's company to hers. What could she do about it? Nothing at all, except cry into Argos' fur and wish that everything could be as it used to be.

A few days after the Remembering Nana said, 'The queen's asked to see you. Go quickly now.'

Klymene left the kitchen at once. She always went quickly when Penelope summoned her, happy to be away from the cooking smells and the boring work Nana always found for her to do. The door to the bedchamber stood open, and even before she went in, she could see the queen, sitting on her chair, and someone standing behind her: a girl of about her own age, with hair the colour of beaten brass and eyes somewhere between green and blue. This person was holding a comb and twisting Penelope's hair into curls which she then anchored to her head with pins made of bone. Even before Klymene had been introduced to her, she decided that she didn't like her.

'Klymene, this is Melantho. She's come to join our household. Her father is a distant kinsman of Odysseus. I hope the two of you will be good friends. And Klymene, I leave it to you to make sure Melantho knows the workings of the palace. When Melantho has finished arranging my hair, and you've tidied up the wool round the loom, Klymene, you may go. I'm sure you're eager to see everything, Melantho. You'll be sharing a bedchamber with Klymene.'

'Yes, my lady,' said Melantho.

Klymene said nothing but bent her head to her task. She began to attend to the loom set up beside Penelope's bed, making sure that the stray ends of wool that had fallen to the floor yesterday were neatly swept up, but a wave of pure jealousy made her feel as though she would choke if she tried to say anything. I must be stupid, she chided herself. Stupid to think that I would be the only one. Of course Penelope must have more than one handmaiden. Nothing will change for me. She won't stop loving me just because there's another girl in the house. Melantho being here won't make any difference.

'There,' said Penelope. 'That's done now. How clever you are, Melantho! I shall put you in charge of my hair whenever I need to arrange it specially.' She turned to Klymene. 'And could you take Argos with you when you go, Klymene? He crept in here some time ago. I think he likes lying near the bed. I sometimes think he can still smell Odysseus in the fabric of the bedcovers. But he's so smelly, poor thing! I can't have him staying here.'

Klymene went to the door and made kissing noises with her mouth to coax the old dog. Penelope said, 'Go on, Argos, good doggie. Go with Klymene. She'll see you're given such a lovely bone. Go on. Out you go.'

Argos made an enormous effort and opened an eye. Klymene moved to his side and pulled gently on his leather collar. He stood up, wobbling a little as he walked.

'He'll come with me, lady,' Klymene said. 'I'll find him a place in the courtyard. A nice shady place, where he'll keep cool.'

'Thank you,' said Penelope. She stood up and went to sit down in front of the loom. Klymene saw that, as usual, she was staring at the frame in front of her, not seeing it. Her hands were in her lap. She was murmuring to herself.

I wish I could stay here, Klymene thought. I wish Melantho would go back where she came from. I wish . . . There's no point in wishing anything. She waited for Melantho to join her in the corridor.

Klymene and Melantho made their way to the outer courtyard, where everything shimmered in the heat of a fierce noonday sun. Klymene put her hand up to her brow to protect her eyes. Argos followed them as they crossed over to the shade, and dragged himself to his favourite cool spot. Klymene made sure that he was comfortable, and turned to Melantho.

'If you follow me,' she said, 'I'll show you where everything is, and where you're going to sleep.'

'How old are you?' said Melantho.

'I'm fourteen years old,' Klymene answered sharply and thought: has this person never heard of thanking someone? She reminds me of a snake. It's because she's so smooth: the way she moves and walks as though there are no bones in her body. Slipping and sliding, that's what it looks like. I wish I didn't have such dull brown hair and eyes the colour of raisins. When Melantho smiled, the smile didn't reach her eyes, even though her mouth was stretched into the right shape. As they walked along together, Klymene spoke because she felt she had to fill the silence.

'Argos is Odysseus' dog.' The girls had come to a place in the courtyard where goatskins and sheepskins were heaped into a kind of nest. Argos looked particularly large and skinny. Klymene saw his fur through Melantho's eyes and it did seem very scanty and flea-bitten. Also, he was dribbling from a mouth that hung open, showing his brownish tongue. She leaned forwards and stroked him gently behind the ears. 'He's very old, but my grandmother says he won't die because he's waiting for his master to come home. He can't hunt any longer, but he used to be the very best hunting dog on Ithaka when he was young.'

'I think the queen's right: he's smelly and

revolting,' said Melantho. 'Are you sure he's not ill? Perhaps it would be merciful to such an old dog to put him out of his misery. He doesn't look as though he can move much.'

Klymene frowned. She wanted to say, *Don't talk about him like that. I love him. He's my friend,* but she was silent, out of politeness. She said, 'He can move when he has to. He sleeps a lot and he enjoys his food. Killing him would be like killing a dear old friend.'

Melantho sniffed, as if to say: *change the subject. I've had about as much talking about dogs as I can stomach.* She began to walk away from Argos, and Klymene ran to catch up with her.

'Who's that?' Melantho asked. She was looking at Ikarios and Telemachus, who were kneeling on the ground near the entrance to the great hall of the palace, playing an elaborate game they'd devised and that Klymene found boring because all you had to do was throw stones and catch them again.

'It's my brother, Ikarios. We're twins.'

'The small dark one? Yes, I can see that he looks just like you. But who's the other boy?'

'That's Telemachus, son of our king Odysseus and Penelope.'

Melantho stopped and stared, and her snake-smile became wider and more snake-like.

'He's our friend,' Klymene added. 'Our grandmother was nurse to him and to his father before him. We were brought up together.'

'Then will you introduce me, please? I'd like to meet him.'

'Now? We're going to see the sleeping quarters and the kitchen.'

Klymene thought, What impudence she has, this Melantho! It isn't up to her to say what she wants to do and when. She ought to be shyer, less brazen. She should be following me, learning from me.

'The kitchen'll still be there in a few minutes,' Melantho said quietly. 'And the sleeping quarters also.'

Klymene nodded, because she couldn't think of anything to say that might delay the introduction. She set off quickly in the direction of the boys.

'This is Melantho,' she called out to them when she was near enough to be heard. They stopped throwing stones and stood up.

'Welcome to our home,' said Telemachus, and to Klymene's surprise, he bowed from the waist.

'Yes,' Ikarios added. 'I hope you'll be happy here.'

'I will, I'm quite sure,' said Melantho, and she fixed her eyes on Telemachus. Klymene felt sick. She could see that if this girl was like a snake, then Telemachus was like a baby rabbit, mesmerized by her, transfixed, unable to move. He's enchanted, she thought. If she asked him at this moment to do anything, anything at all, he wouldn't hesitate. What did it mean?

The heat was blurring her vision. Was that a boy, hiding in the doorway of the armoury? She saw something flying through the air and followed it with her eyes: an arrow shape of blue light that shimmered past her and embedded itself in Telemachus' breast, where it hung quivering for a long moment before it dissolved under her gaze. He was still there, the boy, looking straight at her and holding a finger up in front of his mouth: *Be silent. Don't say a word.* Klymene recognized Eros, whose arrows pierced human hearts with a love they couldn't help and couldn't alter. Had anyone else seen him? No, everyone was staring at Melantho. When she turned back to the God, he had gone and everything was ordinary again. Still, Klymene understood that she had witnessed something important, something that would change all their lives for ever. As she and Melantho walked away to see the sleeping quarters at last, she knew that Telemachus was staring after them.

'He's still watching me, isn't he? I know he is,' Melantho said in a self-satisfied voice. 'He's in love with me.'

'Don't be ridiculous!' Klymene clenched her fists to stop herself from hitting this stupid creature who didn't know anything about any of them. 'He's only just met you. No one falls in love so quickly.'

'You're wrong,' Melantho said quietly. 'Eros' arrow is swift. It's hit Telemachus. I could almost see it, quivering in his breast.'

They had arrived at the sleeping quarters for the female servants of the household. The rooms were arranged one after another along a corridor.

'That's your bed,' said Klymene, pointing to a low couch pushed up against the wall. The coverlets on both beds were finely worked, by Nana in her younger days, with an embroidery depicting animals and flowers in red and blue threads. The window just above Klymene's bed looked on to the outer courtyard and there was a view of part of the town in the distance.

Had Melantho really seen the God? Klymene wanted to ask her, but the moment passed and she said nothing.

'Oh, well,' Melantho said, sitting down on her bed, making it her own. 'I suppose this will have to do. It's not what I'm used to, of course, but there will be good things about living here.'

Klymene felt that life in the palace would never be quite as pleasant again, but she said nothing. Perhaps Melantho is right about Eros, she thought. I don't like the thought of Penelope growing fond of her, and I hate the thought of Telemachus liking her better than he likes me. Am I jealous? I am. I am, so does that mean that I'm in love with him? Even thinking this made goose pimples break out on her arms. She took a strand of her hair and began to twist it in her fingers. If, she thought, I can be jealous and in love, then so can Telemachus. Everything was going to be difficult from now on. Everything was going to be different.

'Are you seriously telling me,' Laertes said, 'that you're happy to spend all this time shut away in here working on *that*?' He pointed to the picture that was beginning to take shape on the loom in Penelope's chamber.

What can I say, Penelope thought, that won't sound rude and unfriendly? I can't say what's in my heart: that I wish you wouldn't come in here and try and cheer me up when I'm working. That I wish I could comfort you for the loss of your wife, but you've always been a difficult man to talk to, even though I love you: cantankerous and irritable and quick to take offence. She said, 'I'm very happy, Laertes. I find it soothing. And there's little going on in the palace that's of more interest. We lead a quiet life here.'

'Too quiet. I'm thinking of asking Leodes to stay with us for a while. It'll take some time to send a boat to ask him – but in a few moons he could be here. What d'you think of that?'

'You must do whatever you feel is best, and I'm sure a visit will make you feel more cheerful.'

'Yes, it will. It will.' Laertes strode around the chamber and peered out of the window. 'We ought to get the gardeners to cut this fig tree back a bit. It's creeping in over the sill.'

'I'll speak to them,' Penelope said, resolving to do no such thing. The fig tree's branches, where Pallas Athene's owl had sat so long ago, would never be cut back if she had anything to do with it. Perhaps, she thought, the bird might visit me again if it remains as it was. Unchanged and unchanging.

'We could go hunting,' said Laertes. 'And fishing too, perhaps. It's a very long time since I've done that.'

'Lovely,' said Penelope. 'Though Telemachus goes hunting and fishing, you know. You could go with him.'

'No, no – he'd be impatient with me. Don't want to hold back the young. Not good for them. No, Leodes will be a more suitable companion. For both of us.'

'I'll welcome him here as a visitor of yours.'

Laertes pulled at his beard and Penelope felt him staring at her. He smiled and his face was transformed so that he looked the very picture of a benevolent grandfather. He said, 'Leodes used to be a very handsome man when he was young. Do you remember him?'

'Indeed,' said Penelope. 'Though I don't see why Leodes' handsomeness has anything to do with me.'

'Well, well . . .' said Laertes.

'You think you're being subtle, Laertes' – Penelope smiled back at him – 'but I know what you're up to, you know.'

'And what might that be?'

'You'd probably be delighted if I married him. I know you don't believe Odysseus is alive—'

'And you do? Can you tell me honestly that you still think he might return?'

'He will return, sir. I know it,' said Penelope. 'So invite Leodes by all means, but please don't plan my wedding to him.'

Laertes shrugged his shoulders. 'Now I know where Telemachus gets his obstinacy from,' he muttered. 'Well, never mind. I'll leave you to your work.'

'Farewell, Laertes.'

The old man waved a hand at Penelope and left the room. *Obstinacy from me*, she thought with a smile. *That was funny, coming from someone who in all the years she'd known him had never changed his mind about anything. I must stop thinking about him. I must go to the loom.*

She approached her seat in front of the frame and gazed at the threads. They were waiting for her shuttle; waiting for the pattern to emerge. Her hands reached

down to the basket at her feet and found a shade of
blue that was almost silver. Yes.

what is the colour of the wind
silver and white   water and light
the black ship moving   still water

still blue and white   one black thread the ship
back forth   warp weft
the shuttle resting   rest
red wine yellow stars   and blue
deep blue the sea   the midnight sea
the colours lying ready for the loom.

There's Ithaka. There, on the starboard bow.
Tomorrow they will see their homes again.
For now they're drinking, singing, telling jokes.
A leather bag catches one sailor's eye.
'More wine,' he thinks and cuts the binding
        thongs.
Then from the open mouth come long white
        shapes
like scarves of mist and smoke and shimmering
        light
that twist and grow and swirl around the ship.
'Fools!' screams Odysseus. 'You have freed the
        winds
that good Aeolus bound up safe for me,
and now see how the water heaves and swells.
See how our ship is driven out to sea.

Who knows when we will see our home again?'
The ocean roars. The black ship ploughs the
 waves.
The winds, the hungry winds, blow ceaselessly.

green and black   white for foam
purple for storm clouds   one black thread the ship
back and forth   warp weft   back and forth

blue and more blue   nothing but the sea
no brown   no red   no firelight   orange now
a black thread for the ship   no white
warp weft   forth back   and no end to it

Argos dreams

stomach full and sleeping in the dark and silence and some-
thing there that can't be seen or touched or felt but loud noises
and crying and snorting and growling and cawing and
screeching and never mind never mind stay stay and forget
about everything and smell the oranges on fire

LEARNING THE TRUTH

Three moons had passed since Melantho's arrival at the palace and for the most part she had her own work in the household, but the folding of the sheets was a task that she and Klymene always did together in the laundry, a cool, high-ceilinged room in the outer courtyard, near the bathhouses.

'You've been here long enough, Melantho,' said Klymene wearily, 'to know how the sheets are folded. In half lengthwise first of all.'

'It's such boring work. Who cares how we fold them?'

Klymene didn't bother to answer and Melantho went on: 'I'm in a rush today, anyway.'

There was a pause. Klymene thought: she's waiting for me to ask her why . . . I shan't. I don't care if I never discover where she's going. I'm not going to give her the satisfaction of showing curiosity. She won't be able to resist telling me.

'I'm going for a walk with Telemachus,' Melantho said, taking up another sheet and throwing it into the air, so that it billowed out and Klymene had to run to catch it. She gritted her teeth.

'Why can't you just hand it to me? What if it fell on the ground?'

'Well, it didn't, so it doesn't matter, does it? Let's get on. He'll be here soon. We're going up into the hills, I think. We went to the seashore yesterday.'

'I'm sure you'll have a very pleasant time,' said Klymene. She was longing to ask: *What happens when you're together?*

'He sometimes walks very quickly,' Melantho said. 'You should have seen how far we walked the other day. Right across the island, over some really rocky patches. I'd never have been able to manage some of them, but he helped me, holding my hand to steady me, and even carrying me at one point. He's very strong for his age, don't you think?'

Klymene nodded but said nothing.

Melantho went on: 'If I tell you something secret, do you promise not to tell anyone? Anyone at all, even Ikarios?'

She had placed the folded sheet with the others in the basket and was smiling in a particularly smug way.

'Yes, I promise.' Klymene tried to speak calmly, not wanting to show how eager she was.

Melantho sat down on one of the benches near the door and said: 'Telemachus kisses me. Properly. When we're alone.'

'Oh,' said Klymene.

'Is that all you can say?' Melantho frowned, peeved at the lack of reaction to her revelation. 'I'm sure no one's ever kissed you, have they?'

'Do you like it?' Klymene had no intention of telling Melantho she was right. She had never been kissed; not properly.

'It's blissful. You feel as if you're melting away. The first time he did it, I went all trembly. I couldn't stand up properly, but he held me and it was all right then. I've got much better at it.'

She stood up, went over to Klymene and whispered in her ear: 'When we kiss, we have our mouths open. I can taste his tongue. In my mouth.'

'Horrible!' said Klymene, making a face. She glanced away, pretending to look for something in the depths of one of the baskets, but her body felt hot when she tried to think what it must be like: wet, open mouths. In her head, all at once, there was a picture of Melantho standing on tiptoe and pressing her body right up against Telemachus as he leaned down and put an arm around her. Klymene could imagine her with her back arched and felt suddenly weak with an uncomfortable mixture of jealousy and desire. What if it was me? she thought. How would his lips feel? She took a deep breath and found she was shivering, in spite of the heat.

'Greetings!' said a voice and there he was: Telemachus, standing in the doorway. 'Nana told me you were both here. You ready, Melantho?'

'There's not much more to do, is there, Klymene?'

Klymene nodded. Seeing Telemachus immediately after thinking about his mouth, about kissing him, filled her with confusion. She said: 'Yes, do go, Melantho. I'll finish up here.'

'Thanks,' said Melantho, taking Telemachus' hand.

'Bye, Klymene,' said Telemachus, and he and Melantho left the laundry together. I'm not going to watch them cross the courtyard, Klymene told herself, but she couldn't help it. No sooner had they gone than she flew to the window. They were still hand in hand. Klymene found that her eyes were misty with tears. How stupid I am to cry over him, she told herself, but I can't help it. She sat down next to the baskets and began to cry in earnest.

Towards evening Ikarios and Klymene were sitting together in the outer courtyard when Telemachus came back from his walk with Melantho.

'Telemachus!' Ikarios said. 'Back from your outing, eh? You might have asked us, you know.' Klymene was amazed. How did her brother, who was usually so shy and tongue-tied, dare to speak out so bravely. 'We wouldn't have minded coming for a walk to the hills, where it's cooler, but you've only got eyes for her, right?'

'You'll understand more easily when you're older.' Telemachus laughed and clapped Ikarios on the shoulder. 'It's nothing to do with you, Ikarios, truly. It's just that sometimes there are other sorts of things I prefer to do than spend my time playing children's games.'

'You're only one year older than we are,' Ikarios answered, frowning and kicking at the base of a pillar with his foot. 'And anyway, you know we don't play children's games any longer. You just want to moon after Melantho.'

'I don't moon, as you call it,' Telemachus said, and Klymene thought how pleased with himself he looked. 'I can't tell you what we do, but I promise you, I've got a lot further than mooning with Melantho.'

'Then why don't you become betrothed to her?' Klymene burst out, unable to stop herself from speaking and dreading the reply.

'My mother wouldn't let me,' Telemachus said. 'And in any case, I'm only fifteen. But you,' he couldn't resist adding, 'are both even younger than I am.'

He hadn't denied it. He hadn't said: *What nonsense, I don't really love her.* Klymene wanted to go on; to ask Telemachus directly what his feelings were, but he was already walking away towards his bedchamber before she'd gathered her thoughts and found the right words.

'Ikarios, don't look like that,' Klymene said, seeing that her brother seemed not much less upset than she was herself. 'He's still fond of us, you know. He's just . . . besotted.'

'You don't understand anything,' said Ikarios. 'You think I care about that spoiled brat Telemachus? He can set out in his stupid boat and never come back as far as I'm concerned.'

Ikarios stalked off in the direction of the carpentry workshop. Klymene stared after him. What did he mean? Could it be that he was in love with Melantho as well? She went to find Argos, wondering bitterly whether it was possible for any man to lay eyes on that girl without suddenly being pierced by Eros' arrow.

Argos waits

nights cooler sun dimmer water washing over rocks rocks in the sky rolling thunder more days more nights more moons more waiting more

IN THE ALMOND GROVE

Klymene lay under one of the finest almond trees in the grove behind the palace, where the leaves grew thick and the grass was pleasant to sit on. She stared at the pattern of leaves and branches above her head. The weather was unusually warm for the season, almost like summer. She and Ikarios, Telemachus and Melantho had come out together to eat in the shade of the trees, carrying a basket of cheese and bread and fruit and two stone bottles of cool water. It was Melantho's idea. She had been living in the palace for nearly a year, and in that time she had begun to get her way more and more often. She decides what she wants to do, Klymene thought, and then we do it. She seemed able to make everyone follow where she led. Today they'd all been persuaded to go for a picnic in the almond grove.

For a long time Melantho had sat next to Klymene and fiddled with her hair.

'You ought to have it twisted up like this,' she'd said, as she anchored a fat braid of hair on top of Klymene's head with one of her own bone hairpins.

Telemachus was leaning against the trunk of the tree and looking at the girls, and then Klymene had drifted into sleep, soothed by the touch of Melantho's hand on her head. Now she was astonished to find herself alone. She sat up. How could she have fallen asleep? Perhaps it was the heat. She looked around her. All the others had disappeared and the basket was gone too. Maybe Melantho had taken it back to the palace. Or Ikarios. Why hadn't her brother woken her up? Wait till I find him, she thought. He'd better have a good excuse.

There was no point staying here if they'd all decided to go back to the palace. Klymene stood up and began to walk through the grove, and then she caught sight of her brother, sitting on a tree stump with the basket on his lap. He was staring straight ahead of him.

'Ikarios? What's wrong? Is anything the matter?'

'No. I'm going back, that's all.'

'You don't have to lie to me, you know. I can see that there is—'

'Then you don't need to ask, do you? Go away and leave me alone.'

Klymene took no notice. She knelt down and took his hand. 'Tell me. I'm not going away till you do. You've been crying.'

'It's ridiculous. When I tell you, you'll see it's nothing to cry about.'

'It's Melantho, isn't it? What's she done?'

Ikarios shook his head. 'Nothing. Nothing wrong. She went for a walk with Telemachus. That's all.'

He stood up and, speaking over his shoulder, said, 'I'm going back now. Ikmalios will be waiting for me. Don't worry, Klymene. I'm perfectly all right.'

But I'm not, Klymene thought. She stood up and looked around. Melantho and Telemachus . . . the knowledge that they'd gone walking together was upsetting to her brother, but why? He'd hinted before that he was interested in Melantho, but Klymene thought he was more likely to be jealous that she'd taken up most of Telemachus' attention. Klymene sighed. Ikarios had always known what she felt about Telemachus, though he rarely mentioned it. And I must feel more than I admit to myself, she thought, or why am I so anxious about where they are now?

She set off in the direction of the mountain, away from the palace. Beyond the almond trees was the olive grove and that went on and on, but then she was out of it at last and walking towards the farms on the other side of the island. Huge oleanders grew on either side of the dusty path. These bushes were covered with pink and white blossoms and the air was filled with a heavy, bitter fragrance. A few drowsy bees buzzed drunkenly around the flowers. A heat haze shrouded the landscape, and Klymene shielded her eyes from the sun with one hand. A sound, some kind of animal noise, broke the silence and she stopped in the middle of the path and listened. There it was again: not like any creature she'd ever heard before. From behind one of the bushes came rhythmic grunts and breaths. Then there was a cry like someone being torn in half, and after that everything was quiet.

She felt cold, understanding suddenly what the sounds meant and who had made them. She knew she ought to run away, to leave them there together, because what they were doing was private between a man and a woman and no business of hers. But what if she was mistaken? What if this was some shepherd and his love and not Telemachus and Melantho at all? No one would ever find out. She had to know.

She crept up to the bush and looked into the tangle of leaves. At first she saw nothing, and moved her head a little to the left. A mist came down over her eyes and she blinked to clear them, and then peered through the branches again. There she was: Melantho, stretched out on the ground with her skirt pushed to the top of her legs. Her dress had been pulled down over her shoulders: Klymene was near enough to see her bare breasts. If she put her arm out, if the bush weren't there, she could have touched them. Klymene shivered, a mixture of longing and disgust making her want to vomit, turn away, escape from the sight of the two of them. Telemachus lay on the other side of Melantho, on his back, with his eyes closed and an expression of bliss on his face, but Klymene stared at *her*: her white skin, her red mouth still open, her legs still apart. She was panting, trying to catch her breath. Klymene's eyes filled with tears. Hopeless, she thought. The very first time Telemachus saw her – the day I brought her across the courtyard to where he was playing with Ikarios – I knew. Melantho's gaze had gobbled Telemachus up, and I knew even then that he'd been struck. I saw the arrow with my own eyes,

Eros' arrow, and there's no defence against that. He would never, Klymene knew, love her. Not like that. Not in the way he loved Melantho and while her face was constantly before his eyes.

She backed away as quietly as she could, and began to run back to the palace. The sound of laughter, Melantho's laughter, followed her as he ran. What am I going to do, she thought, with all the love I feel for him? What will become of me?

LEODES COMES TO ITHAKA

Klymene was helping her grandmother prepare for Leodes' arrival, and wishing she didn't have to.

'I don't see why the other servants can't do this,' she said. 'I hate bed-making. And who is this Leodes anyway? Where's he from?'

'You'll do as you're told, girl,' said Nana. 'Everyone's busy. I know you're always trying to get out of housework and go and sit at the queen's feet and spend your life dreaming, but not today, I'm afraid. Leodes is lord of one of the islands to the south. Best sheets for him, and good ones for his servants too. He was a childhood friend of Odysseus, but I haven't seen him for many, many years. A good man, they say.'

He was certainly an important one. Everyone in the household had been rushing about ever since they knew he was coming, making things ready. Klymene spread the fine linen over the bed. Maybe there'd be a bit of gossip to ease the boredom; an explanation, or some kind of a story that might explain why this guest had decided to visit now. Klymene supposed he had been invited by the queen, but perhaps he himself had suggested it and then, of course, Penelope would have had to agree. The palace had been swept, and Klymene had been charged with keeping Argos out of the public rooms. Penelope said that the old dog's smelliness was enough to make any guest run home at once. There was new oil in every lamp and the cooks had been working since morning to prepare sides of lamb and roast boar, basting them with oil and fresh herbs and squeezing over them the juice of the lemons that grew on the tree outside the kitchen.

'You see to the other beds now, Klymene,' said Nana. 'I'll go down and deal with the wine. It needs to be cooled before the feast.'

'Yes, Nana,' Klymene said, and made a scowling face at her grandmother's back as she left the room. She hadn't been gone very long when Melantho came in.

'I'm exhausted!' she sighed, sitting down on the very couch that Klymene was in the middle of preparing. She thought of saying something sharp like, *Can't you look where you're sitting? I've only just smoothed that coverlet and strewn it with fragrant herbs and see what a mess you've made of it all,* but she decided not to, hoping that Melantho might have some titbits of gossip from Penelope's chamber. Part of her felt bitter that she was never chosen to dress the queen's hair, but she had to admit that Melantho had a special gift. She could take an ivory comb and some pins and construct curls and falling ringlets with no trouble at all. Klymene knew that however good she might be at many things, arranging hair wasn't one of them. She turned her attention to the pillows and pretended that she wasn't particularly interested. She didn't want Melantho to think she cared one way or another why she might be exhausted, and she was sure she'd get the reason anyway.

'The queen's hair is very difficult to deal with, you know. It's heavy and straight and it takes all my skill to make it behave in the way I want it to, but I managed at last. She looks better than I've ever seen her. I wonder why she's going to so much trouble?'

'We haven't had guests here for a long time,' Klymene said. 'Perhaps she'd like to talk to someone who isn't her son or her father-in-law or one of her servants. Everyone's excited. Everyone likes a change, don't they?'

'Yes,' Melantho said. 'Telemachus says— No, I can't tell you what Telemachus says. I promised him, you see.'

Klymene nodded. She was accustomed to this tactic of Melantho's because she used it all the time, sensing that it drove Klymene nearly mad with fury. She'd never given her the satisfaction of begging her to reveal Telemachus' secrets, but Melantho knew the effect of her behaviour. She realizes that I'm longing to know, Klymene thought. And I hate knowing that Telemachus takes her into his confidence now and not me.

'Doesn't matter,' she said, as nonchalantly as she could.

'Shall I do your hair for you, Klymene?' Melantho was all sweetness and friendship now. A nasty dig was often followed by an equally cordial offer or statement, which made it nearly impossible for Klymene to pick a fight. There was no denying how clever she was.

Klymene hesitated. Part of her wanted more than anything to be made pretty; to have her hair dressed in curls on top of her head. There was also the possibility (remote, certainly, but still a possibility) that Telemachus might notice her if she were thus transformed. No, that would never happen. She knew Telemachus very well, and hair was the last thing in the world he was concerned with. If there was one thing that she knew it was this: boys didn't care about such things.

'No, thank you, Melantho,' she said, trying to sound uninterested.

'Never mind,' said Melantho, getting up slowly and making her way to the door. 'I'll go and do my own. I'll do yours another day.'

Klymene stared after her. It wasn't too late. She could run after Melantho and say she'd changed her mind, but she didn't do that. There was a voice in her head that whispered, I'm right not to let her do my hair. She'd probably work hard to make me even less pretty than I am already. I don't trust her.

The storm broke as Klymene was crossing the court-yard and she ran into the laundry room to take shelter from the rain. She could see black clouds sweeping in from the direction of the shore and the wind was blowing hard. Lightning forked across the sky and thunder rolled like boulders being thrown around Olympus.

'Argos! What are you doing here?'

He was cowering behind a basket, whining and crying like a young puppy. Poor Argos, fearless in the face of every enemy throughout his long life, was terrified of storms.

'It'll soon be over,' Klymene said as she watched him bury his head under the dirty sheets in the basket, having failed to climb into it. 'I'll close the shutters so that you can't see the lightning, and in any case, look, the storm has nearly passed.'

Outside, the sun was beginning to shine from behind the clouds, huge masses of which were racing towards the hills behind the palace. Argos left his shelter and staggered out to a puddle and began to drink eagerly.

Klymene called out, 'Silly dog! Anyone'd think you hadn't got your very own bowls of fresh water all over the place. Why do you want to drink water with earth in it?'

Argos went on drinking and took no notice at all of Klymene.

Every fishing vessel that had gone out the day before was back in the harbour now with its sails furled. They were bobbing about on the far side of the breakwater, their masts like a forest of thin black sticks. Nets lay spread over the decks to dry, and near the jetty where the fish was landed a gang of skinny cats sat hoping for scraps to pounce on. Some were apricot-coloured with white patches, some brownish and striped, and others grey. Biggest of all were two or three black tom-cats with bright green eyes; the fishermen always said that these were sacred to the God Poseidon.

Stallholders had left their stalls in the market to come down to the harbour; mothers had brought their children; the whole town had gathered to greet Leodes.

'So many people,' said Ikarios. Ikmalios had given him time off from the carpentry workshop to go down to the harbour with all the others. A few days ago Laertes had told everyone that they were awaiting the arrival of an important visitor and had posted a sentry on the southernmost tip of the island to announce the sighting of Leodes' ship. Now, here it was, clearly visible, and sailing into the harbour, its white sail bright against the blue water.

Telemachus stood with his mother and grand-father under a canopy that was supposed to keep off the heat. This was a kind of tent without sides that had been set up the previous evening. They'd all been standing there for a long time. The progress of a ship from the outer harbour to the dock was slow, but as Laertes said, it would never do for Leodes (who, of course, would be standing on the deck, watching the approach to Ithaka and waiting to disembark) to see them all scurrying down to the waterside at the very last minute.

'It must be clear to him that we have prepared a welcome,' the king said. 'That we are waiting for him eagerly.'

Klymene, who was standing very close to the royal party, could see small groups of children holding bunches of flowers to give Leodes as he landed. The musicians were ready with their drums and flutes, and Penelope was wearing one of her finest robes for the occasion. Melantho stood behind her, and Telemachus had made sure, Klymene noticed, to position himself very close to his beloved.

I don't care, she told herself, and knew this wasn't true. How can I stop feeling like this about him? she wondered, and shook her head to clear it of these unhappy thoughts. There was Leodes at last, making his way along the plank that had been placed between his ship and the jetty. He was a tall man, wearing a cloak of scarlet woven with golden threads. His hair was fair and shone gold in the bright light. His servants followed him, carrying chests full of his belongings. The musicians started to play, the little girls ran up and presented their flowers, and Leodes thanked them and strode over to where Laertes and Penelope awaited him.

'Welcome, welcome,' said Laertes. 'It gladdens my heart to see you on Ithaka again. It has been a long time since you were here last, and we rejoice that you are well.'

'Thank you, Laertes. And greetings to you, and to you, my lady.'

Klymene saw him bend his knee and kiss Penelope's hand.

'Greetings, Leodes,' she said. 'Our house awaits you.'

Now that he had come closer, Klymene could see that he was handsome. His teeth were white in his sunburned face when he smiled. Perhaps his ancestors came from more distant lands, Klymene thought. His hair is nearly as fair as Melantho's and his eyes are very blue.

When the greetings were over – after Leodes had listened politely to the music and acknowledged the musicians with a nod and a wave of his hand – everyone turned to walk up to the palace. Klymene ran ahead, wishing she could stay with the others but knowing Nana would be waiting for her to help with the refreshments.

Argos was waiting in the outer courtyard.

'Argos! What are you doing out here? You never come out during the day. And you've never waited by the gate before. Can you tell we've got visitors coming?'

Argos, happy to see Klymene, pushed his nose into her skirt and she stroked his head.

'You sit here, with me, in the shade. Everyone else has greeted Leodes and so will you!'

When he saw the king and Penelope and Leodes coming through the gate, Argos began to bark.

'Argos! Bad dog!' Laertes shouted. 'Stop that noise this minute.'

'No, no, Laertes, he's a good dog!' Leodes said, coming right up to Argos and presenting his hand to be sniffed. Argos decided at once that this was a friend and rolled over on to his back. Leodes knelt down beside him and rubbed his ears. 'This is surely not the same dog who used to come hunting with me and Odysseus? How can he still be alive?'

'We say the Gods have him in their care,' Penelope said.

'Long may they protect him.' Leodes stood up. He smiled at Klymene. 'He has a good friend here to look after him. What's your name, young woman?'

'Klymene, sir.'

'I'm happy to meet you, Klymene.'

'Thank you, sir.'

She and Argos watched the royal party crossing the courtyard and going into the great hall. In a corner of the courtyard, half hidden by one of the pillars, Klymene caught a glimpse of a glittering white dress; a flash of silver and then it was gone. Artemis had been watching them.

'Leodes is a kind man, isn't he, Argos?' she said, stroking the old dog's neck.

She was sure that Argos agreed with her, and she wondered whether the old dog really did recognize Odysseus' friend from those distant days when they'd all been young together. She thought it was perfectly possible that he'd known all along exactly who Leodes was. Maybe he'd been expecting him too, and that was why he'd come out into the courtyard.

'You're a special dog,' she told him. 'With special powers, granted to you by Artemis. I think I saw her. Over there.'

Argos made a woofing sound deep in his throat.

'I think you saw her too, didn't you? Good dog. Lovely dog.'

*

The great hall was decorated with flowers from the gardens of the inland farms. Every pillar was twined around with vine leaves, and the table was set with the finest pottery plates. Klymene had helped to place them on the table and she and Ikarios were to be allowed to help the other servants serve the food: the roasted lamb, the whole fish garnished with herbs. She had helped to heap the bowls with grapes from the island's vines, and now she stood near the door, waiting for Laertes and his guests to arrive and take their place. Where was Ikarios? He must, Klymene thought, be helping Nana in the kitchen.

The king came in with Leodes walking beside him and Penelope following them. Klymene had never seen the queen more beautiful. Melantho had done her hair with great skill, and her robe was made from thin, gauzy fabric, in a colour like the flowers on a wild lavender bush. She sat down next to Leodes, who had Telemachus on his other side. The others at the feast, friends from all over the island, took their seats and began to eat and drink.

Klymene was ready to start pouring more wine when she saw her: a tall woman standing just inside the door. Perhaps she was a guest who had been delayed. She wore a gown of palest pink, with silver threads woven through the fabric and silver bells dangling from bracelets on both her wrists and from the hem of her robe. Her beauty was dazzling and looking at her was like trying to gaze at the sun.

'May I help you to your seat, madam?' Klymene asked.

'I won't require a seat, child. Do you not recognize me? Perhaps you are too young still, though I doubt it. I am Aphrodite, Goddess of Love.'

'Goddess!' Klymene looked around the hall, but everyone was talking and eating and paying no attention whatsoever to their conversation.

'I've come to help your queen. To bring her a little comfort. There is no need for you to disturb yourself.'

The Goddess moved off towards where Penelope was sitting. A thin tinkling music followed her as she moved. She went to stand behind the queen and leaned over to touch her hair. Then she passed to where Telemachus was sitting and whispered in his ear. She walked past the other guests, and then drifted back towards the door, leaving behind her as she left the hall a fragrance of new roses and almond blossom.

Klymene went to pour more wine. As she passed behind the seats of the royal party, she caught snatches of the conversation. The queen had turned her whole body to speak to Leodes. Her eyes were shining and she leaned towards him to catch what he was saying.

'. . . many nights when we didn't come back at all. Such good hunting up there in the hills. Were you ever worried about us?'

Penelope spoke too quietly for Klymene to catch her answer, but it made Leodes laugh. He put his hand out and touched the queen briefly on the arm. She was smiling. Klymene wished she could stay and listen to what Leodes was whispering. He'd leaned over and his lips were so close to Penelope's ear that he could have kissed her if he'd wanted to. Klymene blinked. It's nonsense, she told herself. Aphrodite has cast some magic over everyone. It doesn't mean anything.

She moved over to where Telemachus was sitting.

'I'm bored, Klymene,' he said to her. She followed his gaze and found herself looking at Melantho, who had just come into the great hall. She was leaning against one of the pillars, with a basket of bread over her arm. As Klymene watched, she saw Melantho smiling and Telemachus raised a hand to greet her. At once, she made her way towards the table and came to stand beside Klymene.

'More bread, Telemachus?'

'No more bread, thank you,' he said, and Klymene saw him put out a hand and touch Melantho's breast. She smelled of the fragrant oil she always wore: essence of jasmine, which she kept in a tiny vial under her pillow.

'I'm thinking,' he said, 'of making my excuses and leaving. D'you think anyone will mind, Klymene?'

Klymene said, 'Ask your grandfather. He'll tell you if he wants you to stay.'

Melantho drifted off towards the door again, distributing bread wherever it was wanted and smiling over her shoulder. Telemachus went to speak to Laertes and then rushed to catch up with Melantho. Klymene gritted her teeth and turned back to look at the table. The king was speaking to Leodes now, but Penelope was leaning forwards, so that her arm was lying alongside his.

'Remember, child. It's perfectly possible to love two men at the same time,' whispered a voice in Klymene's ear. Aphrodite had returned. Before Klymene could answer, the Goddess had floated over the heads of the guests and her filmy skirts grazed the heads of Leodes and Penelope as she vanished.

Ikarios had come in and was standing right beside her. She wondered whether he'd seen the Goddess and thought of asking him, but decided not to. He said, 'D'you know anything about Lord Leodes?'

'He's from a neighbouring island, Nana says. He used to be a friend of Odysseus' when they were young. He's handsome, isn't he?'

Ikarios nodded. 'I see Telemachus has left already.'

'He told me he was bored. He's gone after Melantho.'

Ikarios frowned. 'He said . . . Never mind. I'm used to taking second place to Melantho. Everyone has to, don't they?'

Klymene thought: Ikarios is also jealous, in his way. Telemachus is neglecting him as well in favour of that enchantress. This thought didn't make her feel any happier.

Penelope, Leodes, Laertes and the others had stood up and were starting to leave the hall. They would make their way to their chambers, and Klymene remembered how she herself had sprinkled Leodes' bed with fragrant herbs earlier in the day. He would sleep well there. She watched him following the queen out into the dark courtyard.

*

Klymene woke up suddenly and wondered how long she'd been asleep. For a moment she was confused and tried to remember what had happened after the feast. Telemachus and Melantho had left the room. Then the others went to bed, and she'd taken some water and a lamb bone to Argos, who was so pleased to see her that he actually stood up and nuzzled her skirt as she put the bowl down on the floor for him. Melantho's bed had been empty when Klymene came into their chamber, but she was in it now. That was her body under the light cover, and her golden hair was spread out and caught what little light came in through the window. There was a moon, but it looked like a thin slice of lemon low in the black sky and shed only a dim light so that it was difficult to see anything clearly. Melantho was breathing deeply, almost snoring.

I should go back to sleep, Klymene thought, but she knew that there was little hope of that. She was wide awake and thirsty too. Perhaps the cooks had added too much salt to the oil tonight. It had tasted good as she ate it, but now her mouth was dry. She decided to go quietly to the kitchen and find some cooling water. How hot the night was!

Klymene didn't need lights to show her the way. She knew every stone in the palace. Every passage had been mapped in her head since childhood. If only I could see them, she thought, there are probably hollows worn into the floor by all my footprints.

The great hall was thick with shadows. A smell (spilled wine, herbs, the memory of a fragrance Klymene recognized as the perfumed oil Penelope wore sometimes) hung in the darkness. The servants had removed most of the bones and fruit rinds, but there were still bits of food left lying here and there, and in the morning, she knew, her grandmother would be up as soon as Phoebus Apollo led his horses over the horizon to make sure that the whole room was washed down and made clean again.

A movement in one corner of the room caught Klymene's eye. There was someone there, just by the open door that led to the outer courtyard, and she stood frozen for a second. Perhaps I imagined it, she thought, peering into the shadows. She would have cried out, called to whoever it was, but she didn't want the whole palace waking up in alarm so she shrank back behind a column and watched to see whether whoever it was moved again. Nothing.

It can't be a stranger, she thought. Argos would bark. Even in the armoury, he would have heard an intruder and woken up. The fact that he was fast asleep reassured her that there were no enemies walking around Odysseus' palace.

She made her way towards the kitchen. What she'd seen, or thought she'd seen, made her forget for a moment where she was going, but now her thirst was worse than ever, and she began to imagine how good a ladleful of cold spring water would taste. Suddenly a hand seized her upper arm and she gasped, shocked and terrified.

'Klymene! What are you doing? You should be in your bed. You gave me a fright.'

'Telemachus! You startled me! What are *you* doing,

if it comes to that? I'm going to the kitchen. I'm thirsty.'

'Too much salt in the oil as usual,' Telemachus said, and Klymene could see that he was frowning. 'I'll come with you. I can't sleep.'

They walked together in silence, and Klymene wanted to say: do you remember how we used to do this when we were younger? You and me and Ikarios? Do you remember how we used to creep into the kitchens to see what good things were being prepared, ready to steal some when the cooks' backs were turned? This hadn't been in the middle of the night, but during the lazy time after the midday meal, when all the adults closed their eyes and slept a sweaty, deep sleep for a while. Still, Telemachus had organized these expeditions as though he were a general in a war, and we all, Klymene thought, felt like Prometheus on his way to steal fire from the Gods themselves.

'Sit down,' she said, when they reached the kitchens. 'I'll pour you a drink.'

'Thank you, Klymene,' Telemachus said. He sounded tired and angry. Klymene could judge his moods from listening to the tone of his voice. Sometimes she knew how he was feeling before he spoke. She could tell from the set of his chin, from the way he walked, from what she saw in his eyes.

'You can tell me anything,' she said. 'I can see that you're—'

'What? You can see that I'm what? Truly, Klymene, you're becoming like one of those interfering crones that my mother fills this house with.'

'What interfering crones? D'you mean Nana?

You'll get this cup in your face, Telemachus, if you speak disrespectfully of her. I know I do sometimes, but you shouldn't.'

Klymene felt her face turning red with fury. How did Telemachus dare to be so unkind to her? When all she'd done her whole life was follow him devotedly wherever he went. When all she felt for him was love.

'I'm sorry, I'm sorry,' Telemachus said now, and Klymene instantly forgave him. 'I know that you and Ikarios are the best friends I have, and I have no right to spill my anger over your heads.'

'Just *my* head, Telemachus. Ikarios isn't here.'

'I know he isn't, Klymene. I was just saying—'

'I know what you were saying.' She turned away to fill her own cup again. Why did everyone, *everyone*, have to lump her together with her brother all the time? As though they were one person, when they were not.

'Tell me what's the matter,' she said at last. She could see that Telemachus was hesitating, and added, 'I won't speak of it to anyone, I swear.'

'I know you won't.' Telemachus pushed the hair from his forehead with one hand and, dipping his fingers into the cup in front of him, touched his brow with the cool water. 'You were there, weren't you, when Leodes arrived?'

'Yes, I was. He was good to Argos.'

'Do you like him?'

'Yes, I do. He's very handsome.'

Telemachus snorted. 'You can't see further than a

106

man's face and figure, then, like all women. I don't trust him.'

'Men are worse than women when it comes to judging by appearances,' Klymene said mildly. What she really wanted to do was shriek: *what about you and Melantho? You can't see further than her shining hair and her greenish eyes and all her deceitfulness is hidden from you, because you're led by your desires*, but she kept silent because she wanted to hear what else Telemachus had to say. Having this conversation with him was like looking at a butterfly. Klymene had the feeling that if she moved too quickly or said too much, he'd get up and walk away, so she waited. She knew that he would speak again soon. She could feel the words rising in him, pushing their way up from his heart to his mouth. She could see that he was struggling with them, wondering how to lay his thoughts out in front of her in the most persuasive way. She said, 'Anyway, you seemed perfectly happy to talk to him tonight at the feast. You looked interested in what he had to say. Was he speaking of Odysseus?'

'Yes. They used to go everywhere together, he told me. They went hunting with Argos at their side. I wish . . . Well, never mind. He was happy to tell me stories of their youth, but he very soon turned his attention to my mother. Didn't you notice?'

'She's Odysseus' wife,' Klymene said quietly. 'He has to be attentive to her.'

'You're right, of course. He has to be polite, but did you notice my mother?'

'She looked beautiful. It's the first time I've seen

her dressed in that robe, though I've seen it in the chest and even asked her why she didn't wear it.'

'What did she answer, when you asked her that?'

'She said she wasn't happy enough to do justice to such fabric, to such embroideries.'

'There you are, then. I'm right. She must have been a little happy to put it on, wouldn't you think? That's what I noticed about her tonight. That she looked happy.'

'Well, yes, but why d'you mind that, Telemachus? Don't you want your own mother to be happy? Even if it's only just enough to wear a particular dress?'

'She wore it to impress Leodes. She wanted him to look at her.'

'Nothing wrong with that. What's she supposed to do? Shroud herself in plain robes? Don't you want her to be admired?'

'No!' Telemachus shouted, and Klymene put her hand over his mouth.

'Sssh!' she said. 'You'll wake everyone up!'

'I'm sorry,' Telemachus said. 'Only I can't bear it. This Leodes, you say yourself, is a good-looking man. He's kind to dogs. My mother likes him because she takes out a dress she hasn't worn in my lifetime and puts on perfume and acts as though . . .'

'As though what?'

'As though she likes him.'

'Well, maybe she does,' Klymene said. 'I don't understand why you mind so much.'

'Then you're stupider than I thought. But why should I blame you when I've been even stupider.

108

Melantho told me. It spoiled the time I had with her, I can tell you that. She showed me the truth. She says he's after Ithaka. He's after my father's lands. He's after my mother. He wants to marry her and take everything that belongs by right to Odysseus. I didn't see that till she pointed it out to me, and neither did you, and so we're both fools. He has a plan and he's come to ask my mother to marry him. I've heard the talk around the palace. He thinks – lots of people think – that my father isn't coming back. They say he's dead, and that it's my mother's duty to marry someone who can look after Odysseus' lands and also take care of his wife. She shouldn't be shouldering the whole burden of ruling Ithaka on her own. That's what they say, but what they mean is, she's only a woman and so how can she manage to do a man's work? And also – Melantho says everyone thinks this but no one will say it aloud – she's been all on her own for years and years and she must be longing for love. Surely she can't seriously be waiting for a husband who's not going to turn up? They say that Leodes probably thinks he's the answer to a grieving widow's prayer.'

'Perhaps . . .' Klymene knew that she shouldn't say what she was about to say, but the darkness, and Telemachus' closeness to her as they sat at the cooks' table, made her brave. 'Perhaps she's beginning to wonder whether Odysseus is ever coming back, and if he is not . . .' She couldn't say, *If he is dead*, but Telemachus knew what she meant. He turned and took hold of her by both arms, squeezing the flesh above her elbows till she nearly cried out. She wondered how it could be that she felt two things at the same time: pain where Telemachus was hurting her, and a longing to go on feeling his hands on her body, to have his face so near to hers. She took a deep breath to stop herself from trembling.

'He's not dead. He's not. I can feel it. I'd know if he were dead. Don't you dare say that, Klymene! Don't utter such things. My mother thinks he's alive too. You know she does. Don't you know that she believes that?'

Klymene nodded. It was true. Penelope never ever spoke of Odysseus except as a living person who was simply delayed on his way home from the war, but sometimes her actions belied her words. Sometimes Klymene saw that she had tears in her eyes as she gazed at the white wall behind her loom. She'd press her lips together till her mouth was no more than a thin hard line in her face, and there were many afternoons when she lay on the bed staring up at the carved headboard and not seeing it. Klymene told Telemachus that she, too, had seen that his mother had seemed different. She said nothing about Aphrodite.

'I couldn't stay and look at them,' Telemachus said. 'Did you notice how she was leaning towards him? She couldn't take her eyes off him. It was disgusting.'

'You're imagining it, Telemachus. You're thinking of your father and that's natural, but you mustn't see things that aren't there. She was being polite. Pleasant. Friendly. Really she was.'

Klymene watched Telemachus considering what she said. Would he believe her? He sometimes did, when she spoke firmly enough, as though he were waiting to be told what was really true. He seemed calmer. In the end he sighed and put his head in his hands, covering his face.

'I miss him, Klymene. Can you miss someone you've never really known? I pretend . . . I sometimes pretend that I'm speaking to him, and that he can hear me.' He laughed, without mirth. 'That's childish, isn't it? I go and take the bow down from the wall in the armoury and try and bend it, and I can't. I don't think I'll ever be strong enough to do that. Do you and Ikarios ever think about your father like that?'

'No, because we know he is dead. The bodies of all his crew were found, and so we knew he too must have drowned. I can remember Nana weeping and weeping. Now if I imagine him, it's in Hades, with the other shades of the dead.'

'That's it! You have a place in which to imagine him and I haven't. I believe my father is alive, I *do* believe it, but sometimes – don't tell anyone, Klymene – sometimes I think he must be dead, as so many people have been trying to tell my mother. But she doesn't believe them. She says she knows he's alive. She says he promised her that he'd come back. I have to believe too, don't I?'

'It's late, Telemachus. You should try and sleep.'

'Yes, you're right,' he said. 'I'm very tired. I'm going to my bed now, and in the morning you'll see, I'll be as hospitable and charming as my mother could wish. But you wait, Klymene. The time will pass and very soon I'll be old enough to go and find out where

111

my father is. I'll pray to the Gods to help me. If he *is* dead, then I must know how he died, and if he's alive and perhaps unable to reach his island, then I'll rescue him. You think I'm babbling. You think I've been drinking from the wine at the feast, but I haven't. I'm nearly old enough now. All my life I've been thinking of what I have to do to see my father again.'

'If he's alive, Telemachus, then I'm sure you'll find him. Let's go now. It's nearly dawn, look.'

The night was almost over. Already pink and blue streaks had started to appear above the bulk of the mountain that rose behind the palace. Telemachus stood up and touched Klymene briefly on the shoulder.

'Thank you for listening to me, Klymene,' he said. 'If I had a sister, I couldn't love her better than I love you. You know that, don't you? You're like a younger sister to me.'

Klymene smiled at him as he left, holding back the tears that had filled her eyes while he was speaking. Sister! Hearing the word hurt her. She felt a burning in her breast that was partly rage, partly jealousy of Melantho and, more than either of these, a sense of the impossibility of ever loving anyone else as she loved Telemachus, and the horror of having to watch him bewitched by someone who didn't deserve him. That, she thought, was a torment as terrible as the ones devised by the Gods to punish wicked mortals in Hades.

Klymene left the kitchen and walked slowly back across the courtyard, through the public rooms of the palace and up the staircase to the servants' quarters.

As she passed the queen's bedchamber, she saw that the door stood open. She looked in, thinking that perhaps her mistress had been too tired to close it, and there she was – sitting on the edge of the bed, still wearing her lavender-coloured dress, but with her hair loose now and falling down on to her shoulders.

'Klymene!' she whispered. 'What are you doing up at this hour?'

'I'm sorry, lady,' said Klymene. 'I couldn't sleep. I went to the kitchen to get some water. Please don't be angry.'

Penelope smiled. 'Of course I'm not angry, child. I must take off these clothes and lie down now or morning will be here and I won't have closed my eyes.'

She fell back suddenly on to the pillows and said, 'Go to bed yourself, Klymene, and don't worry about me.'

'Goodnight, then, lady,' said Klymene, and as she made her way to her own chamber, she realized that never before had she seen Penelope smiling in that way: lazily, comfortably, as though there wasn't a single thought in her head that might worry her. She's happy, Klymene said to herself. I wonder what could possibly have banished the dark thoughts that have haunted her days and nights for as long as I can remember? From somewhere in the distance came the silvery tinkle of bells, fading away into the dawn.

Penelope stood by the window, breathing in a fragrance like new roses and almond blossom that filled the chamber like a mist. Where is it coming from? she

113

wondered. It's nothing like any of the perfumed oils I use. She shook her head. The feast was over, but everything she'd felt was still with her. It doesn't mean anything, she told herself. It doesn't mean that I've forgotten about Odysseus just because I've enjoyed the company of another man for an evening. That means nothing. Leodes is a friend of my husband's. I remember him from the days when we were young. It's natural for me to be hospitable and kind to him. That's all it was. Hospitality and kindness.

Penelope went to sit down on the small stool beside the loom, facing the bed. I wish I knew. The owl . . . Sometimes I think that I dreamed all that I was told that night but I can't take that risk and leave the weaving. If it's true, if Odysseus' life is truly tied to the threads on my loom, then I can't stop believing. If only I were certain that Odysseus was dead, then everything would be easy. Pallas Athene is his protectress. He always believed that, so why shouldn't I? But Poseidon is his enemy, the enemy of everyone who laid siege to Troy. That was what the priests said, and who could tell which God was more powerful and whose will would prevail. She sighed. She liked Leodes. He was handsome, there was no doubt of that. The heat from his body had reached her as she sat next to him, and she remembered how her breath came faster; how a sort of weakness had seized hold of her limbs. And did the way she'd felt make her love Odysseus any less? Of course not. The wine was probably responsible for this confusion of her senses.

She went to stand by the window again and thought

about Odysseus. If he were alive, then he must be somewhere. Wherever he was, there would be women. Just because she was faithful to him, did it mean that he would be faithful to her? Men were easily moved to lust. Perhaps he would see nothing wrong with taking another woman to be the companion of his bed. *If I'm never to reach Ithaka*, he might tell himself, *then what's the harm?*

Penelope smiled. How easy it was to understand the mind of a man! Dawn is rising, she thought. I will lie down for a little while. She stretched out on the wide bed, still in her lavender dress, closed her eyes and fell into the soft darkness of deep sleep.

On the morning after the feast Leodes and Laertes set off to walk in the olive grove and talk about old times, and Penelope returned to her weaving. Klymene had come to help her, and with her came Argos. Now the only sound in the chamber was the rhythmic snuffle of the old dog snoring on the floor on Odysseus' side of the bed. Penelope sat in front of the loom and looked very carefully at the fabric that was growing under her fingers. My hands are moving in a way that's not connected to my brain: all by themselves, like two living creatures which are not part of me. Where did these colours come from? Did I choose them? She turned to ask Klymene, who had taken all the wool from the basket beside the bed and was searching for something.

'This scarlet, Klymene – did I ask for it?'

'Yes, lady,' the girl answered. 'You said you wanted

115

warmth. Heat, even. You said you'd dreamed of spices and perfumes and honey. I'm looking for a particular pink that you asked for. Like flesh, you said.'

Penelope nodded. 'Yes, I remember.'

She'd told Klymene only a part of her dream. The rest was not suitable for such a young girl, even though the person she'd been used to thinking of as a child was becoming more like a woman every day. A bed. That's what she'd dreamed about. Not their bed, hers and Odysseus', but a low, wide couch piled with soft cushions, smooth to the touch. The covers were disturbed, and the scent of something wafted from the rumpled linen: burning spices, a thick, syrupy fragrance that made her melt inwardly and nearly swoon. She woke from this dream sweating, panting and weak. The smell disappeared as soon as she opened her eyes, but the colours that had surrounded her in that bed (Oh, how the coverlet slipped like water over her skin! How drowsily her head sank into those cushions!) stayed in her mind: honey-gold, apricot and orange, and thin, lemony yellow. Brown and red and the pale pink of flesh.

Penelope shook her head to clear it. 'I hardly ever use these colours, Klymene. And what am I showing? Can you see what it's going to be? I can't tell . . .'

'Flames, lady,' said Klymene.

'Are you sure?'

The girl nodded. 'Yes, flames. But not bad flames. Not a fire that destroys, but a good fire. One that warms you and calls you to be near it.'

'Well,' said Penelope. 'Thank you, Klymene. And

I'd be so grateful if you could remove Argos. It's difficult to concentrate with all that snuffling he does.'

'And the smell, lady!'

'Yes, indeed, the smell.' Penelope smiled.

Once Klymene and Argos had left the room, she took up another strand of wool and began to weave it in with the rest. This will be beautiful, she thought. So why is it that all my feelings are stirred up? Why do I feel restless and uncomfortable? What is the weaving telling me today? I don't understand.

Her thoughts returned to the dream again. She was sure that Aphrodite had sent it into her mind. But did it show that Odysseus was alive? And if he was alive, did he still remember her? The kisses they'd shared, the caresses: did his body relive them as hers did? Or had he forgotten her hands on his skin? Don't think of the dream, she told herself. Think of the threads. They will show me what I want to know. They may reveal what I dread, perhaps, but I cannot stop my hands from moving on the loom. The threads will tell the story.

where is the black ship?   quiet on the shore   hot flames
food   more darkness on the water   stars out in the sky

there is purple there is milky white
no blue orange hot as flames   warp weft
black and brown and spotted
striped and grey   yellow for the eyes

Here is a garden full of animals.
But look more closely. Look into the eyes
of wolves and bears and foxes; pigs and dogs.
Under the fur, in unfamiliar shapes
creatures who once were men are bound: entranced,
bewitched, enthralled, transformed by sorcery.
The enchantress, Circe, waved her magic wand:
made for herself her own menagerie.

white red flames of hair
back forth   lying sleeping   dreams   forth back
gold and red   weft warp   white and dreaming blue

He lies asleep in Circe's soft white arms.
Her hair like amber winds about his throat.
Her breath moves like a zephyr on his face.
Pillows are soft. Covers are smooth and warm.
A thousand roses make the air so sweet
that breathing it brings on a swoon of lust.
Odysseus turns; drowns in another kiss.
Tides of this woman close above his head.

red lips on his   weft warp   thin black line for the ship
sailing again   back and forth   weft and warp

Argos dreams

blood meat roasting on the spit yellow sand and leaves and smoke rising from the fire sleep the high cliff climb and climb perfume wine spices

AT LYSANDER'S TAVERN

'I'm bored, Ikarios,' said Telemachus, leaning against a pillar in the outer courtyard. 'Let's go down to Lysander's. You've never been, have you? No, of course you haven't. You wouldn't dare. Nana would skin you alive if she caught you, so you'd rather miss out altogether.'

Ikarios didn't know what to answer, because what Telemachus said was true. Everyone knew what went on at Lysander's: drinking till all hours and fights breaking out between gangs of youths with too little to do and too much passion burning inside them. There was also the matter of the women who sat about under the vine-clad trellis that served as an awning and tried to lure men to their side: women who wore very few clothes and a great deal of paint on their faces. He'd passed the tavern sometimes on his way back from the market with his grandmother, and she always said, 'Don't look, Ikarios. You're too young to go anywhere near such a place.'

But to be asked by Telemachus . . . Ikarios was so happy at this sign of friendship that he would have gone anywhere. Truly, there were days when it seemed as though the Gods were smiling down from Olympus. It was sad, of course, that Melantho was lying sick in her bed after a meal of shellfish that must have been lying in the kitchen too long, and unfortunate that Klymene had been charged with her care. Still, it left Telemachus at a loose end. Ikarios knew that if Melantho were well, Lysander's Tavern would have been the last place he would have wanted to visit, but this was a stroke of good fortune. He said, 'Nana's busy. Klymene's looking after Melantho. No one'll miss me. What about you? What about your mother?'

Telemachus grimaced. 'Too busy listening to Leodes and my grandfather. Or to be fair, my grandfather alone. Once he gets going it's hard to escape. And Leodes doesn't seem in a hurry to leave, does he? He's been here for days and days. No, everyone'll think I've gone off with one of my friends.' He flung an arm around Ikarios' shoulders and smiled at him. 'Which is no more than the truth, right?'

Ikarios nodded, ridiculously pleased at being called a friend.

They crept across the dark courtyard and out of the palace. They almost ran down the hill to where Lysander's Tavern stood, just near the fish market. You could see it from quite a long way off: lanterns hanging from the trellis shone out in the darkness and the sound of laughter and singing reached them as they came closer. Ikarios noticed two or three harbour cats prowling around the door, waiting for someone to throw them a bone or a scrap of meat or fish. He watched as a huge black cat slipped inside and disappeared among the legs of the revellers.

'Sounds like a good crowd in there tonight,' Telemachus said.

'Have you been before?' Ikarios asked.

'A couple of times. Lysander knows me. He won't tell anyone at the palace. I've made sure of that.'

They passed a stone wall on which someone had scratched the words: DIONYSUS RULES! and Telemachus laughed. 'That's true,' he said, 'but I've never seen it written up on a wall before.'

The tavern was crowded. Groups of men gathered around all the tables, and others lounged against the walls and sat in the street outside. Telemachus pushed his way through them and waved above the heads of the drinkers at someone Ikarios presumed was Lysander: a big, plump man with a red face and enormous hands who was carrying a leather bottle of wine in each hand.

'Make way!' this person shouted, and the crowd parted to let them through. Before long they were sitting at a small table squashed into the corner of the room.

'Very busy tonight, sir,' said Lysander, placing a bottle of the best wine on their table, together with a bowl of oil and some bread and olives. 'Crowd of people came in on three boats on the last tide. There's a couple of them.' He leaned down to whisper to Telemachus, even though the noise all around was so deafening that no one would have heard him if he'd spoken normally. 'Beware of those two,' he said, jerking his head behind him.

Ikarios looked at the two men sitting at the table Lysander had indicated. One of them was enormous. You could tell he was tall, and he was also fat, with eyes set too close together in his head. His hair stuck up like a brush and his chin was covered in short bristles that didn't quite make up a proper beard. His companion was better looking. He was very thin and could have been called handsome, except for the fact that his black eyes were full of cunning and his nose was as sharp as the blade of a knife.

'I put some of them outside on the terrace – this lot had a whole gang of ruffians with them,' Lysander continued. 'I told them I was full and sent them packing. They're outside now, on the street, spoiling for a fight, I shouldn't wonder.'

'Where are they from?' Telemachus asked, but Lysander's attention had wandered to another group of men and he didn't hear the question.

Ikarios looked at the men drinking and laughing all around them. He wouldn't have a chance to talk to Telemachus. It was too noisy. His friend was busy anyway, pouring wine into the goblets Lysander had provided. Something near the small door to the kitchen caught Ikarios' eye. A man with a long, bluish-silver beard that glittered a little in the light of the lanterns was standing there, not moving. He was wet all over and his arms were covered in fish scales. Poseidon again, Ikarios thought, trembling with a sudden fear. What's he doing here? Is he working out the plan he spoke of? I can smell him. He's looking straight at me. He opened his mouth to say something to Telemachus and closed it again. Better to say nothing. Now the God was walking towards the two men Lysander had pointed out to them. He was coming closer and closer to their table. Surely now Telemachus would see him . . . smell him. The whiff of the ocean was everywhere. The air was heavy with the reek of fish and salt and slime and it was all Ikarios could do not to faint. Was he really the only person in the whole tavern who could see Poseidon?

Telemachus was speaking to someone he knew. This was the way it was wherever he went: there were people ready and happy to speak to him; to wish him well.

'Don't be envious,' said Poseidon. Suddenly he was standing at Ikarios' elbow and whispering into his ear. 'His days are numbered, just like his father's. See those two?'

He pointed at the two men Ikarios had noticed. 'Those are my agents,' he said. 'They'll do it. They'll bring down the house of Odysseus, if all goes according to my wishes.'

'Odysseus is protected by Pallas Athene,' said Ikarios, trying to sound braver than he felt.

'I am heartily sick of Pallas Athene,' said Poseidon. 'And you – you should have a care to these two . . .'

The God brushed his scaly hand over the heads of the two men as he passed and then he was gone. All that was left of his presence was the lingering smell and then that faded away as though it had never been.

The two men began to sing.

'Is she ready? Yes, she's ready
'cos she's waited years and years.
Will we show her? Just hold steady.
Lead me to that famous bed-y
where she'll soon feel newly wed-y.
She'll be gagging for it. Cheers!'

'Listen, Ikarios.' Telemachus' face was white. 'They're singing about my mother.'

'Not necessarily. They're drunk, Telemachus. It could be . . . well, it could be just a song.'

'Are you deliberately being thick, Ikarios?' Telemachus was almost spitting in his rage. 'Didn't you hear it? The *bed*? Waiting *years and years* . . . They're insulting my mother.'

He stood up and left the table. Ikarios caught at his tunic and pulled. 'Leave it, Telemachus. You'll be smashed to bits and your mother and grandfather will find out and they'll . . . they'll . . .'

'I don't care what they do. These bastards can't be allowed to get away with stuff like that.'

He stood directly in front of the two men as he spoke. The fat man smiled nastily and said, 'And you are?'

'I am Telemachus, son of Odysseus, king of this island, and of Penelope, his queen. You've just sung a revolting song about my mother and I've a good mind to take you out of here and put you back on the boat you came in on and push you back out to sea.'

The fat man laughed. Then he stood up and put his hand out to Telemachus. 'Bloody brave, I've got to admit. Your father's son, eh? Delighted to meet you. Amphimedon. That's me. This is my friend, Antinous. We're lords of a kind ourselves. Not in the same class as Odysseus, but still. He's dead, right? Everybody says so. And sorry for that song before, mate. Just a joke. In bad taste, possibly, but that's the wine speaking. Don't mean the lady any disrespect. In fact, tomorrow morning we're going up to the palace to offer to marry your esteemed mother. No harm done, eh?'

'Marry my mother?' Telemachus looked as though the fat man had hit him over the head. 'Dionysus has robbed you of your senses, you idiot. As if my mother would look at a creature like you.'

He pulled his arm back and then drove his fist straight towards Amphimedon's face. The man moved a little and Telemachus' blow landed on his shoulder. He turned, quickly for a man of his size, grabbed Telemachus' wrist and pushed it down on to the wooden table.

'Bloody pipsqueak! How dare you take a swing at me!'

Telemachus wrenched his arm away and began to hit out blindly, not much caring who he hit or how hard. Two of Amphimedon's men came roaring through the crowd and threw themselves at Telemachus, hanging on to him as he flailed and wriggled to try to get away from them.

'Calm down, calm down,' said Lysander, pushing through the throng. 'Don't want trouble here, if you don't mind. Telemachus, are you hurt? What's the matter?'

'My friend,' said Antinous, 'was just explaining to this young man that we're here to see his mother. Queen Penelope.'

'Fine kind of welcome you get on Ithaka, I must say,' said Amphimedon. 'When you're here to pay sincere court to someone and their son gets on his high horse and starts hitting out at people all over the place.' He sat down heavily again and took another gulp from his goblet.

'Perhaps you'd better apologize,' said Lysander to Telemachus.

'In your dreams,' said Telemachus, and leaning over the table so that his face was inches away from Amphimedon's he spat out, 'My father is *not* dead. My mother would row herself to Hades with no help from the ferryman before she'd marry you. You might as well go back where you came from. Come on, Ikarios, we're going home.'

He stalked out of the tavern, wiping the sweat away from his brow. Ikarios ran to catch up with him.

'See you around the palace, young Telemachus,' Antinous called after them. 'We'll be arriving tomorrow. Tell them we're on our way.'

Telemachus walked along the dockside with his head down. Ikarios recognized the mood he was in: furious and terrified at the same time. He wondered what he could say that would make things better and then decided that it was probably best to say nothing. Telemachus stopped walking and turned to Ikarios.

'Bastards. They're wrong, Ikarios. You believe me, don't you? Odysseus isn't dead. He isn't. How can they come and offer to marry my mother?'

'It'll be all right,' Ikarios said and hoped he sounded convincing. He wasn't altogether sure he agreed with Telemachus about what had happened to Odysseus, but he would never tell him so. 'Your mother'll send them away, I'm sure. Come on, Telemachus. We don't want to get caught.'

'I don't care,' Telemachus muttered. 'I wish I'd thumped that pig even harder while I had the chance.'

He clenched his fist and punched it into the empty air. Ikarios felt, all at once, as though someone were staring at them and he whirled round to see who was behind them. There was Poseidon again, sitting on the low wall they'd just walked past. Ikarios could hardly see him in the dark, but in the moonlight his skin had a strange bluish glow, and that smell was everywhere. Breathing in was like swallowing a mouthful of sea water.

'Let's hurry, Telemachus,' he said. 'It's late.'

They began to run up the hill to the palace.

THE SUITORS ARRIVE

'Greetings to you,' said Laertes. 'You are welcome visitors and my house is your house.'

He was standing on the dais at the far end of the great hall and twelve men were lined up in front of him. Penelope and Telemachus were seated next to him. Leodes stood a little apart from them behind the king. The queen was wearing her widow's robes of dark purple and white, and Telemachus was staring at the men and scowling. He had a cut on his cheek and his knuckles were bruised. Klymene stared at him and wished she'd been there yesterday in the tavern to comfort him. Ikarios had told her what had happened. For a moment she let a fantasy of herself binding up Telemachus' wounds form in her head, but then other members of the household began to gather near the doors to look at the visitors. Klymene had been watching as the strangers marched through the gates, looking around as though they'd never seen a king's house before.

'D'you know who they are?' she whispered to Nana.

'Chieftains from some other islands,' the old woman answered.

'Those two in the middle,' Ikarios whispered into his sister's ear. 'They're the ones I told you about – in the tavern. That fat one, he's one of the ones Telemachus had a go at. And the skinny one's his friend.'

'Amphimedon at your service, King Laertes.' The fat man spoke. 'I thank you for your greeting. We have come to beg a favour.'

'Speak, Amphimedon. I am listening. I will do everything I can for you.'

'We have come to ask for the Lady Penelope's hand in marriage.'

Penelope, Klymene noticed, had turned pale. Amphimedon continued, 'We are all saddened at the loss of the great Odysseus, who was our friend, but we feel that now may be a good time for the lady to take another husband.'

Laertes sighed. 'My son has not come home, that is true. However, I am still hoping that he is in the land of the living, and in that case, of course, my daughter-in-law cannot marry. However, you have come a long way from your homes and you must stay as our guests for as long as necessary. My servants will show you to the guest chambers. There are certainly enough of them to accommodate you all comfortably.'

'The hospitality of the king of Ithaka is well known,' said the thin man. 'My name is Antinous and I thank you, on behalf of us all. But of course we have travelled with our own servants and they too have their needs.'

'Where do you think we're going to put your servants?' Telemachus burst out, his face scarlet and looking, Klymene thought, as though he might rush off the dais at any moment and hit somebody.

'Forgive my grandson,' said Laertes. 'But it is true. We cannot accommodate crowds.'

'We've come equipped with tents, sir,' said Antinous. 'We would not presume on your kindness to such a great extent.'

'Very well, then,' said Laertes. 'I will doubtless break bread with you all tonight in this hall.'

Nana frowned. 'A feast for twenty people or so at this notice? I don't know how I'm expected to do that.'

'I'll help you,' said Klymene. As the chieftains strode out of the room, she saw a thin, grey-cloaked figure standing quite still next to one of the pillars that held up the ceiling. She shivered in the heat. Hades . . . What was the God of death doing here, in the presence of so many people? His place was in the cemetery, not in the great hall. As she watched, the God began to follow Amphimedon and Antinous out of the room, so close to them both that his cloak, flapping like the wings of a great grey bird, seemed almost to engulf them.

'Get out of the way, you bloody stupid girl!'

Klymene ducked as an arm struck out and nearly hit her across the face. Amphimedon – she could hardly believe that he'd struck out at her. Now that she was close to him, she could see how enormous he was. And he smelled bad too. As he spoke, she caught his breath in her nostrils and turned her face away.

'What're you making faces for, girl? Don't you know to be polite to your betters?'

'Excuse me,' Klymene mumbled. She could see a group of men milling about in the courtyard. One of them was spitting out orange pips and throwing the pieces of peel on to the ground. Another was urinating quite openly against a wall, and it took all Klymene's self-control to prevent her from rushing over to him and pushing him out of the gate. Even Argos had better manners and knew exactly where to go for such business.

What was happening? She'd been carrying a basket of laundry from Penelope's chamber to the laundry room and dodging the blow had made her stumble. She nearly dropped the basket and it took her a little time to gather her thoughts and collect herself. The visitors, the suitors for Penelope's hand, had been in the palace for three days. At first they seemed to be keeping out of the way but now, suddenly, where she'd been expecting to cross an empty courtyard, there was something like a crowded market. She put the basket down and looked around.

Where had they all come from? Was this what Amphimedon meant when he spoke of servants? From where she stood she could see more men making their way through the outer courtyard as though they owned it. This was like the invasion of a small army.

'Say: *Excuse me, Lord Amphimedon*,' said the man. 'That's me. Who are you?'

'Klymene.' She thought, Where are they now, the

fine manners and the smooth voice you used in front of Laertes? I will never, ever call you by your name, whoever you are. You are nothing more than an animal. A bear. That's it. The Bear. Your title for ever.' She smiled. 'I must go and deliver this laundry.'

'Don't you know who we are?'

'I was in the great hall when you spoke to King Laertes.'

'Then you know that we've come to visit the queen. I saw that Lord Leodes is here already, and that's not fair, is it? We're just as good as he is. Better. Anyone with any sense knows that Odysseus is down there in Hades with the rest of the dead and will no more come back to Ithaka than I'll waft up to Olympus on the next breeze. So we've come to put our case, as it were.'

'You had an answer from the king.' Klymene felt cold suddenly, in spite of the sun's heat.

'Total crap. Stands to reason: that queen of yours might be a queen. She might think she's faithful to her husband, but you can't tell me she doesn't miss a man in her bed. Wouldn't be natural otherwise . . . Anyway, that's Laertes, isn't it? We've come to ask her what *she* thinks. Ask her to choose one of us and allow us to take upon our shoulders the management of the lands and wealth that Odysseus left her in charge of. Not right for a woman to have to look after all that. Right, Antinous?'

Amphimedon's thin companion had come up to join them. His hair was greasy and his nose thin and prominent. He wasn't as revolting as his friend, but there was something stone-hard and dangerous about him, as though he was just waiting for the opportunity to draw the sword that hung down at his side. He looks like a rat, Klymene thought. The Rat and the Bear . . . She shivered.

'I can see,' said the Rat, 'that our time here is going to be more pleasant than I thought, if you're the sort of girl Ithaka produces. Perhaps you'd be willing to serve my men and me on a – shall we say – a more personal basis?'

Klymene knew what he meant exactly. If she hadn't been in the palace, but down in the market by the harbour, she'd have put this Antinous in his place. But here he was a visitor to the palace. Nana had told her many times that it had always been a point of honour with Odysseus and his wife to offer hospitality to visitors, and if a chieftain from a neighbouring island set foot on Ithaka, he was always welcomed as a friend, but these men hadn't come alone. Was Laertes really prepared to be host to so many people? She could see what was happening over the Rat's shoulder as he spoke: gangs of men were setting down bundles of clothes and weapons and bedding and laughing loudly and calling for wine and water. Some of them had stretched out in the shade of the palace, and soon the whole of the covered stone terrace outside the great hall was going to be crowded with loud, smelly men. She breathed in deeply, trying to quell her rising irritation and said merely: 'Someone will bring you some drinking water.'

'Drinking water? You think we've come all this way to drink water? When the wine from Odysseus' vineyards is famous throughout the islands? Bring wine, girl. As much of it as you can carry.'

A shout and the sound of a scuffle on the terrace made Klymene turn her head just in time to see a large earthenware pot sail through the air and crash to the ground, exploding in a shower of earthenware fragments, spilled earth and crushed scarlet flowers.

'Stop them!' she cried to the Rat and the Bear. 'Why don't you do something? How dare you let your men wreck my grandmother's garden? She's spent days watering those plants and now look – they're kicking them aside with no thought . . . Just do something, can't you?'

'Too much to do to bother with flowerpots.' The Bear scratched himself under one arm as he spoke, and then spat a fat gobbet of phlegm on to the sand at Klymene's feet. Klymene tried not to look at him and took a step backwards. He went on, 'Got to get settled in, find the best place to camp. It's only high spirits. The men mean no harm. They'll be quieter once they've eaten and drunk. What does one have to do to get them some grub around here?'

'I'll find them some food,' she said, choking back her rage, 'once I've delivered this laundry and cleared up the mess your people have made of my grandmother's garden.'

She picked up her basket and walked away from them, fuming. Why am I so powerless? she thought. I'd like to take a stick and beat them around the legs till they run out of the gate and go back to their rotten ships and sail away. How long will they be here? And how many more will come, now that they know the Rat and the Bear are here to put their case to the queen? She can't marry one of these monsters. She would no more take such creatures to her bed than lie down with a thousand scorpions. Klymene was sure of that at least.

'May I help you?'

Klymene whirled round to see who was speaking. She was sweeping up the earth that had been strewn around when the flowerpots were broken. A young man was standing a little way away and staring at her. She could see from the way he was holding his hands that he felt awkward and uncomfortable. He shifted his weight from one foot to another and hung his head, as though he felt ashamed. And so he should, Klymene thought. He's one of them. Why's he offering to help me now?

She muttered, 'I don't need help,' and returned to her work, hoping that this person would see how unfriendly she felt and go away. She went on sweeping, looking only at the earth under her broom.

'If you make a pile of all that,' the youth continued, 'I can pick it up and put it in one of the other flowerpots. Here's the plant that was in that pot – I found it over there by the wall. I'm sure it'll survive, if there's another pot it can be transplanted into.'

'I'll try to find one. You seem to know a lot about plants,' said Klymene sharply. 'Are you one of the B— Amphimedon's men?'

'I'm of Antinous' company. But not really one of

his men. I don't come from his island. I'm . . . well, Antinous took my mother in when she was fleeing from the sack of Troy. She's dead now, but I owe a debt to Antinous for rescuing us. I was only a baby then, but look . . .' He held out his arm and Klymene saw a white band around his wrist, like a bracelet made of scarred skin. 'That's where I was burned in the fire. It always remains white, even though the rest of my skin is brown.'

What was she supposed to say? She looked at the outstretched hand and saw that the fingers were thin and strong. He seemed to be the sort of person who would know how to put things in order. She had a sudden picture in her head of how those hands would look, planting her grandmother's flower in a new pot. She said: 'D'you know what I call him? Your master? The Rat. Amphimedon is the Bear. I don't know why I'm even speaking to someone who's come here with them, but you've been kind. I wish you'd never come to Ithaka, any of you. I'm not going to tell you lies. Not when you've offered to help me.'

'My name is Mydon,' said the youth, and as Klymene turned to sweep another scattering of earth, their eyes met. 'I'm not a rat.'

He smiled then, for the first time, and his teeth were very white against the dark skin of his face.

'No, you're not,' she said, noticing that his eyes were exactly the colour of the chestnuts that grew on the trees to the north of the island. He was tall and thin, with brown skin and wide cheekbones. His face was broad under the eyes and came to quite a sharp point at his chin. His hair, which was mostly brown, had been dyed red-gold by the sun and his nose was rather sharp. He looks like a handsome fox, Klymene thought, but she was determined he shouldn't know her opinion of him. 'I'm sorry. I'm very bad-tempered and cross today. My name is Klymene.'

'I know. I asked.' Mydon went over to the pile of earth that Klymene had swept together and picked up a handful. He poured it into the nearest flowerpot. Then he did it all over again and didn't stop until every bit had gone. 'There. That's better.'

'Yes,' said Klymene. She swept the faint scattering of earth that was too fine to pick up out into the courtyard. 'I'm grateful to you. I have to get on with my work now.'

Mydon nodded and walked away to where Antinous' men had set up some tents. Klymene watched him go and felt suddenly dizzy. The sun was very hot. She sat down in the shade and thought about Mydon. He'd asked her name. He wanted to know who she was. She remembered his brown eyes and the way he had spoken: so kindly and with such respect for her in his voice. His hands . . . she liked his hands. He was not of the Rat's party. She was stupid, she knew, to think like this, but she believed there was a link between Mydon and Odysseus. Both of them had been in Troy. Mydon bore on his wrist a sign of the destruction of the city. He isn't one of the horrible ones, Klymene decided, and the thought made her feel happier than she had felt since the arrival of the suitors.

Argos waits

and the night follows the day and the day brings a night and they go on and on and the sun shines down and the fruit ripens on the trees figs pears and on the vines the grapes the waiting

QUARRELS

Nana was at the door of the storeroom. She had just been to inspect it, worrying that there wouldn't be enough corn, oil, and olives for the household. The harvest was a moon or more away and these days there were so many more mouths to feed. The situation wasn't as bad as she'd feared, but still, she'd made up her mind to send someone up to the farms inland to see if there was anything more they could send to the palace. Those men – she couldn't think of them as guests – had been in the palace for forty days and forty nights. Nana knew, because she was counting the time away like someone imprisoned for a crime.

'You! Old woman!'

'Are you addressing me?' Nana turned round and saw a young man standing over her. He was tall and, if he'd bothered to wash, might have looked like a decent person.

'Can't see anyone else here, can you?' he said.

'Your mother, young man,' she said, 'would be ashamed of you for speaking to an old woman in that tone.'

'And you watch your mouth, talking to a guest like that. Open that door.'

'Certainly not. That's the storeroom. I keep the key.'

'Not any more you don't. Hand it over.'

'You'll have to take it from me by force,' Nana said. She pulled herself up to her full height and stared at the youth. 'What's your name?'

'It's none of your business, but I'll tell you anyway. I'm Ilos. Kind, that's me. Give me the key. We need more oil.'

'You're not getting it, so you may as well go back to whoever sent you and tell them that.'

Ilos lunged forward suddenly and grabbed at Nana's wrist. He pulled her to him and squeezed her hand, forcing her fingers to open. The key dropped to the ground and at once he let go of Nana and pounced on it.

'Help! Someone help me! I'm being attacked!' she shouted.

Telemachus came running from across the courtyard, screaming as he came.

He flung himself at Ilos and locked an arm around the man's neck. 'Get up, you bastard. Give her back whatever it is you're hiding. Go on. Or I'll squeeze the life out of you and I'd enjoy doing it, I promise you.'

'Stop!' Ilos squeaked. 'I can't breathe. What's the matter with you? I wasn't doing anything. I've come to get the key, that's all.'

'Give it here.' Telemachus let go of Ilos' neck, twisted one of his arms behind his back and prised open his hand, which was clenched into a tight fist. The key fell to the ground and Telemachus kicked it towards Nana.

'There it is, Nana. Pick it up. He won't bother you again. Will you?'

'Will I what?' Ilos snarled.

'You won't come near Nana again. And I'll tell you why not. Because if you do I'll come and find you. Remember that.'

Telemachus let go of Ilos and he slunk away. Before he was out of sight he shouted at Telemachus, 'That woman of yours – that Melantho. Tasty bit of skirt, she is, isn't she? I reckon she is. She's no stranger to my bed, I can tell you. Ask her.'

Telemachus started to run after Ilos, but he'd vanished out of the courtyard.

'Don't listen, Telemachus,' said Nana. She made her way over to Telemachus to thank him, but he'd gone running off in the direction of the laundry room.

'I'm telling you what he said!' Telemachus shouted. 'Is it true or isn't it?'

His face was contorted with fury as he took hold of Melantho and shook her. Klymene, who was standing with Argos next to the water trough behind the kitchen, could see and hear them quite clearly.

Melantho said, 'Don't shout at me, Telemachus, please. And take your hands off me. We're not alone.'

'I don't care who hears me. I certainly don't mind Klymene hearing what I have to say. She's like a sister to me. If you want to know the truth, I'd like to gather everyone around so that you can tell them as well. Is it true? Do you go down there? D'you know this Ilos?'

'I don't know what you're talking about.' Melantho shrugged and began to run her fingers through her hair, which lay over her shoulders like a scarf of golden threads. 'I have taken wine down to Amphimedon's camp from time to time. Somebody has to. I talk to them. They're not so bad when you get to know them a little. I think they're bored, that's all.'

'And drunk. There's altogether too much wine being sent down there. But Ilos – do you know him?'

'Speak to your mother about the wine, Telemachus. It's the famous Ithaka hospitality. No one must be allowed to go without anything.' Her voice was full of scorn.

'Don't talk about my mother like that!' Telemachus shouted, and Klymene saw that Melantho was considering what to say next. When she spoke, it was obvious that she'd decided to be sweet, because she knew that Telemachus hated his mother to be spoken of with disrespect.

She said, 'You're making a huge fuss about nothing, Telemachus.' She went to stand beside him and began stroking his hair and smiling up at him. 'I do know Ilos, but so what? He doesn't mean anything to me. It's you, Telemachus. It's always been you, ever since I first saw you. Don't you know that?'

'He said you'd been in his bed. I almost killed him. Maybe I will kill him.'

'And you believe him and not me? I think I'm the one who should be angry. Such a lack of trust! I'm hurt, Telemachus.'

She pouted and looked as though she was about to burst into tears. Telemachus sighed and said, 'Oh, Melantho, I want to believe you. Kiss me and I'll try to forget. But you must promise me . . . promise me not to speak to Ilos ever again. Will you swear?'

Melantho stepped back and frowned. 'You don't believe me. I can see that you'll still think badly of me, whatever I do. I certainly won't promise not to speak to Ilos. Why should I? He's not so bad. Why shouldn't I speak to him sometimes just because I'm in love with you? Do I ever stop you speaking to Klymene? Going off on walks with her and Argos?'

'It's not the same thing at all!' Telemachus said, growing red in the face with anger. 'Klymene, tell her it's not the same!'

Klymene hurried to where Melantho and Telemachus were standing. 'You two shouldn't be quarrelling. Not when there are all these strangers making life difficult enough.'

'Oh, never mind! I'm sick of talking about it. I'm not staying around here listening to all this pointless crap any longer.' Telemachus stamped away in the direction of the gates.

Melantho laughed and started to braid her hair. 'He's mad. He's like all men, Klymene. Wanting everything. Who does he think he is to tell me who I can talk to and who I can't? I'm not his wife, nor am I ever likely to be. Why shouldn't I go down there sometimes – to the tents?'

Klymene could think of a thousand reasons to keep well away from those unsavoury groups of smelly men.

She said, 'He loves you. He's jealous, that's all. Were you telling him the truth?'

'You understand nothing.' Melantho smiled her most enigmatic smile and leaned forward to whisper in Klymene's ear: 'Ilos is exciting to me. It's a matter of bodies only, not souls. He's . . . he's not like Telemachus. He's . . . well, I can't explain it to you, but his flesh calls to mine. It's like drinking to quench your thirst. You can't know what I mean because you've never been with a man. You'll see I'm right when you know more.'

Klymene said nothing. She wondered privately what it would be like and found she could imagine it rather too easily. She said, 'I thought it was supposed to be different if you love somebody? D'you love Telemachus?'

'Yes, I do love him, and I don't love Ilos. If Telemachus never finds out, I don't see where the harm is.'

'Aphrodite's used her powers on you, Melantho, and twisted your desires.'

Melantho laughed. 'My desires? Oh, Klymene, they're not a bit twisted. They're perfectly straightforward. I want everything, that's the truth.'

She smiled and walked away, and Klymene stared after her.

Klymene knew all about the Land of the Dead. Nana had told her stories of the special torments reserved by the Gods for men who had done great evil in their lives. There were certain punishments that never ended. She knew that Sisyphus, for instance, had to push a huge boulder up a steep hill, which then rolled back down the slope, and then the poor unfortunate man had to start all over again. For ever. Pushing and pushing for ever.

Now, she thought, the suitors have turned Odysseus' palace into a place of torment. Almost overnight, the home Klymene had known all her life had been transformed into a stew of large men who hardly ever washed, drank all day long, snored and spat and lay sprawled about in the sun, littering the courtyard with chicken bones and melon peel and piles of dirty clothes. There were servants in with the rest: personal guards and washerwomen and attendants and hangers-on of every sort. And, of course, it was the Rat and the Bear who'd brought the greatest number of followers with them. Whenever she wanted to walk down to the seashore, Klymene had to tread a path between groups of people who'd all made small camps where they burned fires and sang songs. Some of the rougher men were also only too ready to grab at a passing skirt. She'd become quite accustomed to kicking out at grasping dirty hands with her feet as she passed, but life had become so difficult. Now even Nana wasn't safe from them any longer. She had made light of what had happened outside the storeroom, but Klymene knew she had been in danger. And now Telemachus was angry with Melantho. She couldn't help feeling a small thrill of satisfaction about that.

THE SHROUD

Laertes was pacing up and down in his chamber. Penelope sat quietly on a chair near the door, knowing that soon a storm of words was going to break over her head. That was what Laertes did: he sulked for days and the anger built up in him until he couldn't keep it hidden any longer. That moment was approaching. His face was growing redder and redder, and Penelope dared not look at him directly but kept her eyes fixed on the floor.

'Those men,' said Laertes at last, 'the ones who call themselves friends of my son, they're nothing but animals. Look at them! I know I asked them to stay but I'm sick to death of them. They've been here too long. They're camping in our courtyards, eating everything in sight and drinking our wine to the dregs. Every few days one or another asks to see me and presents his case. He should be the one allowed to marry you. I say nothing, of course, because that's what you've asked me to do. And I don't know what's the matter with *you.* You keep to your room and ignore the whole thing, and all around you the very fabric of the palace is crumbling. Well, I'm not prepared to sit here and watch it any longer. I've decided. You must do something about it.'

'What would you have me do, Laertes?' Penelope spoke quietly but she could feel herself growing hot with rage. How did Laertes dare to speak to her as though she were a naughty child? She decided not to add that it was Laertes who had welcomed the first of the suitors as honoured guests, and therefore perhaps it was his duty to tell them all to leave.

'Why,' said Laertes, 'can't you choose one of them to marry and let the others go back to their own homes? Or marry Leodes – I suggested it long ago, do you remember? He's a good man. A friend of Odysseus when he was alive. What's wrong with him?'

'Nothing is wrong with him, but I can't marry him and I told you why the last time you spoke of it.' Penelope took a deep breath. Was he really saying what she thought he was saying? 'I'm waiting for my husband to return.'

'Then you're bloody stupid as well as being irresponsible.'

Penelope stood up. 'I don't have to listen to this, Laertes. I'm mistress here, and Odysseus' queen, and you're nothing but an old man with a filthy temper.'

'Mistress here? While I'm alive? You've lost your reason, woman. Living alone for so many years has addled your brains. Not natural. I say it again: why in the name of Zeus and Hera don't you marry someone? Anyone, and then we'd be shot of this scum at a stroke.'

'Because I'm still married to your son!' Penelope

shouted. She sat down again, shocked at her own out-burst and trembling all over. I never shout, she thought. She said, 'I'm sorry, Laertes. I didn't mean to scream at you, but you can't say such things. They go against everything I believe. Everything I thought *you* believed too. Odysseus is alive. I know he is.'

'Rubbish! How can you possibly know such a thing? Only the Gods know the truth of it – the truth of how he met his end. You must listen to me, Penelope. Listen to reason. My son – and it wounds me to say it, I swear – has crossed the river and is in the kingdom of Hades with his mother.'

Penelope shook her head. 'The owl visited me. I've never told you before. Years ago. Pallas Athene's owl came to me one night and told me . . . it doesn't matter what she told me, but I have to stay here and change nothing and then Odysseus will return. I can't choose someone else.'

'Dreams! That's all that was. A dream. You say yourself that it was night time. You'd probably had a little too much wine. Antikleia was forever doing that: saying she'd seen this or that God here or there. I don't believe a word of it. It's dreams. All you women are the same. You believe anything that suits you.'

'I'm going, Laertes. There's nothing to say. Except, why don't *you* get rid of the suitors if they distress you so much? Gather a few farmers from inland and take up your swords and charge at them. Maybe they'll all flee in terror.'

Laertes stopped pacing and stood quite still. He covered his eyes with his hands and sank on to the bed, looking suddenly frail and white-faced, an old man with no strength left. Penelope sank to her knees in front of him.

'I'm sorry, Laertes. Sorry with all my heart. I should never have said such a thing. I didn't mean—'

'No, you're quite right. That's what hurts me most. I *can't* do anything. I'm powerless. Do you know how that feels? Like a knife to the heart, Penelope. That's what it's like to know you can do nothing – nothing to save those things you treasure. The bastards'd kill me and anyone I could muster without a second thought, and take you by force when they'd done with me, I've no doubt. As things are, they think there's some hope. I suppose we must be grateful they're just sponging off us and not murdering us in our beds. Which they easily could. Oh, I'm no more use than a baby.'

Tears were pouring down Laertes' cheeks now and he wiped them away with his hands. 'Take no notice of me, child. I'm going. I won't worry you any longer. I'll go to one of the farms, over the mountains and far away, so that I don't see it every day under my eyes. I can't bear it, and that's the truth.'

'Yes, go, Laertes, and live quietly in the country and rest. I'll stay here and wait for Odysseus, and when he comes, I'll send Telemachus to bring you home.'

'I'll be dead by then.'

'Don't say it, Laertes. I'll pray that Pallas Athene will protect you too!'

'You and your Gods . . . Well, I don't want to offend any of them, of course, but I haven't got your faith. I admit it. I'm too old. I've seen too much. I've lost my wife and now my son . . . well. Let us hope you're right.' Laertes sighed as he embraced her. 'I don't know any more. I used to think I'd be aware if my only son were dead. I used to think I'd feel it somewhere on my body, but I'm near death now and perhaps I'm deceived. It's been so long, Penelope. We must at least consider the possibility, mustn't we?' He was speaking quite calmly now.

'You may if you wish,' Penelope answered. 'But I'll never, never stop waiting for him. I don't know how I know it, but I'm sure he's alive. Somewhere.'

'There's something else, though, that you may not have considered, my dear,' Laertes said. 'What if he *is* alive, just as you say, but has deserted you? Found another bed to lie in. Other eyes to gaze into. It hurts me to admit it, but he *is* only a man, and you know how weak we all are.'

'I've thought of that,' Penelope answered quietly. She brought to mind certain dreams she'd been having, which stayed with her all through the day sometimes. She'd had visions of her husband with his face and neck entwined in long strands of red hair, and while she could sometimes dismiss the images, they were like tiny stones in a sandal, always irritating and impossible to ignore. She went on, 'I don't care what he's doing, as long as he's alive.'

'So when he arrives, send Telemachus over the hills to tell me the news, and visit me from time to time.' Laertes stood up. 'That chest over there belonged to Antikleia. I don't know what she kept in

151

it – women's stuff, I'm sure. Get rid of it. Burn it, I don't care. I don't care about anything any more, and that's the truth.'

Laertes left the room, and Penelope went to stand next to Antikleia's chest. During her lifetime the old woman had guarded it jealously, not allowing any of the servants to come near it. There's probably nothing more interesting in it, Penelope thought, than a few blankets.

She opened the chest and picked up one garment after another: robes from the days before black became the only colour for the mother of a missing son to wear. Penelope sighed and thought that she would ask Nana to distribute the garments to poor widows in the town. There were many down there whose husbands had been taken by the sea.

But under the dresses and shawls there was something else. Penelope reached in and took out two long strips of knitted fabric and laid them on the bed. Then she reached down and brought out skein upon skein of white wool, spun into the finest strands.

She sat down on the bed. Antikleia's handiwork, she thought. How could I have forgotten it? A few moons before she died the old woman had begun to make a shroud for Laertes. She'd even shown her how to do it one evening, and Penelope began to remember. There was wool and there were pins fashioned from bone. That's it, she thought. You wind the wool around and pick up one loop and place it over the next nail. Then the next in a kind of pattern. It's boring, but it's not difficult.

What Antikleia had already made looked like fine-meshed fishing nets. How many strips would you need to stitch together to make a shroud? Five, or six? Perhaps, thought Penelope, I should continue her work and finish it. She could remember thinking that making a shroud was a strange thing for a wife to be doing when her husband was still hale and strong, but maybe Antikleia knew she would die before her time. A feeling came over Penelope that perhaps Laertes ought to be wrapped in the garment his wife began for him when he crossed the river to Hades' kingdom. It would be pleasing to the Gods.

But what of her weaving? The pictures? She dared not neglect those. No one would blame her if she didn't finish this shroud. She could do what Laertes had suggested and burn the chest on the fire. Penelope stared at the knitted strips for a long time and then began to roll them up. An idea, as shapeless and misty as clouds over water, had begun to form in her mind. She thought, Some good may come of this. This work may save me in the end. She bent to replace the beginnings of the shroud in the chest and smiled. Perhaps Antikleia has sent me a gift from the grave. She left the room and hurried to give instructions to the servants to move the chest to her own chamber.

Argos waits

and the moons turn and change and the winds blow colder and the nights come and go and the waiting

LIFE IN THE PALACE

Klymene sat with Argos in the shade of the fig tree that grew against the wall of Penelope's bedchamber. The rain that had fallen in the night still lay on the ground in puddles, but a watery sun was shining now and soon she would be able to put aside the warm shawl she had wrapped herself in. She had brought the old dog to sit in the sun for a while because, now that everywhere was so crowded and noisy, he didn't dare to venture out by himself at all, but waited for someone to take him. As they'd approached the bench, Klymene thought she saw the shining figure of Artemis disappearing into through the gate that led to the orchard.

'Did you see her?' The dog lay with his head in Klymene's lap. 'I think I did. But maybe I was day-dreaming.'

'Greetings, Klymene. Don't get up and disturb Argos.'

It was Mydon. Since they'd first spoken, almost two moons ago, Klymene noticed him almost every day on the fringes of Antinous' gang, never part of them, always by himself. She'd exchanged a few words with him occasionally but never enough to make a real conversation. She would not have admitted it to anyone, but there were times when she looked for him. Now, she pretended to be picking a burr out of Argos' fur as she said, 'You know his name.'

'I hear you speaking to him. Do you mind me speaking to you?'

'Why should I?'

'Because . . . because I know how you feel about them. About *us*, I suppose I should say. I can't do anything to prevent what's going on, but I wish I could. And more than that I wish *you* knew that I wish I could. If you see what I mean. I'm getting a little muddled. It's confusing.'

'No, I know what you mean. Thank you. But Mydon . . .' Klymene hesitated. 'You said you were born in Troy. Talk to me about that. What did your mother tell you? Odysseus, our king, was a hero of the war.'

Mydon nodded and sat down on the ground on the other side of Argos, so that the dog was lying between them. 'That's why I wanted to come here. To see where my rescuer came from. My mother said Odysseus plucked us out of the flames that he himself had started. As if, she said, that would make up for the destruction of our home. Antinous didn't want to bring me to Ithaka, but he agreed eventually.'

Klymene said nothing but she could imagine Mydon being quietly stubborn and simply standing and staring at Antinous till he gave in and allowed him to board the ship with the others.

156

'The queen thinks Odysseus is still alive.'

'Everyone says that's impossible,' Mydon said. 'But if she feels it, then maybe it's true. We don't understand what the Gods do. Argos, for instance.'

'What about him?'

'Some of Antinous' men say he used to belong to Odysseus.'

'He did. He's very old.'

'That's impossible, Klymene. Dogs don't have such long lives. Are there any other dogs as old as Argos on this island?'

'What are you saying, Mydon?'

'If it is Argos, then one of the Gods is looking after him. He is not a dog like all the others.'

Klymene frowned. 'Artemis looks after him. Because he was such a good hunter when he was younger.'

She wondered whether she should admit to having seen the Goddess and then decided to be silent. She began to stroke Argos, running her hand down his body from his head to his tail. 'I've got to go,' she said. 'There's so much to do.'

'We'll speak again, won't we?' Mydon said. He took her hand as it lay on Argos' back and squeezed it.

Klymene didn't know what to say. In the end she murmured, 'I'm glad you came to Ithaka with Antinous.'

Mydon sprang to his feet and helped Klymene pull Argos to a standing position.

He waved at her as he walked towards the Rat's encampment.

'Come on, darling dog,' Klymene said. It was good to have a friend among all the enemies who swarmed in the palace.

One day followed another. Penelope had decided to work on the shroud outside. Klymene helped to carry the basket that held the wool and the pins and she sat next to the queen on the bench under the pomegranate tree.

'This work is boring, Klymene,' Penelope said. 'I might as well enjoy the air and the view.'

Klymene watched as Penelope practised the new handicraft of winding wool on to the bone pin and moving it between one nail and the next. The pictures she was weaving in her chamber were being neglected and the queen seemed tired whenever she approached her loom.

'I wish I could do more on the weaving,' Penelope said; gazed with longing away from the boring work on her lap and towards the blue patch of ocean that they could see from the bench. 'White wool, when I could be choosing colours! But it has to be done.'

Klymene only nodded and smiled but Penelope was right. There was nothing to see but more and more white holey fabric growing into yet another strip for the shroud. She too missed the days when she used to place the skeins tidily in the basket with everything arranged according to colour, from the palest to the darkest. There was so little for her to do while Penelope was working on the shroud that she found herself more and more often in the kitchen, helping her grandmother, where she did any task Nana had for her, and secretly wished she could escape.

Every day she looked for Mydon as she went about her work, and often she saw him, somewhere in the palace grounds, but it seemed to her that he was surrounded by others in the Rat's company. Though he raised a hand in greeting, and sometimes smiled at her, he hadn't come near her again. Still, every time she caught sight of him, she felt better: less oppressed by the noise, mess and drunkenness that seemed to be going on all around her.

Now, Nana was sitting at the kitchen table. She sighed and pulled her scarf over her head. She said, 'What am I supposed to do with them all? How will I go on managing? We feed them and feed them, and they've taken over the entire palace. I can't bear to look at them lying on the ground on blankets and filthy matting like a pack of dogs. It's been going on too long and I can't abide it, Klymene. Sometimes I think I'll run away, like Laertes. Poor old man! Driven from his home by rage, as much as anything. That was what it was – rage that he was too old to rid the palace of this riff-raff. He was too old and Telemachus isn't strong enough and the queen has no power . . . Oh, it's no use talking about it. Nothing helps. Nothing will ever help, and they'll devour everything we have, those beasts, and still come back for more.'

She stopped speaking, exhausted by her anger. Her hands trembled and Klymene noticed how frail she seemed suddenly and how old. The hair that had once been thick and dark was now white and sparse, and

Klymene was grateful that a scarf covered it and hid it from view. I don't want to grow old, she thought, if my hair vanishes and my scalp is as bare and pink as a baby's. She felt guilty at wishing to be anywhere but in this kitchen; guilty at wishing Nana would stop moaning so much. If only I could work in Ikmalios' workshop instead of Ikarios, and he could come and help Nana. She smiled to herself. She'd never been taught to work with wood, so that was impossible, and the very idea of Ikarios in the kitchen was silly. He'd let the food burn while he lost himself in a daydream. Still, he spent more and more time with Klymene and Nana these days, because he wanted to escape from what was going on outside. When he wasn't working, he often came to the kitchen.

'People will say we don't know how to treat guests, because, of course, guests should be given beds in the house,' Nana went on. 'Our hospitality is famous throughout the islands. I don't know what's become of that.'

'They're not guests,' Ikarios muttered, appearing in the doorway. Klymene felt as though she'd conjured him up by thinking about him. 'You said it yourself, Nana. They're scum.'

He sat down on a stool and, taking a piece of wood and a sharp knife from a leather bag slung over his shoulder, he began to carve the shape of a wolf into the wood.

'Those men you're talking about, they're leeches. They're sucking our blood. They're after Penelope and not just her but the whole island. They're after

160

Ithaka. Telemachus wants to send them away, but there's only one of him and too many of them. They'd kill him soon as look at him, some of them, if they weren't after his mother.'

'They don't have to worry about him now,' Klymene said. 'He's not here all that often.'

As she spoke, she realized that what she was saying was true. Ever since his quarrel with Melantho, Telemachus had gone hunting by himself much more often in the hills behind the palace. Sometimes he didn't even come back at night, but slept in shepherds' huts or with his grandfather on the farm where Laertes had chosen to live. Melantho said they'd kissed and made up, but Klymene knew that Telemachus was still angry. She smiled. There might be a chance for her now. Maybe she should speak to him. Fleetingly, she thought of Mydon. Would he be unhappy if he knew how much she still longed for Telemachus?

Now she said to Ikarios: 'Telemachus hates the suitors more than anyone. The Rat and the Bear especially. The other day he told me he wouldn't be surprised to find a tail sticking out of Rat's garments.' Klymene shivered. 'I hate him. He's always there right at the front when the food's served.'

Ikarios smiled. 'What about the Bear?'

'He's disgusting!' Klymene said, not hesitating. It was true. Amphimedon had grown more and more like a bear. It seemed that every bit of skin you could see was thick with hair: his arms and legs were almost black with it, and when he went lumbering around the courtyards the earth shook from the weight of his body. There were other suitors, it was true, but Klymene knew that the Rat and the Bear were Telemachus' main enemies.

'He told me once he'd take a boat and go looking for his father,' Ikarios said, 'but that was long ago – and now he's got Melantho. He thinks of nothing but her.' Splinters fell to the floor as he continued to gouge at the wood with his blade. 'Anyway, Odysseus isn't coming home. Something must've happened to him or he'd have returned by now. Ridiculous to keep on hoping.'

'That's just like you!' Klymene cried. 'Why d'you always expect the worst?'

'Because it happens. Often,' Ikarios answered. 'And when it doesn't, well, I'll rejoice, won't I?'

Klymene said nothing but went on ladling olives into terracotta jars and pouring green oil over them. She added some fresh thyme and rosemary to each jar, to give the olives fragrance, and tried not to think about what her twin brother was saying. Make sure the olives are neatly placed in their jars, she thought, and maybe the chaos everywhere else won't look so bad. That was what Nana thought. She sighed and wished she could be walking on the seashore, in the mountains, anywhere that was far away from this kitchen.

Shouting and raucous laughter came from the courtyard outside and Klymene put down her jug of oil and went to look out of the window. Two of the suitors were lying about on the ground, after some kind of brawl. They'd been in the palace, these strangers, for nearly half a year, and Klymene found it hard to remember a time when the palace hadn't been overrun.

'The queen'll never marry any of them,' she said. 'Never.' She believed this in her heart, but still she could understand that the suitors would think Penelope a prize worth fighting for. And Ithaka, its trees heavy with fruit, its fishermen the best in the Ionian at bringing home nets loaded with a harvest of the glittering silver creatures which swam in Poseidon's kingdom, its fat livestock wandering over the rocks, and its plentiful supplies of wine and grain and oil, why, Ithaka was worth dying for.

'I've got to go now,' she said to Nana. 'The queen will have woken from her rest, and she'll be needing me.'

'She doesn't rest,' said the old woman. 'She pretends all's well for the sake of harmony, but I know her. I know when she's troubled. She wishes the whole lot of them' – Nana waved a hand in the air to indicate everything that was going on outside the window – 'would be swept up by some storm and tossed away, anywhere at all, but not here. She can't say that, but that's what she thinks.'

'She should choose,' Ikarios said. 'What's she waiting for? They'd be gone in a moment if she'd only say which one of them she fancies.'

'She doesn't fancy any of them, stupid!' Klymene made a face at her brother. 'She's waiting for Odysseus.'

'I don't know what's to be done, I don't really,'

Nana fretted and pulled at a loose thread in the fabric of her scarf. 'Sometimes I think maybe she's right and the master will come home. Some Goddess may have him in her care.'

Ikarios laughed in a way that showed he thought Nana had taken leave of her senses, and Klymene scowled and pushed past him and out of the kitchen.

'No need to lose your temper with me just because I'm telling the truth,' he called after her, and she turned and shook her fist at her brother before covering her head with her scarf and starting to make her way to Penelope's chamber.

Penelope was troubled. She tried to summon the image of Pallas Athene's owl to mind; tried to recall how she had felt on the night when the bird came to her chamber. I was terrified then, she thought, as well as relieved at his survival, and although I've grown used to the work the Goddess has placed on me, perhaps I'm mad, and what I saw was what Laertes said it was: nothing but a dream. It's possible that I've clung to this hope because I'm not brave enough to bear the truth. They all say he's dead – my husband, my dear love – and there are times when I'm trembling with fear because part of me wants to believe them. Because of Leodes, part of me wants to put it down, this burden of love. The making of Laertes' shroud has to be done too and I have neglected the weaving most shamefully. When I sit at the loom, my hands are finding black threads more and more often and the threads never lie. They weave more than pictures. They weave the story.

how cold the night air is
black everywhere   and floating bodies   water and bones

The dead are everywhere: pale, flapping shapes
float like white mists above the river bank.
Odysseus shivers in the freezing damp,
and peering through the gloom he sees a shape
known to his blood, remembered in his heart.
'Mother!' he cries. 'Tell me it isn't you.
Speak to your son. Say words to comfort me.'
'I cannot comfort you, Odysseus,
for I am dead. I wearied of my life,
but you are breathing still and I rejoice.
The sight of you is balm to my poor ghost.'
Her shade dissolves. Odysseus is alone
save for the sighs of the unnumbered dead.

nothing but the shuttle   back and forth
no colours   warp and weft   black grey
bones white as breath

White skeletons of men who once stood tall
wear breastplates rusted by the seeping damp.
They carry broken swords with blunted blades
and cry out: 'Oh! Odysseus! Look at us!
Remember when we fought with you at Troy.
Were we not brave then? Were we not fine men?'
Odysseus weeps to see his comrades here,
the living flesh stripped from their noble skulls,

their bodies ruined, and where there once were
    eyes
nothing but black holes rimmed with ancient
    blood.
He nods, his heart too sore and full of grief
to speak real words. Tears blur what he can see,
but everything has gone, shrouded in mist.
Odysseus turns and leaves the dead behind.

grey green   black thread for the ship   sail between banks
scarlet   warp weft   listen to the loom   grey   bone white

Argos dreams

drip drip drip and trees with black roots growing in mud and creatures with no bones walking in the rain and a wailing that makes my hair rise on my back and mist hiding the way and howling and the smell of something rotting in moss and leaves and hanging vines and long bones grinding together and cold cold cold and shifting shadows and cold and weeping and cold and cold

A VISIT TO THE TAVERN

'Stop it! Oh, stop that at once. Go away! Leave him alone!'

Klymene was crying and shouting and running as fast as she could towards a group of men who had gathered near the gate. She could hear Argos whimpering, and she knew, even before she saw him, that he was there, in the middle of a tight circle of tormentors.

'What're you doing to him? Stop! O Gods, make them stop!'

When she reached the men, she pulled at their garments and kicked out at their legs, not seeing properly, nearly mad with fury. Argos was crying now, making a sound she'd never heard him make before, which tore at her heart. She sobbed, 'Argos! Argos, don't cry! I'm coming.'

She elbowed her way roughly between two men, her rage making her suddenly strong. And then she caught sight of a figure all in white. Artemis had arrived to help her, and Klymene watched, astonished, as the Goddess held out one hand and sent the men who'd been thronging around her tumbling to the ground. By the time Klymene had turned to see what had become of Argos, the Goddess had disappeared, but the men were now gathered some distance away.

'Argos!' she cried. As soon as she saw him, she sank to the earth on her knees and started to weep. He was squatting on his haunches, his head down, and she could see small stones all around him. His fur was thick with dust. His mouth hung open and his tongue lolled out of it, and he was panting. Klymene could almost see his heart beating through his ribs. She stood up and started screaming, 'Monsters! Disgusting monsters! What's this poor animal ever done to you? Answer me! How could you? How could you be so cruel? Oh, if I were a man . . .' Klymene's voice failed her and she turned to Argos and began to stroke him gently.

'I'm here now, darling dog. Stop crying. I'm taking you away. You'll be all right now. Come on, come on, Argos!'

The dog had stopped whimpering and nuzzled Klymene, licking her hands, and his tail – his poor, skinny, almost furless tail – was starting to wag again. She could see that it was going to be hard for him to stand up. I'll die, she thought, before I ask any of these vile men to help me. She noticed that they were all still there, staring at the spectacle. Even more of their friends had arrived to cheer them on, to look at what had been going on. They'll laugh, she thought, when I try to pick him up. But I must because I'm not leaving him here and they're not going to go away. I must take him somewhere else.

'I'll carry him,' someone said, and Klymene looked up. Leodes was standing next to her, and she scrambled to her feet.

'Lord Leodes,' she said. 'Thank you. I don't know why . . . those men. Those men, who hurt Argos. I don't know how they can.'

'They're bored. And stupid, most of them. It's a game to them, I'm afraid. They've been here too long – almost six moons – and they have too much time for idleness. Klymene, that's your name, isn't it? We've met before. Do you remember? You were with Argos when I arrived, and I've seen you attending the queen. I'll deal with them, don't worry. Wait here a moment.'

He strode over to where the suitors were leaning against the wall. Klymene saw him speaking to some of them, though she couldn't hear his words, and soon they were walking away and Leodes was coming towards her.

'You didn't even raise your voice, sir,' she said. 'What did you say to them?'

'I told them if they didn't leave at once, they wouldn't live to see the morning.'

'You'd have killed them?'

Leodes smiled. 'They thought I would, and that's all that matters.'

He squatted down beside Argos and picked the old dog up, like a shepherd picking up a lamb, so that all four of his legs were gathered into his arms and the old dog's head was resting against his shoulder.

'Where should I take him?' Leodes asked.

'To the armoury. He likes it there. Thank you.'

Leodes carried Argos as though he weighed nothing. He also walked very quickly. Klymene ran to keep up with them.

'Let me come with you,' said Melantho. 'I'm dying of boredom.'

The girls were in the kitchen of the palace and Klymene had taken a basket from the corner where they were kept.

'I'm only going to the market,' she said. 'There's not that much to get. I've asked to go because I can't stand it here. Nana says it's full of thieves down there. She wouldn't let me go to begin with.'

'They won't worry us,' said Melantho, 'and it's more fun going to the market than sitting in the court-yard counting the flies on the rubbish.'

Klymene hesitated. She was longing to visit the town, knowing how good it would be to escape the noise and the dirt for even a short while, but Melantho? Did she really want Melantho's company for the whole afternoon? Would she have to listen to more stories of Telemachus? She hesitated, but Melantho was determined. She had turned her most charming smile on Klymene.

'Come on! You almost never have fun – you do nothing but run and fetch and carry for Penelope and your grandmother. It's time you had a few hours to yourself.'

'The market's not what I call fun, exactly,' said

Klymene, but she could see that Melantho had taken her hesitation for assent. She was already wrapping her scarf round her head and had picked up a second basket.

'We'll be able to carry twice as much,' she said, 'if there are two of us. And I'm sure I can get a better price from the stallholders than you! You probably agree to the first thing they say.'

'Very well,' Klymene said. 'Let's go.'

The market was teeming with people, all pushing and shoving and demanding that their baskets be filled first. Klymene was glad Melantho was with her, because Melantho elbowed her way through the crowds in a way she'd never have dared herself. Not an 'Excuse me' or a 'Could you move, please?' came from her lips, and yet she managed to slip between this person and that and somehow always arrived right in front of the stallholder, who was, of course, enchanted by her and immediately lowered his prices by at least a few coins as he helped fill her basket, and Klymene's too.

'Enough!' said Melantho at last. 'I think we deserve to sit down for a while. A drink would be good, wouldn't it? Look over there! It's a tavern – we could sit in the cool shade of the vines!'

'We can't go in – that's Lysander's. You know what goes on there, Melantho.'

'Don't be silly. That's only at night. You're such a coward, Klymene. No one's going to hurt you.'

Klymene decided to ignore the 'coward' remark

and said, 'I know Lysander a little. I used to come here with my father. When I was a baby. He used to carry me everywhere on his shoulders and Lysander was always kind to me. His wife used to give me honey cakes.'

'Well then!' said Melantho. 'Let's go in and tell him who you are. He'll find us a good table when he sees it's you.' She smiled at Klymene, and however hard Klymene searched her face, she could see nothing there except friendship and amusement.

'I'm not going to stay long,' she said, thinking: that's how Melantho does it. That's how she makes everyone do exactly what she wants. She smiles and all you can see is the light in her eyes and not what she's thinking behind the smile.

Lysander came quickly out of the tavern when he saw the two young women approaching.

'Young ladies, young ladies! Come, sit here and take a cool drink. I can see you've been shopping. Thirsty work, eh? I have the juice of peaches and the juice of lemons sweetened with honey.'

'Thank you,' said Melantho sweetly, sitting down at the table Lysander had indicated. 'That sounds blissful. And though you don't know it, sir, you're entertaining an old friend. This is Klymene, daughter of . . . What was your father's name?'

'Halios,' said Klymene. 'A fisherman.'

'Little Klymene! Oh, the Gods be praised! How wonderful! Yes, yes, I can see it in your face. I remember the chubby little baby who used to like my wife's honey cakes. D'you remember those? Well, my

173

wife ran away with another man years ago, but I've found an even better pastry cook. Just try one of her confections! And it's not just her confections that're an improvement, I tell you! She's turned out to be a better wife as well. She's younger than my first and keeps me warmer in bed, if you know what I mean! I'm honoured to see you here, both of you. Please sit as long as you like.'

'Thank you,' said Melantho. 'It's very pleasant here, under the vines.'

Klymene looked around. Every other seat was occupied. Two or three cats were wandering about among the tables and a black one had taken up a position under theirs. It stared at Klymene with wide green eyes, and she bent down to stroke it. She and Melantho were the only women in the tavern and she began to feel a little uncomfortable. In the corner near the entrance to the inner room of the tavern sat an old man dressed in clothes that seemed to be soaking wet. His tangled beard, which seemed to have fish scales caught up in it, was dripping on to the floor under his seat and no one had noticed. Perhaps he was a fisherman from some other island. He raised his glass to her and nodded, and Klymene felt his ice-blue eyes cold on her face and she shivered. She turned to Melantho, to avoid his gaze, but her companion was busy lowering her eyelids and casting flirtatious glances at some young men sitting at a nearby table.

'Melantho! Look over there!'

'What at?'

'The old man – he's wet all over and his beard . . .'

Old men did not interest Melantho. She turned her gaze on him for the briefest moment, saying only, 'Who d'you mean, Klymene? I can't see anyone . . .' before rearranging herself and adjusting her clothing to charm the young men. She removed her headscarf and placed it over the back of her seat. Melantho's clothes were always too loose in some ways and too tight in others and Klymene knew why. As she moved, it was easy for anyone to see the movement of her breasts under the thin fabric. By the time she'd noticed this and looked towards the old man again, he had stood up and was right beside her.

'You are the sister of a young man I met on the beach.'

'You know Ikarios? He's not spoken of you – what is your name, sir?'

'I am Poseidon.'

Klymene felt all the blood rushing from her face. How could she not have recognized him? She had noticed his black cat . . . Where had the creature gone? And why had Ikarios not told her about seeing him? She said, 'Lord Poseidon,' and bent her head. The smell of oceans drifted from his bluish flesh and into Klymene's nostrils, making her feel faint.

'Farewell, young woman. My day is coming.'

He walked slowly out of the tavern and no one looked at him as he passed. Could it be that they didn't see him? Or was he such a familiar figure here that no one was startled at his strange appearance?

When Lysander came to put the sweetened juice

and a plate full of honey cakes in front of them, Klymene thanked him and said, 'The old man who's just left – does he often come here?'

'An old man?' said Lysander, wiping the table with a rolled-up cloth. 'Can't say I noticed. Who's your delightful friend?'

'This is Melantho,' Klymene answered, realizing that Lysander was like all the others, staring at the parts of Melantho's body that were on display.

'Melantho! You're welcome any time,' Lysander said, smiling like a fool.

'You're very kind, Lysander,' Melantho said, and he went back to the inner room grinning all over his face.

Klymene drank her juice. Melantho said: 'Look, Klymene. They're beckoning us over to their table.'

'Are you mad? Don't you know who they are? They're from one of the gangs up at the palace. I've seen them often in the courtyard. I'm not sitting with them.'

'Why not? They're not so bad, really. Some of them are quite fanciable. Honestly, Klymene, you oughtn't to let your prejudices get the better of you – it's only a bit of fun. They look quite polite and clean to me. No one's asking you to *marry* them!'

'You go if you want to. I don't care.' She thought, It's no more than I'd expect of you, because whatever you tell Telemachus, you're always down there. A wave of fury threatened to bring tears to her eyes. How could Telemachus prefer this creature to her? How could he? When she behaved like this? When she clearly didn't care a fig about being loyal, being true?

'Right,' said Melantho. 'I'm off then – just for a bit. We'll go back soon, I promise.'

Klymene said nothing. She watched Melantho weaving between the tables, her hair shining like gold on her shoulders. As soon as she had sat down among the suitors, she waved happily at Klymene, and Klymene gritted her teeth as she raised a stiff hand in reply. Then she held her breath, knowing that Melantho was probably talking about her – about what a spoilsport she was; about how she was never up for a bit of a giggle. It wouldn't be long, Klymene knew, before some remark or other would be shouted at her. I won't answer. I won't look at them, she thought. I'll just finish my cake and my drink and then I'll go. Whether Melantho's ready to come or not.

'Hello, gorgeous!' It had begun. Klymene said nothing. She stared at the grain of the wood under her eyes. A man stood in front of her whom she hadn't noticed before. He must have been sitting at one of the tables behind them.

'I'm talking to you, Klymene. I overheard your friend calling you that. Why don't you answer? It's rude to keep silent when someone addresses you directly, didn't you know?'

'I'd like to be left alone if you don't mind, sir,' said Klymene. She'd added the 'sir', though the word nearly choked her, because above all she didn't want to provoke this man to anger. He was revolting, with a scabby skin and brown teeth.

'*I'd like to be left alone if you don't mind, sir!*' he said, in a squeaky imitation of her voice. 'What I'd like, on the other hand, is *not* to leave you alone. Just the opposite, in fact. Whatcha say to that?'

'I'm leaving as soon as I've eaten my cake.' She thought: why doesn't Lysander come out of the kitchen? Should I call for Melantho? She must have noticed what's going on.

'That's not an answer. I'd like you to come and sit with me. On my lap, preferably. You can eat your cake, and I can have a little nibble at your tits, all right?'

Klymene pushed her chair away from the table and stood up. Her blood was pounding in her head, making her feel hot and sick. She covered her face with her hands.

'Leave the girl alone, you!' said someone. 'You're disgusting. Can't a young lady have a drink and a cake without having to put up with your crap?'

The scabby man slunk into his seat and turned to his friends, shrugging his shoulders.

'Thank you,' said Klymene, looking up at the man who had spoken. The Rat. The Rat had come to her defence.

'It's a pleasure,' he said. 'Antinous, at your service. We meet again, do we not? I've often noticed you around the palace. Here and there.' He smiled at her and Klymene was confused. Why would Lord Antinous disturb himself in order to help her? He was better looking than her tormentor, but his eyes were full of something; some emotion she didn't recognize, and which frightened her. Some of his gang had been sitting with Melantho, but he must have been at a table inside the tavern. Perhaps he was drunk. Still, he'd been kind to her and deserved her courtesy.

'May I sit with you while you eat and drink?'

She hesitated. If she refused, what would happen? And yet the thought of Antinous watching her as she ate made her stomach heave.

'I'm not hungry any longer. And I must go. I've already been away from the palace too long. Thank you for helping me.'

'The least I could do for a pretty girl like you. I'm sure we'll meet again.' The Rat was smiling at her in a way that made her shiver. 'I don't think your friend is ready to go home yet.'

'Then I'll go by myself. Thank you,' Klymene answered, thinking, *I will try not to be anywhere where you are, if I can.* No other words came into her mind. She picked up the basket that she'd put down on the floor and pushed past the revellers at the other tables.

'Klymene! Wait! Wait for me!'

Melantho was calling after her. Klymene didn't pause but kept on walking out of the tavern and into the heat.

'Honestly! You might slow down a bit. I see you've fled, after all. And I see you caught the attention of Lord Antinous.' Klymene heard the thread of envy in Melantho's voice. 'I thought his tastes were a bit more sophisticated. Still, you can't ever tell what someone'll go for, can you?'

'I wasn't . . . I was just . . . Never mind. I don't know how you can stand it!'

'Stand what? For the Gods' sake, stop going so

fast. It's hot, in case you hadn't noticed. And this basket is heavy.'

Klymene stopped in the middle of the road. 'How can you bear to have them all looking at you like that: as though you were naked? You can see that they'd fall on you like dogs in one minute. Sometimes it's hard to see a difference between men and wild animals. Did you see the horrible one who came up to me first? Revolting.' She shivered.

Melantho said: 'But Antinous rescued you from him, didn't he? I think he deserves a little kindness just for that.'

'I wasn't unkind. I was polite. I don't trust him.'

'He's not so bad.'

'Not as bad as some,' Klymene acknowledged. 'But not for me. He's supposed to be courting the queen.'

'Yes, but that doesn't mean he can't amuse himself while he waits, does it? You're too fussy,' Melantho said. 'And men get all bossy if you resist them. Much easier to wheedle them into doing what you want.'

'I don't know how to "wheedle", as you put it.'

'I could teach you. I could give you wheedling lessons. I'm sure you'd soon learn.' Melantho's laugh echoed in the still evening air.

As they hurried back up the road to the palace, Klymene became aware of someone staring after her. She turned to see who it was, and there was the Rat, walking behind them. He was quite a long way away, but Klymene could tell that he was watching her. He lifted a hand to wave at her as she went and she raised her hand in return, not exactly understanding why

180

she felt a thrill of terror rushing through her body. She was cold all over, even though the sun was making the air shiver with heat. I'm going to forget what happened, she told herself. I shall try to keep out of his way.

Argos waits

every night and every day and more and more of them and mornings and evenings and more waiting

A NIGHT SCENE

'Lords of the Islands,' Penelope began, and her voice echoed from the high spaces in the roof of the great hall. 'It is not my habit or desire to speak aloud at such a gathering, but there is something I must say.'

The crowd fell silent. Five years to the day had passed since Antikleia's death and the feast that by tradition marked the Remembering was about to begin. The suitors, who had been in the palace for more than half a year, had been invited too, because on this day that honoured Odysseus, it was good, Penelope considered, for them to be reminded that he was still lord of Ithaka, even though he was not present at the table. All around the walls of the dining hall, lit torches blazed from their bronze holders and the men who'd thronged in to hear what Penelope had to say pressed closer to the throne. Antinous and Amphimedon, the Rat and the Bear, who were most eager to know what Penelope had decided, stood in front of the others, looking up at the woman who, to all intents and purposes, was ruler in Ithaka.

Her hands were clasped together and the knuckles,

Klymene noticed, were white. Melantho had arranged the queen's hair, because that was her particular skill, but Klymene had chosen the robe and the ornaments that accompanied it: a dress as blue as the ocean at midnight, worn with a silver necklace hung with crescent moons set with rough nuggets of turquoise and onyx.

Penelope took a deep breath and continued, 'Today marks five years since my mother-in-law's death. On this day we pray for Antikleia and offer sacrifices to Pallas Athene to beg her to keep my husband Odysseus safe from harm. As you all know, he has not returned from the war fought against Troy. In my heart I hope for his coming, but I know that it is my duty to marry if he does not. You have, all of you, many times asked me to choose from among you, but it is hard for me when my heart belongs to my husband still. Nevertheless, I have decided that after so long the time has come to make a decision.'

The Rat smirked and the Bear shifted his enormous weight where he stood. The listening crowd stirred a little, and Klymene could hear that they'd all breathed in at once, eager for the moment, each of them thinking: *This is it. This is when I might be the one she chooses.*

'I am almost ready to settle on a husband,' Penelope said, 'but you must humour me a little while longer. I am making a shroud for my father-in-law. I wish to do this for Laertes, who has been better than a parent to me. His own wife began the work but died before it was finished. It is my clear duty to finish what

184

she started. I cannot allow him to be buried in anything other than his dear Antikleia's handiwork, which I shall continue. When I have completed that, then I will marry. That is my decision. I wish you all quiet sleep.'

She turned and made her way quickly from the hall. Klymene followed her, shivering at the anger she heard in the voices that shouted after them:

Unfair . . . You said you were deciding tonight . . . You haven't said which of us'll be chosen . . . How much longer do we have to stay here in this dung heap while a woman makes up her mind?

'Quick, quick, lady,' said Klymene. 'Let us close ourselves in your room where they can't reach us.'

They hurried up the staircase and along the corridor and went into the queen's bedroom. Penelope sank on to the great bed.

'O Zeus and Pallas Athene, keep me safe from those men! Let me not ever fall into their hands—'

'But you've said you will choose,' Klymene whispered. 'What will you do when the shroud is made and the time comes to tell them your decision? The work is so quick that it will not be long before it's done.'

'No, I will work slowly. I will take all the time I can. And men don't understand women's handiwork. I shall continue to sit under the pomegranate tree to knit where any passing suitor can see me and watch how slowly it's growing. But I'll spend most of my time on the weaving, Klymene. It'll be a long time before they understand what's going on and anything may

185

happen. Anything. Why, my husband might return, Klymene, might he not?'

'I'm only telling you what I saw,' said Melantho. 'There's no need to be so sulky about it. What d'you care anyway?'

'I *do* care,' Klymene whispered. The two young women were lying on their beds in the servants' quarters and the heat was like a thick blanket you could feel pressing down on you. Trust Melantho, Klymene thought, to make life more difficult by telling stories like the one she'd just confided.

'I'm going for a walk,' Klymene said. 'It's too hot to sleep.'

'Nothing to do with the heat, why you can't sleep,' Melantho said, and Klymene felt that she could hear the smile she was smiling as she spoke: smug and knowing. 'You just don't like thinking such things about the queen, though why you imagine she's any different from any other woman, I really don't know.'

'It's you, Melantho,' Klymene said. 'Just because you're finding it impossible to be loyal to Telemachus, you see such things everywhere. There's probably a perfectly innocent explanation anyway.'

'Like what? Tell me why someone hooded and cloaked should sneak out of Penelope's chamber when everyone else is sleeping and why she should stand in the doorway and stare longingly after him.'

'You don't know anything!' Klymene wanted to scream, but kept her voice low for fear of waking the others who slept in neighbouring rooms. 'How could you tell, if it was so dark, that it was a man anyway? Maybe it was my grandmother! And how could you see her staring *longingly*? What does *longingly* mean? Tell me that!'

'Don't be ridiculous, Klymene! I know what I'm talking about, which is more than you do. I know longing when I see it. And I'll tell you something else. She was naked under her thin robe – the yellow one. I could see her breasts plainly.'

'I'm not listening. I'm going.' Klymene almost ran out of the room. She hurried down the stairs to the kitchen and out of the door that led to the back of the palace. I'm not staying in the same room as Melantho, she thought. Hateful creature! How dare she spread gossip about the queen!

Klymene went to sit on the bench near the wooden gate that led to the orchard. The night air was filled with the smell of the ocean, which murmured around the island. Clouds raced across the sky, and the moon, sacred to Artemis, was nothing but a fingernail of silver on the blue. Beyond the gate she could see the black masses of the fruit trees that provided apricots, figs and plums for the household. Something like silence had fallen at last and even the hordes of men camped out around the main gates of the palace were asleep. It wasn't true. It couldn't be. Penelope would never, never be disloyal to Odysseus. She hated all of them, all the men who'd come to seek her hand in marriage. How many times had she told Klymene so?

Not all of them, said a small voice somewhere deep in Klymene's head. *She doesn't hate them all. She likes*

Leodes. You know that. Why don't you admit it to yourself? They're not all the same. Not at all. Leodes isn't a bad person. And remember how she looked on the night when he first came to Ithaka and feasted at her table? Remember how her body leaned towards his?

Klymene considered this and thought, No, it can't be. Just because she likes one among the chieftains, it doesn't follow that she lets him into her chamber at dead of night. It's much more likely that Melantho is making mischief. And anyway, why should I care so much? It isn't any of my business, what Penelope does.

Klymene reflected on this. Perhaps because her mistress was like a mother to her in many ways, she needed her to be more than other women – better, more loyal, so faithful to a missing husband that she remained chaste for ever, long after the time when anyone else would have taken another man into her bed. Klymene drew her scarf around her. It was a little cooler now and she'd been sitting here for a long time. From far away she could hear a dog barking and, from the depths of the palace, Argos's answering noise, too weak to be called a real bark. These days he only went out when Klymene took him by the collar and led him into the garden for a short walk. She looked down at the encampment and wondered if Mydon was awake somewhere down there. Lately she had spoken a few words to him occasionally, but they had not had a proper conversation for some time.

She closed her eyes for a moment and what Melantho had told her came again into her mind like a painted picture: the man, cloaked and hooded, bending down to kiss the queen's lips and hurrying away. Penelope, her breasts visible under the thin robe, staring after him *longingly*. That was the word she couldn't bear. *Longingly*.

I'm going to forget what I've heard, she decided. She stood up and turned towards the palace, but then she saw something moving in the shadow of the wall, and froze.

'Who's there?' she called out. She wanted her voice to sound brave, but she knew that it didn't. It wavered and shook with the fear that had taken over her body. 'Come out and show yourself!'

A black shape detached itself from the surrounding darkness.

'Don't be afraid, Klymene. It's me. Antinous. You remember me from Lysander's Tavern. I mean you no harm.'

'Lord Antinous.' What else could she say? She could hear her heart beating in her breast.

'Aren't you pleased to see me, Klymene?'

What was she supposed to answer? That seeing him filled her with black dread? She said, 'Good evening, sir.'

She thought, *I must go. I must leave now. I must just smile and say something pleasant and walk right past him.*

'I think you might be a little more friendly to me,' said Antinous, and he laughed in a way that made Klymene's flesh crawl. 'After all, I did you a favour, back at the tavern, only a few days ago, didn't I? Who knows what would have become of you without me.'

'Yes, and I was grateful. Thank you. But I must go inside now. You'll excuse me, I'm sure.'

She made to walk past him and he caught her by the wrist.

'You're one of those, I see. One of those who blow hot and cold. Pull a man towards them and then come over all frigid. Back at the tavern, you were up for it. What's happened since then?'

Klymene was struck dumb. What on earth was he saying? Was he demented? How, in what way, had she been 'up for it'?

'I was polite,' she said finally. 'That's all. No more than that. You were kind to me and I thanked you.'

'Ha, you say that, but I can read the language of your body. That's what you didn't know. I could see how you *really* felt.'

'How . . . how did I really feel?' This could not be happening to her. Perhaps it was dream and she would wake soon in her own bed.

'You fancied me. You still do. I can tell, you see. I can see it in your eyes.'

Should she cry out for help? Who would hear her? This part of the garden was distant from all the bed-chambers. I'll keep him talking, she thought. Lead him nearer to the palace. I'll be pleasant and not make him angry and he might let me go. Should I mention Penelope? *Wheedle*, she could hear Melantho saying. *They will do what you want if you can wheedle . . .* But how? How did you do it?

'I didn't mean to lead you on,' she whispered.

'But you did, didn't you? And it's lucky for me you

190

did, because you're my type,' he said and laughed again.

'I must go back, Lord Antinous,' Klymene said. 'Back to the palace. Melantho will be waiting for me.'

'Don't count on it. She's well known in our camp, that Melantho. Not above a bit of hanky-panky, her.'

'Don't talk like that!' Klymene hissed, anger suddenly joining with her fear to make her forget for a moment that she was trying to mollify him.

'Ask her yourself,' said Antinous, coming closer to where Klymene stood, cowering a little. 'She'll tell you. Don't think she's ashamed. Taken quite a fancy to young Ilos, they say. I say she's too good for him.'

'But—' Klymene was about to object when the Rat seized her by the arms and pulled her towards him.

'Enough talking,' he said, and his voice was rougher now. Klymene could feel his fingers digging into her arms, and his breath, his foul breath, was in her nostrils. She tried to kick out with her legs, and found that he'd forced her to her knees – how had he done that? Should she call out for Telemachus? If he came, he would run the Rat through with his sword. No, no one must ever know her shame. What if Antinous told everyone? How would she bear the disgrace? She looked straight into the Rat's dark eyes.

'Let go!' she cried. 'Let me go, I implore you. If you let me go now, I'll say nothing, I promise. I won't tell anyone. If you hurt me, I'll tell the queen and she'll throw you out, you and all your men.'

'I'm sick of you and your denials. Your lies. Pretending you didn't encourage me when you know that's not true. I don't intend to leave you in any position to talk. I've got a knife, you see, and I'm not afraid to use it. Never told you that, did I? You shouldn't have treated me like this. Big mistake, Klymene. I'm going to punish you now, see? You won't be doing much of anything except wandering among the dead in Hades, come morning. And I will tell your mistress some tale that shows me in a good light. As your protector from one of those young thugs in the tents. She might be so moved by my kindness and my bravery that she decides to marry me. Think of that. Your death might be what helps her to make her mind up.'

Klymene closed her eyes. Perhaps it would be better to die after all. There would be no disgrace. And this is what her death was going to be: torture and dishonour and then nothing. She almost longed for it to be over. She felt Antinous' hands on her neck and shoulders as though everything were happening to someone else. *He's pushing me to the ground on my back – o Artemis, Artemis, save me from this.*

A shriek came from the Rat that was like the noise a pig makes when the slaughterer's knife finds its throat, and Klymene opened her eyes. He was kneeling with his legs on either side of her body and trying to fend off something white that was pulling at his garments, biting his legs. He let go of her for a moment and Klymene twisted herself almost upright. A silver-white hound had his teeth embedded in the Rat's leg. She didn't wait to see more but got to her knees and pushed herself into an upright position. Then she began to run.

'Oh, Gods, help! I'm being torn to pieces! Help

me!' Antinous shouted. Klymene looked back and saw the hound reaching for his throat. The Rat was writhing on the ground, howling and crying out for his mother, for the Gods, for anyone to help him. Not me, Klymene thought. I won't lift a finger. Let him rot there where he's fallen.

As she reached the kitchen door, she turned to look behind her. Her tormentor was getting to his feet and there was someone standing beside him. Artemis, in the tunic that seemed made of the moonlight, raised her silver quiver into the air in triumphant greeting. Antinous was upright now and stumbling in pain towards the courtyard. Artemis' voice travelled through the night like a silver thread and whispered in Klymene's ear. 'He will say nothing, do not fear. Not to anyone.'

The Goddess put out a hand, the silver hound bounded to her side, and together they drifted over the ground and disappeared into the shadows of the trees.

Klymene went into the kitchen. She poured cool water on her face. She took a pitcher of wine from the table and went outside again. Above her head she saw the moon, thin and white and pure in the dark sky, looking down on her. Artemis, who kept young maidens in her care, had watched over her. Klymene poured some of the blood-red liquid on to the earth.

'I thank you for your help, Artemis,' she whispered. 'Accept this libation.'

MOTHER AND SON

'I don't know what the matter is with everyone!' Telemachus kicked at the side of the chest that held his mother's clothes. The midday meal was over and almost everyone in the palace had retired to escape the heat and rest a little.

'There's obviously something the matter with you, Telemachus,' Penelope said mildly, 'but I'd be grateful if you didn't behave like a spoiled brat. What are you talking about?'

'You know what I'm talking about, Mother. I think we ought to do something about those barbarians.'

'And what do you suggest that hasn't been thought of already? You're not proposing that I marry one of them, are you?'

'Course not. You've always told me my father was alive and I've believed you.'

'Thank you for that. You are almost the only person in the whole world who does.'

'But why do we have to put up with no-hopers and low life all over our courtyards?'

'Because the only way to get rid of them is for me

to marry one. You wouldn't want that, I presume?'

'No, I've said I wouldn't but I've had a good idea, Mother. Really.'

Why didn't she say something? She was just waiting for him to speak again. Telemachus leaned against the wall and smiled at her.

'We could put a sleeping draught in the wine. They drink enough of it. And then when they're asleep, we could kill them.'

'Just like that? Kill them while they sleep?'

Telemachus nodded. 'I know it's a bit . . . well . . . a bit underhand, but we can't fight them properly. We haven't got the men.'

Penelope sighed. 'Come and sit down next to me, here on the bed. I'm going to pretend you never said those words. I don't want to think a son of mine could have thought of such a plan. Telemachus, I'm ashamed of you!'

'But why? They've no right to be here. They're like thieves.'

'They're visitors, Telemachus. We have a duty of hospitality.'

'Crap! How can you be hospitable when you're entertaining monsters?'

'You've learned some of their words, I see. Don't learn their behaviour too, Telemachus. If you kill defenceless men while they sleep you are a murderer and not a defender of your property. You'll have to come up with something a little more sensible than that, I'm afraid, if you're to be any help in this situation—'

'What about you?'

'What do you mean?'

'I mean: surely there's something you can do apart from sitting here weaving all day long?' His voice rose dangerously. 'You're doing *damn all*! Anyone would think you don't care—'

'If you can't express yourself decently, Telemachus, then I wish you'd go.'

'I'm not going. You've got to see how it looks. As if you're putting up with everything and just waiting for the time to pass.'

'That is what I have to do,' Penelope said. 'I have to have faith and wait. You think it's an easy option, but I promise you it's not. I'm not going to trouble you with my problems.'

Telemachus aimed another kick at the wooden chest in which his mother kept her clothes.

'This is a waste of time,' he said and, opening the door, he stepped into the corridor and banged the door behind him as he strode into the courtyard. Women! His mother was infuriating but she was probably right and murdering the whole lot of them was out of the question. He felt the blood beating in his head. Who could he turn to who would help him? How could he raise an army to attack the suitors? His hands, he noticed, were still clenched into fists and he took a deep breath and unclenched them.

'Klymene!'

Mydon's voice startled her as she was walking from the great hall to the armoury carrying a pitcher full of water.

'Have you been waiting for me?' she asked. She walked with her eyes fixed on the ground.

'Yes. Let me take the pitcher from you. You look—'

'I'm all right. I can carry it myself.'

'I was only going to say: you look pale. I didn't mean to say . . . well, it doesn't matter. I'll leave you, if you prefer.'

'Yes . . .' Klymene said. 'Maybe you should.'

Mydon blushed and bowed his head. 'Another time, perhaps.'

He walked away quickly. Klymene started to cry out, to stop him, to call him back to her, but the sound died in her throat. She stepped into the armoury and, putting the pitcher on the floor, she sat down beside it and hugged her knees, burying her face. Argos roused himself from where he was lying and came to nuzzle her arms. She looked up with tears standing in her eyes.

'Argos, I'm mad. What have I done? I've sent him away. I can't talk. I'm so . . . last night . . . Never mind, darling dog. I nearly died, Argos. Only Artemis saved me. And now, instead of being happy and telling Mydon, I've sent him away. What if he doesn't come back? What then?'

Argos sat down beside her, sniffing at the pitcher.

'Now I'm neglecting you! Here – here's the water.'

She stood and went to fill the dog's bowl. He followed her and lapped at the clear liquid. 'Good dog,' she said. 'Good dog that I love.'

A flicker of movement caught her eye. Someone was standing against the wall beside Odysseus' huge

197

bow: a man she didn't recognize. She stood up, trembling. Who was this? Another suitor? One she hadn't seen before? How could that be? This person was very tall and wearing a black cloak over a suit of black armour. His helmet was crested with crimson horsehair.

'Who are you?' Klymene asked, trembling with fear and flinching a little at the chill she felt as he drew closer.

'Ares, God of War.' The God's voice was like a knife being drawn across a stone. 'The battle is being prepared. Know that.'

'What battle? Against the suitors? When? How?'

'You ask too many questions.'

As Klymene watched, Ares began to walk out of the door, wrapping his long black cloak around his body. A shadow, dark as bad dreams, spread out behind him, staining the pale stone floor.

'This is where you're hiding.'

Klymene felt all the blood in her body turn to ice. Antinous . . . How did he dare to come near her after what had happened to him last night? She pressed herself close to Argos and decided to be silent for as long as she could.

'I have some news for you, Klymene,' said the Rat, leaning against the wall and looking at her quite without desire. All she could see in his eyes was hatred: cold and terrifying. 'I've decided to send Mydon to work at one of the farms inland. I need someone there . . .'

Why? Klymene wanted to ask but said nothing. She

fixed her eyes on the floor. *Go away, please go away,* she said over and over in her head.

The Rat continued in a perfectly reasonable tone. 'You're dying to ask why, aren't you? Can't you guess?' He sighed and continued: 'Well, you're determined not to talk to me and I can't do anything about that, of course, so suit yourself. I'll tell you anyway. Mydon's a friend of yours, isn't he? More than that, perhaps. So I'm doing you a favour. That's the way I look at it. Sending him away so that your precious chastity may be preserved. Nice of me, right? But then I'm a nice sort of person. Goodbye.'

The Rat was gone, and Klymene waited till she could no longer hear his footsteps before she dared to go to the door.

'He's lying, Argos. He's sending Mydon away because he knows I like him. He's sending him away to punish me. To show me that there's something he can do after what Artemis did to him last night.'

She trembled at the Rat's cunning. He knew exactly what to do that would most upset her. And perhaps he was protecting himself too. Perhaps he realized that Mydon was not one of his most loyal supporters.

PENELOPE AND LEODES

Penelope was sitting in the shade of the pomegranate tree that grew in the furthest corner of the garden. She had laid aside her work for the moment and it was folded into a basket at her feet. How angry Telemachus had been yesterday when she spoke to him! He'd grown into a short-tempered young man and she feared his nature. If any boy had needed a father, it was Telemachus. Perhaps I should have married years ago for his sake. She closed her eyes against the glare of the afternoon sun. I won't think of Telemachus now, she told herself. I'll enjoy the peace here. She noticed that a fragrance of roses and almond blossom hung in the air. Perhaps it was a young servant, being too lavish with the perfumed oil in order to attract one of the rabble who were lying about all over the palace.

This was one of the very few places where Penelope felt she could be alone, or at least free from the intrusions of the suitors. Her chamber, which she kept to more and more, was on a side of the palace facing away from the outer courtyard. But she could hear, if the shutters were open, the noise of fighting, swearing and singing of a tuneless and drunken variety. The worst of the smells didn't reach her, but she had to prevent herself from pinching her nostrils together as she walked about. The melon peel and leftover shreds of meat putrefied in the sun and that drew flies in their thousands, which buzzed about in a noxious blue cloud. How did it happen that these men were oblivious to the stench and the vermin and the whole hideous scene that met her eyes wherever she turned them? Here, in the shade of the late afternoon, she was reasonably sure of being alone for a while. The ghastly creatures who had taken over the rest of her home generally slept in the afternoon and only woke to carouse when the sun had disappeared into the ocean.

She knew she ought to be stronger, but there was little she could do. If she had more men to help her, she might have seen to it that the place was cleared, but the servants in the palace were frightened of the bullies who'd taken up residence and it was as much as Nana could do to stop the women who worked in the kitchen from fleeing to the other side of the island. Penelope knew that it was only a fierce loyalty to Laertes that kept some of them in their posts. Even after all that they had suffered, no one wanted it spread about the islands that the hospitality on Ithaka was inadequate.

Her thoughts went to Leodes. I can't help myself, she thought. She had allowed him to accompany her to her chamber more and more often, and each time they had spoken of the old days, and he had kissed her gently before he left, and she had trembled with fear for a long time when she thought that Telemachus might have seen him slipping quietly out of her door.

'My lady,' said a voice, and Penelope opened her eyes. Leodes stood in front of her, his face in shadow. She started, surprised to see him. It was as though her thoughts of him had materialized in front of her.

'Please accept my apology for disturbing you,' he said, 'but it's difficult to say anything when all the others are in the hall, and I think I should speak with you. Perhaps I ought to have said something when we spoke last night, but the talk was of other matters then.'

Penelope smiled. 'I'm always happy to talk to a friend. That's what you are, Leodes. Not like the others. Whenever I see you, I'm reminded of the days when we were all young: you and me and Odysseus. How we used to laugh!'

'I haven't heard that laughter since I came to Ithaka,' Leodes said.

'Please sit beside me, Leodes.'

'Thank you.' He turned to Penelope and took her hand. 'I want to say something to you, Penelope. My friend Odysseus would have me speak these words, I know it, if he could see you now and what has become of his palace. Marry me. How can it be that your husband is alive and not at your side? Your loyalty does you credit, lady, but you're deluding yourself. My dear friend is in the Elysian Fields with the other heroes of the war and you're suffering for nothing.'

Penelope's heart leaped. She said nothing. Her hand in Leodes' hand seemed to be too warm even for this hot afternoon. She was aware of his blue eyes looking at her and her body – she couldn't help it – grew warm and soft under his gaze. He was kind. He was handsome. And, she told herself, it's no disgrace that I have dreamed of him. I can't help it. I am human and my bed has been empty for so long. Is it wrong to imagine his mouth on mine? Penelope trembled and said only: 'I feel that my husband is alive, Leodes, or I would agree to what you suggest. I can't help it. My heart would know if he were dead.'

'I'll wait,' Leodes said. 'In the end, you'll understand what has to be understood. Meanwhile, I'll do all I can to make your days easier. My heart, Penelope, is yours. Do you know that? And do you know that I mean my friend Odysseus no disrespect?'

'Yes,' said Penelope. 'I know it.'

Leodes brought her hand to his lips and kissed her fingers. 'Farewell then for now, dear Penelope. I'll leave you to your rest.'

She watched him walking away towards the courtyard. How tall he was! Taller than Odysseus. For a moment a picture of how he would look naked flashed across her mind and she moaned and stood up. The fragrance of roses and almond blossom hung in the air. Where did that come from? What is happening to me? she asked herself. I am as foolish as any young girl. Her hand, where Leodes had kissed it, seemed to burn with the imprint of his lips. It was time to return to her chamber. It was time to put such thoughts away entirely.

As soon as she entered her chamber, she felt the picture she had begun to weave calling out to her, summoning her to her work. Does anyone guess at my feelings? Penelope wondered. And does anyone know how seldom I've been attending to the labour the Goddess entrusted me with? The shroud, the white wool, had been taking up all her energy and thought and she trembled for fear that her inattention would be punished. She went to sit in front of the loom, staring at the threads and not really seeing them. She began to hear a hammer beating in her heart and a kind of humming in her blood. Her head was filled suddenly with images of birds and water and bones. She must weave the story. It must be woven.

deep blue   silver and green
a black thread for the ship
warp weft   back forth   the shuttle moves

white   weft warp   weft warp   blue black
songs of home   the beating of your heart   warp weft

They stand on sand ground from dead sailors' bones.
Their wingspan is as wide as a man's arms;
their feathers pearly as the morning light.

They're birds, but standing upright and their eyes
are human eyes. From human lips, rose-red,
come songs to lure all humans to their doom.
They sing love songs; they sing the songs of death.
They sing the darkest secrets of each heart
and the desires no one dares confess.
No ear is safe from their bewitching airs.

feathers float down   back and forth
warp and weft   blue and gold green
float down feathers   weft warp
down float feathers   soft soft

His crew have lashed Odysseus to the mast
and stopped their own ears with small lumps of
    wax.
That was the order, and they've followed it.
They row, heads down, straight past the Sirens'
    Isle
and they hear nothing and Odysseus cries;
shrieks at his men to cut him loose again.
'I want to go and shelter on that shore.
I need the comfort of those magic songs.'
He sobs and writhes and blood flows from his
    wrists.
They're bound behind his back with leather thongs
but he feels nothing. Music fills his heart.
His men can't hear. The black ship moves away.
Odysseus bows his head. The songs have gone.

soft sweet   warp weft   silver silver

blue yellow   black thread for the ship
weft warp   back forth   move the shuttle sweet

warp weft   blue black   round and round
silence   blue green   weft warp   round round
sharp silver white back forth   warp weft

Argos dreams

*where are the fires and where is the blood bones and water
and nothing but smells and a dark place and not moving
sleeping and sleeping and running in dark places and voices
calling and calling whistles and voices and water and bones*

ANGRY WORDS

Telemachus ran his hands through his hair and groaned. 'It's a torment to me, Melantho, and that's the truth. You're driving me out of my mind. All I've been hearing for the last moon or more is stories about this Ilos. You refused to promise me to stay away from him, and now they say you're spending hours down there in Antinous' camp. With Ilos. Is it true?'

'*They say!* I notice you'll believe anyone rather than me. You don't trust me,' Melantho said, looking injured. She bent her head. 'You're away from the palace so often. I'm sometimes bored, that's all. It doesn't mean anything, I promise, Telemachus.'

They were sitting together in the covered passage of the inner courtyard, on a bench outside the great hall.

'Is that all you've got to say?' Telemachus frowned. 'There was a time when we couldn't keep our hands off one another. Remember that, Melantho?'

'I'm quite happy for your hands to do exactly what they want,' she said.

'You're not taking me seriously. You're flirting.

You're always flirting – I've seen you and heard you.'

'Oh, don't be so . . . so *serious*, Telemachus! What's wrong with you these days? You used to be amusing, you know, but now . . . I have more fun with the suitors.'

'So it's true! You admit it! You've just said it didn't mean anything.'

'It doesn't. It's just . . . O Gods, Telemachus, I don't know what you want.'

'Do you love me?'

'How can you doubt it?'

'I do, that's all. I *do* doubt it. In fact I don't know whether you know what love means.'

'Do you? Does anyone? I think we're at the mercy of the Gods. Eros strikes us and we're powerless.'

'He struck me when I saw you, Melantho. We weren't much more than children in those days but I've never stopped loving you.'

'Diddums!'

'Don't dare to laugh at me, Melantho! I'll . . .'

'You'll what? Are you going to hit me?'

Telemachus stood up suddenly and turned his back on Melantho. His hands had formed themselves into fists, and he could feel the fury welling up inside him and knew that if he didn't get a grip on himself at once, he probably would strike her. He said, 'I've had it, Melantho. I can't stand this. I'm going. Perhaps when I'm not here you'll come to your senses.'

'You're never here. That's part of the problem. You're forever going off to hunt and spending the night on one farm or another instead of being with me.'

'That's got nothing to do with you. I hate looking at it – what those damned suitors are doing.'

'Where will you go?'

'I'll take a ship and then . . . Never mind.'

'Running away to sea! How predictable you are! Well, I hope you're in a better temper when you return. They're always very happy down in Antinous' camp. No long faces there!'

'That's because they're pissed half the time!' Telemachus was shouting so loudly that his throat felt raw. 'You can move in there if you like and good riddance!' He strode away from the bench.

'What about a kiss, my darling?' Melantho called after him. Her voice was full of scorn. She was mocking him.

'Get stuffed!' Telemachus called back. 'Get Ilos to kiss you. You two deserve one another.'

He made his way swiftly across the courtyard, kicking out as he went at stones that stood in his path.

Telemachus squinted into the sunlight and threw a small stone as hard as he could at the water where it became flat and still beyond the frothing of the waves. The stone bounced on the surface, and leaped on to bounce again and again. Klymene tried to work out how long it had been since she'd sat on the seashore with him. They'd brought fruit with them, just as they used to when they were children. It was possible to imagine that nothing had changed since then, but everything was different now and the next words Telemachus spoke were full of bitterness.

'I can't bear it, Klymene, not for another day,' he said. 'I'm not sticking around here watching them all grabbing and clawing at my parents' property. I can't understand what's happened to my mother. She's just putting up with it. Saying nothing. Doing nothing. D'you realize how long they've been here? Nearly six moons. It's no use. She says she can't do anything except weave those damned tapestries. Odysseus' life depends on her, that's what she told me. I don't see how it can, but that's what she says. She also says he promised her he'd return. Can you believe a grown woman can be so stupid? As if every soldier who ever went to war didn't say those exact words? Laertes thinks she ought to marry one of them, but I don't. That'd be too disgusting, wouldn't it? Horrible. I'd kill anyone who married her, I think. For two pins I'd take the next stone I see and chuck it at one of their heads and hope I manage to put out one of their greedy eyes!'

'Have another fig,' said Klymene, trying to calm him down. 'It's so long since we've been down here like this. Enjoy your time away from the palace while you can.'

'I can't. Everything I look at, everything I think is spoiled by those animals. Melantho . . . that's the last straw. You know, don't you, Klymene? You've seen how friendly she is with some of them? That bastard Ilos boasting about how she spends most of her time down in their camp these days. I'm sick of it.'

'Has she said anything?' Klymene asked. Perhaps it would be over between them soon. Could it be that

Telemachus had asked her to come to the seashore to tell her that?

'We had a row yesterday. She doesn't deny it, but she says it doesn't mean anything. Pah!' Telemachus made a spitting sound. 'I don't believe her. But I won't have to look at it much longer. I'm going.'

'Going?' Klymene asked. 'Where to?'

Telemachus took up a stick and began to draw a pattern on the smooth sand. 'That's why I've asked you down here, Klymene. Away from all of them. I've got a plan and I'll need you to help me.'

All the hopes Klymene had been cherishing vanished at once. She took a deep breath. 'Tell me what you want me to do,' she said at last.

'The suitors . . . I'd like to take them all on myself but I'm not strong enough on my own to fight them and that makes me furious. I'm leaving. I'm not telling my mother where I'm going nor why, and you, Klymene, will tell her the lies that'll comfort her. You will do that, won't you? I'm going to sea.'

'When?' said Klymene. 'When will you go? Isn't this a bit sudden?'

'No, it's not. I've had the thought in my mind for a long time . . .'

But you never did anything about it till Melantho lost interest in you, Klymene thought.

Telemachus went on: 'I've arranged for a ship to take me to Pylos. The *Sea Nymph*, she's called. I'll tell my mother I'm going on a fishing trip and you can confirm it. Tell her I've spoken about it to you often.

She'll think it's an unsuitable thing for me to be doing but at least she won't worry about me.'

'What *will* you be doing?'

'I'm going to find out if anyone's had word of my father since the Trojan War. I'll go everywhere – Pylos, Mycenae, Sparta. I won't come back till I have some news.'

'What if there's no news?' Klymene asked.

'Then I'll ask for help from my father's friends to rid Ithaka of those parasites. And meanwhile I won't have to see them every day, pass their encampments every time I step outside the palace. Above all, I can stop tormenting myself thinking about Melantho.'

Klymene said nothing. Telemachus knew the truth about Melantho now: she was drawn to men as a moth is drawn to the lantern flame, and her longing was a longing of the flesh. She had no desire to become one half of a couple; to find the missing part of her that wise men said was what real love was.

Years ago, she would have felt fury at Melantho's behaviour, but they'd grown used to one another after working and talking and arguing together for so long. They had shared the same bedchamber for nearly six years. Nothing she can do, Klymene thought, surprises me any longer, and now that she's tired of Telemachus, I don't even dislike her as much as I used to.

She looked at Telemachus as he sat staring out to sea. She felt like crying but bit her lip to stop herself. She'd been stupid to hope that Melantho's behaviour might make Telemachus turn to her instead. He'd never love her. Not in the way she'd been dreaming about and longing for since she was a small girl. Somewhere in her body she felt pain. Perhaps it was the arrow, Eros' glowing blue arrow, being wrenched out of a heart in which it had been embedded for so long. Klymene found that she was looking down at the front of her dress, but she saw nothing and chided herself for being foolish.

Klymene put the stones from the plums they had eaten into a shallow hole and covered them up.

'Let's go back,' Telemachus said, standing up and brushing the sand from his clothes. 'I must talk to my mother.'

'She'll try to persuade you not to go fishing,' Klymene said. 'Are you ready to argue with her?'

'She'll understand,' Telemachus answered. 'I'll tell her the truth about that – well, she knows it anyway. That I can't stand what's going on any longer. She'd probably come with me if she could, but of course she has to remain here and look after the palace. If she went, they'd tear it to the ground in their eagerness to get their hands on my father's possessions.'

'It's a comfort to her to have you here,' Klymene persisted. 'Don't you think it's a bit . . . well, won't it be seen as a kind of running away? If you go and leave her here on her own?'

'I'm not running away.' Telemachus looked furious and he spoke sharply. 'The Gods themselves know what's in my heart, and if any man dares to call me a coward, or any woman too, come to that, they'll feel my knife between their ribs before they repeat the remark. It's my duty, my solemn duty as a son, to search for my father. And I'll tell you something else, Klymene, since you've brought it up. She'll be glad to get me out of the way. When I'm around, she's on edge all the time. Haven't you noticed? As though she's fearful of what I might do to one of her so-called guests. Oh, I'm sick of the whole bloody lot of them, and of everything else as well. Come on, let's go. The sun's going down.'

Telemachus and Klymene set off up the rocky path to the palace, and behind them the chariot of Phoebus Apollo plunged into the sea, leaving the sky streaked with scarlet and gold.

Telemachus told everyone that he didn't want a fuss or any kind of ceremony to mark his departure. He had visited his grandfather to say goodbye, in order to spare him the tiring journey to the palace and the sight of it still overrun by strangers. Nevertheless, not only Penelope and Klymene and Ikarios but also many of the farmers from the other side of the island had come to wish Telemachus well on his voyage. A stiff wind was blowing off the sea and almost from the horizon lines of white-crested waves ran towards the land and slapped against the breakwater, throwing a fine spray up into the air. There were no cats any-where. They'd disappeared, fearing rain, but the har-bour wall was lined with people, and the crew of the *Sea Nymph* were waiting to welcome him aboard.

'Goodbye, Mother,' Telemachus said, holding tight to Penelope's hand and leaning forward to kiss her.

'Take care, my son,' she said. Klymene could hear

from the way she was speaking that she was determined not to cry. The tears would be for later, when she was alone, bent over her weaving.

'Don't worry about me, Mother. I'll be safe and well looked after by these men. They won't let any harm come to me. Klymene, Ikarios, my good friends, farewell.'

He flung his arms around Ikarios' neck and hugged him. Then he came to where Klymene was standing and took her hands in his and looked deep into her eyes.

'You'll look after her, won't you?' he said. 'My mother.'

She nodded and said, 'You know I will.'

'I see Melantho's decided to stay away.'

'She has women's pains,' Klymene said. 'That's what she told me. She wishes you well.'

Telemachus laughed. '*Wishes me well*,' he said. 'Never mind. I don't care. I have other matters to attend to, as you know.'

'I'll pray to Pallas Athene to hold you in her care,' Klymene said.

Telemachus suddenly leaned forward and kissed her cheek. 'Thank you, Klymene. I'll miss you both: you and your brother.'

'And we'll miss you.'

As he walked up the gangplank and into the ship, Klymene glanced at Ikarios. Tears stood in his eyes.

'You're sad, brother,' she said. 'Did you think he might take you with him?'

Ikarios shook his head. 'It's the wind. Getting in

my eyes. I'm all right. I never thought he'd ask me. Why should he? I have my work to do here with Ikmalios and . . .'

There was nothing else to say. Klymene knew why Telemachus had decided not to take a companion. She leaned over and whispered right into her brother's ear.

'I'll tell you later why he's going alone. I can't tell you now. There's a good reason, Ikarios. You must believe me and be happy. Or happier at least.'

'Really? Is that true? I'm glad . . . Thanks, Klymene.'

The ship, which looked large and solid when it was tied up at the jetty, sailed out of the harbour, growing smaller and smaller. The sea was dark and angry-looking and the ship rolled over the waves as it moved towards the distant horizon. Streaks of greyish cloud moved across the sky. Penelope and the others gathered on the dockside waved until the ship was out of sight, their clothes flapping around them. A black cat had ventured on to the wall and seemed to be staring out to sea. Klymene shivered. Telemachus was sailing into the kingdom of Poseidon, his father's sworn enemy. She closed her eyes. Protect him, dear Pallas Athene, she prayed, and hoped that Pallas Athene would send her white owl to watch over Telemachus.

Argos waits

dozing and waking and sleeping again and light and dark
and sleep again

PENELOPE'S SECRET

'Klymene? Klymene, open your eyes! Take this water, child. Can you hear me? Speak if you can, or if you can't speak, then nod. Klymene, say something!'

Klymene tried to nod, and thought maybe she succeeded because the voice stopped all of a sudden. Her head felt as though it were stuffed with rags and she knew that if she tried to open her eyes the sun would burn them, so she kept them closed. What had happened to her? Where was she? Was this Telemachus? No, Telemachus had gone. Fishing and not really fishing, days and days ago. Klymene started to make noises, wanting to ask this person, whoever he was, what had become of Argos. She remembered taking the poor old dog for a walk beyond the palace walls, for a treat. He was far too shaky on his legs to chase rabbits, but he liked going out with her. Most of the time he kept to his hiding place in the armoury.

'Why am I lying on the ground?' she murmured at last, hoping that the sounds coming out of her mouth were intelligible to this man, whoever he was. She ought to ask. She added, 'Who are you?'

219

'Leodes,' said the man. 'You know me well, Klymene. Remember how I carried Argos into the armoury when he'd been attacked? The sun has confused you and you're not yourself. I think you must have fainted in the heat. It's fortunate that I've come back this way. I've been visiting the old king on his farm.'

'Of course,' said Klymene weakly, struggling to open her eyes. 'I know you . . .'

She closed her eyes again. Mydon and Leodes were the only good men from among the horrible strangers whose presence you could never escape as long as you were in the palace. Only two from such crowds of people! Leodes had been kind and polite to her ever since the day when he'd come to her rescue and she liked him. She couldn't help it. He was handsome and gently-spoken and Melantho was always talking about how Penelope herself was fonder of him than she admitted, although Klymene herself had never seen them together. Leodes wasn't one of the chieftains who regularly raided the store for Odysseus' best wine and grain, and as far as she knew none of the serving women had complained about him pulling at their clothes or trying to grab them as they went about their work. The Rat and the Bear, they were the worst, but there were plenty of other big, smelly men with beards that looked dirty and matted. And what seemed like hundreds of hangers-on: whole armies of idle young men with nothing better to do than get drunk and roam about trying to persuade any young woman they found to come to the overgrown part of the orchard behind the palace. Klymene shivered. She knew that some of the women were happy to oblige, but there were others who spoke of being forced at knifepoint. As she would have been, if Artemis hadn't rescued her. Leodes interrupted her thoughts.

'Let me help you,' he said now, kneeling beside her. 'My servants have taken charge of Argos, and I'm going to carry you back to the palace.'

'But . . .' Klymene started to say.

'You'll be lighter than many other burdens I've carried, don't worry. Maybe even lighter than Argos was. You're not much more than a child.'

Klymene wanted to object, to say that on the contrary, many girls of her age were already married, but the effort was too great, and she wanted more than anything to be lying in a cool room with a wet cloth over her eyes.

'The sun must have been too hot for you and made you faint,' said Leodes as he bent down to pick her up.

She tried to answer, but the words wouldn't come. She wanted to tell Leodes that she'd forgotten her scarf and thought it wouldn't matter if she walked in the noonday sun with her head uncovered just this once, even though Nana always said that the heat of the sun could strike you down and even kill you, if you weren't careful. It was too hard. She closed her eyes and felt herself lifted and held against the man's chest. She felt safe. His voice came to her as they walked.

'I shall take you to the queen's chamber. She's very fond of you, I know.'

How does he know? Klymene asked herself sleepily. Can it be that they speak about me? Why would they do that? Everything is too complicated. I'll wait till I feel better, she thought. I'll wait till I'm cooler, till this sun-fever has left me.

At first, when she woke up, Klymene didn't know where she was. This is not my bed, she thought. This is not my chamber. She tried to turn her head sideways but the pain was too great. What has happened to me? she asked herself. She closed her eyes again and tried to remember and gradually things began to come back to her. Falling on the ground and being lifted up by – what was his name? – Leodes. That's right, she thought. One of the suitors, but not at all like the others. He was kind to me and said he was bringing me to Penelope's chamber. Is that where I am now? She opened her eyes again and saw that indeed it was the enormous bed that she was lying in. How long had she been here, and where did Penelope intend to sleep? She turned her head to one side and looked at the window. The colour of the sky outside told her that night had fallen, but whether Phoebus Apollo's horses had long ago dragged the sun down into the sea or whether it had only just left the sky was difficult to tell. Klymene couldn't hear any noise, which probably meant that it was very late. If everyone was still laughing and talking in the courtyard I would hear it from this chamber, she thought. There are so many of them and they make such a racket.

Just then, the door opened quietly and someone came in. Klymene lifted her head from the pillow a little, thinking: it's Penelope. I'll greet her and ask her how long I've been here. Then Penelope laughed. It was a very small, quiet laugh, but immediately Klymene knew, just from the sound of it, that she wasn't alone. Someone was coming into the room with her.

Klymene felt cold all over. Who was it? Why were they here in the bedchamber? Whoever it was must never know I've seen them, and neither must Penelope. O Pallas Athene, make me faint and not see, and not hear anything. She lay as still as she knew how, imagining herself a stone or a fallen branch. She breathed deeply and evenly, in and out, but quietly, so as not to draw attention to herself. Her eyes she kept almost closed. It's so dark in here that no one will notice that I haven't shut them altogether. That would have been impossible. More than she'd ever wanted to know anything, Klymene wanted to know who Penelope's companion was. She could see from the size of the person who came in behind her mistress that it was a man, and everything Melantho had told her, everything she knew for herself, came back to her. This was probably Leodes himself. Yes, that's most likely, Klymene thought, and part of her was relieved that it was him and no one else, and another part of her shouted, *How could you? How could you bring anyone, anyone at all, into Odysseus' bedchamber where the bed that your husband made for you both with his own hands*

223

takes up most of the room. How? Don't you believe any more?
How can you not believe after all you've said to me?

She strained every muscle to hear what the two were saying to one another. They were standing next to the window, very close together, but still both wearing dark, all-covering cloaks. Then the man took his off and it fell to the floor. Klymene dared to open her eyes a little more. She needed to see exactly. She could not risk being deceived in any way. She had to know the whole truth.

It *was* Leodes. He put out two hands and unfastened the cloak from Penelope's shoulders and it spilled down on to the floor. Then, in one movement, as the fabric gathered around her feet, it was she who put out her arms and twined them round Leodes' neck. Penelope brought her body close, close to his, and wound her fingers in his long hair and moaned a little, but from pleasure and not from sadness. That Klymene could clearly recognize.

'Not now, Leodes. We can't. Not while Klymene is still in my bed,' she whispered.

'Somewhere else, then,' Leodes said. 'I'll think of somewhere safe.'

'Nowhere's safe. Not even here.' Penelope moved away from the window and from Leodes and went to sit down by her loom, on which the picture had scarcely changed for two moons or more.

Klymene was terrified that the two of them would hear the beating of her heart. She thought of what she had just seen. What she had just heard. Could she possibly have been mistaken? Her head began to hurt again. Leodes was now with Penelope near the loom and their backs were turned to her. She lifted her head from the pillow a little and saw that his arm was around Penelope's shoulder as she sat and that she was leaning her head against his neck. They were murmuring words to one another that Klymene could hardly hear.

'She's telling him how difficult it is for her,' said a voice, and suddenly, out of the air, there was a woman sitting on the side of the bed, dressed in robes that shone in the gloom and illuminated her beautiful face. A fragrance of roses and almond blossom drifted around her like mist.

'Aphrodite!' Klymene said weakly, wondering what would happen when Penelope heard the sound of voices talking.

'Do not judge your mistress,' Aphrodite whispered to Klymene. 'You have no idea what Odysseus is up to while he's away. I will not soil your young ears with tales about him and Circe—'

'Who is she?' Klymene asked.

'You don't need to know. All you need to do is keep quiet. It would spoil things if you went blabbing about things you've just seen, or are about to see.'

'What am I about to see?'

'Nothing. You will sleep again. But remember: Penelope deserves a little pleasure after years of being so faithful. And she likes Leodes. Look at them now. They won't see you or hear you. And I will reward you for your kindness to your mistress, never fear.'

Klymene sat up a little in the bed and stared at

Penelope and Leodes. They were so close together that with no lamps lit, it was hard to see where his body ended and hers began. They had moved from the stools beside the loom and were now lying on a pile of cushions. Klymene couldn't hear words, but they were whispering together and Penelope's breath was coming faster and faster.

Klymene felt her eyes closing and she sank down on to the pillows again. She breathed in the fragrance of roses and almond blossom and slid into darkness.

When Klymene woke the next morning, it took her some time to realize that she was still in the queen's bed. Her thoughts were muddled, but the fever had gone and she lay with her eyes closed and wondered how much of what was in her mind was a dream. She had seen the Goddess Aphrodite – such a beautiful fragrance surrounded her! One thing she did recall, quite clearly, and that was the sight of Penelope and Leodes standing by the window, close together, and how Penelope had caressed his hair, running her fingers through it, tenderly, lovingly. I'm not sure of many things, Klymene thought, but I do know that I saw that. Should I say something to her? Or should I forget what I've seen and pretend it never happened? If Penelope wanted it known, she would speak about it, surely? Everyone was urging her to choose a new husband. If she loved Leodes, no one would blame her for marrying him. And there would be so many advantages. In one stroke all the riff-raff hanging about the palace would be gone.

Klymene turned her head on the pillow and looked across the room, expecting to see the queen sitting at her loom. The stool in front of it was empty, and the basket of wool looked as though no one had touched it recently. Why had Penelope done so little work on the woven picture? Klymene knew that the queen had used her loom to imagine the places in which her beloved husband might be. The colours changed, but there was always a ship somewhere in the picture: Odysseus' ship. Penelope believed that the threads on her loom kept the ship afloat and her husband alive.

Klymene moved her head again and there, on the other side of the room, in a corner away from the window, Penelope was bent over something . . . The shroud. Klymene watched her silently, and at first the tiny noise of the bone pins moving soothed her and she drifted into sleep again. When she next opened her eyes, she saw a tangle of white wool at the queen's feet. She sat up and looked more carefully. The tangle was growing. More and more wool curled on to the rest. All around Penelope's seat, a wilderness of white lay tangled and heaped up.

'You're undoing the shroud!' Klymene burst out.

Penelope sprang from her chair and ran to the bed. She grabbed Klymene by both her arms and hissed at her: 'Don't you dare say a word about this, do you understand me? Not one word or it will be the worse for you!'

Never in all her life had Penelope ever spoken to her with such rage in her voice. The queen's face was contorted with fury. Her face was white and her lips were pressed together.

Klymene flinched. 'I won't. I won't, only don't be . . . please. I never meant . . .'

Penelope let go of Klymene and covered her face with her hands. She spoke in a thin whisper and rocked from side to side. 'Oh, Klymene, what has happened to me? Will you forgive me? I'm so, so sorry. I shouldn't have. I'm not feeling . . . Oh, I don't know where to begin.'

'Don't cry, lady,' said Klymene. Penelope's face was wet with tears that she didn't trouble to wipe away. 'Please don't.'

'I'm sorry. It's too much. I can't do everything . . . The weaving. The shroud . . .'

'Perhaps if you showed me how, then I could help you? To make the shroud.'

Penelope said nothing. Her hands rested on her knees and she was staring at the wall. 'I'm not making it,' she said at last. 'I'm unmaking it.'

'Unmaking? I don't understand.'

'I've said I'll choose a husband when the shroud is finished. Therefore it can't be finished. Ever. I undo half of my work every night. It doesn't take very long, but there is the weaving – and the new work that has to be done each day so that it can be undone, and every bit of unravelling has to be done in secret . . . I'm so tired, Klymene. So weary of everything.'

'Show me how to do it – the unravelling – and I'll do it in your place.'

'Would you?' A light appeared in Penelope's eyes and then vanished again. 'I can't let you, child. If the suitors discover what's going on, they'll kill me.'

She stood up. 'It's nearly time for me to go and eat with some of the chieftains. I hate doing that. My throat closes up after every mouthful. Do you feel well enough to get up?'

Klymene nodded. Penelope said, 'And be careful when you leave to make sure that the door is firmly closed. I fear that there are people in the palace who are watching me more carefully than usual. As though they are waiting to find me out. I even find myself glad that my son is far away now, so fearful am I of discovery. I must go, Klymene. We'll speak again later. But I thank you, Klymene. We will share this secret, won't we? And tomorrow I will show you how the work is done. You have removed a heavy weight from my heart tonight, child. And I'm so grateful . . . How I wish I could spend more time on weaving the pictures, as I used to! Doing that is still a great comfort to me.'

'I know,' Klymene said. 'Things will be easier when I can help you. And I promise you I'll be careful.'

'Farewell, then,' Penelope said. 'They're expecting me at the table.'

Klymene stood up to bar the door after the Queen left the chamber. Then she went over to the length of fabric that Penelope had made over the last few days. How quick this work was compared to the painstaking labour of the loom! And how easily what she'd done could become wool again with just one pull on the thread! She began to put the white wool back into the trunk.

*

229

The secret she shared with Penelope, the undoing of a good proportion of the work she did on Laertes' shroud, had become a refuge for Klymene. Her work for Nana was soon done, and then, after taking Argos for a short walk, she spent much of the afternoon watching as her mistress twisted the wool into fabric on her seat under the pomegranate tree, and she prayed to Pallas Athene every night that Laertes would live for many more moons and not require the garment that she was so carefully unravelling every night. She had to be careful. Enough of the knitting had to be undone to prevent the shroud from ever being finished, but too much and someone would notice, perhaps, that the fabric wasn't growing as quickly as it should. If Laertes were to die now, Penelope would have to stop the work, and choose someone to marry. Klymene used to worry that it would be either the Rat or the Bear or one of the others who hung around the outer courtyard, but now there was Leodes. Secrets upon secrets, she thought. There's such a lot I mustn't mention to anyone. How fortunate that Telemachus had left Ithaka! He, more than anyone, believed in his father's return, and what his mother was doing had to be kept hidden from him more than from almost anyone else.

Klymene rolled the wool she was unravelling into a ball, and put away her work.

Penelope dried her eyes and offered up a prayer that Telemachus would be safe, wherever his journeyings took him. The fishing trip he was on was taking a very long time. Was it really a fishing trip? Or was he simply escaping from Ithaka? She no longer knew what was true and what wasn't. One thing was certain: her son hadn't been able to bear to stay in the palace any longer. Sometimes Penelope wished that she too could set sail in a ship and make for the horizon. Everything was confused now, and her head was like a bag of torn rags: full of different dreams, and the black ship was always on the far edge of her mind and she had to go on weaving. Lately she'd been having dreams of Odysseus as he was before he went to war. She heard his voice promising to return. And the owl . . . She would obey Pallas Athene's owl whatever it cost her in anguish. That was her duty, and she'd never let herself forget what she had to do. The picture was less clear in her head than it once was, and all the colours were muddled and muddied, but the shuttle had to move because the threads wove more than pictures. They wove the story.

too much blue
and round and round
and there is blood and more blood   silence and black
*   rocks*

round and round   back forth warp weft
sharp hard   white blue   silver   weft warp
so much red   too much white   white
round and round

On one side of the strait, Charybdis lies:
a whirlpool ready to trap every ship
and suck it down into the night-black depths.
And opposite Charybdis, Scylla dwells
in a dark cave carved in the white cliff-face.
She is a monster with six hideous heads
on six long necks that writhe like fattened snakes
all ready to twist down and pluck a man
up from the deck he's standing on. The crew
have all been warned. There is no other choice.
If they keep closely to the monster's side
then six will die. Another course means doom
for the black ship, Odysseus, everyone.

back forth   warp weft   blue black   scarlet blood
round and round   weft warp   blue blood
warp weft   black white   back forth

A fig tree grows on top of Scylla's cliff.
The sailors see it as they row and pray
that they may pass the cave and not arouse
the monster. But the heads have darted out
of their foul hiding place and swooped and struck
and now a sailor hangs from each dog-mouth,
his life-blood dripping on the deck below.

blue grey   white green   warp weft   forth back
blow blow   grey and more grey
warp weft   green black red

Odysseus can hardly see to row
and steers the ship and the remaining men
back to Charybdis' side. Poseidon laughs
to see the vessel whirling in the foam
and every sailor sucked beneath the waves.
The ship is lost for ever. Many men
but not Odysseus make the journey down
to Hades, clammy Kingdom of the Dead.
Odysseus is washed up on a shore
of a small isle he doesn't recognize.
This is not home, he thinks. I've dreamed of home.
What was the dream? The dream was Ithaka.

back and back and back
warp and weft   back back
round and round   no one left   blue black   white
nothing else   white white

Argos dreams

small winds and sweet breathing and whispering birds with murmurs like the sea in and out of caves underwater blue and purple feathers humming humming bees and growling in the water round and round and up and sucking down with teeth biting snatching claws clawing tongues licking and up and up and sucking down sing songs to sleep to dream to lull thoughts and pain sing songs

A VISIT FROM MYDON

'What's the matter, Melantho?'

Klymene had recovered sufficiently to venture outside when the sun was past its hottest. *But you must
stay in the shade*, her grandmother had told her. She
and Melantho were sitting under the trees, and
Melantho was uncharacteristically quiet.

'What's happened?' Klymene asked gently.

'Nothing,' said Melantho. 'Nothing's happened.
I'm thinking about Telemachus and wondering
whether we'll ever see him again.'

'Of course we will. I pray to Pallas Athene to protect him.'

'And so do I, but maybe Poseidon will prevail. It's
very dangerous, to go sailing about on the ocean. I
have to consider my future.'

'What d'you mean?'

'When we were children, I used to think
Telemachus would marry me one day. I must have
lost my senses. He's never going to marry me. It's not
just that he won't be allowed to by his grandfather
and his mother. The truth is he thinks he's better

than us, Klymene. He's a prince. We're nothing but his servants, and I see that now. I know you think you're special, you and Ikarios, because of having been brought up with Telemachus and Nana being Odysseus' nurse and so on. But when all's said and done, you're one of us. A servant. Telemachus never used to be the kind of person who thought about rank, but he does now. Just in case you fancy your own chances with him.'

Klymene sat quite still and tried to work out her feelings. She minded about Telemachus' departure much less than she would have done even a short while ago, because of Mydon. It was true that he spent most of the time on the farm Antinous had sent him to, but even though they spoke only rarely, she thought of him as her friend.

'Telemachus isn't part of our lives any longer,' Melantho went on. 'Not really. He's moved into the world of kings and princes and people with power.'

She sat up straighter, took Klymene's hand and said: 'I've got to look after myself, though, haven't I? I must tell you something, Klymene. It's not just Ilos who's interested in me. Antinous . . . well . . . he's promised me everything . . . everything. He'd marry me, I think, if he really believed Penelope wasn't going to choose him—'

Klymene burst out: 'Choose *him*! He can't seriously believe it. He must be mad.'

'No, I don't think he does believe it, not really. Which is why there's a chance for me.'

'And you'd do it? You'd marry Antinous?'

'Why not? Surely it's better to be a chieftain's wife than a servant? Any chieftain's wife?'

Klymene disagreed more profoundly than she could possibly express. How did Melantho bear it? She shivered at the thought of his touch. Hideous, unspeakable. And how would Ilos feel if he was thrown over? Might he not strike out at Melantho in his fury? There were too many horrible possibilities, so she said only, 'And when Telemachus comes home? What then?'

'We'll see how he is when he returns. Perhaps being without me for a while might bring him to his senses. Or, of course, Poseidon may deal the ship a deadly blow. Anything might happen.' She smiled. 'And I have powers of my own. I could have my own vengeance, you know. I can hurt him if I choose to. And even if I can't get to him I can hurt someone he loves.'

She picked a small flower from the grass and began to pull at its petals. For a long moment she was silent, and then she smiled at Klymene and said, 'Perhaps I'll harm his beloved mother. Oh, he adores her, doesn't he? More than any woman he'll ever marry. In fact, I pity a wife of his, and that's the honest truth. She'll always take second place. Yes, I could see to it that Penelope pays for her son's treatment of me. Somehow, I don't know how at this moment, but it'll come to me in time. Yes.'

Klymene shivered. Melantho, more than anyone in the palace, must never know what went on behind the barred door of the queen's bedchamber every night. She said: 'Melantho, you can't really blame

Telemachus for thinking you weren't interested in him any longer.'

'What happened with Ilos didn't mean anything. I did tell him, before he ran off like that in his stupid ship, but he didn't want to believe me. I'm worth something better than Ilos, though he's devoted enough. And, of course, Ilos knows nothing at all about my . . .' She hesitated and then said, 'My relationship with Antinous.'

Klymene knew that Melantho still met Ilos almost every night, outside the gates. That's probably, she thought, why she hasn't found out about me unravelling the shroud. If Melantho's about to turn her attention to Penelope, both of us are going to have to be very careful.

Horrible, Klymene thought. Everything was horrible. Horribleness was never-ending. You couldn't go anywhere to escape it. On the morning after her conversation with Melantho, Klymene was down on her hands and knees scrubbing at the stones of the courtyard just outside the kitchen. Someone had been the worse for drink last night and the vomit had spread all over the floor. They're all full to the brim with the stuff, she thought. All these disgusting people who have moved in here and changed our lives. One drink too many and fountains of vile-smelling, lump-filled, yellowish liquid came spewing out over everything and there was nothing to be done but throw buckets of water over it and scrub it away, over and over again.

She put her cloth away at last and went to do what

she did every day. As soon as the morning meal was served to the queen and the rest of the household, she had to go to the storeroom to hand out provisions to the various packs of men who had settled in all over the palace.

'Bit more corn, darling,' one of the Rat's company said to her when it was his turn. 'Can't keep a man satisfied with this. Be a bit more *generous*.' As the word 'generous' left his mouth, he put out a hand and fondled Klymene's left breast, lingering on it and laughing. She pushed it away roughly, and went on doling out the rations, pouring corn into the upturned bowl he was holding out.

'No need to be so nasty,' said the man. 'Nice girl like you could do with a bit of the other, I reckon. Waste your youth, you will. I could make you happy, you know.'

'I'll tell—' She nearly said 'the Rat' but caught herself in time. 'I'll tell Antinous how rude you are and he'll see that you're beaten.'

'Why don't you save him the trouble?' The man took his corn and handed the bowl to one of his companions. He then lifted his shirt and bent over, showing his bare buttocks and thrusting them so near to Klymene that she could smell his foul stench. 'You could beat me yourself. I'd enjoy that – truly I would.'

She didn't see at first where it came from. A sandalled foot caught the man on the side of his body, lifted him a little into the air, and sent him flying into the watching crowd. Klymene turned to see Mydon, who went to stand over the fallen man. His foot, it seemed to Klymene, was all ready to strike again.

'You impudent puppy,' said the man, struggling to his feet. 'Mydon, isn't it? I know you. You can bloody well tell Antinous that if he doesn't keep proper discipline over his rabble, I'll come and beat them all to within an inch of their lives. Personally. Tell him that.'

'My master will believe my story and not yours, and what I tell him will send him straight to Amphimedon, who will punish you, as you well know, for improving my master's chances over his.' Mydon smiled pleasantly at him. 'With the queen.'

'I'm going!' said the man, 'I haven't got time to bandy words with scum like you.' He scuttled off with his bowl clutched tightly to his chest.

Mydon turned to Klymene. 'I'm sorry about him,' he said to her. 'He's an animal. Are you hurt?'

'No,' said Klymene. 'Thank you.' She went back to pouring the corn into one bowl after another. 'When did you come back from the country? How long are you staying?'

'Not long,' said Mydon, 'but it's good to see you, even for a short while. Maybe your grandmother could do with something from the market?'

'She might. I'll suggest it to her.' Klymene laughed. 'Thank you for helping me.'

'When you've finished your work here, meet me at the gate. We can go down to the dockside together.'

Klymene almost ran to the kitchen, already rehearsing what she was going to say to Nana.

Argos waits

sun and moon day and night sleep and waking more and more waiting more days more nights

ON LAERTES' FARM

'I confess, Leodes,' said Laertes, draining the last of the wine from his cup, 'I had hopes when I invited you to visit us here on Ithaka.'

The old king, Leodes and Penelope were sitting in the cool of the evening at a table set outside the door of the farm that was now home to Laertes. From this high place they looked over terraces planted with fruit trees down to the distant sea that stretched in one wide swathe of silvery-grey as far as the black line of the horizon. Vines grew along the trellised roof that provided a canopy for the table, and bunches of heavy, purple grapes hung down over their heads.

'What hopes, sir?' Leodes smiled. He had accompanied Penelope and the man who drove her carriage on this visit to Laertes, riding with her behind a pair of elderly horses.

'Why, hopes that you two would find favour with one another and marry. Hopes that my son's widow would be able to find happiness again.'

Penelope spoke into the silence that followed the king's words. 'I'm not a widow, Laertes. There will be

242

time enough for me to seek happiness, as you put it, when I become one.'

Laertes made a spluttering noise. 'Gods on Olympus, but you're obstinate, Penelope! How can you believe that Odysseus will return?'

'I do,' said Penelope. 'I'm not going to explain again. I've told you often enough.'

'Some nonsense about owls and Goddesses. Never heard such piffle in my life. Fat lot of good the Gods are when it comes to keeping my palace safe from those locusts. You're being difficult, Penelope, and I must say, I would have expected better of you, as a dutiful daughter-in-law. You should think of me.'

'I do think of you,' said Penelope. 'I wish I didn't have to, but it's impossible. You have no idea how – Never mind.'

'Speak, Penelope,' said Leodes gently. 'Tell us what you were going to say.'

'Very well then. Don't be offended, Laertes. I know I could pick someone today and all your troubles could be over. But think of me. Think how I would have to . . . well, be a wife to whoever it is I choose.'

'But you don't have to do that!' Laertes burst out. 'It's what I've just said: marry Leodes and put an end to all this.'

'Perhaps you ought to let the queen decide such things for herself,' said Leodes gently. 'She may not be as fond of me as you are.'

'What's the matter with her then? You're a good man. And women would doubtless call you a hand-some one. And look, Penelope – only consider how kind it is of Leodes to have stayed with us for so long. Almost as though he's protecting you, wouldn't you say, Penelope?'

'Leodes is a good friend. I'm grateful to have his friendship, but I cannot marry him. Or anyone. Not yet.'

'You'd marry her, wouldn't you? Tell me that you would, Leodes.'

'Father-in-law, I beg you.' Penelope spoke while Leodes was still considering what to say. 'Don't ask him such a question. If you care for me at all.'

'Can't understand you young people.' Laertes stood up. 'I'm off to my bed now. It was kind of you to visit an old fool like me. Have a care as you return to the palace. I hope your driver has not been too eager to drink my wine. Goodnight to both of you.'

He bent to plant a kiss on the top of Penelope's head and went inside. The evening sky had darkened to violet and the first stars had come out. For a long moment there was nothing but the thin music of the crickets to break the silence. Then Penelope said, 'He doesn't know, does he? He couldn't have guessed . . . just by looking at us?'

'No, my love. How could he have guessed? We hardly speak to one another when we're not alone.'

'We're alone now.' Penelope sighed. 'I wish we could stay here and never go back. Imagine how that would be. How peaceful it is, Leodes! No shouting, no drunken quarrels . . . lovely.'

'There's something I want to say' – Leodes leaned forward – 'and not just because Laertes has mentioned it.' He took Penelope's hand and held it. 'Marry me.

244

Marry me now and stop this madness. You know, do you not, how I feel for you?'

'I can't, Leodes. I'm sorry, truly.'

'Don't you love me?'

Penelope took her hand away. 'I . . . I'm not allowed to answer that . . . You know how I need you.'

'Very well, don't say the words. I don't care if you're in thrall to the Goddess, and powerless before her. I'll say it whether you do or not. I love you, Penelope. I'm Odysseus' friend but he is dead, my sweet one. You know I'd never declare my love for his wife if I thought he would return, but he will not. Your palace and your lands are suffering, Penelope. You're suffering. It's wrong for a woman like you to live alone, to go to sleep alone and to wake up with no husband's head on the pillow beside yours. Choose me, my dear one. Let us stop hiding in the shadows. For you do love me, Penelope. I feel that when we're together, however careful you are to say nothing.'

Penelope got up from her seat and tried to walk but stumbled. She covered her eyes with her hands and leaned against the wall of the farmhouse.

'Leodes, stop. I can't move. I can't stop crying. Please stop saying such things. Please, I can't bear it.'

Leodes left his seat. He stood behind Penelope and kissed her neck and put his arms around her. She turned to face him and raised her lips to his.

'No more words,' she whispered. 'I don't want to hear any more words. Just kiss me, Leodes. Never stop kissing me.'

Leodes said nothing but buried his hands in Penelope's hair and drew her closer to him.

Klymene felt there was almost nowhere where she was completely safe. Here, in the queen's chamber, she thought, and in the armoury with Argos I can drop my guard, but everywhere else I feel that I'm on show, and that eyes are following me wherever I go. Whenever I'm not here, I'm worrying about whether anyone has guessed, whether anyone knows, but in this room and while I work I can think of other things.

She began to pull at the fabric that Penelope had made. Her grandmother was already starting to look around for possible husbands, for what use is a girl (so Nana said constantly) if she doesn't marry into a good family and bear children to carry on after she is dead? Nana's refrain went like this: *Many young men would be only too glad to marry you, dear child, because you're such a good girl and so pretty, and besides, we're a part of the royal household in Ithaka, and I'm sure any sensible boy would jump at the chance of allying his family with ours.*

Well, that may be true, Klymene thought, but what about me? I don't feel like marrying any of them. Her thoughts went to Mydon. He had spoken to her kindly; he'd shown her by his actions that he was willing to do anything for her; and yet something, some kind of shyness had kept him from acting on his feelings. And Klymene didn't know whether the friendship she felt for him could properly be called love. Telemachus . . . She'd loved him for so long and suffered as she watched him and Melantho together. I've spent years, she thought, being unhappy over Telemachus, but now, strangely, thinking about him doesn't hurt me as it once did. I'm different now from what I used to be. I used to think Telemachus was the one. He was the one who made me tremble and faint. Klymene smiled as she recalled the dreams she'd had about him, about the two of them together, but he'd made it quite clear before he sailed away that he wasn't interested in her as anything but a friend. A good friend, but never a lover. And as the days went by, the way she thought about him changed. She almost never imagined him kissing her now, and she'd stopped wondering how his arms would feel around her. She simply worried about his safety, as she would have done if Ikarios had gone with him.

Mydon . . . She liked him, she was quite sure of that, but Melantho had told her often that liking someone wasn't enough. *You have to be sure that your bodies sing together*, she'd said once, and now Klymene found herself growing impatient to find out what true love between grown men and women was like. Would Mydon ever ask her to kiss him? What would it be like if he did? Did she want him to? She'd only know how she felt if he kissed her. These thoughts confused her, and she turned her mind to the problem of Nana.

Her grandmother hated the suitors so much that she wouldn't even have their names mentioned in her kitchen. How, Klymene asked herself, am I supposed to break the news to her that I'm friendly with one of them? I must do it soon. I'll bring him to the kitchen next time he's down here in the palace, and she won't be able to send him away once she's met him and seen that he means us no harm.

Klymene stopped winding wool and began to put everything away. She remembered what she'd seen on the night that Leodes brought her to Penelope's chamber. Some of it was most probably a dream, but he had been there in the chamber, very late, and the queen had spoken to him kindly. Aphrodite had been there that night, because Klymene could remember the fragrance of roses and almond blossom in her nostrils.

Melantho's right, she thought. Penelope does like Leodes. He's the kindest of them and he'd be a good husband, even if he could never take the place of Odysseus in her heart. It would save us all so much trouble if she married him. Klymene let herself imagine how quiet and clean the palace would be when the suitors took to their ships and sailed away. Yes, she thought. I'll talk to her tomorrow. Try to persuade her. Odysseus must be dead. He must be. Penelope should face the truth and mourn him and then turn her attention to the kingdom he left in her care. Ithaka would rejoice at her marriage. Tomorrow, I'll do it. She'll be angry at first, but I must. It's my duty.

TALKING TO PENELOPE

Klymene set off to Ikmalios' workshop with a basket of food for her brother. It was too early in the day to speak to the queen, as she had decided to do the evening before. She crossed the courtyard and left the palace, happy to be out of the noise and dirt for a little while. The workshop was some way down the road to the town, set off the path in the midst of some scrubby grasses and along a short stony track. It was a small, whitewashed building, and since Ikarios had been working there, the cat population of the place had grown. He shared his food with them and would have given some to the birds as well, but the sleek furry bodies stretched out in front of the door in the sun frightened all but the bravest away.

'I've brought you some food, Ikarios,' Klymene said. Her brother never left the workshop when he was engaged on a piece of work and today he was carving the ornamental border on a chest. Two of the cats had come in out of the heat and were lying curled up among the planks in the corner. She placed the basket on a nearby table and said, 'You're not to give this all to those greedy creatures, please. Nana'll be upset if you don't eat it.' She looked at her brother and added, 'You don't look very happy today.'

'I'm not,' Ikarios answered. 'I'm spending my time down here because everywhere else is so uncomfortable. You can't move a step without bumping into one of those oafs. You'd think they'd be bored by now with shouting abuse at me every time I go by.'

'You let them!' Klymene said. 'Hit one of them. Just once. That'd stop them!'

'No, it wouldn't. They're like pack animals. They'd all have a go if one of them was attacked. While Telemachus was around, they knew they had to keep their taunts to themselves, but now . . . No, I'd rather stay down here and get on with some work.'

'Well, eat at least. And have a drink too. It's thirsty work with this wood dust flying about.'

She sat down on a stool and said, 'Is there any news of Telemachus? The queen said she's heard nothing for some time.'

Ikarios shook his head. 'He wouldn't send a message to us. He's not really interested in us any longer, is he? Not in the way he used to be when we were children. D'you remember how we used to spend all our time together? How we enjoyed ourselves? What's the point of being a man if there's no pleasure left in your life? We used to live by the sea, and I never go there now.'

'I go down to the shore with Argos sometimes. Or with the other women in the palace. You could come with us.'

'But it's not the same, is it? We're too old to climb the rocks, and imagine how everyone would laugh if I told them I wanted to build a garrison in the sand.'

'I'd laugh too, Ikarios. It would be ridiculous. You're supposed to be fishing, or hunting. Or running races. Or throwing things. Men seem to find all sorts of ways of passing the time. What about drinking? Or flirting with the girls? You're meant to like that too, Ikarios, aren't you?'

Ikarios blushed. 'The person I'm interested in won't look at me. She thinks I'm insignificant. And so I am, so maybe she's right never to look in my direction.'

'Tell me who she is,' Klymene asked. 'I won't tell anyone.'

'I can't. I feel a fool even thinking about her.'

'You don't have to say a word. I know who you mean.'

'Go on, then, say.'

'It's still Melantho, isn't it?'

Ikarios looked at his twin and his eyes widened. 'I told you years ago what I felt for her.'

Klymene laughed. 'I know, but I thought that that might have faded away. You don't talk about it ever.'

'You've never asked. And anyway, I don't see the point of discussing it.'

'I could have cheered you up, if you'd talked to me. Or persuaded you that it wasn't worth the effort. She's not a very nice person, Ikarios. You can do better than her, really. She's not to be trusted.'

'I thought you quite liked her now,' Ikarios said.

'We rub along together because we have to,' Klymene said, 'but I still wouldn't trust her. She'd hurt you in the end, I feel sure of it.'

'And what about you, sister? Have you no one who lights up the day for you?'

Should she say something about Mydon? Perhaps not yet. Klymene shook her head. 'No, I'm afraid not. Apart from you and Nana, Argos is the one creature in the world I'm most fond of. And Penelope, of course. I worry most about her.'

'Why?' Ikarios said. 'Why do you concern yourself with her problems?'

'Because I work with her every day, and I can see how unhappy she is.'

Ikarios said, 'Most of her problems she's brought upon herself. We wouldn't have this mess on Ithaka now if she'd behaved properly and simply decided on one of the suitors to be her second husband.'

'Oh, you don't understand!' Klymene said. 'No one understands. She believes Odysseus is coming home. She's still married to him. She still loves him. Her loyalty and devotion are the talk of the islands.'

'Her obstinacy's the talk of the islands. No one understands how she can let her husband's property go to rack and ruin. Which is what she's doing. Nothing's being done right. The farms aren't properly looked after and everything they do produce is devoured by that army of hangers-on who've turned the palace into a market place. It's revolting and you ought to try and get her to change her mind. Everyone's sick to death of it.'

'I'm going to. I'm going to speak to her now. I'd decided to do it already, before you mentioned it. I'm sorry, Ikarios. I suppose you're right. I'll talk to her.'

A soft breeze was blowing through the leaves of the pomegranate tree as Klymene sat on the bench next to Penelope and watched her. The queen was bent over her work: winding the wool round the nails, pulling through one strand after another, knitting together the fabric as she did every day. I should speak now, she thought. The queen looks happy. There's no one around and she looks as though she's thinking pleasant thoughts. From time to time she starts humming a tune, which shows she's really taken up with what she's doing. Is it fair to her if I speak now? Maybe I ought to leave it until later. Klymene knew that if she did that, she might well not say anything at all, and she was determined to speak of what was in her heart. Where to begin, that was the problem. She took a deep breath and spoke.

'Lady, may I say something to you?'

'Of course, Klymene, what is it? I'm always ready to listen to you.'

'I'm not sure you'll want me to speak of this.'

'Now, Klymene, what could be so bad that I wouldn't want to hear about it?'

'It's about Leodes, lady.'

Penelope put down her wool and looked searchingly at Klymene. 'What about Leodes?'

'He's very kind,' Klymene began. 'I'm grateful to him for rescuing me and bringing me safely home.'

'That's not what you wanted to say about him though, is it?'

Klymene shook her head. 'No, lady. It isn't. I wanted to say . . . it's difficult and I hope you won't be angry with me, but I couldn't help it. I woke up, that's all. When you both thought I was asleep. I woke up and . . . and saw you.'

Penelope looked at Klymene in silence. Then she said: 'What did you see exactly?'

'You were standing very close together. He . . . you . . . had your arms around one another.' Klymene was shocked to see how frightened her mistress looked and added, 'I haven't said a word to anyone. Not a single word.'

Penelope let out her breath in a long sigh. 'I know you wouldn't, Klymene. It's not that I don't trust you, but I'm so scared. If Telemachus finds out, he'll kill me. He believes his father is alive and is just waiting for an excuse to fight those men out there, but they'd kill him at once. I don't know what to do for the best. I just go from one day to the next, and this work, this shroud, is the only fixed thing in my life. As long as I have that to attend to I can put off making a decision.'

Klymene said, 'You think that Lord Odysseus is dead, don't you?'

Tears sprang to Penelope's eyes, and she wiped them away with a corner of her scarf. 'Look at me! What kind of a queen am I for a hero like Odysseus? Crying at the least little thing? Of course he's dead. All reason, everything in my mind tells me he must be, or why has he not returned after all this time? And yet, Klymene, when I lie alone in my bed in that dim space between sleeping and waking, I see visions of him and hear his voice and I know. He promised me he would return.'

'But—'

'I know. I know. It's what every man tells his wife when he's going off to war. But there's something else. I've spoken of this to very few people, Klymene. I'm telling you because you are like a daughter to me and I think that maybe you have . . . experiences of your own that might make you believe me. Years ago, Pallas Athene sent an owl to visit me. She told me . . . she said I must stay in my chamber and work at my loom. And I have, Klymene. I haven't disobeyed the Goddess. I've trusted, all through the years, that Odysseus will come back, but . . .' Penelope's face was a mask of anguish. 'I don't know what I believe any longer. Sometimes I think the owl was no more than a dream I had, and that my husband has gone to join the shades of the other heroes in the land of Hades. Perhaps everyone else but me has been right all along.'

Klymene wanted to ask: what about Leodes? What do you feel for him? What do you tell him?

As though she had read the young woman's mind, Penelope said, 'You're wondering about Leodes. I can see that you want to ask about him and are too polite to mention it. Am I right?'

Klymene nodded. 'Do you love him, lady? If you believed that Lord Odysseus was dead, would you marry him then? Ithaka needs it. Doesn't it upset you to see what's become of the palace? Of the whole island?'

Penelope bowed her head, and her tears flowed freely now. 'I can't bear it. I walk from room to room and see nothing but dirt and destruction where once there was order and beauty. I hate every minute of every day because I have to live with what's going on out there.'

'So put an end to it, lady. Marry Leodes. Tell everyone it's your decision and then all the others would go home. Surely Pallas Athene would forgive you—'

'It isn't as easy as that, Klymene. You've forgotten something. Someone.'

'Who? You're the queen. You can do what you like, can't you? For the good of your kingdom?'

Penelope shook her head. 'If I marry Leodes, or even confess to liking him a little, Telemachus would kill him. He would never have anything to do with me ever again. I don't think I could bear that, and I know it to be true. He believes his father is alive and he's said many times that he would rather I were dead than married to someone else. Well, perhaps that's just youthful exaggeration, but certainly he would treat me as though I had passed into the kingdom of Hades.'

'But he loves you so much, lady. Doesn't he want you to be happy?'

'No,' said Penelope. 'He wants me to be perfect. Wants me to be faithful for ever. He'd kill Leodes. I couldn't . . . I wouldn't. Well . . . I can't let that happen. That is why you must say nothing to anyone about . . . about what you saw that night, Klymene. Do you promise me?'

Klymene nodded. Penelope had contrived to say nothing about her feelings for Leodes. I asked her directly, Klymene thought. *Do you love him?* I said, and she chose not to answer me. This conversation had made everything even more unclear than it had been before. They would have to go on knitting and unknitting this shroud until the Gods decided what was to become of them.

Argos waits

round and round and more and less and back and forth and nights and days and nights

KLYMENE AND MYDON

The seashore was one of the only places that was still exactly the same as it used to be. Klymene felt that the palace had become like a kind of tavern. It was full of drunken, filthy men who were only interested in lying about in the shade and fighting and spitting and eating and playing silly games on which they'd wager the last of their belongings. Certain areas were so dirty and neglected now that it was hard to walk in the courtyards. Piles of bones lay about everywhere, and just outside the palace gate flies swarmed in black clouds round leavings of decaying fruit peel, and the section fenced off to provide latrines for everyone smelled worse than the flesh of rotting corpses.

But the seashore was the same as ever, and in the early mornings, before the sun made the sand too hot to walk on, even in sandals, there was a silence and peace here near the water's edge that soothed and comforted her.

She had come down to the sea as a companion to Penelope, who sometimes met Leodes there even before the sun came up. Several days had passed since she'd spoken to the queen and begged her to marry, without any effect whatsoever. But Penelope was still determined to meet Leodes whenever she could. These secret meetings were dangerous. What if some drunken lout took it into his head to wander down here? Klymene was the only person in the whole of the palace who knew how precious these trysts were to her mistress. Penelope had confided in Klymene. *I must tell you*, she'd said, *because I need someone to stand guard for us sometimes. And I'll die if I can't speak of him to another human being. Forgive me, Klymene! Do you understand how hard it is to be alone for so many, many moons?*

Now, Klymene was alone. She had watched Leodes come out of the cave a short time ago and hurry up the path towards the palace gates. Penelope emerged some time later, flushed and dazed.

'I'll go back with you, lady,' said Klymene. 'At least as far as the gate.'

'There's no need,' said Penelope. 'No one's awake yet. I won't be disturbed at this hour. Stay a little longer, if you like. The Gods know how hard you have to work when you start on the shroud. It's never-ending . . .' She sighed.

'Thank you,' said Klymene. 'I'll be back soon.'

She watched the queen making her way slowly and languidly up the path, and turned back to look at the sea. I'll just walk as far as those rocks, she told herself, and then I'll go back. Her feet sank into the wet sand, and as she looked behind her she saw how her footsteps disappeared almost as soon as she'd made them. She felt the cool water rushing in round her ankles and then withdrawing. The only sound she could hear was the whispering of the waves as they swept in and broke in small frills of white on the pale sand.

Up ahead of her, she saw that someone was sitting on one of the lowest rocks. She squeezed her eyes together to see better: whoever it was was waving at her. She walked a little further along the shore and soon the figure on the rock became clearer.

'Mydon?' she called. 'Is that you?'

He was running towards her now. When he reached her, he took her hands and spun her round till they were both dizzy. They sank down together on to the damp sand. Mydon lay on his back with his eyes open. Klymene said: 'We used to do that, me and Ikarios, when we were very young.'

'The whole world's going round and round,' Mydon said. 'I feel as though I'm going to fly away, like a bird.' He sat up. 'I was thinking of you and then there you were, like a vision sent by a God.'

'I'm happy to see you.' Klymene stared out at the horizon so that she wouldn't have to look Mydon in the face. 'When did you come down from the farm? I've missed you. Are you well? Are you staying for a few days?'

'No, only for today. My new master, Eumaeus, is a kind man and I like working with the pigs. But I miss you too, Klymene. I want to tell you something.'

Klymene nodded. The sun was nearly over the shadow of the mountain, but she had caught sight of it: a quivering blue arrow flying over her shoulder and burying itself in Mydon's heart. Had he seen it? She didn't dare to look round for Eros but said only, 'I'm happy to listen.' Her mouth was suddenly dry.

'I've been meaning to say this for many days. I'm very brave when I'm alone, but when I'm with you it's hard to speak. I want . . . there's more . . . I don't know . . .'

'You want to kiss me.'

He nodded. 'How did you know?'

'I just do.'

'I don't know where to begin. How . . . ?'

'Nor me.'

'Close your eyes. I'll kiss you if you close your eyes.'

Klymene obeyed. She could feel Mydon coming closer. His hand . . . his hand was on her cheek. His breath. She was aware of his breath on her skin. Then his lips – soft, dry, on her own – touching her lips as gently as a butterfly brushing a flower. Then he kissed her again, and his hands were on her shoulders. She opened her mouth and leaned into his body. I'm going to faint, she thought. The arrow – there must be one in my heart too. She could feel it: a shivering glow entering her body and spreading through her veins. She put her own hands at the back of Mydon's head and they were lost in an embrace that seemed to go on and on, without the need to breathe or speak or move. At last the kiss was over and Mydon drew away a little and smiled at Klymene.

'It's not difficult,' he said. 'Is it?'

She shook her head. 'Not a bit difficult.'

'And I think it'll get easier,' Mydon said. 'With practice.'

He wrapped his arms around Klymene again and they fell back against the sand. She thought: it feels as though we're still spinning and spinning round. The small waves came foaming up over her feet and she scarcely noticed.

'Nana, I'd like you to meet someone.' Klymene stood at the back door of the kitchen. Behind her, Mydon waited in the shade of a small fig tree.

'Meet?' Nana looked up from where she was sitting. For once she wasn't working but resting with her feet up on a stool. 'I don't want to meet anyone ever again. Too many people, that's what's wrong. I'd like to say goodbye to a few of them, instead of greeting them.'

'But this is a friend of mine . . .'

'Where did you find a friend? Poor child, you haven't got a moment in the day to call your own, what with all the help you give me and what you do for Penelope . . .'

'This is Mydon, Nana. Mydon, this is my grandmother, Eurykleia. Everyone calls her Nana.'

The old woman staggered to her feet, her eyes wide. 'Klymene, you've taken leave of your senses, child. He's one of them. Didn't you know? Didn't he tell you? I've seen him down there, in that foul encampment . . . Oh, Klymene, Klymene, what's to become of us?'

Mydon stepped past Klymene and went to stand in front of Nana.

'My name is Mydon and I was born in Troy. I came to Ithaka with Antinous, but I'm not one of his men.'

'He's the one who put your plants back, Nana – don't you remember? I told you there was a kind person who helped me . . . Here he is.'

'Well . . .' Nana didn't appear persuaded. She spoke grudgingly. 'Welcome to our house, then. And I thank you for your help. Those pigs with their boorish behaviour. Imagine destroying a garden!' She shook her head. 'Forgive me. I'm not as hospitable as I once was. Please sit and drink something. It's very warm today.'

Mydon sat down at the table and Klymene went to fetch the water pitcher.

'Troy, did you say?' Nana said.

Mydon nodded and held out his hand. 'My mother, who died when I was a young child, told me that Lord Odysseus rescued us both when the city was on fire. When I was a baby . . . This is the scar of a burn I've had since then.'

'Poor boy!' Nana put out a hand and stroked the white skin of Mydon's wrist. 'But what are you doing with that Antinous, then, if you're from Troy?'

'He took my mother in. I suppose he rescued us.'

'Then you must be loyal to him, if he is your preserver.'

Mydon shook his head. 'No, I feel no loyalty. He's too harsh a master. My mother was like a slave in his house. I came to Ithaka to see the island that was once home to Odysseus.'

'Well,' said Nana. 'I'm sure you're welcome. But mind now' – she grasped Mydon's other hand, his unscarred hand, by the wrist – 'Klymene is my granddaughter and I don't want her hurt. D'you understand? I mean it.'

'Nana!' Klymene hurried to stop what she knew would be a long lecture about how Mydon should and shouldn't behave. She tried to keep the irritation out of her voice. 'Please!'

'What d'you mean *please*? You've no mother and it's my duty to see that any young man who is friendly to you knows that he's got to behave himself!'

'I promise you, Nana,' said Mydon, 'that I'll always be kind to Klymene and care for her in every way. And besides, I'm at Eumaeus' farm most of the time. Far from the palace.'

'Eumaeus!' Nana beamed at Mydon. 'An old friend of mine and a good man. Well then, I've no objections to your friendship.' She was, Klymene noticed, very happy now that she knew Mydon wouldn't be in the palace to tempt her granddaughter into what she considered bad behaviour. For her part, Klymene felt angered all over again at Antinous' cruelty. Now that her feelings for Mydon had changed, how would she get through the days without even a sight of him?

Penelope sat on the edge of the wide bed and sighed. The days were going by and there was still no news of Telemachus coming home, though he did send messages with fishermen, telling her that he was well and would return soon. The nights were full of dreams

that she could scarcely remember when she awoke.
Every moment at the loom was precious. There were
other things to be attended to, but the story had to
be told. The threads weave the story.

blossom pink   pale green leaves   white sand
flat sea   warp weft   wood bound together
black cave   back forth   weft warp   set sail

Calypso saved Odysseus from the sea
when foul Charybdis stole away his ship
and sent his men to a black watery death.
She loves Odysseus and keeps him safe
deep in a cave hung over with sweet flowers.
Her kisses bind him, but he longs for home.
He sits where waves spread over the pale sand
planning a vessel: how to fashion it.

weft warp   blue green   bind the wood
set sail   stars   black ocean   weft warp

Athene tells Calypso: *Let him go.*
Odysseus makes a raft to take him home.
He sets off. Poor Calypso cries her love
into the pillows she has shared with him.
Her body misses his. She cannot sleep
and longs for him who soothed her with his flesh.
Odysseus on his raft is floating free.
Where the sun rises, there is Ithaka.
The dream of home will soon be coming true.

warp weft   back forth   the black ship gone
weft warp   green pale   yellow stones and sand
back forth   no longer tie the threads
finish the picture   no more   no more ever

Argos dreams

nearer and nearer and the water on him and woodsmoke and sand there also dung and fire and soon it will be soon because of blood and sweat and too much wine and shouting but soon it will be over and I will sleep and not hear the crying any longer

APHRODITE TRIUMPHS

Penelope opened her eyes and for a moment couldn't remember where she was. Then she saw that above her head there was nothing but darkness pierced by the brilliant sparkle of the stars. Oh, dear Gods on Olympus, she thought to herself, sitting up quickly. We fell asleep. We could have been discovered here together, and then I would have died of the shame. She turned to her right and saw, stretched out on the ground very close to where she had been lying, the figure of Leodes. What had possessed them?

'Wake up!' she whispered. 'Leodes, wake up. It must be the middle of the night. Someone will see us. What if one of the servants comes knocking at my bedroom door?'

'They wouldn't dare,' said Leodes lazily. 'You shouldn't worry so much, Penelope. Don't you remember what happened? You whispered some words to me at dinner.'

Penelope nodded, blushing and thankful that he couldn't see the redness of her face in the darkness. She recalled only too well what she'd whispered to

Leodes. I must have drunk too much wine, she thought now, or how could I have been so brazen? She'd been sitting listening to one of the more boring suitors droning on and on about some war or other and suddenly she was overcome with a wave of desire for Leodes, a strong need to feel his arms around her and the taste of his mouth on hers. She stood up and went to speak to him where he stood near the doorway.

I can't bear this, Leodes, she'd said. *Let's go outside. Have you ever been to the vineyard? It's very dark there. The vines have been neglected and there are places that are quite overgrown. I'll die if I stay here any longer.*

I know the vineyard, lady, Leodes answered, looking not at her but at something on the other side of the hall, in order to make it seem as though they weren't talking.

Then meet me there soon. As soon as you can. I will wait for you.

Now, in the black shadows of the vineyard, Penelope had returned to herself, her more sensible self, and she was fearful, remembering how she'd fled from the hall and run without telling anyone where she was going: out of the palace and up to where they were now, hidden by the fragrant leaves and caressed by the night winds. What if someone had noticed them? What if that someone were waiting now, under the cover of the night, to jump out at her and confront her with the truth of what she'd done? She hadn't behaved as a queen was supposed to behave; more like some young woman with her senses deranged by lust, driven by Aphrodite to feel nothing except the need to be embraced, held, kissed by a man who loved her. Leodes claimed to be such a man. He said so, over and over again, and his words were always there in her heart. She took some comfort from the fact that she'd never told Leodes she loved him, even though her actions must have been clear enough. She had not been able to govern what her body did: how it moved when it was near his; how her breathing changed when he approached her; how her eyes closed almost without her knowing it when they came together in an open-mouthed kiss.

'We must go back,' she whispered to Leodes. She could feel his eyes on her in the half darkness. 'The Goddess of Dawn will soon come over the mountain and then anyone walking past on the way to the palace will see us.'

'I don't care if they do,' Leodes said. 'But I know you are still uncertain so I will go first, and not towards the palace but in the opposite direction. I will not return till evening.'

'Thank you, Leodes. I am grateful,' said Penelope, pulling her scarf over her head and adjusting her robes. She looked down at him, at his golden hair, which was so unlike Odysseus' hair, and she smiled because she saw that he was smiling.

'You are very beautiful,' he whispered, putting out a hand to touch her arm.

'Stop!' she said. 'You must stop. If you touch me now, I'll . . .' She paused.

'What? What will you do?' He was sitting up now, laughing gently and pulling her towards him. She leaned in to his body, unable to prevent herself, and he wound his arms around her neck.

'Stay,' he breathed, so quietly that she couldn't hear the word but felt it rather on her skin. 'Stay an hour longer. Dawn is not so close.'

'Oh, Leodes, what will become of us?' Penelope groaned and they sank together on to the earth, and forgot everything.

Klymene sat on the stool at Penelope's feet and wondered why no one in the palace had noticed what was perfectly clear to her. The queen's mind was completely taken up with her relationship with Leodes and she was growing careless as a consequence. If anyone came in now, she thought, they'd know at once. Look at her! Penelope was meant to be knitting the shroud, under the pomegranate tree, but at this very moment she was sitting at the window of the chamber looking out at the sea, with the handiwork still in its basket at her feet. There was a smile on her face as though she was recalling something especially pleasant, which perhaps she was. Last night Klymene had found it hard to sleep, and she'd seen the queen returning to the palace very late, and all alone. Perhaps she'd slipped out when she thought everyone was asleep to meet him, Leodes, her new love.

What about Odysseus? Klymene wanted to ask. *What about him?* Penelope still believed he was alive. She must, because if she thought he was dead, there was no reason on earth that she couldn't stand up in the great hall and say, *I want to marry Leodes.* She could have done that a long time ago and spared everyone the horror of what the palace had become: no better than a slum.

Klymene sighed. There was no point going over the arguments again. They were trapped in a situation that didn't seem to be changing as the moons waxed and waned.

'May I ask you something, lady?' she said, just to bring Penelope out of her daydream.

'Certainly, Klymene. I'm sorry . . . I'm lost in thought.' She smiled, and Klymene could guess exactly what she'd been thinking about.

'If you knew . . . if you really knew . . . that Odysseus was dead. If there were certain proof, would you marry Leodes?'

Penelope was silent for a moment and then she covered her eyes with her hands and shook her head. 'I don't know, Klymene. Part of me yearns to finish all this . . . this deception, and this chaos in the palace. I have the power to stop it, and I want to. I *do* want to. And Leodes? Well, I have not said so to him, but he knows my feelings. He would be a good master in Ithaka. The thought of living with him here comes into my mind every day. Every day and every night. But there's no proof that my husband is dead and therefore . . . there's nothing to discuss. Not yet. Not quite yet. Perhaps a God will tell me what I must do. But you, Klymene. You've seemed . . . well, sometimes I think you're happier than you were.'

'There's someone called Mydon,' Klymene said, so quietly that Penelope had to lean forward to catch her words.

'Mydon? Is he from one of the inland farms?'

Klymene shook her head. 'He's with the Rat – I mean Antinous. That's what I call him. But not of his party. Not really. He came to Ithaka with the others because Odysseus rescued him from the fire at Troy when he was a baby.'

Tears filled Penelope's eyes. 'You see? He's everywhere, my husband. No one can forget about him and what he did in the Trojan War, and I can't believe he's dead. Forgive me, Klymene. I'm happy for you, truly. Perhaps you can bring Mydon to meet me one day.'

'You're kind, lady. Nana's met him.'

'And does she approve?'

'She's letting me see him,' Klymene answered. 'That's all I care about now. But he's been sent to one of the farms on the other side of the island to help the farmer. That's what Antinous says, but he's sent Mydon away on purpose, because . . . well, the Rat enjoys hurting people. But Mydon visits from time to time, and when the harvest's over he'll come back. I'll wait till he does and then you can meet him.'

'Both of us are waiting, then.' Penelope smiled. 'And what about Telemachus? When you were children, you loved him so much.'

'I still do. But he's like a brother to me. We grew up together. And besides . . .'

'Besides?'

'There's Melantho. Before he went away, he loved her.'

Penelope sighed. 'I've been too taken up with my

own thoughts, but I knew he was very friendly with her. I never thought that was serious.'

Klymene shook her head. 'They quarrelled before he left. She . . . she's been seeing someone from the Rat's camp.'

'That's a good name for Antinous,' Penelope said. 'It's exactly what he looks like.'

Klymene picked up the wool and handed it to Penelope. 'We should go out, lady,' she said. 'You must do some more knitting or I'll have nothing to unpick tonight.'

'You're right, Klymene,' Penelope said. 'O Gods in Olympus, how tired I am of all this boring wool. How I long for colours! But you're right. We should go.'

Klymene picked up the basket and followed the queen out of the chamber. The fine-meshed white net would soon be spread out for anyone who might be interested in seeing whether or not it had grown. However much Penelope adds to the length, if I take out half of what she's done, they'll never know and the shroud won't ever be finished. Men don't look closely at what women make with their hands.

Argos waits

light follows dark dark follows light more and more sleeping and waking and sleeping again and more waiting more waiting

IN THE WORKSHOP

Ikmalios the carpenter had gone to visit his daughter on the other side of the island and Ikarios was alone in the workshop. He never minded being on his own and enjoyed sitting among the logs and planks and pieces of this or that tree that had been brought in to be carved or shaped into something else. It was always peaceful in this place, and the fragrance that hung in the air reminded Ikarios of forests. The sun was low in the sky and a square of reddish light fell across the floor. One of the cats who always visited him, a tiny black-and-white creature, was curled up fast asleep in the corner and her soft snores and the noise of his chisel were the only sounds to break the silence.

Suddenly something huge and dark filled the doorway, and Ikarios looked up to see who it was coming to speak to either him or Ikmalios so late in the day. He felt a kind of dread come over him as he recognized Amphimedon, and he shivered in spite of the heat. The man strode into the quiet room and the black-and-white cat woke up suddenly and fled through the open door. The Bear, Klymene called this man. Behind him, Ikarios could see the one she called the Rat: Antinous. I hate him, Ikarios thought, because Melantho speaks well of him. Some say she has been seen in his company more and more often recently.

'Where's your master, boy?' the Bear said, not really looking at Ikarios but making his way to a pile of logs at the back of the room. 'He said we could come and collect firewood today. You don't mind if we help ourselves, do you?'

'No,' said Ikarios, thinking, A fat lot of good it would do me to object.

'Right. Get out then.'

'But—' Ikarios was on the point of objecting, when the Rat said:

'We don't like anyone around while we're deciding what we need. Haven't you got something to do somewhere else?'

'Yes, I'll go and find something to eat while you're busy.'

'Right. Scarper, then.'

Ikarios left the workshop, making a great point of banging the door closed as he went. He had no intention of finding food, or anything else. The Rat and the Bear must think I'm stupid, he thought. They'd never come down here to get wood. They'd have sent servants. That means, Ikarios thought, that they're up to some mischief. They've come to talk where no one will overhear them. They're hatching some plan between themselves. He intended to overhear what they were saying.

He ran to the back of the workshop and peered through the window. There they were, the two of them, deep in conversation near the woodpile. They won't hear me, Ikarios thought. I'll slip in and hide behind the planks leaning against the wall near the door. It's very quiet. I'll be able to hear what they're saying.

He went back to the front of the workshop and opened the door, thanking the Gods that Ikmalios was such a fine workman. All the wooden joints were so well made that it opened without a sound.

'He's borrowed a ship from some loser or other in the harbour.' The Rat's voice, Ikarios decided. 'I've got my spies down by the boats and that's the word. He's gone to find news of his father. But he won't learn anything, that's clear. No one knows what's happened to Odysseus, or they'd have said something by now, right?'

'Right.' That was the Bear agreeing. 'But maybe he's also on a mission to raise some kind of force to fight us. That's not impossible.'

'Whatever his intention, he can't be allowed to live. He makes no secret of wanting the whole lot of us dead. She hasn't managed to talk him out of that, which is odd, isn't it? She'd be quite happy if we all set sail and left the island, but that won't satisfy Telemachus. He'd like every one of us down in Hades with his own father. I reckon I take some men and one of my best ships and wait. He has to pass through the straits that lie between Ithaka and Same on his way home. They say he's returning to Ithaka soon. I'll set an ambush for him. He won't escape.'

The Bear laughed. His laugh was famous throughout the palace and it was a sound that made Ikarios' flesh creep. 'A good plan, Antinous, my brother. A most excellent plan! And once that young man is feeding the fishes down in Poseidon's palace, Penelope'll have to choose. There'll be no one left to help her organize matters here. She'll be helpless. Nothing I like better than a helpless woman, me.'

Ikarios could hear them picking up logs. From where he was hidden, he saw them slinging the leather carrying bags over their shoulders. They left the work-shop and Ikarios held his breath as they passed.

He emerged from his hiding place and went to sit down on a stool. He sat without moving for a long time. Telemachus was in grave danger, and even though Ikarios had been angry with him lately for ignoring their old friendship and neglecting both him and Klymene, still, the prince was almost like a brother to them both. How was he supposed to warn Telemachus of this horrible scheme? Even if there was a way of finding some vessel and getting to the straits before the Rat (which there wasn't), anyone who was foolish enough to be there when he arrived would soon be chopped up for fish food and their boat sunk to the bottom of the ocean.

'What's the matter, Ikarios?' Klymene had come in without him seeing her.

'Nothing,' said Ikarios.

Klymene sounded exasperated when she spoke. 'Don't be ridiculous, brother. I know you're hiding something and I know you're troubled. It's me, your sister and your twin. I can read your mind, you know.'

'The suitors. The Rat. He's planning to kill Telemachus.'

Klymene sank to the floor and hid her head in her hands. Then she looked up. 'Tell me everything. Every single thing you know.'

Ikarios told her what he'd overheard. She listened, aghast, and when he'd finished speaking she said: 'There's no hope for Telemachus unless a God protects him. But how wonderful if he really is coming home. We should pray to Pallas Athene. Perhaps,' she went on, 'we should tell Melantho. She is . . . friendly with some of them, isn't she? Perhaps she would persuade them—'

'What she felt for Telemachus has changed. You told me,' said Ikarios, 'that she is someone who can't be trusted.'

'You used to love her, brother.'

Ikarios glanced up at her. 'Melantho might as well be on another island for all the attention she pays me,' he said. 'She's taken up with the Rat now, did you know? Which is another reason we can't say anything to her. She's moved up from Ilos to his master. Probably it was always her intention to find her way into his favour. I'm never sure what she tells you and what she doesn't. She didn't seem to be hiding it from anyone. I saw her with him in the inner courtyard yesterday and it was hard to see where he ended and she began, she was clinging to him so closely. I couldn't bear to watch them. I had to come back here immediately.'

The Rat . . . Well, Melantho had confessed as much to her, but how *could* she? Imagining the two of them in an embrace made her feel sick to her stomach. How could she bear to have that thin rat mouth on hers? And poor Ikarios!

'It must be so hard for you,' Klymene said. 'If only these monsters would leave our island, then maybe Melantho would be able to appreciate you.'

'Why should she?' Ikarios said. 'She's known me for years and never seemed to notice me.'

'You're too quiet,' Klymene said. 'You should make yourself more conspicuous.'

Ikarios sighed. 'She must take me as I am,' he said.

'But you could make more effort to catch her eye. Make her a present . . . carve her a figure she could admire. Show her you like her. Be there when she's sad . . . Oh, Gods, Ikarios, you need help from Aphrodite. You should sacrifice to her and beg her to come to your aid.'

'Maybe. Maybe I will. Meanwhile, I'm worried for Telemachus. And all our prayers must be to Pallas Athene.'

'Yes,' said Klymene. 'My prayers will be for him. But I must go now. Farewell, brother.'

She stood at the door of the workshop and looked at Ikarios. 'I have never said it to you because you know it as you know all my thoughts, but I love you more than I love anything else in the world. You know that, don't you?'

Ikarios smiled. 'Of course. As I love you. We are part of one another, Klymene.'

'Two flowers from a single seed. That's what Nana says.'

Klymene's heart was heavy as she left the workshop. I can pray and pour libations, but what if Telemachus never comes back? She felt tears coming to her eyes. I've stopped loving him in the way I used to, she thought, but he is still like my brother. Ikarios . . . What would become of him if Telemachus was drowned? And what would become of his mother? How would Penelope bear the death of her only son?

Klymene hurried up the path towards the palace. O Athene, she thought, preserve Telemachus. Let him come home safely and not be killed by the monsters who've taken over our kingdom. Protect him.

Ikarios sat on his bench in the workshop, and it seemed to him that he was carrying a black weight on his back. Was there something he could do to save Telemachus? Klymene believed in the power of prayer and so did he, but finding the right words to say was difficult. He picked up a smooth piece of olive wood and a chisel and began to carve. The yellowish splinters fell to the floor and the shape hidden in the wood revealed itself slowly: a small owl, with folded wings and enormous eyes, turned in his hands as he worked.

When it was finished, he placed it on the windowsill, looking out towards the sea.

'You are Pallas Athene's owl,' he whispered. 'Fly to Telemachus' ship and warn him. Keep him safe.'

Argos waits

*and more days and nights and more waiting and more waiting
and more and rain and fruit ripening on the trees.*

TELEMACHUS RETURNS

'Look there, Telemachus!' said the captain of the *Sea Nymph*. 'What's that on the mast, can you make it out?'

Telemachus squinted. The light was leaving the sky, but he could see quite clearly what was clinging with its talons to the top of the sail. He said, 'It's an owl. A white one.'

The captain frowned. 'Hope the men don't notice, that's all.'

'A bird can't hurt them,' said Telemachus.

'They're superstitious. An owl here, so far from land . . . a bird of prey. A night bird. Bad omen.'

The captain went about his work silently, and Telemachus stood leaning over the side of the ship, staring into the water. He glanced up from time to time to where the owl sat, far above the deck. The sailors had spotted it, that was obvious. They sat at their oars, muttering and pointing upwards. He sighed. Some of the crew had left their places and gone to talk to the captain.

'Kill it,' said one. 'It's a bird of ill-omen. We'll be wrecked if it stays there, I'm telling you.'

'No, no,' said another. 'You can't kill a bird. That'd bring us misfortune quicker than anything.'

'We're nearly home,' said the captain. 'Ithaka's just past that headland. That's Same on the port side.'

Then a shout went up, 'Pirates! See, two ships making straight for us.'

Telemachus stared at the ships that seemed to have appeared from nowhere, sailing out of a mist that had sprung up on the Same side of the straits. They were both making for the *Sea Nymph*.

'They're armed,' the captain shouted. 'And they're going to ram us.'

The marauding vessels were so close that Telemachus could see the contorted faces of the men who lined the decks. One or two of them looked familiar. Could they possibly be from Ithaka? Why would anyone want to attack the *Sea Nymph*? he wondered, and turned to find a weapon. The captain was running up and down the deck, handing out broadswords and knives to the crew, and then the whole ship trembled with the shock of impact.

'They're going to board us, men!' the captain shouted. 'Prepare to defend yourselves.'

Telemachus wondered whether he was the only person to taste fear in his mouth. Was everyone else as terrified as he was? I'm Odysseus' son, he told himself. I'm not going to be scared. Not now. He gripped the sword he'd been given and stood as close as he could to the captain. And then, it happened. Later on the whole crew agreed that they'd seen it: a violent wind springing up from the west and blowing the pirate

286

vessels away from the side of the *Sea Nymph* as easily as though they were leaves drifting on a stream. One moment they were there, close enough to touch, and then they were gone, driven before the storm and moving with astonishing speed further and further; past the Same headland and out of sight before anyone had time to understand what was going on.

'Did you see our sails?' one man asked.

'Flat, they were. No wind blowing anywhere. Did you see that?'

'Couldn't have been flat. Storm nearly blew those bastards straight up out of the ocean.'

'He's right,' said the captain. 'We haven't moved, have we? Why didn't the wind affect us, eh? Tell me that. We were near enough.' He glanced up to the mast, where the owl was still perched. 'That's Pallas Athene's messenger, I reckon. Someone on Olympus is taking care of us. Taking care of you, Telemachus.'

Telemachus nodded. 'I thank you, Goddess,' he shouted up at the bird on the mast, and the owl unfolded its wide, white wings and flew away across the black water.

'No more adventures,' the captain said to Telemachus. 'I'm setting course for Ithaka.'

Telemachus strode into the gates of his father's palace and looked about him. The rain was lashing down, and the earth in the courtyard had turned into a field of reddish mud. The filth of the area in front of the kitchen was unspeakable: like the most badly-kept market. Melon skin, dirty goblets, oddments of clothing lay about everywhere. The palace cats had made their home among the leavings and seemed to be growing fatter. Dirty washing was piled high near the trough. Nana had evidently decided not to do laundry any longer and quite right too. Let them wear dirty garments. It was no more than they deserved.

Where are they, he wondered, the scum who made this mess? He hesitated. He ought to go and see his mother first, reassure her that he was safely home, but an even stronger urge came from the hatred he felt towards the men who had spread themselves everywhere. He couldn't help himself. He stood in the middle of the outer courtyard and shouted with all the strength of his lungs: 'Amphimedon! Antinous! Come out and talk to me. Telemachus, son of Odysseus, has returned to his father's island. Come out and greet me!'

From all over the palace, it seemed, people came running. Klymene flew out of the kitchen crying, 'Telemachus! Is it really you? Have you been to see your mother? Oh, Telemachus, I'm so happy to see you! You're safe! You're safe – they didn't kill you . . .'

'How do you know about it, Klymene? My ship was ambushed . . .'

Klymene drew Telemachus behind one of the courtyard pillars.

'Only seven days ago Ikarios overheard them – the Rat and the Bear planning to ambush your ship . . . We prayed to Pallas Athene. Our prayers were answered. I'm so happy, Telemachus.'

Telemachus stared over Klymene's shoulder. 'I didn't know who it could have been, but of course it's them,' he murmured. 'I'm going to find Antinous and Amphimedon.'

'Let me go and tell Penelope you're here. She'll want to see you immediately. She'll be so happy . . . we're all so happy.'

She embraced Telemachus and then hurried away in the direction of the queen's chamber.

Argos, who had been sleeping in the doorway of the great hall, staggered to his feet and tottered into the outer courtyard with Nana beside him. Telemachus knelt down in the mud to stroke the old dog. He looked up at Nana and the others and said: 'It's good to see you all. And Klymene's right. I must go and find my mother. But there's Amphimedon. I've got something to say to him first. Bastard!'

'Lord Telemachus!' The Bear came over to where Telemachus was kneeling and smiled, showing dirty teeth. 'I see that Poseidon has sent you safely home. Your mother will be much relieved.'

'No thanks to you that I'm home.' Telemachus stood up. 'My ship escaped an ambush. Who d'you think might want me at the bottom of the sea? You perhaps?'

The Bear laughed. 'The waters around this island are full of pirates, as well you know. Nothing to do with me, any trouble you might have had at sea.'

The group gathered round Telemachus parted to allow the Rat to come and stand next to his friend. He was smiling the smile that made his face look less rather than more friendly and said, 'Welcome, Telemachus!'

Telemachus said nothing but stared over the Rat's shoulder towards the gates and the tents that had been erected in their shade. Melantho . . . Surely that was her hurrying out of one of them? He couldn't see more than the flash of a woman's garment, but he recognized her. Why should I care? he thought. We quarrelled before I left and I have no real claims on her any longer. Still, Telemachus found it impossible to feel anything but disgust at the idea of her lying with this villain.

'I want you gone from my father's palace,' Telemachus said quietly. 'As soon as possible.'

'Not part of our plan, I'm afraid,' said the Bear. 'And actually, none of your business. Your mother must make a decision. And we're not going anywhere without a fight. You ready to take us on?'

'I'm not bothering to answer that. I'm going to see my mother. You'll hear from me.'

Telemachus went into the palace and tried not to hear the laughter that rose up at his departure. The rain was still falling and he was soaked to the skin and shivering. I look like a drowned rat, he thought. I wish I'd never come back.

'You can't!' Penelope looked at her son, suddenly so much a man, so different from the little boy she still saw in her mind's eye when she thought about him. 'You've only just arrived, and you've told me nothing. Not where you landed, not what you've been doing, nothing. And I still don't understand why you couldn't have sent a messenger ahead of your ship. We'd have got ready for you; prepared a suitable welcome.'

'Honestly, Mother! How is it you still don't understand when I've explained and explained. I wanted to see *you*. To greet *you*. That's all. A few other people. I didn't want what you call *a suitable welcome*. I didn't want that nonsense that goes on with musicians and garlands and everyone waiting on the harbour wall. It's ridiculous. And since the whole of the palace is still overrun with vermin from every corner of the Ionian, they'd have been there too. Don't pretend they wouldn't. They'd have come down to greet me in order to impress you. Well, they can get stuffed, the whole bloody lot of them.'

'Telemachus! You've become so . . .'

'So what? I don't feel like talking gently, Mother. I feel like getting pissed and swearing and running round the courtyard screaming at everyone I meet. Don't worry – I'm not going to do that, but I'm certainly not going to bow and scrape and *pretend* any longer.'

Penelope sighed and picked at a corner of her scarf. How complicated everything was. She'd been longing, yearning, to see her son, and when Klymene told her he was in the palace, her happiness had overflowed into a storm of tears. But here he was and within moments of them greeting one another again, everything was immediately difficult and problematic. Now she didn't know how she felt about Telemachus' return. What was going to happen? She decided that it was probably unwise to interrogate him about what he'd been doing while he was away. She knew her son well enough to know that she would get the information when Telemachus was ready to tell her and not before. He'd be sure to accuse her of nagging if she asked questions now.

'You won't be able to ignore them for ever, Telemachus.'

'I will. I'm not staying, Mother. That's hard for you to hear, I know. And I'll miss you. I'll come and visit you often, but I'm not living here. I'm going to Eumaeus' farm.'

Penelope smiled. 'He's fond of you, that's true. When you were a little boy, you used to spend days and days helping him with the pigs. You really loved those pigs!'

'They're a lot more intelligent and pleasant than most humans. Cleaner than some of our esteemed guests too.'

Penelope laughed. 'Have you asked his permission?'

'No, but he'll be pleased to see me, I know. He always needs help. And it'll be easier for me to visit Grandfather if I'm over there. I'll be all right. Peaceful. Away from this racket.'

The shouts and laughter of drunken men could be heard through the window.

'I thought—' Penelope began and then stopped.

'Thought what?'

'That you'd want to see your friends. Ikarios and Klymene.' She paused. 'And Melantho.'

'I've seen Klymene. I'll go and find Ikarios and speak to him, of course. As for Melantho . . .' He flung himself down on the bed with his face buried in the coverlet.

'Telemachus?'

He sat up at once. 'It's over between us, Mother. She seems to have taken the enemy to her bosom. I'd have thought you'd be relieved. You surely wouldn't have liked her as a daughter-in-law.'

'Did you love her, Telemachus?'

'I don't feel like talking about her. I simply want to be quiet for a while. I need to work out what's to be done about them.' He nodded towards the window. 'Ithaka has to be restored to what it once was. I'll find a way to do it, Mother. Don't worry. And I'll visit you often. Promise.'

He got off the bed and opened the door. Penelope said, 'A feast, Telemachus? Won't you allow me to pre-pare a feast in your honour?'

'No feast,' Telemachus said, kissing his mother's cheek and hugging her. 'I couldn't bear it. I'd choke on every mouthful.'

After her son had left the room, Penelope stood by the window, keeping her gaze high so that she was looking at the ocean in the distance and not at the mess that was there under her eyes in the palace court-yards. With Telemachus gone to Eumaeus' farm, she thought, it'll be easier for me to be with Leodes. She sighed. What have I come to? How can I be so unnat-ural a mother: finding reason to rejoice that my son will be away from home? Nevertheless, she couldn't help but be relieved that Telemachus would not be there to observe her too closely.

She went to the stool in front of the loom. If I sit here for a while, she told herself, perhaps a picture will come to me. She closed her eyes and there was nothing there. Not a single colour in the whole of her head. The threads on the loom were blue and green and there was nothing but that – more blue, more green. There is just a space in my head where the story was, she thought. I must be tired. I'm preoccupied. The pictures will return. I won't worry about it now. Later. I'll go back to the pictures later.

ON THE OTHER SIDE OF THE ISLAND

The man opened his eyes and found himself looking up at the darkness. Stars in their multitudes were scattered on the blue and made him feel dizzy. There was the moon: Artemis, the Goddess of the Chase and the Protector of Virgins, was abroad in her night fields and driving her silvery chariot across the sky. He was lying on a surface that hurt his back: stones or pebbles. In his ears he could hear the rhythms of the ocean. He was alone. He was freezing cold. He was naked, except for a necklace of shells. A memory of someone (who was it?) putting it round his neck came into his mind and drifted out again before he had time to follow the thought. Never mind. He was alive. He sat up and pinched the flesh of his legs to make sure that he hadn't died and gone down to Hades. No, he was definitely alive and on a beach somewhere. He looked more carefully at his surroundings: at the cliff behind him, at the caves hollowed out of the living rock, at the one rock in the shape of a lion's head which he remembered from his boyhood. He looked again. Could it be? Was it truly, after all these wanderings? Ithaka.

He must have breathed the word aloud because there was a voice in his head that whispered, *Yes. You have come home.*

Startled, he jumped to his feet. 'Who's there?' he cried. There was no answer. A white owl was perched at the entrance to one of the caves. He blinked. 'Is anyone there?'

Go to the cave, said a voice that he now understood was not a voice at all but more like a thought in his own mind. *You cannot be seen as yourself. You must hide who you are till it's safe. There are dangers ahead. Go to the cave.*

'You are Pallas Athene's owl and you are speaking to me,' said the man, and chuckled to himself as he made his way to the cave. Was he hearing a Goddess's voice or was he drugged or drunk? Perhaps the person who had put a necklace made out of shells around his neck had also poisoned him in some way so that now he was hearing words that came from nowhere.

He went into the cave and there was a pile of clothes just inside the entrance. Filthy rags they were too, and the man wrinkled his nose at the smell.

'I can't wear these. They smell.'

You are a beggar, said the voice. *No one will take you for who you truly are if you're in those garments.*

'No one will be brave enough to come near me,' the man said. He put on the shirt and the cape and tied the stringy leather belt around his waist. 'Nevertheless, in this cold I am happy to have any kind of covering for my body. Show yourself, Pallas Athene. Tell me all will be well.'

The white owl fluttered into the cave and brushed past the man, touching his head with her feathers. Then she flew out and over the sea, disappearing into the starlit night. The man put his hand to his face and discovered that his beard had grown. It was now long and matted and grey and hung down over his chest.

He stepped out and sat down on the beach again. Ithaka. He was here at last. He knelt down and picked up a handful of sand and brought it to his face, breathing in the fragrance of his own place, his home. Why had the Goddess, or whatever power had brought him here, not washed him ashore on the beach below the palace? From there it was only a short step to his gates. There must be a reason for him to be on the other side of the island, where there was less sand and more pebbles that hurt the feet of anyone trying to walk on them. She is trying to keep me safe, he thought. The time to admit who I am is not here yet. I'll think. I will work out what to do before I go rushing in to find them. I've always acted with good sense. I've always been both daring and careful. Now is not the time to be reckless.

The man stood at the water's edge, looking at the black mass of the island. The dream is still and always Ithaka, he thought. I have returned.

'It's strange, isn't it?' Melantho was braiding her hair and speaking over her shoulder to Klymene in the bedchamber they shared.

'What is?'

'How you can have something – or someone – in front of your eyes for years and years and not even notice him. Then suddenly you look at this person again and see all sorts of things you never noticed before. Like how handsome they are. And how kind. Also how gifted.'

Klymene rolled her eyes to the ceiling and laughed. 'I see. You've gone off the Rat. Pardon me, I mean the Lord Antinous. Someone else has taken your fancy. Well, I don't understand it, but I'm used to the way you behave. I know that Telemachus was only here for a short while, but you were never around when he was. Why was that?'

'Oh, Telemachus! Well, it's true, I did love him once, but that was over long ago. He didn't exactly seek me out either, you know. This other person has never in his life been rude to me.'

'Go on. Tell me his name, though it's unlikely I'll know him. I keep as far away as I can from all those losers lying about in the courtyard.'

'Oh, you know this one. Better than anyone, I think.'

Klymene was puzzled. What could Melantho mean? Surely not the hideous Akamos, whom she saw sometimes out of the corner of her eye and tried her best to avoid?

'Who on earth are you talking about?' she said.

'You're being silly. Of course he must have spoken to you about me. He tells you everything that's in his mind, I'm sure. Everything you can't guess already.'

A sick, cold feeling came over Klymene. She

298

couldn't mean Ikarios, could she? But who else told her everything? Melantho fell back on to the bed and smiled at Klymene.

'I can see from your face that you've guessed. Also that you're not best pleased, though I can't see why you should object. I do mean Ikarios, your brother. Hasn't he mentioned it?'

Klymene sat down on the end of her own bed. 'He's told me how much he admires you. He told me a long time ago. But what's happened all of a sudden? You used to ignore him completely. Something's changed. What is it?'

'I often change my mind. I just looked at him properly, that's all. And he spoke to me for almost the first time. That makes a difference, when someone actually speaks to you.'

'But we've known one another for years! You've often spoken to him.'

Melantho shook her head. 'You're so close to him that you maybe don't notice, only he doesn't ever say very much. He sits about on the edge of things and looks at people, and scarcely ever talks. But yesterday he did. He came to me when I was alone for a moment and told me how much I had meant to him, for years and years, it seems. And he gave me something beautiful. I'll show you.'

She sat up and lifted the cushion that served as her pillow and picked up a small cloth-wrapped bundle.

'Look,' she said. There, sitting on the palm of her hand, was a tiny wooden sculpture of a cat, sleeping and curled up into an almost perfect circle. 'Isn't it beautiful?'

Klymene stroked the curved back. Ikarios had made the creature from olive wood in such a way that the pale striping of the grain exactly matched the markings of a cat's fur. The eyes were closed. The paws were daintily carved. He'd even chiselled delicate whiskers on to the face.

'Yes,' said Klymene. 'Very beautiful.'

'He said I reminded him of a cat.' Melantho sounded triumphant. Klymene said nothing. She still thought her companion was more like a snake than a cat, but she'd never shared this opinion with anyone, not even Ikarios. It just goes to show, she thought, that there *is* a difference between us after all, and that we can't truly read one another's thoughts. It's probably a good thing that we can't, or Ikarios would be able to find out secrets that I don't want him to know. He'd know about how Penelope and I unpick some of the knitting every night. She stood up.

'It's lovely, Melantho. He's very gifted with his hands, unlike me.'

'No, you're gifted too. The queen has said how much she depends on you to help her with her handiwork.'

Klymene wondered whether there was any deeper meaning in the words – a hint that their deception had been discovered – but Melantho looked quite innocent and had got off the bed and turned her attention to her hair again.

'I must get ready now. I'm meeting Ikarios in his

workshop. To thank him. It's all arranged. An assignation, you could call it. I'm looking forward to it.' She smiled. Anyone else seeing her face would have said there was nothing in it but friendship, so why, Klymene thought, do I see a creature stalking its prey? I'm becoming more fearful of everything as I grow older. She felt something like a shadow falling over her. I must grow up, she told herself. I'm tired, that's all. She shook her head to rid herself of a vague feeling of dread.

'I must go now,' she said. 'The queen's expecting me. Farewell.'

'Farewell,' Melantho answered, and Klymene hurried along the corridor to Penelope's chamber.

TELEMACHUS AND THE STRANGER

On his first morning at Eumaeus' farm Telemachus was sitting outside the farmhouse on a wooden bench with a pail of leavings for the pigs when a young man appeared, carrying two baskets of eggs.

'I recognize you,' Telemachus said. 'What're you doing here? You're one of Antinous' men! Aren't you satisfied with overrunning the palace without extending your foul influence over the countryside as well?' He sprang up from his seat and looked as though he was ready to knock the baskets out of the stranger's hands.

'My name is Mydon,' the young man said mildly. 'Has Eumaeus not told you I was working for him? I sleep over there, in the outhouse. And I came to Ithaka with Antinous, it's true. Nevertheless, I don't count myself as one of his men. I'd never hurt you, or your mother, I swear by the Gods.'

'Why should I believe you?' Telemachus was still standing with his hands bunched up into fists.

'Next time you speak to Klymene, ask her about me. She will tell you that I don't have Antinous' interests

302

at heart. I came to Ithaka with him because I wanted to see the island that was home to Odysseus. He's my hero. I was born in Troy and your father rescued my mother from the city when it burned to the ground. Look!'

He held out his hand. 'See that scar? That's where the fire found me. It's always white – never catches the sun's rays.'

Telemachus said sulkily, 'All right then. If that's all true, I suppose there's nothing to be done.'

He let Mydon go into the kitchen, grabbed hold of his pail of pig food and strode off in the direction of the pigsty. When he got there, he stood looking at the swine, who were rooting about in the dirt, scuffling and snuffling among the tasty morsels he'd just thrown down for them, and thought how different this place was from the palace. Even with that Mydon here, who'd have to be watched whatever he said. Down there, the mess and noise were unbearable. Melantho was practically married to the Rat, as Klymene and Ikarios called him. She'd made sure to keep out of his way while he was at the palace. One of these days, he thought, I'll see her when I go down there, but I'm not going to make a special point of looking for her or asking for her. Let her stew in her own disgusting juices. Telemachus picked up a fallen tree branch and hit the side of the pigsty with all the force he could muster. He took a deep breath to calm himself.

Everything was peaceful here. It was a beautiful place. Olive trees grew behind Eumaeus' small house, which sheltered in the shadow of the mountain, and terraces of vines led from his fields almost down to the sea. His mother hadn't put up nearly as much of a fight as he'd expected her to, and he wondered why that was. He'd managed to persuade her very easily. She liked the idea that he would be able to visit his grandfather more often. The longer he could be away from the palace, the better things would be. He could take his time to decide what had to be done about the suitors. When I next see Laertes, he thought, I'll ask him about the chances of raising an army from somewhere to fight those bastards.

The farmhouse itself was clean and quiet, and Eumaeus was kind.

'It's a pleasure for me to have your company,' he told Telemachus as he showed him where the pigs lived and explained what his duties would be. 'The swine are my friends of course, and you couldn't wish for more intelligent companions. It's my opinion they are more intelligent even than my cats. Still, pigs can't speak, and neither can cats, though they all make their own noises, that's certain. It'll be good to have someone to talk to. Someone to tell the old stories to.'

Telemachus sighed and brought himself back to what he had been doing and threw some more of the vegetable peelings into the pen. Because there was no one else there to speak to, he addressed the animals.

'Eumaeus is a good man,' he told them, 'but he does tell a lot of stories, doesn't he? I'm sure I've heard some of them three times. I'll know them by heart soon. Here, Beauty!' He made a wheedling, cajoling sound with his lips to call over his favourite pig. Beauty likes me, he thought. She came trotting over to where he was, stuck her snout through the wooden palings, and made a snuffling noise.

'Good girl! Good Beauty!' He threw some acorns down on to the ground next to her, and smiled to see how eagerly the creature ran to eat them up.

When the feeding was over, Telemachus turned to go back to the house, then stopped. From where he stood he could see the olive grove around the farm quite clearly. He frowned. He'd never, in all the days he'd spent here in the past, ever seen anyone walking there, but now there was a man coming through the trees, dressed in filthy rags. A beggar. He had a crudely fashioned walking stick in one hand and was making his way slowly to where Telemachus stood, almost as though he'd seen him and was trying to reach him. As he approached, he was waving his stick frantically and shouting something.

'Young man! Young man! Is this the farm belonging to Eumaeus?'

'Yes,' said Telemachus. He could smell the beggar from a few steps away. Clearly he hadn't bathed for many moons. Still, he was old and thin and he knew Eumaeus' name. 'Do you know Eumaeus?'

'Oh, yes.' The old man leaned against the wooden palings of the pigsty. 'Eumaeus and I knew one another years ago. Many years ago. Perhaps you'd be so good as to accompany me to his door? I find it hard to walk sometimes.'

'Certainly,' said Telemachus, sounding more eager

than he felt. There was nothing for it. If this creature was an acquaintance of Eumaeus, it wasn't his business to send the old rascal packing.

They walked slowly down the path to the farmhouse door. Neither of them spoke. As they came closer, Telemachus called out, 'Eumaeus! Come out, Eumaeus, you have a visitor.'

Eumaeus opened the door and peered at Telemachus and the old man whose elbow he was holding.

'Never seen him before in my life,' Eumaeus said. 'Still, I expect we can find him a bowl of food somewhere, and a drink. Perhaps even a bath. That wouldn't come amiss, by the look of him.'

The beggar stood directly in front of Eumaeus and stared at him. 'I know you, Eumaeus. The years have whitened your hair but they haven't really touched you. You're just the same. Don't you recognize me?'

At the sound of the man's voice, Eumaeus took a step backward, reeling. His hands flew to his mouth and he stared at the stranger out of wide eyes. At last he said, 'It can't be . . . not after all this time. Is it? O Gods on Olympus, it's *you*! How did I not see it? Your eyes – oh, your eyes are the same eyes . . . the same eyes. A happy day . . . so happy. I don't know what to say . . . what to do.'

Suddenly Eumaeus froze, as though the shock had turned him into a statue.

'What is it, Eumaeus?' Telemachus said. 'What's the matter? Aren't you pleased to see your friend again? It's clearly many years since you last met.'

Eumaeus pointed at the beggar and tried to speak. His words came out as though something in his throat had torn them into rags. 'Don't you see? It's him! It's your father, Telemachus . . . Odysseus. Your father . . . your son . . . can't you *see*? Both of you. Say your names. Tell them aloud!'

The farmer staggered to a bench beside the farmhouse door and sat heavily down on it, mopping his brow with his sleeve. The beggar said, 'You are Telemachus, son of Penelope and Odysseus?'

Telemachus nodded. He could feel his heart suddenly begin to beat loudly in his chest and his mouth was dry. He blinked. 'And you are Odysseus. You are my father.'

'I am. I have waited years to see you and now I have no words. No words to say.'

'Nor have I.'

'And now that we've found one another, you're wishing I were different. You're thinking: this is not what the king of Ithaka is supposed to look like. Am I right?'

'No,' Telemachus said quietly. 'I don't care what you look like. I'm . . . I'm happy to see you.'

'Then come and embrace me, my son, and we'll sit down together and tell one another stories.'

Telemachus let himself be hugged and, surprisingly, the smell had almost vanished. He sniffed again. How could that be? Smelly and foul one minute and clean and fragrant the next? He looked at his father again, at the clear grey eyes that were nearly hidden under shaggy white eyebrows and felt a flutter of love like a dove rising up in his heart. *Odysseus.* His father had returned to Ithaka. All at once a burden Telemachus didn't even realize he was carrying fell away from him. Tears rose in his throat and he choked them back. A hero's son didn't weep. Never, not even when they were tears of joy.

Later that day, as the sun was setting in a blaze of gold, Odysseus came out of the farmhouse door. 'Who's this, Telemachus? A neighbour? A friend?'

'He says he's a friend. His name's Mydon. He says you rescued his mother from the fire at Troy . . .'

'Mydon? Mydon?' Odysseus came closer to the young man and peered at him. 'There were many. Many people, all running from the flames. But a young woman with a small baby . . . yes, yes . . .'

'That was me, sir!' Mydon's eyes shone. 'That was my mother and me. Oh, I have lived all my life waiting to see this day. I didn't dare to hope you were alive.' He sank down to his knees and his forehead touched the earth.

'Do you really remember him, Father? Is it true?'

Odysseus nodded. 'I think I do. There's been so much in my head that I no longer know what I'm sure of . . . but I think maybe. Never mind, Telemachus. We need all the friends we can get, don't we? If we're going to defeat those bastards who are preying on my property. Who are lying in wait for my wife.'

He leaned down and pulled Mydon up by the elbows. 'Are you with us or against us, young man? I have to know. And you have to tell the truth or Pallas Athene will strike you dead.'

'I'm with you. I'll always serve you faithfully. I give you my promise.'

'Then welcome, Mydon. You must stay for the feast tonight and drink with us.' Odysseus smiled at his son. 'Telemachus, be a friend to this young man.'

Odysseus, Telemachus, Mydon and Eumaeus were sitting together round the table in the courtyard outside Eumaeus' kitchen. A plump young pig had been slaughtered in honour of Odysseus' return. While it was roasting, it had been Mydon's duty to turn the spit and baste the flesh with olive oil in which herbs had been standing for so long that their fragrance had passed to the golden liquid. With the pork there were bowls of fresh vegetables from the farm and figs from the trees around the house and bread baked by Eumaeus himself. Telemachus poured the wine. The night air was warm and the dark sky bright with stars. The waning moon shone dimly, but a lantern stood on the table among the platters and cups and it shed a warm, yellow light and made black shadows move on the walls.

'I've never been to the Elysian Fields,' said Odysseus, smiling at his son. 'But I doubt they'll be pleasanter than this. I've journeyed on the oceans of the world so long that my son, my little baby Telemachus, is now a man and I'm proud of him. If only my beloved Penelope were here, then I'd want nothing more in this life.'

'We'll go, Father, won't we? Tomorrow. I've kept silent about the suitors, telling you only the bare facts and not the horrible details, but I will. When this feast's over, when we start planning our revenge, I'll tell you things that'll freeze your blood. You wouldn't recognize your palace.'

'But your mother? She is well? Does she still think of me? And my beloved father? Has he followed my mother to Hades?'

'Laertes is still alive,' said Telemachus. 'He's in a cottage just beyond the hill there. He's become like a hermit – doesn't like seeing anyone from the palace, though I go and visit him whenever I can, and Mother sends him whatever she can think of that he'd enjoy. Wine, mostly.' He helped himself to another piece of bread and a few more olives.

'You say Amphimedon is one of them,' Odysseus said. 'I remember him. Big fat youth with a mouth as foul as a cesspit.'

'That's him,' Telemachus said. 'Only he's not a youth any longer. We call him the Bear. And his friend is Antinous – the Rat. He's the one I'm going to get if it's the last thing I do. He sent that ship to ambush me in the straits. I hate him.'

'He's wicked,' Mydon added. 'He sent me away from the palace because he knew I wanted to stay there. He enjoys cruelty.'

'We must be cunning and careful,' said Odysseus. 'They've no idea that I'm here on Ithaka and they think you're safely hiding in the countryside, Telemachus. They know you visit the palace, but you're safe enough. They're not going to attack you there if they intend to woo your mother. You must go back ahead of me. That'll give me a great advantage. No one cares where a feeble old beggar man goes. Am I right?'

Telemachus nodded. Odysseus went on, 'Don't tell your mother you've met me. I want to show myself to Penelope in my own way. Mydon and I will walk to the palace after you. But as soon as you see your mother, you must tell her that you now think I'm dead. Tell her that you've reconciled yourself to her choosing a husband from among the suitors, just in order to get rid of the rest and restore some order in Ithaka. You must persuade her to host a feast.' He took a piece of bread and chewed it thoughtfully. 'And during the feast, there must be a contest, so that she may choose her next husband. Is my bow still hanging in the armoury?'

'The huge one?'

'That one, yes,' said Odysseus.

'It's still there.' Telemachus took a sip of wine.

'And do they still sing the song? They were singing it on this island when I wasn't much older than you are. *Humble or wellborn, swift or slow, only our king can bend the bow.*'

'Yes,' said Telemachus. 'We all know it. But . . . what if one of the bastards somehow finds out who you are?'

'Pallas Athene will protect me,' Odysseus smiled.

NIGHT TIME IN THE WORKSHOP

Ikarios was finding it difficult to breathe. When he'd followed his sister's advice and carved a gift for Melantho, he never expected it to lead to anything like this. She had been kind to him when he'd presented it, and that was more than he'd hoped for. Then she'd continued to be friendly and more than friendly, coming into the workshop and talking to him, and taking an interest in everything. Ikarios had just begun to wonder whether Melantho's friendliness meant something like affection or maybe even love, when she suggested this evening meeting. He remembered how she'd emphasized that it must be in the evening. *We wouldn't like to be interrupted by Ikmalios, would we?* she'd whispered and smiled the smile that made something in his stomach jump and twist in a way that was half painful and half pleasurable.

Now here they were, together and alone. The workshop was in almost complete darkness, but one lantern still burned in a corner, almost hidden by the chairs and tables that Ikmalios had been mending that day.

The light was golden and dim, and the two of them were close together on the low bench that Ikarios sat on while he worked.

'You're pleased to see me, aren't you?' Melantho's voice in his ear was delicious but seemed to have the effect of paralysing him completely. He found that he couldn't move his limbs. I'm frozen, he thought. What do I do now? What shall I say?

'Don't say anything,' Melantho murmured, putting both arms around him and somehow twisting his body so that he was facing her. 'Just kiss me. Look, like this.'

She took his head between her hands and pulled it close to her own. Her mouth was suddenly on his, and her lips were open. Like a thirsty man plunging into a pool of water, he opened his own mouth and felt himself drowning in pleasure. He could smell her: the fragrant oils she put on her skin filled his nostrils and, as she wound herself closer and closer to him, his limbs regained their movement and soon his own arms had twined themselves around Melantho's body and there was no knowing where one of them ended and the other began.

'Lovely! A truly lovely and inspiring sight! Love's young dream. Isn't that what they call it?'

Ikarios sprang away from Melantho, who immediately covered her face with her scarf and ran to a dark corner of the workshop. He stood up and peered at the person standing in the doorway. It took him only a heartbeat to recognize the Rat.

*

Something was amiss. Penelope sat at the loom and stared at it. She had a basket of wools at her feet and her hands, which normally longed to weave the colours, lay on her lap, idle. Klymene was busily occupied unpicking the latest handiwork, and she was sitting on a stool on the other side of the bed, talking under her breath to Argos; singing him a song, as though he were a little baby she was trying to lull to sleep.

There is nothing in my head, Penelope thought, and shivered. Nothing. Every story, every picture, had gone. Where to? And why? She closed her eyes, praying that the colours would appear there, telling her which of them needed to be threaded on to the loom. Nothing. Black and blank and empty. Did this mean that her husband was dead? She picked up a skein of black and held it up to the light. Not this, she thought. Not black. I refuse to admit that black is the colour the loom is waiting for. Red then? No, not red.

One after another, she held each colour up and considered it. I don't want to weave, she thought. How can that be? Weaving is like breathing to me, and yet if I could walk out of this room and away from my handiwork, I would. I wish, she thought, that I could run away, like Telemachus. How comfortable it would be to sit at Eumaeus' fireside and talk about nothing. Or Leodes. She could almost hear Aphrodite speaking to her: *Life is short and pleasure is all there is. Go with Leodes. Love him. Forget Odysseus.* We could flee to his island on his ship. I could leave them all behind me. Leave everything: the palace, the suitors, Telemachus,

Laertes, this bed that has bound me to the earth of Ithaka. I could run away.

She stood up and went to the window. Where are you, Pallas Athene, to reassure me? How long ago it was, that night when you sent your owl to tell me Odysseus would return. I'm tired of waiting for something that is not going to happen. There is nothing in my head: no pictures left to weave. What can that mean but that my husband is dead?

She sighed.

Klymene said, 'Is something troubling you, my lady?'

'No, no, Klymene. All is well. It is just that . . . well, my head is hurting somewhat. I think I will lie down now. You may continue with your work. I don't mind you being here. Is anything worrying you?'

Penelope looked carefully at Klymene. She had jumped up from her stool and was staring at a patch on the wall as though some monster were painted on it. 'What are you seeing? Klymene?'

'I'm sorry, lady.' Klymene tried to make her voice light, to sound as though nothing were wrong, but she couldn't disguise the trembling that shook every word. 'I feel . . . I don't know what I feel. Cold. Sick. I can't say what's the matter. I don't know. But I must go. I must find Ikarios. I think . . . I don't know, but I think he may be in some danger.'

She placed the white length of the shroud she'd been unpicking on the bed beside her and stood up.

'Are you ill, child? You've turned quite white.'

'Yes,' said Klymene. What else was there to say? She

had never been able to explain exactly how she was bound to her twin. Now, what she felt was icy terror. She could see something. Some iron thing glittered in the corner of her eye, and she could smell blood. A thousand slaughtered creatures: lambs, chickens, pigs and goats had lain in the kitchen and her grandmother had often called on her to help prepare them.

She knew the smell of blood and now it filled her nostrils.

'Forgive me, lady. I must go.'

'Go at once, Klymene, but take every care. I will pray to the Gods on Olympus for you. And I will see that Argos is looked after.'

Klymene ran out of the room.

'Argos,' Penelope said, 'everything is wrong today. No pictures, no stories. Nothing but pain and sorrow.'

Ikarios tried to breathe normally, though his heart was beating so loudly in his chest that he thought the Rat must hear it too. Antinous, who, everyone said, had been Melantho's favourite for a while. He's jealous, Ikarios thought. He's mad with jealousy and that's why he looks so angry, but I don't care. I'll fight him for her. I'd do anything.

'No use hiding, sweetheart,' said the Rat to Melantho. 'It's thanks to you that he's here for me, and I'm grateful for your help in keeping him in this nice dark place where I can deal with him.'

Deal with me? Ikarios thought. What does he mean? And what did he say about Melantho? Confusion filled his head. Did Melantho bring him here for some other reason? Why? He said, 'Melantho, tell me the truth. Why did you come here?' He wanted to hear her say the words: *To be with you, quietly, because I'm so fond of you. And you wanted us to be alone.'*

'You shouldn't ask, Ikarios. But I *do* like you. We've known one another for a ages and I feel as though I'm close to you. Truly. And I don't want you thinking for a moment that I'm not grateful for your lovely cat and your . . . well, your attention to me. But I should tell you the truth, shouldn't I? Antinous wanted to see you alone, so that's why I asked you to come here. I love him, Ikarios. D'you understand?'

How could you kiss me like that if you love Antinous? he wanted to say, but couldn't find the words. In any case, he knew the answer. He didn't have much experience with young women, but he knew well enough that it was perfectly possible for them to be treacherous. To pretend to love someone when they didn't really. Klymene had always said that Melantho was sly and wicked and would stop at nothing to get her own way, but why in the name of all the Gods on Olympus had Antinous come here to find him?

'What d'you want with me?' he asked, turning to the Rat, vowing never to speak to Melantho again if he could possibly help it.

'You're good at playing the innocent, you,' said the Rat, his thin lips stretched in a smile that showed his sharp, yellow teeth. 'You know why. It must have been you. We've worked it out, me and Amphimedon. You must have hidden away and heard us talking. No one else could have warned Telemachus.'

317

'That's not true! How could I have warned him? You've seen me every day . . . What are you saying: that I got hold of a ship somehow and sailed off to tell Telemachus of your plans?'

'You admitting you knew them?'

Ikarios turned away. 'I'm not admitting anything.'

'What if I just scratch my initials on your arm? Will you admit it then?'

The Rat drew his blade gently down Ikarios' arm and a trail of blood appeared on the skin. Ikarios went white, sank to his knees and cried out, 'Stop! I did hear. I hid myself and I heard every word. But I didn't warn him. I swear I didn't warn him . . . you *know* I couldn't have done.'

'Don't know anyone else who could have, do you? However you did it—'

'I didn't . . .' Ikarios was screaming. 'I swear.'

'I'm sick of this,' the Rat said. 'You're going to be punished.'

He held the short, wicked-looking blade up in front of him, and Ikarios saw it gleaming in the lantern light.

'You heard us plan the ambush of Telemachus' ship and you must have told him about it – told him that we were lying in wait on Same – because suddenly there was a wind that swept our boats away and didn't touch him. Funny, right? Then he gave us the slip and landed somewhere else on the coast. Now he's here and throwing his weight about. If you want to know the truth, I'd rather put a knife between his ribs than yours, but there's a problem there. Penelope's not going to marry me if I skewer her son, right?'

'I never told anyone about your plans. I swear . . . only my sister.'

'I don't believe you. Funny that, don't you think? Melantho, you should go. Things are about to get nasty round here.'

'I'm going too,' said Ikarios, taking a couple of steps in the direction of the doorway. Melantho came running out of the corner and fled from the workshop without a backward glance at either of the men.

'Melantho!' Ikarios called. 'Come back! Say something.'

He was so busy staring after her, so busy wondering what had happened, how it had come to pass like this; so busy accustoming himself to the fact that Melantho cared nothing for him that he hardly noticed when the Rat took hold of him by the shoulder and spun him round. He wished that he didn't have to know the truth: that she loved someone else.

'I'm going,' the Rat said to Ikarios, 'to kill you, but I'll do you the honour of killing you face to face.'

'Go on, then,' Ikarios said, smiling. 'Do whatever you like. I don't care.'

'It'll be a pleasure,' said the Rat, and jabbed his knife into the soft flesh between Ikarios' ribs. 'You won't be spouting your rubbish ever again.'

Spouting rubbish? This thought struck Ikarios as ludicrous. He was well-known for his silence, wasn't he? He started to laugh, but something was piercing his side. He closed his eyes, gagging at the smell of his own blood.

*

'Ikarios!' Klymene saw her brother lying on the ground and knew at once that she was too late to save him. He was trying to say something, and she flung herself on his body, holding him and weeping and saying his name over and over again: 'Don't speak, Ikarios. I can't bear it! Don't die, oh, Ikarios, please don't die. I can't live alone. We're one person, Ikarios, only split into two. Help . . . I must help you. I'll call the queen. We'll mend you . . . we'll take care of you.'

Klymene tore at her own skirt, thinking to make a bandage for Ikarios' wounds, and then she saw him: a man in a grey cloak, sitting next to the woodpile in the corner.

'Go away,' she shouted at him. 'Don't take my brother, I beseech you! Please, kind Hades, let him live.'

The God made no answer but stood up and walked over to where Ikarios was lying with the his own dark blood forming a shadow all around him. Klymene wept as she saw Hades drape his grey cloak over her brother's face.

'No, oh, please no,' she wailed. 'I won't let you . . . oh, Ikarios, my brother. Don't leave me.'

His eyes were closed now. Klymene saw the God bend down and put out a bony hand to touch Ikarios and take his hand.

Argos dreams

blue everywhere and nothing to smell but sand and water and old seaweed and bones and something blood and tears and where is she going remember a voice his voice saying Argos here good dog Argos come here and no more noise only his voice her tears her voice his tears

TELEMACHUS PLANS A FEAST

Klymene ran. She had no clear idea of where she was going, but she knew she had to go, to escape from the palace and everyone in it. She'd been walking with everyone else from the cemetery to the palace after Ikarios' funeral, when something like a cloud came into her head and she thought: how can I live now? What will I do? How can I bear it?

Mydon, she thought. Oh, Mydon, where are you? If I could find him, she thought, he'd comfort me. I must find him, wherever he is. She knew that there was no real consolation in the palace. From the time she'd run back to tell Nana the black news, there'd been nothing but weeping and sobbing and cries of vengeance, although no one knew who had murdered Ikarios. The queen promised justice, but how could she find out which of the swine, which of the suitors, it had been? Klymene was sure it was one of them. The Rat or the Bear, most likely, but she couldn't think about that now, nor begin to work out how to prove what she suspected. There was no room left in her for anything but grief and a longing to get away.

She wanted not to have to see Nana's face drained of life. Not to have to listen to her sobbing and her sighs. She wondered what was left in the world of mortals that could make her happy to go on living without her brother. She was filled with anguish when she remembered how often he had irritated her: his silence, his pessimism. It hurt her to recall how often she'd envied him his work with Ikmalios, and the freedom that was his and which he didn't seem to need. I'll find him in Hades, she told herself. He'll wait for me there.

She ran away when the others weren't looking, just as they left the cemetery. When Antikleia was buried, long ago, Penelope had nearly flung herself into the grave, and while the rites were being performed, Klymene was on the point of doing so. There was a moment when all she wanted was for the earth to be piled up high over her living body, but then she'd caught sight of Hades standing under a tree, and he shook his head at her and held out a hand as if to stop her. She felt a chill go through her body and turned away. The God wasn't ready for her. She was condemned to staying alive.

Tears blinded her as she ran, but she didn't stop to wipe them away. Her mind was empty, scrubbed clean of everything. Her grandmother, and Lady Penelope, and even Argos would look for her and not find her and she didn't care. Ikarios is dead, she told herself. You should be there to comfort Nana. You can't run away. The queen depends on you. Argos will pine – oh, my poor darling dog! The shroud, the work

323

that needs to be constantly undone. Go back. Try to discover who killed Ikarios. Klymene shut her ears to the voices clamouring in her head, and opened her mouth to wail at the night like a deer that has been struck by an arrow to the heart. Mydon, she said. I must find you. You are the only one who can help me.

She ran through the trees, pushing aside branches that overhung the path and scratched at her arms. I'm in the olive grove, she thought, and there's nothing except twisted tree trunks between here and the upper slopes of the mountain. There was space between one tree and another, but very little, and her arms brushed against rough bark as she ran. When she and Ikarios were young, they used to stay out of the olive grove at night. Nana told them that the dryads would tear a person to pieces if they damaged the precious wood, and Ikarios said: *We wouldn't. We'd never hurt a dryad.* Ikarios, where are you now on your journey down to the River of Oblivion?

Klymene stumbled and fell. She leaned against a tree and saw that her sandals had fallen off. When had that happened? She couldn't remember, but now her feet were bruised and bleeding. How strange pain is, she thought. My heart is so full of sorrow that I can barely feel anything else. My whole body is numb. She glanced down at her clothes. Her dress and scarf were torn and muddy and the hem of her skirt, she knew, was dark with her brother's blood. Oh, Ikarios, Ikarios, she thought. How could you leave me and go down to Hades without me?

It would have been easy to lie there under the

olive branches and never move, but she went on, deeper into the grove. The darkness covered her now. The night birds cried but she heard nothing. On and on she went, not thinking, not feeling, until at last the Goddess of Dawn started to climb slowly over the mountain in her pale rose-coloured garments.

I'll rest for a while, Klymene thought, and sat down on the ground. I'll get up soon and go on. I wish I could lie here for ever. I wish I could die here in the wilderness and let the beasts devour me. I've lost my brother, and no one has come after me, and I've been running all night. Where am I going? To find Mydon. She closed her eyes and stretched out with the ancient trees all around her. Soon she was dreaming.

It seemed to her that she was lying in the middle of a circle, and that there were creatures dancing round her, and she trembled because in her dream she recognized the dryads Nana spoke of: the tree spirits who must always be appeased. They were almost transparent: brown and thin and wavering, as though she were looking at them through moving water. Strands of green hair streamed over their shoulders, and their voices made a sound like dry leaves moving in the wind:

'Dryad sisters, come!'

'We are here.'

'We are coming.'

'We will watch over this child till she is taken into the care of someone who will tend her.'

'We will guard her.'

'We will keep all harm from her.'

Klymene knew nothing more as the dreams left her and she sank into a black and silent sleep.

Penelope lay on her bed with her eyes closed. She wanted to weep. When Telemachus came to see her, they would talk of Ikarios' murder. Ikmalios said there was nothing missing from the workshop, but what reason would anyone have to kill such a quiet young man? Surely, surely robbery must have been the motive, Penelope thought. Ikarios. The twin of her beloved Klymene was dead and buried and Klymene herself was nowhere to be found. Penelope had given orders for a search of the beach and the caverns along the shore, but there was no sign of her. Tomorrow she would ask Leodes to lead a party of men to see whether she'd taken it into her head to run away to Laertes' small farmhouse beyond the mountain. That was the only place Penelope could imagine she might be making for. Tears fell from her eyes, and she wiped them away with a corner of her scarf. How can I be happy when Klymene is grieving? She's like a daughter to me. And how will we manage without Nana?

The old housekeeper had wailed and torn her clothes and fallen on the ground when the news came to her of her grandchild's death, and since the funeral she'd been like a ghost, creeping round the palace with a face contorted with pain. Truly, it was hard sometimes to understand the Gods. There was no end to sorrow.

*

Penelope looked at her son. He was standing with his back to her and looking out of the window. She could see from the way his head was bent forward, from the way his shoulders were hunched over, that he was sad, and not allowing himself to weep. He was the one who had spoken at the funeral; who had led the mourning for his childhood friend. Now he went to sit on the edge of the bed and pushed both hands through his hair. 'I don't know who killed him, Mother, but when we find out, I want to be the one who avenges him. It's one of those bastards, I know it is, but how do I prove it? And why would anyone want to kill Ikarios of all people? But I've got something important to say. I came here to visit you, it's true, but I've also come to tell you of my decision about them.' He waved his hand in the general direction of the courtyard. Penelope knew who he meant: the suitors. She felt herself grow cold. Had he found out about Leodes somehow? Could Klymene have said something before she ran away? Telemachus went on, 'I lied to you about my fishing trip. I wasn't fishing. I went to visit every ruler I could think of, to ask them about my father. No one had any news of him. No one thinks he's alive. I've given up, Mother. I'm not going to delude myself any more and I think you should open your eyes too. Just acknowledge that you won't see your husband again in this life.'

Penelope nodded but said nothing. What could have happened to Telemachus on his travels that had so changed him? He'd been even more determined than she was that Odysseus was still alive, and now this. She said, 'Perhaps you're right, Telemachus.'

'I *am* right, Mother. And I think the time has come for you to choose.'

'Choose?'

'One of that rabble out there. To be your husband. Then all the others'll go away. There'll be nothing to stay for. You should announce it at a feast, I think.'

Penelope turned to her loom. Don't speak at once, she told herself. Don't, above all, say a word about Leodes. She knew that she could stop this feast talk if she chose. She could admit to her son that she'd decided on Leodes, but if she did that, then it would be obvious to him that she had fixed her affections on him long ago, and then, perhaps, the jealousy that she'd noticed between the two of them would lead to something dreadful. To fighting. Even to killing. Men lost control so easily. I must think, she told herself. I must think what's the best thing to do, and if I agree to a feast, that doesn't necessarily mean I have to announce my decision straight away. Her son was still talking.

Some time later, after Telemachus had told her of his plan, Penelope sighed. 'I'll speak to Nana and arrange for everything. I wish Klymene would come home. And I'll do as you say and not mention what you've told me to anyone.'

Telemachus said, 'I'm going now, Mother. I've got things to do.'

He stood up and went to where Penelope was sitting. 'Don't cry, Mother. All will be well. You must believe that Pallas Athene will be looking after us both.'

Penelope nodded. 'I didn't realize I was crying. I'm sorry. And you're quite right. We're all in the hands of the Gods.'

Telemachus left her, in his usual whirlwind style, slamming the door of the chamber behind him. Penelope went to the bed and lay down on it and stared up at the ceiling. This bed: it had tied her to the room, to the island, to the memory of a husband whose face was growing dimmer and dimmer in her memory. The carved wood behind her, the heavy, embroidered coverlet, the soft pillows: it must be possible to sleep in another place that didn't wrap her round in dreams. Sometimes when she lay here, she imagined the olive tree still growing. She could almost feel roots and branches sprouting from the bed linen to tie her to the mattress. Leodes must have a bed of his own, she thought. A fine bed. A completely different bed. I could share it. I've decided. Whatever happens at the feast, I can still choose Leodes. Telemachus would have to accept it, wouldn't he? And if the suitors all leave, and he's still unhappy, we don't have to stay here. I could sail away with Leodes. Sail away from Ithaka.

The idea of leaving her home, this chamber, filled Penelope with a kind of despair. Would she be content to live with Leodes in his own smaller, much less prosperous domain? I can't think about that now. Telemachus has ordered a feast, she told herself, so I must put everything aside and help poor Nana to arrange it. I must find Leodes and tell him what is happening. Where can we meet, when the household is in chaos? We'll all be preparing for the banquet just after celebrating poor Ikarios' funeral rites. I must go and see Nana. Oh, Klymene, where are you? What's become of you?

Penelope went to the loom on which no pictures had appeared for some time. She closed her eyes, testing to see if any colours had returned to her mind, and there was nothing. The inside of my head is entirely white, she thought. She trembled to think of what this might mean.

TWO REUNIONS

Odysseus was walking slowly along the rough path over the mountain, using the stick that went with his beggar's disguise. Mydon walked along at his side.

'Your adventures,' he said. 'What you were speaking of last night – everything that happened to you on the way to Ithaka – I dreamed about those stories all night long.'

'What we're about to do now will be more dangerous than anything that's happened to me till this moment,' Odysseus said. 'But I have the energy for it, I promise you. Pallas Athene has made this disguise so thorough that I can't move as quickly as I'd like to. But I'm like a young man under all these rags. As for seeing my wife and palace again, well, there are no words to tell you what I feel. Just being here, on the island, has made me young again. I'd forgotten things: the smell of the earth; the way the clouds lie over the mountain. And as for my son . . . I cannot express what I feel when I see Telemachus is such a fine young man. And the pigs . . . who'd have thought pigs could make you cry, eh? But seeing them, seeing Eumaeus still tending them after so long, well, anyone would become womanish, don't you think?'

Mydon nodded without speaking. 'I wish my mother was still alive so that she could know that I'd found you.'

'Sorrow,' said Odysseus, 'has to be borne, or we might as well die on our way out of our mothers' wombs. Life is threaded through with it, but you must face it, and grieve and carry on, if you're to be a real man. It's easier to do that when you've got your family around you. When you're in your own house. Home . . . that's the best that we can hope for this side of Hades, and it's worth fighting and even dying for. Ithaka is worth every bit of agony I've gone through to get here.'

Mydon nodded. The undergrowth was thick on either side of a narrow path. Soon they'd be in the olive grove with the twisted trunks of the trees all around. He said nothing but feared that Odysseus might have underestimated the power of the suitors. There must be more than a hundred men down there. Could Odysseus trick his way past them all, and come out alive?

'Maybe you ought to announce yourself,' Mydon said. 'Perhaps the suitors will be so happy to see you alive and well again that they'll all go home quietly. After all, most of them claim they were friends of yours in the old days.' As soon as the words were out of his mouth, he knew the idea was ridiculous.

Odysseus laughed. 'Oh, no, they'd kill me at once. They've invested so much time waiting for Penelope.

Or my lands. Or both lands and woman together. It would be admitting they'd been wrong from the very beginning to give up now. No, they'll stay, never fear, but I'll have the element of surprise on my side. And the help of the Goddess, of course. Never underestimate her powers.'

'I don't,' Mydon said. 'You've told us that you owe her your life.'

They made their way through the grove in silence. Then Mydon whispered, 'Odysseus! Look – there's a scarf caught on this branch . . . and here . . .' His words faded away as he sank to the ground. There, lying face down in the gap between two enormous trees, was the body of a young woman. Her dress was torn and the soles of her feet, which stuck out into the path, were covered with deep scratches that had bled and dried into dark scabs.

'Turn her over, Mydon,' said Odysseus, taking control at once and sounding as though finding young women under olive trees was not in the least unexpected. 'She's probably had a fight with her parents and run away into the grove. I can remember doing that as a child. Be gentle.'

Mydon knelt down and leaned over to pull the girl's body on to her back. Even before he saw her face, he knew who it was.

'Klymene! It's Klymene. Why is she here? Klymene, speak to me.'

'You know her?'

Mydon nodded.

Odysseus said, 'Right. You don't have to say another

word. It's written in your eyes. I'll go over there and eat some of the bread that Eumaeus prepared for us. I'll save your portion, and you can eat it later. But keep the water bottle. Your Klymene will need that more than anything.'

'Thanks . . .' said Mydon weakly, wondering how it was that Odysseus knew so much. He'd walked away very quickly and was now sitting in the shadow of one of the most distant trees. He's out of earshot, Mydon thought. That's the important thing. I can say whatever I want. His heart was beating.

'Speak to her, Mydon. I am the Goddess Aphrodite. Listen to me. Tell her you love her. Those are the words that will revive her.'

Mydon looked up to see a beautiful woman dressed in veils of mauve and pink and surrounded by the fragrance of roses and almond blossom. As he stared at her, astonished, she drifted into the trees and was gone. He bent down and spoke to Klymene.

'Klymene? Klymene, wake up. It's me, Mydon. Please, Klymene, wake up.' He looked around and added quickly, 'I love you, Klymene. Can you hear me? Speak to me, please. Wake up. It's me—'

Her eyes opened so suddenly that Mydon, kneeling beside her, almost lost his balance. She was staring at him but her gaze was horror-struck, as though she were looking into the face of a monster.

'Oh, Mydon, I've found you!' she said, in a hoarse whisper. 'I've been running and running to find you. I can't bear to tell you. I can't bear to think of what's happened. Oh, hold me, keep me safe. My heart is in pieces.'

Mydon didn't hesitate. He pulled Klymene to a sitting position and put one arm around her. With his other hand he smoothed the strands of hair that had fallen over her forehead.

'Don't be sad. I'll hold you. For ever, if I have to. Did you hear what I said? Did you hear me say that I love you?'

'I thought it was part of my dream. Is it true? Oh, Mydon, how did you find me? I could have died, lying here.'

She began to weep and sob, and turned to bury her face in Mydon's shoulder.

'He's dead. My brother's dead. No one knows who killed him. No one knows why. Oh, Mydon, I can't bear it. What shall I do? How will I avenge him?'

'I will help you to find out who killed Ikarios, never fear. And there are so many things I have to tell you. Come Klymene, I'll carry you. Your feet are bleeding.'

For the first time since she'd opened her eyes, Klymene smiled. Her mouth was very near his own.

'Kiss her,' said the Goddess's voice in his ear and Mydon looked around but Aphrodite was nowhere to be seen. He bent to kiss Klymene, and honey and sunlight spread through his veins.

Odysseus stood on the rocky path and said nothing. He stared at the palace gates, which were open, and at the crowd of men lounging about outside them. Some of these had the excuse of selling something – fruit, meat or old bread – but most, he knew, were no more than hangers-on with nothing better to do than sit on the ground and fiddle with their knives or throw stones in elaborate games of their own devising.

'Home,' he whispered so quietly that Mydon and Klymene barely heard him. 'In all my imaginings, I didn't see this. This isn't what I dreamed of.' He sighed. 'Doesn't matter. All will be well in time.'

Klymene had managed to walk some of the way, with her feet bound up in rags taken from the bundle Odysseus carried on his back. He was now transformed into a beggar again. She was still stunned and delighted that Odysseus had come home at last. Klymene had been grateful to be carried for most of the distance by both Mydon and Odysseus, but her heart leaped when it was Mydon's turn. This was not only because being near him made her feel safe and happy. Pallas Athene had seen to it that Odysseus stank like the old beggar he was supposed to be.

'Something's strange,' Mydon said. 'What's happened to the light?'

It was a little past midday, but suddenly the air was darker: amber-coloured and thick all around them. The people at the palace gates had become statues. Nothing moved. There was not a breath of wind. A silence fell on everything so that the barking of a dog sounded loudly in their ears.

'It's Argos!' Klymene said, and burst into tears. She had scarcely thought of the old dog since Ikarios' death – how cruel and unkind that was! Poor old Argos, who loved her and who didn't know about Ikarios.

How was it now that they could hear him barking when he must be far away in the armoury?

'Argos?' Odysseus looked puzzled. 'I had a dog called Argos, oh, long years ago when I was young. I've thought of him so often. How kind of Penelope to call a new dog by that name! It brings tears to my eyes.'

Klymene was about to speak when they all saw him. The dog they knew, the dog who could hardly walk, whose coat was patchy with age and mange, who dribbled and drooled and lay all day on a heap of dried skins, had vanished, and in his place, a healthy animal with a gleaming coat and bright eyes was bounding out of the palace gate, barking and barking, his tail wagging with joy. He came straight to the beggar and jumped up and put both front paws on Odysseus' shoulders.

'My Argos! It's you, really you . . . just as you were when I left you. How can this be? Argos, stop licking my face and let me see you. Let me stroke you. Impossible. It's impossible and yet here he is . . . Klymene, this is Argos. My beloved dog – oh Argos, Argos!'

Argos put his paws to the ground and rolled over with his legs waving in the air.

'Look!' Klymene said, and pointed. Standing behind Odysseus was the figure of Artemis.

'Yes, listen to Klymene, Odysseus,' said the Goddess, and Odysseus stopped rubbing Argos' stomach and stood up.

'Queen of the Hunt, honoured Artemis,' he

breathed and bowed his head. 'This is your doing, is it not?'

'Of course,' she said. 'Argos is near death. I have kept him alive long, long after his time so that he might have one glimpse of you; a short spell of perfect happiness; his reward for the love he has shown you through the years. He has waited for you. Any creature who loves so much and is so loyal deserves a fond goodbye from his master. Say goodbye to him, Odysseus. Say it now.'

'No, Goddess, I implore you. A little while longer. I've hardly had a chance—'

'Speak the words, Odysseus,' said Artemis. 'Hades is waiting for him . . . look over there. He will take him to another life. You will join him in the dark kingdom when your own days come to their end.'

Klymene recognized him: the same grey man who had been there when her brother died. She shivered and closed her eyes. Better not to look too closely. Odysseus didn't even glance in Hades' direction. Instead he buried his face in Argos' neck. 'Goodbye, old friend. Go easily with Hades.' There were more words he would have spoken, but for the tears that choked him.

'Argos,' said Klymene, throwing her arms around the dog's neck. 'Lovely, lovely Argos. It'll be better for you to go. And you'll see Ikarios. There, in Hades' kingdom.'

She started to sob. Mydon drew her close to him and she buried her face in his shoulder. Then the Goddess lifted her arms high. The sunshine dimmed to a yellowish glow and not a breath of wind stirred the air. Silver tears ran down the Goddess's cheeks and her dress of radiant white shimmered in the light. Argos lay with his head on his front paws, as though he were stretched before the fire. His eyes were closed. Artemis took an arrow from her silver quiver and shot it up into the sky, where it hung like a silver feather for a while and then vanished. Odysseus bent down and picked Argos up and held him in his arms.

'It's not the same dog,' he whispered. 'This is such an old, old dog . . .'

'That's Argos,' Klymene said. 'That's what he's like now.' Her voice was thick with tears.

'Half dead, mangy, and so thin that I feel as though I'm holding nothing but a bundle of old bones . . . oh, Argos!'

'Give him to the boy, Odysseus,' said Artemis. 'Let Mydon take Argos. You are nobody, nothing but a beggar. Remember that.'

Odysseus passed the lifeless body to Mydon, who took it and started to carry it away from the palace gates. Klymene was crying so hard she could scarcely see to walk. Argos would be buried with every honour, she knew, when everything was more settled in the palace, but how she would miss him! How sad life would be without him!

'I thank you, Artemis,' said Odysseus, as he watched Mydon disappearing, 'for allowing Argos to be happy.'

'Much awaits you now, Odysseus,' Artemis said. 'But Pallas Athene will be at your side. Remember that.'

'I know it,' said Odysseus.

Artemis raised a hand in greeting and then she was gone, running lightly over the ground and disappearing into mist that had gathered around her. The air was bright again, and the sun shone. The crowds near the gate had returned to life. Heat, noise and the smell of too many people reached Odysseus on the breeze that had started to blow once more.

A SHOCK FOR NANA

Nana had fallen into a decline since the death of her grandson. She sat at the table in the kitchen, her head covered with a black cloth, weeping silent tears that she sometimes forgot to wipe away. First Ikarios had been brutally murdered, and now Klymene was missing. How could she leave her own grandmother and run away? She went through the work she had to do like a statue who had been given some movement, and not like a human being at all.

She peered out of the window. Two men – rapscallions and no-good beggars by the look of them, so ragged and filthy that she could almost smell them from where she was – were shouting at one another. In a moment it would come to blows, but she wasn't really paying them any attention. She was gazing at someone else: a young woman with dark hair, looking anxiously at the goings-on. Could it be? O Gods, Nana thought. It is. That's my Klymene. O Gods be praised and thanked! It is. It's my beloved Klymene. And Mydon too. She rushed out of the kitchen and stumbled down the path, shouting.

'Klymene! Klymene, it's me! Your grandmother. Oh, Klymene, come and kiss me. I thought you were dead. Gone down to Hades to be with your poor brother. Come, Klymene. It's me.'

'Nana!' Klymene ran to meet the old woman. As they clung together, the words tumbled out of her mouth: 'I would never have left you, Nana, only I had to find Mydon. I couldn't stay here. I couldn't bear to think of Ikarios put into the earth. But Nana, I'm so happy to see you. Why aren't you with the queen? Who's looking after everything at the palace?'

'I haven't been myself, as you may imagine. Others have done everything. Who's that beggar man? I've never seen him before.'

'I promised to take him into the palace. That hideous Irus, who hangs round the gates asking for alms, has already had a go at him. Imagine: he said that particular bit of earth was his pitch and no one else was allowed to sit and beg there. Impudence!'

Nana wasn't interested in beggars and their doings. She said, 'Promised? Who did you give this promise to?'

'It doesn't matter. He's a good man and deserves to be treated well.'

Nana frowned at the beggar, who smiled at her and bowed from the waist.

'I'm honoured to make your acquaintance,' he said, and Nana, taken by surprise, said, 'Thank you, I'm sure. Now come along out of the sun, both of you. I'll give you some water and there are figs and grapes in plenty.'

They made their way back into the kitchen.

'Come and sit down here,' Nana said, her arm around Klymene's shoulders. 'Eat. Drink.'

She pointed at the table. 'You must be very thirsty.' She peered at Odysseus and sniffed. 'I dare say you must be thirsty too, old man, but I can't let you sit down at my table in that state.' She pushed the sleeves of her dress up and said, 'Follow me.'

Odysseus followed her out of the back door of the kitchen.

'Sit there,' said Nana, and she pointed to the wooden bench pushed up against the wall. 'Don't move. I'm coming back.'

She returned almost immediately, carrying a large jug of water and a length of cloth.

'Feet first, I think,' she said. 'They smell dreadful. Take your sandals off.'

'I can't,' said Odysseus, pretending to be even weaker than the Goddess had made him. 'All my strength is gone.'

Nana sighed. 'Nothing for it, then. I'll have to do it. I'm not having that stink in my kitchen.'

She knelt down and removed Odysseus' sandals. Then she dipped the cloth into the water and wrung it out.

'I don't know why you couldn't have found a stream or something,' she muttered, as she began to scrub at his shins and feet with the wet cloth. 'It can't be the most difficult thing in the world to keep your feet clean. These smell as though they've been resting in a pigsty.'

343

'Which they have, in a way,' Odysseus chuckled. 'Eumaeus, the old swineherd, put me in with his livestock, and very grateful I was too.'

'Hmm,' Nana said, and dipped the cloth into the jug. 'You remind me of someone I haven't seen for many, many years, old man. Something in the way you speak brings back my beloved Odysseus.'

She wrung the cloth out again. The water was now dark with mud, but she hadn't finished. She began to scrub the beggar's leg all over again. Then her face turned white and she dropped the cloth and covered her mouth with her hand. Her eyes widened, and she stared up into Odysseus' face.

'This scar' – she pointed at a scar shaped like the blade of long knife, which ran down the inner part of the leg she had just washed – 'I have seen this scar before. Odysseus had just such a one. He got it when he was a very young man, during a boar hunt. I had to bind the wound myself.' Her voice dropped to a whisper and she said, 'Is it really you, lord? Is it Odysseus?'

'Ssh, Nana. It's me. Of course it is! You've found me out. Well, I'm not surprised. I never could keep a secret from you, could I? Your eyes were everywhere. Even the Goddess Pallas Athene, who's disguised me as a beggar, can't fool you. But you mustn't say a word, dear nurse. Promise me. Not even to Penelope. I need to keep this form for a little while longer.'

Nana began to tremble and mutter. 'Odysseus . . . my baby. Returned to us after all these years . . . oh, I can't believe it. I can't really believe it – how wonderful.

The Gods were protecting you. I never thought to see you in this life, my baby boy – how wonderful!'

She was flushed now and her hands shook. She covered her face and drew a few shuddering breaths to steady herself.

'I'm sorry. I'll stop babbling now. It's a shock, a very great shock, but I'm getting used to it. And you can trust me, Odysseus, you know you can. I won't say a single word to anyone. May I be struck down by Zeus' lightning bolt if your name crosses my lips.'

'It won't be long now. You'll be able to speak my name all day long soon enough. I have a plan.'

'Of course you do! You always had plans, some more mischievous than others. You're going to throw that riff-raff out of your palace, am I right?'

'Something like that, Nana, but we should go back now. The others'll be wondering what's become of us. And remember: complete silence, I beg of you. Do not, I implore you, tell anyone at all that you know who I am. Especially not my wife. Will you promise?'

'You can trust me. I won't say anything to anyone. I'm known for my quietness. Now, throw the water from this jug over your feet and wipe them on the step to dry them a little before you go in. You couldn't call them the most fragrant feet in Ithaka, but they're better than they were.'

Odysseus smiled at the woman who had nursed him in his infancy and crossed the threshold into the kitchen of his palace.

*

'I've seen everything now,' said Amphimedon, moving away from the beggar who had just come into the great hall of Odysseus' palace. 'This cur walks in here as though he had a right. What's happened to the guard, eh? All drunk and asleep, I suppose.' He turned to Antinous, who was standing beside him, and said, 'If you want something done properly, you've got to do it yourself. And I want this verminous piece of shit out of here. Now.'

He was standing close to Odysseus in his beggar shape.

'Are you going or d'you have to be thrown?' he said, pushing his fleshy face almost into the old man's.

The beggar smiled through a tangle of filthy beard. 'You may try to throw me if it pleases you, sir, for certainly I shan't go alone. The man who was once master here would give shelter to anyone who came to his door. I knew him. I fought beside him at Troy.'

Penelope stepped out suddenly from between two columns. At once Amphimedon and the beggar both withdrew a little and the suitor bowed from the waist.

'What's going on here, Amphimedon?' she said. 'Who is this poor creature and why are you tormenting him?'

'A beggarly scoundrel, lady, and a smelly one at that. Just walked in here as though the place belonged to him. I was teaching him a lesson, and I feel it's my duty to send him packing.'

Penelope took no notice of these words. She approached the beggar and took him by the hand.

346

'Forgive this man, who is nothing to do with me, or with the palace, but merely a visitor,' she said. 'I heard you speaking a moment ago. I heard you say that you'd fought beside my husband Odysseus at Troy. Is that true?'

'True, gentle Queen. I knew him well and he spoke of you often. He told me of your beauty, but surely the Gods have had you in their care for you are still, if I am allowed to say so, young and very lovely.'

'You are kind,' she answered, smiling, 'but as you're so old you cannot see perhaps as well as you used to. I'm not what I once was, believe me. And you are most welcome in my house. Come, sit down here beside me and tell me everything you remember about Odysseus. Every single thing. I have longed to hear word of him for years and years.'

The queen went to sit on her usual chair beside the throne where Odysseus once sat, and the beggar man lowered himself to the ground at her feet and began to tell his story.

Penelope listened to the beggar, who told her the stories she had been longing for.

'I knew Odysseus was a hero,' she told him with tears standing in her eyes, 'but to hear you speak of him – it's as though I were close to him once again. And I believe . . . well, most of the time I believe, that he will return to me. That he is still alive.'

The beggar sat on the stool at Penelope's feet and looked at her searchingly. 'There is much that is troubling you. You can talk to me about it if you will. I would not speak of what you told me.'

'It's a dream I've been having lately, that's all. For many years I had no dreams except about my husband. I saw pictures in my head . . . well, that's gone now and for the last few nights I've had the same dream.'

'Tell me.'

'It's always the same,' Penelope said. 'I'm out in the courtyard, feeding a flock of grey geese. Suddenly a golden eagle appears and swoops down to the trough where they're all drinking.'

'Then what happens?' the beggar asked.

'The eagle speaks to me. I can't hear what he's saying. What can it mean?'

The old man smiled at her. 'The eagle,' he said, 'is your husband, Odysseus. He comes back and drives the geese – that's the suitors – from the palace.'

'But I haven't kept geese for a long time,' she said. 'There was a flock I used to tend as a girl in my father's house.'

'The ways of sleep are strange,' the beggar said. 'Mortals do not understand them. But the eagle is your husband and your suitors will flee when they see him. That is what I think your dream means.'

'And you knew him. D'you think Odysseus could still be alive? After all this time?'

'No one has told me of his death.'

'I am eager to believe you, old man. I don't know why.' Penelope looked at the beggar and wondered whether perhaps he might be a God come down from

Olympus to guide her. The Gods sometimes did that – visited mortal women for purposes of their own – and the shapes they took to do so were often very strange.

A LIE TOLD OUT OF KINDNESS

Telemachus went to find Melantho to discover more about his friend's death. Melantho always knew everything that went on everywhere, and she'd told him that Ikarios had picked a fight with someone. The quarrel had got out of control, she'd said, but he could hardly believe it. Ikarios was so mild and gentle: who on earth would pick a fight with him and about what?

'I'm pleased to see you, Telemachus,' Melantho said. She was in the great hall, preparing the table for the evening meal.

'Come with me to the orchard,' Telemachus said. 'I don't want to speak here.'

He left the hall and Melantho followed him, out of the palace and through the gates to the orchard. Neither of them spoke till they were sitting under one of the pear trees.

'How did it happen?' Telemachus asked Melantho. The sun had dipped behind the crest of the mountain and the air was cooler than it had been all day. 'Ikarios dead . . . it's hard to believe. Who'd pick a fight with him?'

Melantho turned her smile on him, and she could see that even now it had the power to move him. He was sad and angry, certainly, but he was softening under her gaze, she knew it. If she could speak to him for a little while longer, he would be hers. She realized that the gift she had of making men weak with desire in her presence was just that: a gift. It probably came to her from Aphrodite, and it was something that a lot of other women seemed to lack. Melantho was grateful for it. She edged closer to Telemachus and let her blouse fall open a little so that he could see the curve of her breast as she spoke. To make sure of this, she also stretched one arm above her head in a false yawn. Yes, yes, there he was. Just like a fish, taking a hook into his mouth. Only a few more sentences now and he'd be hers. She smiled.

'If I tell you, you must swear not to say a word. I'm as good as dead if anyone finds out I've spoken about what happened. Do you promise, Telemachus?'

Telemachus nodded. Melantho went on, 'I just happened to be there, in the workshop. It's not a place I'd visit normally, only Ikarios had given me such a pretty little carved cat that I had to thank him. Antinous came in while I was there, that's all. That's why I saw what I did see. Ikarios attacked him. It was quite unprovoked. No one's asked me, but this is what I think. Ikarios was angry that our meeting was interrupted. He was very jealous of Antinous, because I'm a friend of his – of Antinous', I mean. And you know how jealousy can make men mad, don't you?'

Telemachus turned away from her suddenly and

leaned forward, hiding his head in his hands. 'Poor Ikarios! He and I and Klymene have been friends from the cradle. We hadn't been seeing much of one another lately because my whole head has been filled with the need to get rid of those animals.' He waved a hand in the direction of the palace. 'You know who I mean. The bastards who're after my mother and our kingdom. I'm going to see to it that his death is avenged. I swear it.'

How dare he? Melantho thought, feeling the heat of rage, feeling her skin grow red from the fury that filled her. How could he? Here she was, putting herself in danger by telling him who killed Ikarios and laying herself out for him. She was practically begging him to turn and take her in his arms and do whatever he wanted, and she would have melted in his embrace; but no, his stupid head was filled with the usual male rubbish about revenge and fighting and death, and she might have been a hideous crone for all the attention he was paying her. I'll show him, she thought. I'll do it. I'll break every part of his life into pieces with my words. Listen to this, Telemachus. She made sure that her voice was soft and sweet as she spoke, 'They're not all bastards. You may think they are, but that's not an opinion shared by your mother.'

Silence. Melantho waited for the stone she had thrown to fall to the bottom of the well of Telemachus' mind. After a few moments he turned to face her. He was frowning.

'What do you mean, Melantho?'

Splash, Melantho thought, and composed her face

to answer. It was difficult not to smile. 'She and Leodes are very close. Everyone knows that. It's common gossip.'

'How close?' Telemachus' eyes had narrowed, and he was pale. He'd pressed his mouth into a thin line. Melantho brought her hands together, interlaced the fingers and twisted them a little.

'Close close,' she whispered. 'Extremely close close.'

Without saying another word, Telemachus stood up and began walking towards the palace. Melantho fell back on to the grass. He'll kill them, she thought. He'll never let her get away with screwing someone who isn't his father. Serve him right. Serve them all right. If it comes to a fight between Antinous and Telemachus, Telemachus hasn't got a chance. What do I care? She closed her eyes and let her thoughts turn to Antinous, who could be relied upon to respond in the ways that she intended.

Penelope thought, I am unravelling. Just like the shroud I've been making for so long, every night I feel as though parts of me are being pulled away, undone. Soon there will be nothing left, and I'll be glad to be done with a life that's become harder and harder.

She had been neglecting the shroud. That hideous item lay folded in the chest, and she hadn't had the heart to work on it by herself. She'd put it away when Klymene disappeared, and soon someone would notice that she wasn't sitting under the pomegranate tree every afternoon working on it. If they discovered she was shirking, what would become of her?

Her hunger for Leodes was like a strand of scarlet wool. I should pull at it and throw it away, she said to herself. It colours everything it touches. Pale yellow, that's pain, and there's mauve for devotion to duty, and this white, why that's the hope I still have that I may see my husband again. She smiled. What kind of nonsense was going through her head now? None of this would be happening, if only Klymene were here. She yearned for the girl as though she were a true daughter. Telemachus is my son, she thought, and it was wonderful to welcome him home again, safe and sound, but o Gods, protect my Klymene and bring her back to me. Do not let me weep over her grave as I have wept over her brother's.

Her thoughts were interrupted by a gentle knocking. Klymene used to do that: rap three times with her fingers. Could it be? Was it possible? Penelope ran to the door and opened it.

'Klymene! Oh, my child, it's you! It's really you and you're alive and well and smiling. Come and kiss me, dear girl. How happy I am! You can't imagine how I've longed to see you. I've missed you so much. At times I've thought you must have followed your brother down to Hades, for I believed you'd never leave me. Such sorrow! I couldn't have borne such sorrow.'

'Lady,' Klymene said, clinging to the queen's neck, as tears came into her eyes. 'I wouldn't have left you, only a kind of madness of grief took hold of me and I had to find Mydon. I knew that you'd worry, but I couldn't help myself. Something drove me to run and run. He found me – Mydon. I'd have been devoured by wild beasts if he hadn't stumbled over my body. And have you heard that Argos is dead? Poor old dog. He died . . . Well, he's been near death for a long time and now he's at peace. Mydon took him to a quiet spot, where no one will find him till we're ready to bury him.'

'Poor Argos! He hasn't had much of a life lately, has he? Odysseus would wish him to be buried with all honour and I will see to it. But come and sit down, Klymene. Have you seen your grandmother? She'll be even happier than I am, if such a thing were possible. And now that you're back, I can start on that hideous shroud again. I've not touched it since Ikarios died.'

Klymene looked at Penelope with horror in her eyes. 'What if they find out? They'll kill you, lady.'

'Do you know, Klymene, I've been thinking that I wouldn't care if they did or not, but suddenly, now that you're back there's a reason to live again. And Telemachus has ordered up a feast for tomorrow. You can help me prepare myself for that.'

Penelope went to the door of the chamber and looked out at the corridor. 'I'm making certain that no one can overhear us. You know, don't you, Klymene, some of the secrets of my heart?'

'Yes, lady, but I've told no one.'

'I know you haven't, child. But I'll whisper this to you and don't tell a soul. Tomorrow at the feast, I'm going to say something. Telemachus has decided that I must choose one of the men, simply to make the others leave, and I've chosen Leodes. He has begged me to run away with him. His ship is waiting, but I can't leave Telemachus here to deal with the rest of them. We will wait till they have all left Ithaka, and then, maybe, we can sail away and leave Telemachus to rule in his father's place.'

Klymene said only: 'The Gods will see that justice is done. I'm sure of it now.'

'If I left Ithaka, Klymene, I'd miss you. More than anyone else on this island, except for my son.'

Klymene lay on her bed, unable to sleep. While she had been making her way to the palace, while she and Mydon had been together and in the company of Odysseus, it had been easy to banish all thought of Penelope and Leodes from her mind. But now, now that the queen had made her plans, it was clear to Klymene that everything was in turmoil. What would Penelope do if she knew that her husband was already here in Ithaka and ready to take his revenge on the suitors? What would Odysseus say and do when he discovered that his wife, far from being the most faithful and devoted of spouses, was actually in love with another man? And she herself: what ought *she* to do for the best? It was difficult to think. She considered going to find Mydon and talking to him about it, but her promise to Penelope stopped her. She would have to work everything out all by herself.

She got off the bed and tiptoed out of her chamber silently, so as not to wake Melantho. I'll go to the kitchen, she thought, and tears sprang to her eyes as she remembered how, when Ikarios was alive, they would always meet there if sleep was long in coming, or if one of them had been woken by a bad dream. And Argos: he would sometimes wake from a deep sleep to greet her. Telemachus too was often there, talking to them both late into the night.

A lamp was burning in the kitchen. Someone's probably preparing something for the feast, Klymene thought, and went in.

'Telemachus! I was just thinking of you . . .' she said. Telemachus turned to see who it was, and then went back to gazing at the goblet he had in front of him. He didn't say a word.

'Aren't you going to speak, Telemachus? What's the matter with you?'

The only answer was a shrug, and Klymene sighed. She was used to the way men sometimes behaved, but it was exhausting. They wouldn't ever admit, straight out, what was wrong, but waited for the *thing* – whatever it was that was troubling them – to be drawn out slowly like a thorn from an animal's paw. You had to ask questions. They had to be the right questions. You had to guess and cajole and tease the pain out of them, and it could be a tedious business. Klymene sat down opposite Telemachus and took his hand across the table.

'This is how it used to be, isn't it? Like when we were children. D'you remember?' she said. He nodded and muttered something. 'What?' Klymene asked.

'I miss Ikarios,' Telemachus said. 'I'm sorry now that I didn't see more of him when he was alive. I

357

didn't notice him enough. I'm sorry, Klymene. You must miss him much more than I do. It's I who should be comforting you.'

'You should be happy, Telemachus.' She leaned closer across the table and whispered, just in case there was anyone hiding in the shadows. 'You came to the palace before I did, but you should know that I returned to the palace with a beggar man,' she said. 'You know who I mean. I just want to tell you that I'm in his confidence as well.'

Telemachus spun round in his seat to make sure they were unobserved and then turned back to face Klymene. 'You haven't said anything to my mother? She mustn't know that . . . the person we mean is here, under her roof. Not yet.'

'No, I've not said a word.'

Silence fell between them. Klymene thought, surely he ought to be happier? This is what he's been dreaming about, hoping for, ever since he was a boy. Why then is he so sad? Surely it can't be all because of my brother? She said, 'I've known you all my life, Telemachus. It's not just Ikarios, is it?'

'It's Melantho,' he said at last. 'She told me something tonight that . . . Never mind. I don't even want to mention it.'

'Melantho often lies,' Klymene said. 'You should take that into account. She's got her reasons usually, but what she says is untrue a lot of the time. I wouldn't trust her if I were you.'

'No, perhaps you're right. I think she was . . . well, you know. Trying to get me to . . . well, I don't have to spell it out. I showed her I wasn't interested, and then she just lashed out with the first thing she could think of that would hurt me. D'you think that's what's happened?'

'What did she say?'

'I'm not repeating it. It's disgusting. Unthinkable. And you're right. I shouldn't pay any attention to her bleatings. She never *was* trustworthy, so why should she change now? I'm going to bed. I need my strength for tomorrow. Everything will come right, won't it, Klymene?'

'Certainly it will,' Klymene said, surprising herself by how confident she sounded. 'Good dreams to you, Telemachus.'

'And to you, Klymene. Sleep sweetly.'

As she watched him leave the kitchen, Klymene thought, He knows. That little bitch Melantho has told him about his mother and Leodes. O Pallas Athene, see to it that he doesn't tell his father, I implore you. Protect us all from what is to come.

Klymene put her head in her hands and sat without moving in the silent kitchen. After a while she became aware of someone in the room with her. She looked up and there was Pallas Athene, sitting in the place that Telemachus had just left.

'Goddess!' Klymene said, and started to stand up.

'Sit down, child. Let me speak to you of the queen. She is going through torment now, but it will settle itself in the end.'

'I never thought to find you in a kitchen,' Klymene said.

'A table is the one place where men and women can sit together and talk and look into one another's eyes. But I wanted to tell you this: Melantho will be punished for her unkindness to your brother. For her cruelty.'

'But she wasn't the one who murdered him.'

'It was Melantho who lured him to the workshop at night, and it was she who told his murderer that he would be alone there. She prepared him for his death like a farmer preparing a goat for slaughter. You should know this.'

Klymene felt herself turning cold, and then heat ran through her veins and she felt her face grow red. Words came to her mind but her lips opened and shut and she couldn't say them.

'Do not distress yourself, Klymene. I know what you are thinking. You want revenge but I will tell you this: wait. It will come. Melantho will regret spreading her poisons, I promise. Rest now. I have you in my care. Remember that.'

In her anguish, Klymene started to cry. 'Weep, child, and do not hold back your tears, for you have reason to be both sorrowful and angry,' said Pallas Athene, and she stood and gathered her glittering bronze garments about her. Klymene watched the Goddess drift out of the kitchen, then she laid her head on the table, resting it on her folded arms. Evil Melantho – how would she ever speak to her again without wanting to tear her limb from limb? Klymene's eyes closed. Melantho was partly to blame for Ikarios' death. And Melantho was in love with Antinous. Was he the murderer? Why had the Goddess not told her everything? Poor Ikarios, who loved Melantho for so long – how could she? How much wickedness there was in the world! It was a wonder people found even a small amount of happiness in the midst of all the anguish.

THE FEAST

The entire household was upside down. Every piece of furniture in the great hall had been dragged out to the courtyard while the servants scrubbed the floor and prepared new fleeces for the benches and seats. Kitchen maids were polishing the gold and bronze platters that were only used on ceremonial occasions and Nana herself had opened the secret cellar hidden deep under the outer courtyard and she stood watching carefully over the menservants as they brought out several enormous stoneware jugs of the best red wine.

The cooks had been sweating since dawn. Buckets of silver fish stood about in the kitchen, ready to be put into the ovens. Sheep and pigs were turning on spits set up in the gigantic fireplace in the kitchen, and the smell of meats, basted with herbs and oil and roasting slowly, spread through the rooms and reached the nostrils even of those who were occupied out-doors.

'We haven't had a feast like this since Odysseus' and Penelope's wedding day,' said Nana to Klymene, after she had greeted her granddaughter and set her to work as well, polishing the knives to be used at the table. Mydon, who had come into the great hall with Klymene, had been sent to help the men bringing in more benches from the courtyard.

'I'm glad to see you're feeling better,' said Klymene, gazing at a slice of her own face reflected in the blade of the knife. Was it possible to see in such a tiny space how happy she was? Yes, it was. Her eyes were shining and her hair had a lustre to it that she did not remember from the last time she'd looked carefully at it. Mydon. When he found her, he'd set something alight. She could taste him on her mouth, and every part of her still hummed with the memory of his mouth on hers. When would they be together again?

'Klymene, you're not paying attention, child. Did you hear a word of what I've been telling you?'

'What a feast it's going to be . . .' Klymene tried hard to recall what Nana had been saying only a moment ago, but it had almost disappeared.

'No, silly girl. That was before I told you that the queen has asked me to be in charge of her dressing tonight. And she's particularly asked for you. She says she trusts you in the matter of jewellery and orna-ments.'

Klymene smiled. 'I'm honoured, Nana. We'll make sure that Penelope is dressed as beautifully as she was on her wedding day. It's very important that she should look her best.'

Nana said: 'Indeed it is.' She looked searchingly

at Klymene and added, 'D'you know something you're not telling me, child?'

'No, no, Nana. Nothing at all really.' Klymene said, thinking: may I be forgiven for lying to my own grandmother. I wish Odysseus would hurry up and reveal himself to the queen and then I won't have to watch every single word I say. She picked up another knife and began to rub it with a soft cloth. Thinking of the queen and Odysseus worried her. Poor Leodes! What would his feelings be when he saw his old friend come back to Ithaka? Surely his affection and comradeship for Odysseus was not as strong as his love for Penelope, and in that case, Leodes was destined to leave the island and go back to his own home and never see his beloved again. Klymene couldn't help feeling sorry for him, but she worried even more about the queen.

Penelope loves Leodes, she thought. But she also loves Odysseus. Or she *would* love him if she believed he was still alive. What if it came to a choice? What if she has to choose between her husband and Leodes? What then? Perhaps Leodes will be noble and stand aside so that the king of Ithaka may be reunited with his queen. And perhaps not.

'Have you finished, Klymene?' said Nana. 'It's time to go to the queen's bedchamber and dress her for the feast.'

'I'm ready, Nana. I'm coming.'

Klymene put the last of the polished knives on the table and took the old lady's arm to guide her along the corridors.

*

'The white robe with the edges embroidered in purple,' said Penelope.

'Worn with the amethyst pendant and your silver headdress,' Klymene added and Penelope nodded. She was sitting at the loom in her undergarments. She had anointed her body with rose oil and the scent of it was heavy on the air. Her lips were reddened and her cheeks too, but in spite of the coloured salves she wore, Klymene could see that she was very pale. Melantho had already arranged her hair into an intricate arrangement of curls, held together by small silver pins and clasps. The queen seemed preoccupied and sat silently, staring at nothing.

'You will be beautiful, lady,' said Nana. 'Come, put on your robe and I'll let Klymene fasten the silver chain round your neck.'

She took the white robe that was lying on the bed and held it out to Penelope. The queen raised her arms and Nana drew the heavy linen garment carefully over her head so that her hair was not disturbed. Then she turned her attention to the folds of the skirt and made sure that they were draped to the best effect.

'I thank you, Nana,' said Penelope. 'You may leave now, if you wish. Klymene and I will go down to the hall together shortly, but I'm sure the servants will need you there to supervise the place settings.'

When Nana had gone, Klymene took the amethyst pendant and fastened it around Penelope's neck.

'You look lovely tonight, lady,' she said. 'Every eye will be on you.'

'I'm so afraid, Klymene. What if . . . ?'

'All will be well. Don't think about it,' Klymene said, and added to herself, *O Pallas Athene, tell me I'm doing the right thing by not speaking of what I know!*

The jars of wine were nearly empty. The suitors, at their places around the hall, had drunk their fill and more. Their words were slurred as they spoke and even the most disgusting of the insults they were in the habit of trading with one another turned into nothing more than drunken babble. Every morsel of meat had been stripped from the bones of sheep and pigs, the cakes dipped in honey and sesame seeds had all disappeared, and now nothing remained of the feast but smears of grease on every platter and on most faces and fingers as well. Stomachs were so full that even the smallest movement was an effort.

'I don't see why *he* had to partake of this . . . this . . .' said Amphimedon, pointing down to the end of the table where the beggar had been allowed to sit. 'Whatever next, eh? Beggars eating and drinking with the likes of us. Not right. 'Swhat I say. Not right at all. Chucked out, he should be. Right?' He waved a knife belligerently about but he was so drunk that it clattered to the floor. 'Hmm . . .' he muttered, looking down, trying to find it again.

'Lords of the Islands,' said Penelope. She was standing in the centre of the hall and holding an enormous bow in her hand.

'Bloody Hades, what's that when it's at home?' said the suitor sitting next to Amphimedon. 'And what's the queen doing? I ask you. Going to make a speech, it looks like, doesn't it?'

'Shut your mouth!' said Amphimedon, batting his neighbour across the face with his hairy right hand. 'Bad manners to speak when a lady's speaking. I want to hear wha' she's go' to say.'

'I am holding my husband's bow,' Penelope said. 'It has lain unstrung for more years than I like to remember. Odysseus didn't take it to the Trojan War for it is, as you can see, too big to carry into battle. However, when he was a young man, my beloved husband used it for hunting, and I have seen him with my own eyes, stringing it on many occasions.'

She paused and looked around at the suitors. 'You may all be wondering why I'm telling you this. This feast is being held in honour of my son Telemachus, who is visiting us for a while. I am taking advantage of his being here to make an announcement. I have decided that the time has indeed come for me to choose a new spouse. It's clear to me now that Odysseus is in the Land of the Dead, and I need a man to help me rule in Ithaka.'

''Bout bloody time, bitch!' someone shouted, and a scuffle broke out around him in a corner of the hall. Two of his companions took him by the arms and dragged him away to the courtyard. When the noise had died down a little, Penelope continued.

'The fairest way for me to choose from among so many worthy suitors is by holding a contest of the kind my late husband enjoyed. My son has set up two rows of axes in a line here . . .'

'I never saw anyone laying out those axes,' Amphimedon muttered. 'I'm more pissed than I think I am, me.'

'. . . and whoever can string Odysseus' bow and shoot an arrow between the axes without touching one of them will be king in Ithaka. Is it agreed?'

'Agreed!' came a roar from all the suitors at once, and someone cried, 'Give us a turn at that bow!'

'They're all out of it,' Mydon whispered to Odysseus, who was still sitting quietly at the bottom of the most distant table from the throne. 'Just look.'

'Hasn't it been good to watch, though?' Odysseus whispered back. 'I can't remember when I've enjoyed something so much. But Leodes – he used to be a friend of mine and now here he is, sitting next to my wife at a feast. At least he hasn't tried to bend my bow. It seems he's still got a bit of loyalty left.'

Mydon nodded. It had indeed been quite difficult not to keep from laughing at the contortions of the suitors. One after another they'd tried to bend the gigantic bow and not a single one of them had even come close. They swore, they cursed, they railed against the Gods, they protested that they were only unable to bend it because they were so drunk and if the contest had been held on any other day, they'd have succeeded, no problem.

Odysseus stood up. 'Wish me good fortune, Mydon,' he said. 'I'm going forth to war again.'

He made his way across the floor. Shouts of *What's that beggar doing? Get him out of here, the impudent bastard!*

rose to the rafters as he dragged his old man's body to the foot of the throne and looked up at Penelope.

'You remember me, lady,' he said.

'Of course. Of course I do. My husband's comrade in arms during the war against Troy. I enjoyed my conversation with you.'

'Let me try to string my old friend's bow, I beseech you. I may look an old man, but I am strong too.'

Penelope bowed her head. How happy she looked tonight! Odysseus knew that this was because she thought she'd won. She can see that she'll never have to marry any of the suitors now, he thought. They've all agreed to abide by the rules of the contest and no one has won. Not yet.

'I don't think you'll succeed where so many other young, strong men have failed,' the queen said, smiling at him. 'But please, take the bow and try, if you are determined to do so.'

'Hasn't a hope in Hades! Silly old fool. It's only the kindness of the queen that's stopped him being thrown out. Thinking he can string Odysseus' bow! Now I've seen everything.'

Mydon wanted to tell the man sitting beside him to shut up, but he didn't. He wished that Klymene could have been sharing the bench with him, but she'd been charged with attending the queen. She was on the other side of the room, half hidden by a column, so that Mydon could do no more than catch sight of her from time to time, when she leaned forward to take some food. He was trying very hard not to call attention to himself, and had shrunk back against the wall, waiting to see Odysseus shoot his arrow straight through the two lines of axes without touching any of them. Of course he was going to do it. I must have drunk more than I should have as well, Mydon thought. He could see . . . he thought he could see . . . a shadow in the shape of a woman at Odysseus' side. Now the shadow was behind him, and it seemed to Mydon that she was putting her hand over his. He blinked and when he looked again, there was nothing to be seen but the beggar man, bending the bow as easily as though it were a child's toy. He strung it quickly and turned to face the throne. Who was that helping him? Could it have been Pallas Athene? Odysseus claimed he was under her protection, but had he really seen something or was it just the kind of waking dream that came to men when they'd drunk too much wine?

'There, o great Queen,' he said. 'And now I'll shoot the arrow, just as you've decreed.'

From every seat in the hall came loud cries of astonishment. Penelope half rose from her seat, with a hand in front of her mouth, and her eyes widened. Odysseus turned to Amphimedon and said, 'Silence, please.'

'Don't you go telling me when I can speak and when I can't, flea-ridden wretch! Why, I'll get my men to toss you into the trough outside, whether you've strung the bow or not. You might impress others round here, but I know it's just a fluke. Happens sometimes.'

Mydon smiled as the fat man sank back on to the bench and took another gulp of wine from his goblet.

Odysseus pulled back the bowstring and let one arrow fly. It moved so quickly between the axes that Mydon couldn't follow it with his eyes, and then it reached the wall and embedded itself in a beam, where it hung, vibrating. Out of a corner of his eye, Mydon saw a shadow move near the doorway.

Everything happened very quickly after that. Leodes summoned the servants who were still in the hall and said, 'Take the queen away to her chamber at once, please. All the women should leave now. There's going to be trouble. They ought not to be here to witness it.'

The servants gathered round the queen and hurried her out of the hall. All her maidservants followed her. Mydon caught a glimpse of Klymene. She looked around as she went through the door, searching for him, and he raised his hand in greeting. She hasn't seen me, Mydon thought, and now she's gone. I pray to you, Pallas Athene. Reunite us after this is finished.

When he was a boy, Mydon had seen ceremonial dances, where every step and movement was set down and in which each dancer knew what to do and where to go. Amphimedon seized a spear from where it was hanging on the wall behind him and threw it with all his strength in the direction of Odysseus, and something like a battle dance began.

Suddenly everyone was brawling. There were obviously some men among the suitors to whom Odysseus had spoken before the feast – perhaps those he'd managed to find in the outer courtyard – because Amphimedon and his cronies were not the only ones who were attacking. Soon spears and swords were raised against them and it wasn't long before the first death. Someone Mydon didn't recognize was stuck through the neck by a flying dagger; a scarlet fountain sprang up from the gash, and he fell across the table, his blood soaking into the wood.

'Mydon!' Odysseus was there beside him. How had he moved so quickly? 'No time to talk, boy. Just go. Don't wait round here. I'll meet you outside . . .' A spear whistled past Odysseus' head as he was speaking and Mydon cried out, 'It's Amphimedon! Beware!'

Odysseus took hold of the spear that had nearly struck him and wheeled round. With no visible effort at all he threw the weapon back towards Amphimedon. There's no chance, Mydon said to himself, rooted to the spot and disobeying Odysseus in his anxiety to see what happened next. No chance he'll hit the fat slob.

He couldn't see anything, but it must have been Pallas Athene who moved the lightly-flung spear and bore it with her own hands to where Amphimedon stood, grinning stupidly. Odysseus had scarcely made any effort at all when he threw it. It must have been the Goddess who pushed it gently and easily into the fat chest like someone slicing into a slab of butter with a warm knife, and Amphimedon made a sound, Mydon thought, such as his namesake, the bear, would make when a hunting knife was quivering in his chest.

'Know who has ended your days, scum,' said Odysseus. 'I am the ruler of Ithaka and husband of Penelope. Odysseus. May you rot in the foulest swamps of Hades.'

Amphimedon, lying on his back with blood bubbling out of his mouth, managed to repeat Odysseus' name before his eyes turned up into his head.

'You shouldn't be here, Mydon.' The old beggar man was drenched in sweat and covered in dirt. 'I've other matters to attend to, but you must go. At once. You shouldn't see any more of this carnage. Go on, run. Anywhere, just run.'

Mydon ran, and others ran too. He noticed that just ahead of him, Antinous the Rat was hurrying through the door. Antinous. He remembered certain things Klymene had told him about. He remembered years of cruelty and harsh treatment at his hands. He remembered his mother's face and how her eyes darkened when his name was mentioned. A rage he'd never felt before flooded through every vein in his body.

Mydon picked up a long dagger that someone had dropped, and stuck it into his belt. I'll have my revenge, he thought. I'll be as brave as Odysseus. The Goddess will protect me.

He rushed into the corridor. Antinous was turning a corner, making for the sleeping quarters, and Melantho was with him, running alongside him, her hand in his. Where had she come from? She must have been waiting at the door. Mydon chased after them.

Where was Leodes? Why had he not followed her out of the hall? Men were all the same. It would have been impossible for him to stay quietly here while the fighting was going on somewhere else. Penelope stood at the window and looked towards the sea. She could hear the sounds of fighting from here, and it seemed to her that she was no longer flesh and blood but had been turned to stone.

'He's not coming, Penelope,' said a voice she half recognized. Who was it? How had someone managed to get in here, when she'd given orders that she wanted to be quite alone? Not even Klymene had been allowed to come with her. She turned to her window, and there was the owl, sitting as it had done so many years ago in the branches of the fig tree.

'Goddess . . .' she whispered, and sank to her knees.

'You must be ready, Penelope, for everything. There is a battle – can you hear it?'

'Tell me, Goddess . . . what will happen?'

'Poor Penelope,' murmured the owl. 'Your lover, your Leodes, is doomed to die. And your own son will kill him.'

'No! Oh, I implore you, Goddess. Tell me none of this is true. How can I bear it? Oh, Leodes, why . . . ?'

'Do not ask why, Penelope, unless you want to know the answer.'

'Yes. Tell me. Tell me everything. I will be brave, I promise.'

'You have been more faithful than any husband has a right to demand. Years and years went by before you even looked at another man. Your weaving has kept him alive. The stories you have told in your work.'

'This is no story, Goddess. It's my life. It's what I

live every day. Why are you speaking of stories, as though what I'm going through is some sort of . . . amusement for children?'

'Every life has a line it must follow. Every life is the story of that person told from beginning to end. And for us on Olympus, why, some lives and the stories that belong to them are more interesting than others. That is all I meant. I only repeat: your threads have been important to this tale.'

'Speak to me of Leodes. Why would Telemachus want to kill him?'

'Because he has turned you into an unfaithful wife. Telemachus will not forgive him for that.'

'Then will my son kill me as well? I was the one who wanted it; who wanted Leodes. Perhaps he's coming after me with a knife.'

'Telemachus would never believe a woman could initiate such passion, much less his own mother. No, he will assume that the man was responsible for everything and that weakness is the most he can blame you for.'

'But who told him? I never breathed a word to anyone . . . well, Klymene knew, but she would never have betrayed my confidence.'

'Melantho. She knew about you and Leodes even before Klymene did, but said nothing until Telemachus showed her he was no longer interested in her. Then she vowed to hurt him, and she has. Be comforted, Penelope. Try to remember what you had, and not what you might have had if matters had worked out differently.'

'But I'm all alone now!' Penelope cried, putting out a hand to touch the owl.

'Wait and see,' said the bird, and it flew away into the darkness, its wings luminous in the silver moonlight. Penelope took the edge of her scarf and dried her tears as she looked around her chamber. She was quite alone. Leodes will die. That is what the Goddess said. Penelope flung herself on to the bed and buried her face in the pillow, weeping as though she would never stop.

DEATH AND DESTRUCTION

'You! Stop! Turn round and face me.'

Telemachus, holding his unsheathed knife in his right hand, ran down the dark corridor towards a shape he recognized. It was Ilos, staggering from too much wine and leaning against every pillar he could find. He said, 'Going to try your luck with me, pipsqueak? Come on then.'

Ilos put out his hand and beckoned Telemachus, making kissing noises with his mouth, as though he were calling a beloved dog to his side. Out of the corner of his eye, Telemachus glimpsed a tall figure swathed in a black cloak and wearing a bronze helmet with a red horsehair crest, and had time to wonder briefly who this could be and where he'd come from, but then Ilos was on top of him and he was struggling to escape his clutches.

If I can get him in the gut with this knife, Telemachus thought, then he won't hurt me. I can kill him. Ilos was punching him in the stomach and it was all he could do to stay upright, and harder than he thought to control his hands and for a terrible moment he was sure that the knife was going to slip from between his fingers and then he'd be dead for sure. He imagined Ilos and Melantho together and this made him so angry that he began to bite the arm that had tightened round his face. He tried to speak, and then suddenly someone else was there, pulling at his legs and then at Ilos' legs – who was this? Telemachus twisted and twisted himself, trying to wriggle free, and at the same time to stab at whatever he could.

'Telemachus! Let me help you . . . I'll hold him. You run away while I hold him.'

Leodes. It was Leodes. Why was he helping him? Melantho said . . . could what she told him be true? He couldn't get hold of any of his own thoughts. Everything he tried to fasten on slid away and disappeared and all he could think of was putting his knife between Ilos' ribs or somewhere, anywhere. He pushed as hard as he could with the hand that held the blade and Ilos let go of him. Telemachus stood upright and roared his fury at the sight of his enemy running away into the courtyard. I haven't hurt him. Maybe only grazed him. But he'd felt something. His knife had gone somewhere, into something. And he himself was wounded too. Blood ran down from his shoulder and he felt pain he'd not noticed while he was in the thick of the fight. Ilos must have got a blow in before he ran away. Telemachus looked around. The warrior he'd seen before, the one in the black cloak, was there in front of him.

'Look there,' said this person.

Telemachus followed the pointing finger and saw Leodes lying near the wall with blood pouring from a wound in his chest. Had he done that? To Leodes? He sank to his feet and cried, 'Leodes? Speak to me. It's Telemachus.'

'I'm done for, boy,' said Leodes. 'I meant to help you. He got me. But he didn't get you. That's only a scratch. I'm glad of that, for your mother's sake.'

'He got you? Are you sure?' Telemachus was confused.

'Sure.' Leodes was having some difficulty in speaking and the blood was pouring from his side. 'You must have stabbed him in the arm. Go now. Don't stay here. They'll find you. But promise me something.'

Telemachus leaned close to the fallen Leodes to hear his words. His speech seemed to bubble, as though there was blood rising in his mouth. 'Your father and I were boys together. Say . . . say Leodes sends his dying thoughts and greetings to Odysseus. Tell him . . . tell him there was no disloyalty in my heart. You'll do that for me?'

Telemachus nodded, then stood up and walked away, thinking that if he could find his father, all would be well. Odysseus would know what to do. The black-cloaked warrior strode along beside him and whispered in his ear, 'I saw what happened. Your blow wounded him.'

'Then why's he lying?'

'He has his reasons,' said the warrior.

'Who are you? How come you know everything?'

'I am Ares, God of War. I know where every blade comes to rest.'

'Why's Leodes protecting me? Because he loves my mother?'

Ares said nothing, and as they came to the door of the great hall, the God disappeared and Telemachus was left by himself.

'Help! Someone help me!'

Who was calling? The voice seemed to be coming from one of the smaller chambers off the main corridor, a place used only to store old furniture and ornaments. For a moment Klymene hesitated. Lady Penelope was sure to be needing her at this very moment. She'll be wondering what the uproar coming from the hall is all about. I could ignore it, couldn't I? She stood quite still, and the cry came again, accompanied by a groan that made her skin crawl. She stepped over the threshold and saw Leodes, lying on the floor. A trail of smeared blood led from the door to his body. He must have dragged himself here after being wounded outside in the corridor.

'Lord Leodes . . .' Klymene said, and ran to his side. 'Who did this to you?' As soon as she spoke she remembered that Odysseus didn't know that his own father had invited Leodes to the island. Perhaps he would think his friend had become an enemy like the other suitors. And of course he had no idea of Penelope's feelings for this man. 'I'll help you,' Klymene said. 'We'll go to the queen's chamber. I'll call my grandmother. Please don't die . . . please. Be brave. Look, I can bind your wound till help comes. It's me. Klymene. You remember. You rescued me once when I was lying in the sun. Let me go for help.'

'No, Klymene, listen. It's too late for me, only tell my lady that I died loving her.'

Klymene couldn't answer because her throat and mouth were filled with tears. 'I'll tell her,' she managed to whisper. 'And they'll bury you with honour, Leodes. I promise.'

The face in front of her was now white and blank, and the eyes saw nothing. She took hold of his hand, but the warmth was leaving it, and it felt like clay to her touch. In a corner of the room the figure of Hades was waiting, his grey cloak gathered round him. Klymene covered her eyes and stood up. I must go and find someone to take him away, she thought, but not yet. No one will come here, so I can leave him for a short while and go and tell the queen the terrible news. The God of Death will watch over him.

She left the room and ran towards the kitchen. It was dark in this part of the palace, and although the sounds of the fighting were growing fainter, she could still hear shrieking and the clash of metal on metal. Someone was following her. She stopped to look behind her, and there was Telemachus.

'Oh!' she cried. 'You've scared me half to death! Why are you creeping after me like that? What's happened?'

Telemachus said nothing. It was hard to see much, but there was something black all over his face and arms . . . blood. Scarlet turned to black in the dim light.

'Telemachus, sit down. Sit down here – look, on this step. Are you wounded?'

'Maybe. I don't know. I don't care.'

'What do you mean, you don't care? Of course you care! Who did it? How?'

'My fault.'

'How could it be?' Klymene tried to keep her voice kind, but really, Telemachus was infuriating. How could the wound on his shoulder, which looked truly terrible – so much blood – be his fault?

'Tell me,' she said, and began to use the scarf that covered her head to wipe his brow and cheeks clean, or at least cleaner. His forehead was burning hot to the touch.

Telemachus began to speak. 'I killed him. It wasn't like I thought it would be. I thought it would be easy, but it wasn't. I was meaning to kill Ilos. We . . . we were struggling. I couldn't see properly. Hard to keep track of where everything was. I didn't know how hard to push the blade. Push it in, you know? And then Leodes was there suddenly, and I put my hand out to hold him off and that must have been the hand that had a dagger in it and he fell on the floor, and when Ilos ran away, I wanted to help him. I didn't want to kill him. Ilos had gone and he was the one I was after. Not Leodes, who's always been good to me, and anyway how did Melantho know that my mother . . . ? I hate her. Melantho. You told me not to trust her, and yet when I saw him lying there, what she told me stuck in my mind and I couldn't forget about it. My mother and Leodes . . . I killed him. My knife killed him, but it wasn't me. I didn't . . . it was an accident. Really, Klymene, believe me. I didn't want him to die.'

Klymene couldn't think of a word to say. She had no idea what to do, either. Should she take Telemachus to his mother? Or to Nana? Should she leave him here and go and get help? Or should she forget about Penelope for a moment and clean his wounds herself?

'Come with me, Telemachus,' she whispered at last. The longer Penelope didn't know about Leodes' death, the greater the chances were that someone else would discover his body and break the terrible news. But how could she leave her oldest friend when he was feverish and delirious, and in pain and so unhappy? Klymene took him by the arm and they walked slowly towards the kitchen, with Telemachus leaning his full weight on her, groaning and dragging one of his feet.

'I think I've also twisted my ankle,' he muttered, and then, 'D'you know where my father is? Are all the suitors dead, or running to their ships?'

'I don't know. I haven't seen him. And I haven't seen Mydon, either.' Klymene shivered, and in her mind said a prayer to Pallas Athene to keep him safe.

'Here we are,' she said. 'Sit down there, on that bench. I'm going to wash your face, and then I'll find some olive oil to clean the wound on your shoulder. Nana uses it for the worst wounds.'

'Let me drink first,' Telemachus said.

Klymene poured water from a jug into a small cup. 'There's not much left here,' she said. 'Everything's in the hall. The feast . . .'

She sat next to him and began to wipe his arms and legs with a cloth wrung out in water.

'Listen, Telemachus,' she said. 'You must stop tormenting yourself. Your mother won't be made happier by seeing you like this. And anyway . . .' *O Artemis, tell me I'm doing the right thing. Show me that this is wise!* 'Melantho's a lying cow. You know that, don't you? I told you not to trust her. How could you believe a word she said even for a heartbeat? She wasn't telling you the truth, Telemachus. Your mother . . . your mother would never look at another man. Don't you know that?'

Telemachus gazed at her as though she had just lifted a rock from his shoulders. 'Really? Is that true? Does she still wait for my father?'

'Of course she does. Why, she's famous all over the islands for her devotion and loyalty. Listen, I'll tell you a secret, only you mustn't breathe a word. We've been undoing our knitting on the shroud every single night. I've been helping her. The suitors all thought it was growing and that she'd finish it eventually, but we've undone a little bit each night, so that your mother wouldn't have to decide. Doesn't that prove she wants nothing to do with any of them? If she'd loved Leodes, she could have said she'd marry him, couldn't she? We'd have been spared all that trouble.'

'She wouldn't have wanted to upset me,' Telemachus said, and his words were so true that Klymene didn't know how to answer.

She said, 'No, she wouldn't have wanted that, but' – *What now, Goddess?* – 'you'd have heard something from someone else in the palace if there was any truth in the story. You know how hard it is to keep anything private. Don't say a word to her, Telemachus. Not a single word. Don't even mention Leodes' name. Do you promise me? Forget the whole thing. Put it out of your mind.'

'If you say that's what I should do, Klymene. I'm so tired. I must rest. Tomorrow I'll think about what to do.'

'I'll tell your mother about the fighting. I'll tell her Leodes is dead, but I won't say a word about how he died, I promise. Don't think about it any more, Telemachus. It won't help anything.'

'You're so kind to me, Klymene. I . . . I thank you.'

Before she could answer, Telemachus suddenly cried out and flung his arms around her. 'Oh, Klymene, what's happened to us? Ikarios – how can you bear it without him? I never . . . he never . . . we didn't speak about such things.'

Telemachus was groaning now, his head on Klymene's shoulder. 'There's only you and me left and it was always the three of us, wasn't it?'

'Oh, Telemachus,' she said, thinking how woefully useless any words were; how ridiculous. As if you could stop yourself groaning when the pain was so huge that it threatened to engulf you and drown out every other thought. There was a time when having Telemachus in her arms would have made her faint with happiness. Now she hugged him and said, 'You're my only brother now, Telemachus. We'll comfort one another.'

'And you're my sister, Klymene. I'm sorry if I . . . if I've disappointed you ever.'

'You haven't,' Klymene said firmly. 'You never have. Let's go now, Telemachus. Come on, I'll help you.'

He stood up and shuffled painfully out of the door, and Klymene followed him and turned towards Lady Penelope's bedchamber. There was someone standing next to a pillar . . . Who was it?

'Pallas Athene!' Klymene breathed, bowing her head. A waxing moon had come out from behind a cloud, and the Goddess's tunic glittered in the silver light.

'You have acted wisely, Klymene. Soon, soon it will be over. Olympus is tired of playing games with Odysseus. We are weary of the whole story, and therefore it will end.'

'And Penelope? What'll become of her?'

No answer. Silence and moonlight. Klymene looked around. The Goddess had disappeared. Penelope. Leodes. I must go and tell my lady that Leodes is dead. I know I have to do that.

'Sod off! I don't have time to stick spears into little boys. Apart from that Ikarios. I made an exception for him.' Antinous was out of breath. He'd been running, that much was clear, but some of his breathlessness was because of Melantho. Somehow, in the midst of all the uproar and the carnage, they'd managed to sneak away into this corner, where Mydon had found them so closely entwined together that they might have been one creature.

'Ikarios? What are you talking about?' Mydon paused to take in what he'd heard. 'Did you kill him?'

'What if I did? He deserved it. He'd— Oh never mind what he did.'

Mydon took a deep breath. If he spoke now, he couldn't be sure of coming out with anything that had any sense to it. At last he said, 'It's no good hiding behind a woman, Antinous. And if you're a man, you'll leave the woman alone and come and face me.'

'Face *you*? You're not worth the effort, to be honest. Why don't you push off to wherever it is you came from?'

Mydon lunged at Antinous. 'I'm going to kill you, Rat. I'm going to avenge Ikarios.'

Antinous let go of Melantho and pushed her behind him as he stepped out into the corridor. 'Come on then, you little turd. Let's see what you're capable of.'

Mydon found that he couldn't see clearly any longer. There was a film of red over everything he looked at. Antinous, Melantho, hanging on to his left arm, everything in his line of vision was scarlet. He ran at the body in front of him, not thinking of anything but how to stick his weapon somewhere, anywhere, and then all at once every movement was both too fast for him to control and so slow that Mydon felt he must be asleep and dreaming. He could hear someone screaming. Melantho. She was pulling at Antinous; Antinous had his right arm round Mydon's neck; Mydon was twisting and wriggling to get free, and at the same time trying to stick a blade into

387

Antinous' flesh, anywhere, anywhere at all, and then the three of them were in a twist of limbs and he could feel the breath from Melantho's mouth on his face and she was still screaming, only this time it was easy to see why. There was a deep, long cut running down the side of her face from her hairline to her chin, across one eyebrow and all along her cheek. Blood streamed out of it and you could see the bone like a white stripe in the middle of the wound, and the blood was running in lines down her neck and it soaked into the fabric of her garments, turning the pale linen dark and sticky.

She fell back, holding her hand in front of her face.

'Bastard! Scum! O Gods, my face, my face!' The words came out garbled, torn, difficult to understand, because Melantho was sobbing as she spoke and she'd fallen to the ground and was writhing with pain.

Antinous kicked out with his foot. 'Go, woman. What d'you think you're doing, eh? Piss off. Back to the kitchen. Go on. I've got things to do here.'

Melantho crawled away, still shrieking. Mydon felt the thick arm tighten around his neck. I must – I must get this dagger somehow behind me. I must move. The arm was squeezing. Breathing was hard. He kicked out with one leg. Kicked out behind him. Advice from long ago, from the days he'd almost completely forgotten, when Antinous himself had trained him in the basics of fighting, came back to him and he remembered what he'd been told: *Get 'em where it hurts. Spoil their wedding night for them. Kick 'em in the goolies and run like Hades*. Can't breathe. Can't kick. Klymene. Kick. Knife. Where. Darkness. Where.

Mydon opened his eyes and saw a beggar looking down at him.

'Mydon? You all right? Bit of a narrow shave there.'

Mydon tried to sit up but dizziness and sickness forced him to lie down again and close his eyes.

'Odysseus? Is that you? Where's . . . ?' The name of the man he'd been trying to kill had gone from his head. There was nothing in there but burning rocks and thorns and red stuff.

'Antinous. I killed him. Came up behind the two of you. He wasn't exactly alert. Too busy trying to murder a young lad. There he is, just a hunk of meat now, and not able to hurt anyone. You'd nearly had it by the looks of things. Bastard had you in an arm lock and wasn't going to let go, I promise you. Come on, boy. Try and get up. We'll find Nana. She'll sort you out.'

Mydon took the hand Odysseus held out and struggled upright. How was he going to put one leg in front of the other, when each one had been turned into something like a flower stalk? Suddenly there was an arm round him, and he was being yanked along as though he were a bundle of old rags. Maybe he was. He closed his eyes again and leaned all his weight on Odysseus.

'Lady.' Klymene held Penelope close. She had never in her life dared to initiate an embrace with the queen. She half expected her to stand up and shrug off the comfort. Instead, Penelope made a sound that was like the howl of an animal and, turning her whole body towards Klymene, she buried her face in the young woman's neck. The noises that she was making were supposed to be words, but tears had drowned them, and there was nothing to be done but sit and wait for the first pain to subside.

Klymene's garments were already wet, and now Lady Penelope's tears were added to her son's blood. When everything is over, she thought, I'll burn this robe. I will never wear it again. She said, 'Cry, lady. It's good if you can cry. It will pass. The worst pain will pass. I know, because of Ikarios. I never stop missing him, but the worst agony . . . you can't keep on hurting so much and so it stops.'

Penelope sat up suddenly and, taking her ceremonial scarf of linen embroidered with purple flowers, she wiped her eyes and nose with it as though it were a kitchen rag.

'Tell me,' she said. 'Tell me who killed him. Tell me what he said. I want to know every single word he said.'

'He spoke only of you. He said he loved you and would love you even after death. He said . . . he said you should try to be happy. For his sake.'

Forgive me for embellishing the truth, Goddess, she said to herself.

'Greetings, Klymene,' said Pallas Athene. She was standing beside the loom. 'I commend you for your lie to Telemachus. It would have served no useful purpose whatsoever for him to fret about his mother and

390

Leodes for the rest of his life. He will hide the fact that he killed him, because he is ashamed, and it's to be hoped that this shame will prevent him from killing anyone else.'

'You could make Penelope forget as well, couldn't you? Now that her husband is here. Now that they'll soon be reunited.'

'I could, but why should I? Why shouldn't Penelope have memories of something that made her happy? She loved Leodes. I will see that she remembers the pleasure and the grief will fade. Of course she will keep this secret from Odysseus. This story is almost over. Loose ends must be tied in some haste, but that can't be helped.'

She stood up and leaned over the loom, moving her hands gently over the threads. 'Farewell, child. I am gone.'

The window stood open. The sky outside was streaked with apricot and mauve, and Klymene watched as the Goddess's shape dissolved and vanished. Where she had been, a white owl appeared then perched on top of the loom. The bird spread its white wings, looked at Klymene with its amber eyes and flew up and up till it disappeared in the shadows at the top of the carved headboard.

'Someone,' said Penelope, 'is making a fearful noise in the corridor. Open the door, Klymene, and see who it is. Send them away. I want to . . .' She paused. 'Maybe it's Telemachus. Where is he? Where is my son?'

'He's gone to find Nana, I think. He . . . I think

he was slightly wounded. But the suitors'll be leaving soon. The old man, the beggar, after he won the contest you set them all – well, it enraged them. There was bound to be trouble.'

'We must go and find out. I must see Telemachus and see how bad his wound is . . . Have you seen Nana?'

Klymene heard the tears in Penelope's voice. She could see that her hands were trembling. Her mistress said, 'See who it is, Klymene.' She then sat down on a low chair beside the bed and covered her face with her hands.

Klymene led Odysseus into the room, still in his beggar's shape, and Penelope stood up, trying to appear normal in spite of everything that had happened.

'Forgive me, old man. I'm not myself . . . I've had black news. Death news. I don't seem to be in control of my lips . . . I'm glad you're alive.'

Odysseus looked, Klymene thought, worse than ever. His rags were dark with blood and the stench of death and wine rose up from him as though his body had been steeped in both.

'Yes, lady, I thank you. Everyone who has sought to lay waste to your husband's kingdom is dead.'

'Everyone?'

'Everyone.'

'Dead?'

'Dead.'

'All the suitors? They are all dead?'

'Some have fled to their own islands. The others

are dead. With the help of the Goddess Pallas Athene.'

'You're very . . . calm about it,' Penelope said.

'I have to be,' the old man said. 'I defended myself. I defended my kingdom. I put to flight those bastards who were after my wife. After you.'

'No, old man, you're muddled, and no wonder after what you've been through. My husband is Odysseus. Your friend Odysseus, who fought with you in the Trojan War. Do you remember?'

The beggar smiled. 'Forgive me, lady. I deceived you. I *am* Odysseus. I had to hide this from you, I'm afraid. Till now.'

Penelope said nothing. It was clear to Klymene that she didn't believe a word the old man said. She said quietly, 'You must be tired, old man. After all that fighting you say you did. I think I'll have the bed taken out of my own bedchamber and you may rest. Klymene will call the servants and they'll move it to a quiet place where you'll be undisturbed.'

Klymene saw what the queen was doing. She was testing Odysseus. She didn't believe him, that much was clear. She continued: 'And then when you're rested, we'll speak again. I think you're confused now and no wonder.'

'Impossible,' said Odysseus.

'Why? What's impossible about it?'

'Well, unless at some point in the last twenty years or so you've taken an axe to that bed, it won't budge. I made it with my own hands out of a living tree, an old olive, and the whole of this' – he swept his hand round in a circle to indicate the palace and all its chambers and corridors and courtyards – 'was built around it. Mostly by me, though of course I had men in plenty to help me. Don't you remember? When we were betrothed I cut the topmost branches from the handsomest olive tree on the island and from the piece of the trunk that remained in the earth, I carved this headboard.' He touched the wood. 'It's still shining. You've kept it well polished. Do you recall what I said on our first night together?'

'Yes,' said Penelope, putting her hands up to her mouth. 'If it is really you . . . You said: *We'll make our marriage couch here.*'

'I also said, *I'll build our chamber around it, and when I've done that, I'll make a whole palace for us to live in until we grow old together. We'll die in the same bed we sleep in all our lives.* Do you remember those words?'

Penelope had grown pale. She took a step backwards. 'But you are a beggar, and my Odysseus . . . my husband . . . he was . . .'

'A young man when you last saw him, Penelope. But look at me. Look carefully.'

Klymene blinked as the white owl swooped down from where it had been hiding in the shadowy darkness at the top of the headboard and flew out of the open window.

'Madam, I want you to see me properly,' said the beggar. 'Sit here, on the bed, and look carefully at me. Look into my eyes.'

Klymene held her breath. The beggar's filthy clothes had disappeared and his matted, grey beard was gone. His tangled hair was smooth and he held

394

out his hands to Penelope, who was staring up at him from where she was sitting.

'It is you. Is it you? Can it be you? Odysseus? Truly?'

'My beloved,' said Odysseus. 'You are unchanged. Unchanged. I've come home.'

'You promised me you would. Do you remember? Telemachus was lying on a blanket beside me and you made me a promise.'

'And here I am,' Odysseus whispered.

Klymene left the chamber and closed the door behind her. The last thing she heard was Penelope uttering a strangled, doleful, tear-filled cry that rang in her ears as she hurried towards the great hall.

AFTER THE SLAUGHTER

Klymene held a hand up to her face, but it didn't stop the stench from reaching her nostrils. A foulness lingered in the corridors and reminded her of the decaying body of a pig she'd once come across on a rubbish heap behind the palace. The corridors were slick with blood, and Klymene trod carefully. The door of the hall stood open and the silence was like a thick cloth thrown over everything. She stepped inside and then out again at once. No. It isn't possible, she thought. I must look again and I can't bear it. I must. She put her scarf up against her nose and entered the hall again.

There were bodies, dead bodies, flung everywhere, as though they had no more weight or substance than dolls. Dolls, think of them as dolls, she told herself. They're not men. They're no longer men. Don't look. O Gods, protect me from this sight, she thought. An arm. That's an arm . . . No I can't. I can't. I'm not brave enough. She stumbled back to the door. But what if Mydon is lying in there, in small pieces? Hacked to death by silver blades? I'll wait. Odysseus will send anyone who is still alive to find the dead and bury them well; to perform the rites. I can't stomach it. A sour, disgusting taste filled her mouth suddenly and she retched and vomited everything in her stomach out on to the floor, where it mingled with blood and broken weapons and spilled wine. Klymene ran. My bedchamber. I must reach my bedchamber.

Melantho was there, stretched out on her own bed. Her eyes were open and she was staring at the ceiling. Under her head, her pillow was stained with blood. Her whole face had been sliced open – that was what it looked like to Klymene – and as soon as she saw it, the hatred she felt for Melantho left her all at once. She sank down by the bed.

'Melantho! What happened? Tell me. Melantho, speak to me.'

Melantho shook her head. Tears poured out of her eyes, but she said nothing.

'I'll go and get help. Someone will know what to do. Your cut must be dressed. Honey and olive oil. I'll go and get some and do it myself – or better still I'll send Nana. She's so good at nursing the wounded. It'll heal, Melantho. Everyone's dead, but we're alive. That's good, isn't it? We're alive. And Melantho, Odysseus is back. He's with Lady Penelope. Everything will be good from now on. Look at me, Melantho. Speak to me. Please.'

'Forgive me, Klymene. Please say you'll forgive me.'

'What for? You're delirious, Melantho.'

'No . . . Ikarios. It was my fault. I made sure he was there . . . in the workshop to be killed . . . he came to meet me. I pretended . . . he thought I liked him. Oh, I'm sorry, Klymene. Antinous killed him but I . . . I didn't stop him. I helped him. Will the Gods forgive me? What shall I do?'

Klymene was silent for a long time. Then she said, 'I forgive you, Melantho. You've been punished now.'

Melantho groaned and turned to face the wall.

'I'll come back,' Klymene said. 'I must find Mydon first, but then I'll send Nana to you. I promise.'

Melantho will be scarred for ever, Klymene thought as she ran to the kitchen. The Rat . . . the Rat killed Ikarios. I must tell Nana. Let Nana be there . . . and Mydon, please, o Gods, let him be alive, she thought. Melantho will suffer every day. Her beauty is lost. The ragged, bloody flesh of her cheek and brow will heal and the skin will pucker into a white line and men will shudder and turn away from her. She'll live in a kind of torment until she's an old woman. She's been punished for everything. Poor beautiful Melantho!

Penelope lay on her back. Beside her, Odysseus was asleep, his head turned to one side, his left arm flung over her naked body. She wondered briefly how deeply asleep he was, and whether he would be aware of the tears that streamed from her eyes. Her body . . . she felt as though it belonged to someone else. Her husband – such a stranger! – had caressed her, and in spite of herself, he had brought it to some life, but she could not prevent herself from thinking of Leodes as Odysseus kissed her mouth and her hair and the soft places behind her ears.

*'Is this hard for you, wife? Is it strange? There's no
hurry . . . I'll be gentle. I'll wait until . . .'*

'No, no . . . not strange. Kiss me again.'

'But you're crying . . .'

*'I can't help it. My feelings. I can't govern them,
Odysseus.'*

She looked at his sleeping face and remembered
how his name had felt clumsy as she spoke it. I'd been
thinking it for so long that it was surrounded with a
kind of glow or aura but then his head was on my
breast and the word was like a piece of sweet fruit cut
too big: taking up the whole of my mouth.

I couldn't do it, she thought. I couldn't stop
thinking about Leodes. Remembering how it had been
with him. And that made me cry. Odysseus didn't know.
I don't think he knew. He thought the tears were for
him. Tears of joy. Tears of passion.

*'Cry, my sweet wife. Let out all the tears that lie within
you.'*

*'I'm so sorry . . . you deserve better than a sobbing
woman after your journeyings. It will be better, I promise.'*

*'Don't say sorry. There's no need. I understand what
you are feeling.'*

I didn't answer him, Penelope thought. I couldn't.
It was as though my heart were broken into separate
pieces, each one of them tearing into the flesh of my
body and hurting me. And I'm still in pain. Please,
dear Goddess Aphrodite, take this agony away. Let me
forget Leodes and find happiness with my husband
again. Leodes. Oh, I wish I could be wrapped in the
shroud that we've been making and unmaking and be

rowed across the river that divides the living from the dead. I want to see you again. Oh, my darling Leodes, where are you?

'Are you awake, my love?'

'Yes, Odysseus.'

Penelope turned her head and saw her husband propping himself up on his elbow and smiling down at her with the face he had shown her on the morning after their wedding day. 'I'm sorry,' she said. 'It seems I'm crying again. Only you look like our son. You look like Odysseus – the one I remember.'

She closed her eyes and took a deep breath. 'I'll be myself very soon. I will recover my calm, I promise. I won't always be crying.'

'You can be however you choose. I don't ask you to hide your feelings. Only to stay with me, Penelope. To lie in this bed.'

'For ever,' she said. 'As long as I live. I swear.'

Why did the words fill her with both joy and dread? She looked up and saw, above them, the headboard stretching up and up almost to the ceiling, its carvings full of shadows. The sun had travelled across the sky and was now dipping towards the ocean. Penelope rose from the bed. She put on a thin gown and went over to the loom that stood as it always did under the window. Empty. No pictures. Nothing. Nothing on the frame and nothing in her head but memories she could never, ever speak of.

The shroud. That was still there too, where they'd bundled it away into a chest before the feast, and it would have to be finished. She had made a promise to Laertes. She'd undertaken to finish Antikleia's handiwork, but now the very thought of sitting down with all that white wool made her feel faint and ill. Perhaps Klymene would help her. Yes, that was the answer. Her devoted handmaiden, who was more loving than any daughter – she'd finish the cursed thing. She'd become skilled at the work. Penelope felt a little better. In a few days, when the palace had been cleaned and when things were normal again, she would ask this great favour. Then there was the matter of Laertes – he needed to know his son was safely back home. She would see to it tomorrow.

Penelope turned to where Odysseus still lay in the wide bed.

'There's much to be done,' she said to him, trying to arrange her mouth into a smile.

'Come back to me, Penelope.'

She said nothing, but began to walk slowly towards the bed. It seemed to her like the longest journey she had ever taken, but when she reached her husband, he folded her into his arms and she allowed herself to be held, and breathed in the smell of Odysseus' skin, which she had forgotten and would have to learn all over again, like a young bride.

Everyone in the palace was working. Penelope could hear the shouts of the servants as they went about disposing of the dead bodies, and worse, parts of bodies. She shivered. Odysseus had asked her not to leave the bedchamber and she was happy to fall in with his wishes. She had no wish to see the aftermath of what had sounded like a small war. She stood at the window, looking towards the sea. The fig tree was heavy with fruit. As she glanced down at it, she caught a glimpse of white and leaned out a little to see . . . could it be? She held her breath. The owl had returned and sat with its wings folded on a branch just below her. It has come back to comfort me. To take care of us both, me and Odysseus. As she looked at it, the bird flew out of the tree and came to sit on the windowsill just beside her hand.

'Stay for ever,' she said.

The owl stared at Penelope out of its amber eyes and began to preen its feathers.

ON THE SHORE

Mydon and Klymene had gone down to the caves on the seashore together to collect the body of Argos, which Mydon had placed in one of the caves. They had a soft blanket to wrap the old dog in.

'Here he is, Klymene,' said Mydon. 'I put rocks all around him, to keep him safe till we got here.'

Klymene pushed aside the stones and sat staring at Argos. His eyes were closed in death, and his paws stuck out stiffly. His fur was dull and spattered with dirt and sand.

'Oh, poor dog!' she said, and stroked him gently, as she used to do when he was alive. 'I will miss you, good friend. We will bury you with all honour.'

She turned to Mydon. 'I'm sorry,' she said to him. 'I know he was old . . . more than old. But I loved him so much. I wish . . .'

'He will be at rest,' Mydon said. 'And we can find a young dog. Another Argos for you to love.'

'It won't be the same. He will be a different dog. You can't just replace one with another.'

'I know that. I didn't mean to replace Argos. Only

403

to give you a new, young living thing to love as you loved him.'

Klymene shook her head. 'I'll never love another creature as much as I loved this dog. Never.' Her tears began to flow all over again.

'Dry your tears, Klymene. We must take him back to the palace.'

She stood up. 'Not right away. Let's walk for a while. It's so peaceful here. I can't bear the thought of going back straight away.'

'Very well – we'll walk. But we must wrap Argos up first. We'll come and get him when we're ready.'

'Please, you do it. I can't bear to see him,' said Klymene. 'I'll wait for you at the water line.'

Mydon was digging. He was using half of a large shell to scoop sand up and add it to something that looked to Klymene like a small mountain.

'Ikarios used to do that when we were small children,' she said, smiling. 'I didn't think grown men made castles in the sand.'

'Why not? And in any case, this isn't a castle. It's the citadel of Troy. Look, these are the high walls and we can soon find some driftwood somewhere to mark out the Greek lines . . . What's the matter? Why are you crying, Klymene?'

'I'm not. I'm really not. It's salt in my eyes. I was remembering something, that's all.'

'Maybe so.' Mydon put his shell aside and stroked Klymene's arm. 'When the palace is back to what it was, and everything's peaceful in Ithaka again, we'll be married. I'll ask your grandmother about it as soon as I can.'

Klymene looked out to the horizon. 'Is it right, Mydon, to be happy when so many are dead?'

'It's right,' said Mydon. 'How could it be wrong? Come, let's walk a little before we take Argos back to be buried.'

'You wanted to find driftwood. You said so.'

Mydon took Klymene's hand and they began to walk along the sand with the water ebbing and flowing over their feet.